PRASE FOR *The S*

"To say I loved it would be an understatement, this was just the first thing I've read. The one-liners had me laughing nearly every page, and I found it so moving."

—SARAH PENNER, *New York Times* bestselling author of *The Lost Apothecary*

"An empathetic powerhouse, with a plot that will keep you hooked until the last page, *The Second Ending* is the heartwarming, feel-good debut of the year."

—J. RYAN STRADAL, *New York Times* bestselling author of *The Lager Queen of Minnesota*

"Like a sparklingly fresh interpretation of a classic tune, *The Second Ending*'s story of reuniting with your true self never ceases to captivate the heart, right from the opening notes. Prudence Childs and Alexei Petrov are wonderfully offbeat characters, and I relished both the melodies of their paths to musical epiphany as well as the dramatic accompaniment provided by the vivid cast of characters. *The Second Ending* is thoroughly enjoyable, top-class entertainment —just like one of Prudence and Alexei's performances."

—SARAH HAYWOOD, *New York Times* bestselling author of *The Cactus*

"*The Second Ending* is wild, witty, and bright. This is the novel for anyone who has ever wished they could play a 1952 Steinway Model M, abscond to a getaway motel room (with soaking tub), or completely reinvent their lives. I loved every page and even paused between chapters to play the songs lovingly written about by Michelle Hoffman in her glittering debut."

—AMANDA EYRE WARD, *New York Times* bestselling author of *The Jetsetters*

"I loved *The Second Ending*. The descriptions of music are just fabulous, and the ending is delightful. It's been a long time since I've read anything I enjoyed this much."

—JACKIE FRASER, author of *The Bookshop of Second Chances*

The SECOND ENDING

A NOVEL

Michelle Hoffman

BALLANTINE BOOKS

NEW YORK

A Ballantine Books Trade Paperback Original

Copyright © 2023 by Michelle Hoffman

Published in the United States by Ballantine Books, an imprint of Random House, a division of Penguin Random House LLC, New York.

BALLANTINE is a registered trademark and the colophon is a trademark of Penguin Random House LLC.

Library of Congress Cataloging-in-Publication Data
Names: Hoffman, Michelle, author.
Title: The second ending: a novel / Michelle Hoffman.
Description: First edition | New York: Ballantine Group [2023]
Identifiers: LCCN 2022037022 (print) | LCCN 2022037023 (ebook) |
ISBN 9780593599136 (paperback) | ISBN 9780593599143 (ebook)
Barnes & Noble edition ISBN 9780593724941
Subjects: LCGFT: Novels.
Classification: LCC PS3608.O4783 S43 2023 (print) |
LCC PS3608.O4783 (ebook) | DDC 813/.6—dc23/eng/20220824
LC record available at https://lccn.loc.gov/2022037022
LC ebook record available at https://lccn.loc.gov/2022037023

Printed in the United States of America on acid-free paper

randomhousebooks.com

2 4 6 8 9 7 5 3 1

First Edition

Title-page image: yosuke14 / stock.adobe.com

Book design by Victoria Wong

For Steve, Paige, and Drew.
And all the dreamers.

The trouble with music appreciation in general is that people are taught to have too much respect for music. They should be taught to love it instead.

—IGOR STRAVINSKY

The
SECOND
ENDING

CHAPTER ONE

Prelude in E Minor

There were no more children at home. No more overflowing laundry hampers. No more backpacks in the foyer. It was just the two of them. Three if you included Mrs. Wintour, which Prudence did.

A week ago, Prudence and Stuart had dropped their youngest child off at a prestigious Midwest college with a clock tower, granite buildings, and stone statues. Their eldest was already attending a prestigious East Coast college with its own clock tower, granite buildings, and stone statues. Now that they were back home in the Southwest, back in the desert, Prudence wept at tiny boxes of raisins in the grocery store, reached for old bath toys in the closet. Catching a whiff of baby lotion was like being tugged into a time machine.

The absence of her daughters unmoored her. She had not expected how much she would miss those beautiful creatures who could delight her one minute and aggrieve her the next.

A child's world, Prudence had discovered when her girls were young, is only as large as what is around them. Her daughters never cared about their mother's storied childhood, how she'd played for two sitting presidents and had tea with Isaac Stern. They cared only that she could make mud pies and killer vegan tacos. Prudence gave her children everything she herself had been denied. She read them stories, taught them card games, and held them when they were sad. She nurtured them precisely so they would become independent adults. But the opposite had happened to Prudence along the way: She had grown dependent on them.

Prudence had tried to be brave the day she and Stuart dropped Becca off at college, but as she looked around at the cinderblock dorm room, a terrible thought occurred to her. She would never see Becca again.

"You okay, Mom?"

"Promise me you'll come back for Christmas and summer breaks?"

"Only if you don't turn my bedroom into a sewing room. Oh, wait, you already have one!" She hugged her mother. "Of course, I'll come back home."

Out in the hallway, Prudence could hear new roommates chattering while moms and dads lugged boxes and suitcases up the stairwells. The cheerful chaos depressed her almost as much as the worn linoleum floors. *How can they all be so happy?* She had to stop herself from popping her head out the door and yelling, "Which one of you has an extra Xanax?"

In an effort to delay the inevitable, Prudence began taking the clothes from Becca's bags and arranging them in the wardrobe.

"Mom, I want to do it myself."

"Just let me . . ."

Stuart placed a soft hand on his wife's shoulder. "It's time, Prudence. We have a flight to catch."

She squeezed Becca's shoulders. "If you cry, I'll cry," her daughter said.

Prudence wanted to do more than cry. She wanted to let out a guttural wail that would echo down the concrete hallway.

Instead, she said, "Don't forget me!"

To which Becca replied, "That would be hard to do, Mom."

———

NOW, BECAUSE SHE did not have to prepare dinner or run anyone to ballet lessons, Prudence lay listlessly in her chaise by the pool, where she indulged her new obsession with death.

The morbid thoughts had come without warning. She couldn't talk herself out of them. It was like falling in love suddenly and with the wrong person. It became a sickness. A fever. An illness with no known cure. She would die. Her memorial would attract gawkers. It wouldn't rain like it does in the movies. It'd be ridiculously hot. People would wear shorts and flip-flops. They'd bring their stupid water bottles and take pictures on their phones. They'd snap up those cheap plastic dolls on eBay first chance they got. Prudence at the Piano, they were called. Her grandmother had arranged for them, like that awkward Dick Cavett interview when she was eight—he'd asked what her favorite song was and she had replied, "Boogie Fever." Everyone laughed, of course, because he meant, what was her favorite song *to play*. Prudence would be remembered for that interview, which had racked up nearly three million views on YouTube.

"I'm going to die having been merely a circus act," she said to Mrs. Wintour. The eight-pound shih tzu cocked her head, and Prudence nodded the way you do when you're in the company of someone who just gets you. She stared out into the cinnamon-colored desert at the cholla and the brittlebush. It had been a rainless summer. The hot wind blew, the mesquite trees rattled, the yard was kindling. It just needed a spark.

IT WAS SIX when the glass door slid open.

"There you are," Stuart said.

"Here I am," she said.

"Good day?" he asked.

"A day," she replied. "How are the banks?"

"Still up and running. Look, you're burning."

Prudence let out a long breath. "*Je vais mourir.*" For Prudence spoke three languages, often lapsing into French when she was being dramatic.

"What?"

"I'm going to die.")

"How?"

"I don't know yet."

"Ah."

"What a pity." She shook her head. "*C'est dommage.*"

Stuart unclipped his cuff links. "We're all going to die, you know."

"Doesn't that bother you?"

He shrugged, surveying his desert kingdom. He liked coming home to its marble floors and travertine walls. The mahogany-paneled billiard room gave him a thrill he found hard to name. The spectacular cactus garden, visible through floor-to-ceiling windows, was soothing after a long day of asset-backed securities. Then there was the pool, surrounded by teak sectionals and glass tabletops, ceramic pots cascading with succulents. It was a grand residence, and it was their home—a home made possible by the extraordinary success of one little jingle that Prudence had composed at the age of eighteen. And that was Pep Soda, on the air for thirty-one years. Kids turned it into a game in the schoolyard. Fraternity brothers sang it when they got drunk. Gardeners whistled it while trimming hedges. It was very catchy.

"You're obsessing," he told her.

Prudence did what she usually did in situations like this. She blamed her parents. "It's all that LSD my mom took back in the sixties. I'm damaged."

Prudence's parents had been hippies. They'd had long hair and listened to folk music and had not worn shoes.

"Yes, that's true. It was true last week, too, but you weren't baking in the sun talking about death then." Stuart stripped off his suit and jumped into the pool in his plain white briefs. He came up for air and said, "You know what I think?"

"Tell me."

"I think you're having a midlife crisis."

"Really?"

"Mm-hmm."

"I should buy a sports car then."

"You already have a Porsche," Stuart said. "A red one, even."

But a flashy car did not take away the acute realization that in exactly one year and two months, Prudence would be fifty. She was old, her children were gone. So were family dinners around the table, vacations to the lake, and endless trips to the grocery store. That wonderful day-to-dayness that gave Prudence purpose had pried her loose from the clutches of fame. Yet despite this sublime domesticity, she feared that her life would come to an end without accomplishing the one thing that eluded her.

PRUDENCE WOKE THE next morning with a nameless trouble in her heart. She went through a list: Her children were safe; Stuart was well; Mrs. Wintour was at her feet; they had not run out of toilet paper. She tried to tell herself to *carpe diem*, but then, while brushing her teeth, she counted four new gray hairs and saw her mother's face looking back at her. For the rest of the day, she could not find purpose in any task.

When Stuart came home that evening, the dry-cleaning bag with his French-cuffed shirts was still in the hall. There was nothing in the refrigerator except an expired carton of milk, a pint of molded raspberries, and a half-drunk bottle of Cristal he swore had been unopened yesterday. On the mail table was an AARP application ripped down the center.

He went upstairs to where Prudence was in the tub, legs draped over the sides, smoking a thin brown cigarette and reading a self-help book, *You Are a Badass*. From a portable record player, Scarlatti's Sonata in D Major echoed in the marble *en suite*. The Baccarat candy dish they received for their wedding twenty-one years ago, which once held gold-wrapped chocolates, was overflowing with cigarette butts.

Stuart sat on the ottoman in their bathroom and unlaced his shoes. "What's going on here, Prudence?"

"I'm learning how to stop doubting myself and start living an awesome life."

"You need to get out," he said.

Prudence exhaled a tassel of smoke. "I have nowhere to go," she announced. Prudence always had somewhere to go, usually somewhere fantastic and spontaneous. More than once she had caught a matinee on the way to the grocery store.

"I'm flying to London on business next week," Stuart said. "Come with me."

Prudence dipped the cigarette into the bath, where it made a sound like paper ripping. "Could you switch out the record? Mendelssohn, 'Songs Without Words in F-Sharp Minor,' please."

Stuart replaced the disc in its jacket even though other records had been tossed onto the ottoman without being put away. "What do you think?" he said, flipping through the stack of albums. He had no idea what he was looking for.

"About Mendelssohn?"

"No, London."

Prudence shifted in the tub. There was the ten-hour flight and the line at customs and the dog sitter and the packing and the jet lag and Stuart's long meetings. Not to mention the overpriced food. The last time she was in London, she paid twelve pounds for avocado toast. Toast!

"I don't feel like it." She was slowing down. This is what happened with age.

"This cannot continue, Prudence."

"Fine. I'll start a book club."

That sounded a little pedestrian for Prudence. "Really?"

"Sure."

"When?"

"Soon as I find a good book."

—

STUART TRIED DESPERATELY to cheer his wife. First, he cooked her favorite foods, like roasted lemon chicken, tomato basil soup, and tuna salad Niçoise. But the chicken was dry, the soup was bland, and the Niçoise mushy. Not surprising since Stuart's culinary skills were limited to grilling burgers and hot dogs, two things that Prudence would not eat.

Stuart then bought her an emerald ring that he found in the silverware drawer a week later. He tried box seats to *Don Quixote,* dinner reservations at Dominick's Steak House, flowers, chocolate. A rare five-disc record set of Beethoven's *Bicentennial Collection* that he found at the Goodwill, of all places.

All to no avail. His once-vibrant wife was slipping away.

Prudence was in bed every day until afternoon. Her dinner went untouched each night.

This crushing ennui might have gone on for decades, as Prudence was a good forty years from her actual death, but the drinking and the smoking and the tubbing came to an abrupt end one morning when she was awakened by the hiss of hydraulic brakes. Then the doorbell. Then Mrs. Wintour barking.

Prudence answered the door in men's silk pajamas with a long strand of milk-white pearls knotted at her chest. Three large men in blue uniforms, the names Gil and Hector and Fred stitched in red on their left breast pockets, stood on the other side.

"Delivery for a Ms. Prudence Childs," Fred said.

Prudence did not remember any recent purchases that needed a moving van, as she had been consumed with the thought of dying and had not been out. Peeking over Gil's shoulder she saw an enormous truck with the words *Music Box Delivery Services* emblazoned on the side.

"I did not order a music box."

"It's a piano."

"I already have a piano," Prudence said flatly. She did, too—a spinet kept in her study, a room playfully dubbed "the Sewing Room," although it had never seen any actual sewing. It was on this spinet that Prudence had once played Disney scores for her children, where, before that, she had composed jingles for cleaning products. But the jingles had been merely a job—the spinet may as well have been a typewriter.

Hector unfolded a document and handed it to Fred who handed it to Prudence who handed it back to Fred. "You'll have to read it to me."

"Ma'am?"

"I don't have my glasses."

Fred held the document as if a formal proclamation. "Says here, deliver to a Ms. Prudence Childs, 10534 Pricklypoppy Lane, Scottsdale, Arizona."

Indeed, that was her address. Indeed, that was her name.

"Where'd it come from?"

Fred did not care where pianos came from, only where they were going. "I don't know, ma'am."

"It must say on there."

It was eight in the morning and 95 degrees. Not the best sort of weather for moving large objects weighing nearly a thousand pounds. Fred and Hector and Gil wanted to get the piano off the truck and into the house and assembled before the temperature rose to triple digits.

"Says one six-foot, eleven-inch, Model B, grand Steinway, ebony finish from Longmont, Colorado."

A *Steinway*. A Model *B*. From *Long*mont.

It couldn't be.

Could it?

Prudence gasped and Fred frowned. Gil checked the time, Hector wiped his brow, and Mrs. Wintour splayed herself across the cool marble floor.

"Take it back," Prudence said. "I can't have it in my life now."

"Why's that, ma'am?"

"I have to start a book club."

CHAPTER TWO

The Cover of *Rolling Stone*

Exactly eight hours after the Steinway arrived in the Childses' marble foyer, Oscar-winning composer Curtis Lyons was seated on a massive sound stage in Burbank, California, knocking out his own furious arrangement of "Flight of the Bumblebee." Cameras panned to showcase a whir of finger acrobatics. Curtis was a marvelous musician with an excellent pedigree: a Performance Studies major at Princeton with a film scoring degree from the Berklee College of Music.

Curtis Lyons was competing on live television in a one-to-one battle against another pianist, Rakul Nagaraja. The reigning champion, Nagaraja had just completed a kinetic rendition of Scott Joplin's the "Maple Leaf Rag." The show's producers had played up the differences between the two men. They implied that calling Rakul Nagaraja a *pianist* was, perhaps, something of a stretch. He had not attended a prestigious music institute. He had not played with any symphonies. Mr. Nagaraja was an accountant for a large plumbing supply manufacturer. He had been taught by a neighborhood piano teacher in the suburbs of Akron, Ohio, and kept up his skills into adulthood, practicing each morning before work. He could play anything you put in front of him.

Inside the cavernous Burbank Studio 1, massive klieg lights and tiers of descending flip seats allowed the audience to look down on the ample stage. Here in Studio 1, home to game shows and sitcoms, the cameras were busy filming the exciting conclusion of *Alexei Petrov's Dueling Piano Wars!* The discrepancies between its contestants were part of the draw. The very first episode had pitted a Juilliard graduate against a touring keyboardist for the Smashing Pumpkins. Then there was the beloved, white-haired conductor of the Baton Rouge Symphony Orchestra versus a fifteen-year-old wunderkind from Japan. And so on.

Each week, two dueling pianists performed a piece from each of three categories:

- Classical (1750–1820);
- Romantic (1820–1900); and
- Contemporary (1900–current).

The groupings themselves were a surprise to viewers who thought *classical* meant any music without an electric guitar or lead vocalist. They tuned in each week to the now-familiar sight of two nine-foot Yamaha CFX concert grands facing each other onstage. The spotlight shone down on the first pianist, who played something from the classical period. Then the focus switched to the second, who played their own prepared piece. After both contestants finished, the host, Alexei Petrov, critiqued the performances. The show cut to a commercial after each segment, at which time audience members would text in their votes. Whoever won two out of three categories was declared the winner and would go on to duel another pianist the next week.

Few at the network had believed in the show when it premiered in late June. The odds of success are slim for even the most innovative television concepts. Statistically, 80 percent of all new shows fail, and *Alexei Petrov's Dueling Piano Wars!* didn't have any of the stuff that tended to attract a wide audience. It lacked sex, drugs, and anyone resembling a celebrity. No spies. No billionaires. No dead bodies.

What were the chances for an eight-episode competition featuring *classical music,* of all things? Best-case scenario, it would serve as low-budget filler and fade into obscurity by September, pacifying casual viewers through the summer months until the high-budget programming returned in the fall.

But no one had anticipated how much the camera would love the show's host. And what the camera loved, the audience loved. It was hard to stop looking at Alexei Petrov. The twenty-two-year-old Russian pianist had flawless skin and lush, sable-colored hair that gleamed richly under stage lights. His high cheekbones and full lips looked like they'd been carved from a block of the finest marble. He often curled his long, elegant fingers under his chin while he listened to whatever was happening on the stage, his smile as untelling as a da Vinci portrait. But it was Alexei's large, coppery eyes that were his most extraordinary feature. They were deep and roomy and could hide all sorts of things, most notably a long-standing ambivalence.

Nothing in Alexei Petrov's life had prepared him to be a TV star. He had been a gifted child and a hard worker. But it was only at the urging of a well-meaning piano teacher that Alexei's mother got the boy out of Russia. From Moscow to Paris to Los Angeles. The show wasn't his idea, yet here he was, the world at his expensively clad feet and a powerful television network capitalizing on his star power.

The duel between Curtis Lyons and Rakul Nagaraja was the season finale. When Curtis Lyons finished playing, his fingers momentarily hovered over the keyboard as if to keep the song from evaporating. He straightened and took a deep breath. The camera panned to his damp forehead then down to the fingers that he kept flexing as if to relieve a cramp. He took a bow. The audience clapped and hollered.

Dressed in a crisp, collarless shirt that would shortly become an Instagram sensation, Alexei Petrov said, "Mr. Lyons, to take sixteenth notes and play them as octaves at one hundred fifty beats a minute is a musical feat. But your performance tonight made me feel like I was in Cosmo Kramer's head and couldn't get out."

"Cosmo Kramer?" Curtis Lyons replied, flummoxed. "Like . . . Kramer from *Seinfeld*?"

The audience giggled. Even though a tutor had been hired to help Alexei Petrov perfect his English, he'd learned much more from watching old *Seinfeld* episodes on Hulu.

"You gave us one frenetic speed, like Kramer when he gets a not-so-bright idea."

The illustrious Oscar winner was not used to being compared to an unhinged nineties television character. He crossed his arms over his chest and drew his lips tightly together. The camera caught the reaction.

Alexei Petrov continued. " 'Bumblebee' is a balance of crescendo and decrescendo, soft and loud, hurried and constrained. Rachmaninoff's arrangement gives the listener the feeling of one lonely bee, a single bee in turbulent flight. We who are listening imagine it as a kind of . . . ballet with wings." At this, Alexei paused for a few moments, caressing the air with his long fingers as if hearing the notes in his head. "Your version sounded as if an entire hive had been beaten with a mallet and booted off a cliff."

There it was again, that tittering from the audience. Alexei Petrov did not consciously aim to make fools of the contestants on his live television show. The audience, at this moment, had ceased to exist for him. He rose from his seat and strode across the stage, giving full view of his tailored trousers and Gucci loafers. He sat before one of the concert grands and played a passage of "Bumblebee."

"See what my right hand is doing?" he said to Curtis Lyons. "You have to make that right hand . . ." He played three measures over and over, a gold Rolex glinting from the stage lights. (Rolex, a sponsor of the show, had given him the watch but Alexei felt its bulk impeded his playing and had been repeatedly reprimanded for removing it before heading to the keyboard.) "Hear that? It is but the lightest touch, which you will only achieve through repetition."

It was a hallmark of the show, Alexei Petrov springing from his seat and playing the critiqued part of the piece. The first time he did it, producers had a fit. But the audience (and piano teachers the world over) couldn't get enough of Alexei's spontaneity. They were in awe of this dapper musician who didn't talk down to them, as if he expected more of people than they expected of themselves. Alexei was biting, but he was never patronizing, something viewers responded to. "Playing is practicing" was an oft-used line. As was "See how clean that sounds?" He was a master of the catchphrase.

"Mr. Nagaraja's piece may not have been as demanding, physically," Alexei Petrov said, "yet he pulled off the syncopated rhythm that showcases a good rag. Your blitzkrieg of notes could only register as an assault."

Through Alexei Petrov's running commentary, the audience learned new terms like syncopation, *allegro molto, legato,* and *tempo rubato.* They learned that music composed by the Romantics—Liszt, Chopin, Puccini—was more intense and expressive than the heavily structured pieces of earlier composers such as Mozart and Haydn. They learned the difference between a fugue and a prelude, a sonata and a minuet.

They also learned to connect history to the contemporary, discovering that the intro of Lady Gaga's "Bad Romance" was lifted from Bach's "Well-Tempered Clavier"; that Beyoncé's "Ave Maria" was Schubert; that Janelle Monáe's "Say You'll Go" was borrowed from Debussy's "Clair de Lune."

Most live performances of classical music took place in gilded concert halls, in front of an audience of genteel patrons. But *Alexei Petrov's Dueling Piano Wars!* drew in a huge cross section of humanity, with a viewership of fourteen million from around the world. Alexei's biting critiques fueled the interest:

If I ever have to hear that Bach prelude played so unevenly again, I will douse myself in lighter fluid and beg for a lit match.

That sonata was so bland, I won't forget it once you leave the stage. I forgot it right as you were playing it to me.

I slept more during your performance of "Allegretto" than I did last night.

Over the course of two months, Bach went from being a relic from a distant era—exciting to those who championed sweater vests and argyle socks—to alive and relevant. Clips of the show went viral. You could bet the following morning's talk around the office would turn into a heated debate about whether one contestant's rapidly ascending fourths really held up to the other player's whirring theatrics. The show had given classical music a shot in the arm.

ALEXEI PETROV FOLLOWED the instructions on the teleprompter. "We will be right back after a word from our sponsor, Flush 'N Clean toilet bowl cleaner. You flush, it cleans."

During the four-minute pause, Alexei went backstage, where someone handed him his phone and a bottle of water. He sat in the makeup chair and checked his messages while the makeup artist sponged his forehead. Les Strom, the showrunner, clapped his protégé on the back like they were the best of friends.

"Hey, kid, congratulations. What a great season. Blew everyone's mind."

"Thank you, Lester."

"If Mick Jagger and Van Cliburn had a baby, it'd be you."

Alexei Petrov smiled his Mona Lisa smile and continued scrolling through his phone.

Les Strom continued. "Hey, listen, slight change of plan when you go back out there."

Alexei hated these last-minute changes. The producers did it to him by design, so he would not have a say.

"It's no big deal, okay? You know how we'd planned for you to make the big announcement *after* you declare tonight's winner?"

"Yes. First the winner, then the big news, then I play 'Scarbo.' The End."

"Well, we've decided we want you to change up the order. You're going to make the big announcement first, then knock 'em all out with your performance. Your stuff has to happen before you report the winner."

Alexei did not like this. "Won't that steal their lightning?"

"Thunder, it's thunder, won't that steal their thunder."

"Won't that steal their thunder?"

"No, no, of course not. We just want to drag out the suspense. You know, give folks at home a few more seconds to get those final votes in while you give them a taste of what you can do."

That wasn't true.

The network had demanded the reordering because it did not want people tuning out immediately after the week's champion was revealed. Fourteen million people were watching, a bonanza in terms of commercial revenue. Alexei Petrov didn't always do as instructed, so to ensure everything went according to the network's plan, Les Strom would withhold the name of the night's winner until after Alexei made the big announcement and played "Scarbo."

It was crucial that the audience get a mind-blowing dose of what they could expect from Alexei in the future. "Scarbo," the third and most technically dazzling movement of Maurice Ravel's *Gaspard de la nuit,* would give it to them.

Les Strom clapped Alexei on the shoulder, searching the tigerlike eyes that hid everything so well. "We good to go, buddy?"

Alexei would never get used to being called *buddy.* "Sure, Lester."

He knew what was coming next. One minute before he had to go back onstage, his phone chimed with the expected text. Alexei didn't have to look at it to know who it was from (his mother), what it said (to follow Mr. Strom's instructions), and why it was sent (in the interest of the show's success). Without answering the text, he handed his phone off.

Alexei Petrov went back out to center stage, bowed elegantly, and waited for the applause to die down. "Before I announce the champion of *Alexei Petrov's Dueling Piano Wars!* I have a special surprise for you. I would be honored to have you all back again. Would you like to come back?"

The camera panned to an enthusiastic studio audience. "This fall, on October 27, I will be the one in the hot seat. I will perform live on this stage in a duel with a yet-to-be named pianist, maybe the only living person I might possibly lose to."

A roar burst from the audience. Though at this point, Alexei Petrov could have burped the alphabet and people would have approved.

"Cash prize—" He smiled, waiting for the fervor to die down. "The winner will be awarded a cash prize of a million dollars." Message delivered, fever pitched, Alexei sat at one of the enormous pianos and played "Scarbo." When he took his bow, the crowd, again, erupted into applause.

The announcement of the evening's champion, Mr. Rakul Nagaraja, came almost as an afterthought, the response noticeably polite compared to the electricity generated by Alexei's October surprise.

Les Strom couldn't have been happier.

Alexei, however, was not happy. If he had to put a name to what he was feeling, it would have been envy. Alexei envied the clear joy of someone who was motivated by success. (What most people recognized as success.) He even envied its opposite, the disappointment that seeped from Mr. Curtis Lyons like beads of sweat. For Alexei, a numbness had set in long ago. He did not get a rush from the applause that was so charged the floor vibrated. He could not remember the last time he laughed at a joke or cried at the opera. He could not remember how it felt to hold someone's hand. Or sleep together on a Paris afternoon. Even his memories were colorless now. He was on top of his game, adored by millions. But that was just a number to someone who wanted to be loved by only one.

CHAPTER THREE

Sleeping Beauty

Stuart returned from his morning workout wearing a damp shirt and the sweatband his daughters repeatedly told him made him look like a dork. He saw the delivery truck in his driveway. "Oh, wonderful, it came."

Prudence huffed. "This was you?"

"Yes, darling." He put his hands on the top of her shoulders. "Can you believe I found your childhood piano!"

"Where?"

"In your uncle's basement. When I told your uncle's fourth wife, Kaitlyn, I'd take care of all moving expenses, she agreed to let it go. Said it took up too much space."

"Why?" Prudence's eyes were electric with anger.

Stuart shrugged. "Maybe their house is too small."

"No, why did you think I would want it?"

Stuart was confused. He'd gone through an enormous amount of trouble to get the piano and did not understand why his wife was upset. "I thought it would get you out of your funk."

"I'm starting a book club."

That again.

Stuart didn't understand this latest fixation. He didn't know that this was the whole point. A book club was void of expectation. You chose the book, read the book, talked about the book, and ate some cheese.

The piano was an entirely different matter. Prudence had been the youngest pianist to play Carnegie Hall. She had won a Grammy at sixteen. She had performed in the most venerable concert halls in Europe and she had become a magical figure. Admired. Worshipped. Looked upon as if she possessed the powers of gods. Proof of nature over nurture.

The reality was, it had been a hell of a lot of work. She had practiced from morning until night. There were days when young Prudence did not see the sun. Half the time she didn't know what city she was in. Her best friends were piano instructors. They called her an "old soul," which was the exact opposite of what Prudence wanted to be. As she approached adulthood, she feared she'd never fulfill the expectations set by her youth. The world would hold her to an impossible standard. There is no middle road for prodigies. There would be some sort of fall. There always was.

Prudence decided to walk away. She embraced the possibilities of a commonplace life. Pot roast for dinner and baths in the evening. A game of Scrabble on a Sunday afternoon. Too many people spent their whole lives running from the ordinary. They missed out on the best part.

Now the monster was back. The one that had devoured her childhood with sharp teeth.

Gil, Hector, and Fred stood in the marble foyer watching this exchange between Prudence and Stuart, all because Stuart had underestimated how much Prudence hated nearly every minute of her formative years.

He also underestimated how very large the piano was.

Fred checked his watch. "Ma'am, you want us to continue?"

Prudence considered. There was no way she was sending the piano back to her uncle's fourth wife, Kaitlyn.

"Continue," Prudence told Fred.

This made Stuart smile.

"Where you want it, ma'am?" Fred asked.

"Right here, of course."

Fred examined the cathedral ceiling and marble floor. "Sure? There's nothing to absorb the sound. Whole house gonna rattle when you play."

Prudence had no intention of playing. "I'm sure."

The piano had arrived in parts that were wrapped in soft blankets and secured with thick straps. As each large silver buckle was unfastened and each quilted blanket fell away, Prudence watched the monstrous instrument gleam with the sleekness of a killer whale bursting from the ocean. Her stomach felt as if it were filling with ice. Mrs. Wintour had a dog's sense and knew, however dogs know, that her mistress was upset. With a whimper, she pawed at Prudence's leg.

The piano took up nearly the entire foyer, which was large in and of itself. When the instrument was fully assembled, Stuart watched as the movers propped up its enormous lid, revealing an intricate network of metal and wire and pins and hammers. Stuart could not imagine his wife, at the age of five, having utter command of such a colossal instrument. He'd only heard her play the little spinet in the Sewing Room, each note absorbed by the clutter of books and furniture and unhung artwork. Hardly the stuff of concert halls.

"Wow, my love," he said.

"Yep," Prudence said, and she ran her finger along the edge, where two little chips had been made by her two front teeth.

"Mr. Childs," Fred said to Stuart, "just need you to sign some paperwork and we'll be out of your way."

"Right." He turned to his wife. "Play something, darling."

"It'll be too loud."

"Mm, make it good then."

"I don't think so."

"Please. It's so beautiful."

It sure was. It also made the most beautiful sound. This was one of the finest pianos ever built. Why did Prudence think she could resist its powers?

While Gil checked the weather on his phone and Hector folded the moving blankets and Fred shuffled the paperwork, Prudence sat before the old Steinway, its keys oxidized to the hue of old newspapers. Then Debussy's "Clair de Lune" began to flow from her fingertips and a hundred years fell away. Gil looked up from his phone and Hector stopped midfold and Fred nearly dropped the clipboard.

Prudence played with a knowing melancholy. Like having to walk away from someone you believed you'd love forever. If the notes had a scent, they'd smell of gardenias. She closed her eyes and saw images of pale green rooms on empty Sunday afternoons.

It was that kind of a song. Prudence was that kind of a pianist. The feeling of ennui that had gripped her for the past month faded like smoke.

The three large piano movers were seized with tenderness as each nursed an old ache in his heart. Gil thought of eating meatloaf in his mother's kitchen. Fred pined for his grown sons. Hector pictured ballerinas, graceful and strong as they glided across the stage. He had never been to the ballet.

"Ms. Childs," Fred said, "I've been moving pianos for thirty years and I've never heard anyone play that way. You reminded me of the joy I had when I used to take my sons fishing. Why aren't you out there playing?"

"That's very kind of you. But no one wants to hear me play anymore," she said and pulled the fallboard down over the keys.

"I do," Stuart said.

"You have to say that, I'm your wife. Anything less, and you'll be sleeping in the garage tonight."

Oh, but she was wrong. The music had a strange, enchanting power—it had opened the lid of that black velvet box in Stuart's mind, the one where he kept his dream.

CHAPTER FOUR

Damn, I Wish I Was Your Lover

The morning Stuart flew out of Phoenix Sky Harbor Airport for London's Heathrow, Bobby Wheeler was in Redwood City, California, wondering how he was going to come up with the money he owed his former employer. Bobby Wheeler had worked his way up to Regional Mechanic for the Northern California District for Vantage Car Rental, which meant he got to visit all eight shops from San Francisco to Monterey, overseeing maintenance and repairs of the vehicles. He had his pick of the fleet, too. Usually a tricked-out Chevy Camaro or a badass, cherry-red Dodge Challenger. It was the best job he ever had, and he had screwed it all up.

Nobody would hire him now. Not after he ran up $88,642 for what he told his bosses were "travel expenses and invoices for car parts." Not after all the papers ran the story, with variations of the headline: REDWOOD CITY MAN TARGET OF ONLINE SCAM, EMPLOYER PAYS THE PRICE.

Vantage Car Rental had no interest in prosecuting, not if they could get their money back. So they made a deal. A payment plan, actually. If Bobby Wheeler made each and every payment in full and on time, he would avoid jail time. But to make the payments Bobby needed a job. Since he couldn't get a job, he would have to sell his Redwood City townhouse. He was fifty years old and finding an other place to live was going to be tough on his jobless, debt-burdened budget. He already bought his groceries at Dollar Tree.

It wasn't fair. That's what Bobby was thinking when the doorbell rang.

"Mr. Wheeler?" said a petite woman in a blue suit. Her voice was as warm and inviting as a bath.

"Yes?"

"Allison Lin, Zephyr Real Estate. You contacted me about selling your home?"

She shook his hand and gave a bit of a squeeze. Bobby Wheeler felt something inside of him stir.

He stepped aside. "Come in, please. Call me Bobby."

Allison Lin looked around, then turned her attention back to Bobby. It was more than attention, it was focus, and it made him feel special.

"How many bedrooms, Bobby?"

"Two."

"Bathrooms?"

"Two and a half."

"Bobby, you mind if I look around?"

"Be my guest." Bobby liked the way she said his name. She was pretty. She smelled good.

Allison Lin strode through the front room and into the kitchen and down the hallway and into the bedrooms. She opened cupboards, looked into closets, and peeked under beds.

"How much do you want to sell this for, Bobby?"

"A billion dollars."

She gave him a crooked smile.

"Nah, kidding, kidding," he said. "What do you think?"

"Market value on this place should be about $800,000. You're not going to get that, though."

"Why not?"

"There's a lot that needs to be repaired and replaced. The broken light fixture in the bathroom. Those warped cupboards in the kitchen. Potential buyers will think you haven't taken care of this place."

"Okay."

"You're going to have to put some money into this place to sell it."

He hadn't counted on that. "Really?"

"You'll get it all back and then some, trust me. Possibly even multiple bids."

"Multiple bids?"

"That really drives the price up. Listen, this is the most expensive area in the world. The *world,* Bobby. You could make some good money here."

"I could?"

"Just sold a condo in Foster City that went twenty thousand over asking. Another in Belmont—a house—went *fifty* over list in a bidding war."

"No!"

"You're going to need to declutter, though. You've got boxes everywhere and to potential buyers, it makes them think there's not enough storage."

Bobby Wheeler scratched the back of his neck. "I like my stuff."

"You want buyers to be able to imagine themselves in your home, Bobby."

Bobby Wheeler could never imagine people in his home. What a nice thought.

"I've got some great ideas on how to stage it," Allison Lin said.

"Stage it?"

"Sure. We'll put in some furniture that's better suited for the space. Your recliner is great, but it really shouldn't be placed in the middle of the room in front of the television. You want it to feel warm and welcoming."

He sure did.

"What about all my stuff? Get rid of it?"

"What you don't want to get rid of, you can put in a storage unit.

There's a great company off El Camino—Mike's Attic. Tell him Allison Lin sent you."

He liked this woman. She was exactly what he needed in his life—someone who'd get rid of his mess and fix everything broken. "Was just waiting for you, darling."

She rewarded him with a weak smile.

Allison Lin studied her new client. He was a strange one. "I can get you a number for a handyman. In the meantime, start cleaning. I'll run some comps in your area and get back to you. You on board?"

Bobby Wheeler snapped off a salute and said, "Bobby Wheeler reporting for duty, ma'am."

FOR THE FIRST time in months, Bobby Wheeler felt happy. Things were moving in the right direction. He turned on some Van Halen and bounced around the house.

By three o'clock the next day, the closets were empty and the front room full. There were beat-up suitcases and mismatched chairs and dented lampshades. There were plastic crates filled with obsolete computer cords and back issues of *Car and Driver*. A box from that damn ex-wife of his. Of course, he got stuck with her junk. He was always holding on to other people's junk.

At a quarter after three, his phone rang.

He turned down REO Speedwagon. "Y'ello!"

"Mr. Wheeler?" It was Allison Lin.

"Heyyyy, you," he said as if they had already made a date. Like to a Giants game or something. Tickets behind home plate. "Thought I told you to call me Bobby."

"Uh, Bobby . . ."

"Got this place practically emptied out. Ready for tile guys, painters, you name it."

He waited for her praise.

"We're going to have to put a hold on that."

He stopped chewing his gum. "Why's that?"

"Mr. Wheeler, you've got a lien on your house."

"A lien," he repeated.

"As in, you owe someone money and they have possession of your house until you pay it off." He could hear the beep of a key fob unlocking a car door.

"Yeah, that. I was going to sell the house to pay them."

"It doesn't work that way. Legally, they have the right to sell the house."

"And reap the profits from multiple bids?"

Bobby did not like this Allison Lin. She lacked the enthusiasm of her counterpart the day before. "That's *if* we get multiple bids. For the time being, my hands are tied."

"How do I get this lien taken off my house?"

"Pay off whoever put it on in the first place."

"Then would I be able to sell my house and get multiple offers?"

Again, a pause. "Sure, Mr. Wheeler . . . look, when you get the lien paid off, give me a call."

Bobby felt the familiar stab of rejection followed by the tight grip of failure. It was a pattern.

"Shit." He kicked the box that belonged to his ex-wife. *Boof.* His size twelve foot made a crease in its worn side. He kicked it again. Because he was still mad at her for leaving him, even after all this time. He kicked the box again and a seam busted, spilling yellowed sheet music out onto the floor.

PRUDENCE WORE TASSELED loafers (sans socks) and had blunt, chin-length hair when Bobby Wheeler met her in the summer of 1986. He didn't know her as the youngest person ever to host *Saturday Night Live*. She was just the cute girl who worked part-time at Disc World, the record store next to the auto parts place where he worked on Bowen Street in Longmont, Colorado.

It was a regular old lunch hour when Bobby Wheeler first saw her. He had wandered over after eating the sandwich his mother had made for him, intending to buy the new Dire Straits album. He tried to make eye contact with a girl browsing the cassettes, but he was distracted by the loud voice coming from the back of the store. Something about a box of records being dropped on the floor.

"I don't care about your hands, Prudence."

"That would make you the only one on the planet."

The manager continued to hassle her about cracked records and leaving the cash register drawer open. He was being a real asshole. Bobby Wheeler would have popped off at him by now. Not this girl. She wasn't flustered or defiant, just very sure of herself. He wished he had that kind of self-control.

It became a regular thing after that, him going in on his lunch hour. He liked to watch her work. She was great with customers. Always as passionate about their selections as they were and even more knowledgeable. She was smart and understood a shitload about music. She'd tap on the metal cash register with drumsticks to the beginning of "When Doves Cry." "Hear that uneven beat? That's syncopation." Or how classical music could be about sex. Sex! "Listen to Ravel's *Boléro*. It'll make you blush." Or how this composer, Rachmaninoff, loved fast cars just like Bobby.

They got to know each other quickly. She'd take him into the little soundproof room in the back of the store and play stuff he never heard of. John Coltrane, Dizzy Gillespie. Beethoven. A guy could get beat up for listening to Beethoven in 1986. But Bobby was falling hard.

"How do you know so much about music?" he asked her.

"It's always been inside me." She told him she'd only been fifteen when she went away to college in New York City.

"Wow, your parents let you go?"

"I don't have parents. I live with my grandmother."

"Are your parents dead?"

"No, just selfish. Anyway, I didn't last at Juilliard. I flipped out from the pressure. My grandmother won't let me forget it."

Prudence rolled up the sleeve of her pink Izod shirt to reveal a purple bruise on her right bicep. "She never messes with my hands, though."

This was all terribly troubling to Bobby Wheeler. He decided he had to find a way to save her.

But before he could figure out how, Prudence decided she would save herself. To hell with her grandmother's tantrums. She was going to run away from home.

Could she borrow some money?

"Don't leave, Peanut," he whispered. "Let's get married instead."

Prudence took a few days to think about it. The more she thought, the more the idea of marriage sounded good. Very grown-up. Marrying Bobby, she would no longer have to be Miss Prudence Paddington, Child Prodigy. She could be Mrs. Prudence Wheeler, Wife and Composer. She would be taken seriously. She would get away from her grandmother. Finally, she would have some peace and quiet.

Bobby Wheeler would be getting something, too. He had grown up in a house where rusted-out cars littered the yard, where the paint on the front porch peeled like an old sunburn. Until he met Prudence, it did not occur to him that there might be more for him. He could see then, through the window of youth, what he might become with a girl like Prudence by his side. A better, more refined version of himself. Someone the world might expect things of.

OR SO HE thought.

Turns out the young couple didn't have much in common. A month into the marriage, the cracks started to show. These weren't little cracks like you'd find in a teacup. These were big fissures like you'd find in the Grand Canyon.

Prudence complained about his music. "Could you stop playing that stupid record over and over? It's starting to scrape out the insides of my ears," she'd say.

"Seriously? It's Iron Maiden!"

He complained about her friends. "I'm not going to another play with your dumb friends."

"Seriously? It's Tom Stoppard."

Prudence didn't drink beer or watch wrestling on television. He didn't read poetry or eat sushi.

That crazy-ass piano was another big problem. He never did figure out how she managed to drag it around everywhere. It was part of her magic, he supposed. It would appear and disappear, as easily as if she had folded it up and deposited it into her purse.

The garage was the only room at Bobby's house that was big enough for the Steinway. His parents' garage, actually. Bobby lived at home with his folks.

The other Mrs. Wheeler couldn't stand the massive piano that had taken over her parking space. Bobby's mom was forced to park her 1978 Oldsmobile Cutlass Supreme—her pride and joy—on the street, where the neighbor's cat left muddy paw marks all over the hood.

Things got worse once Prudence was fired from the record store. (Could happen to anyone, leaving the keys in the door after closing.) Jobless, she would sleep all day and compose music all night. This drove Bobby's mother crazy. "Anyone smart enough to get into Juilliard at fifteen ought to be smart enough to find some *got*damn work," she said.

Bobby tried to stick up for his wife. "It's what she does, Ma, it's her art."

"Art, my ass." Bobby's mother started humming Prudence's latest melody, a simple tune that would eventually become Double Bubble Dish Soap. "That sound like art? Sounds like crap. If you were any kind of man, you'd learn how to handle your wife."

"Prudence is special, Ma—"

"Special, my ass. You're in for a long road, mister."

What could he do? They were living rent-free. He had to let his mother call the shots. Besides, trying to get Prudence to change her habits was like trying to reverse the jet stream.

There was never a moment's peace in that small house. The two Mrs. Wheelers argued constantly.

"You've been stealing my cigarettes, girly."

"I don't smoke Camels," Prudence said. "I smoke Marlboros."

"Would it kill you to wipe down the kitchen table after you eat? My playing cards are sticky."

Prudence doused the table—and the playing cards—with Fantastik. "That better?"

"Spoiled, is what she is," Mrs. Wheeler said to her son.

One night, it all exploded. When Prudence went into the garage to play her piano, Bobby followed her in, his mother not two feet away and feeding him his lines.

"She needs to get her butt back in bed," the senior Mrs. Wheeler said.

"Peanut, come on," Bobby said, "let's go to bed."

"I'm working." Prudence, pencil in hand, played a few notes then wrote on a pad of lined paper.

"You tell her enough of this nonsense."

"Pru, enough."

"Leave me," Prudence said.

His mom's anger radiated like a furnace. "You're weak," she hissed in Bobby's ear.

Bobby Wheeler never acted so much as reacted, responding to whatever was in front of him. He snapped. "Pru, would you just . . ." He gave Prudence a good shove, causing her to topple off the bench. Oddly, as if it had happened before, she did not use her hands to break her fall, but tucked them under her arms and landed on her face. Dazed, she picked herself up and ran off into the night.

She called the next morning for her sheet music. The day after that three guys showed up for the piano. A week later the three-month marriage was annulled.

Bobby Wheeler revisited that evening often, a wound he kept picking at, trying to convince himself it wasn't his fault.

All these years later, there was a knot of loneliness in his stomach that never went away. He didn't have many friends. Hadn't had a date in god knows how long. The closest he got to female conversation was watching those women chat on *The View* every morning. Was it so wrong to want someone in his life? Someone to love, someone who *got him*?

Bobby Wheeler wasn't a bad guy, he just never seemed to get it right.

Turning off REO Speedwagon, he scrolled through his playlist until he found "Clair de Lune." The first time he heard Prudence play it, he had been drawn to it immediately though he couldn't say why. It was sad and hopeful at the same time. He knew nothing about classical music but Prudence told him that didn't matter. "You have just as much a right to love it as anyone."

It was the only time he could remember not feeling stupid about something he didn't know. More than that, it was the first time he felt he had a right to love.

How can you give someone that feeling then take it away?

Sitting down in the middle of the dented lampshades and back issues of *Car and Driver,* Bobby Wheeler wept for Prudence. He wept for the magic in her fingers, for the poetry in her soul.

Bobby Wheeler gathered up the sheet music. That's when he noticed the envelope. The postage was dated November 14, 1986, a week before she'd run out on him. He snatched the letter from its envelope. "Dear Prudence . . ." he read out loud. "I'm writing to you because I've learned of your current circumstances and I strongly encourage you to get out of them. Your talent is the rarest of all and must not be wasted. Isaac Stern once said, people who have a God-given talent have the obligation to share it. They must not withhold their artistry. Please consider returning to Juilliard. Use this jingle for your great escape. Success awaits you."

It was written in rolling cursive that reminded him of the way his grandmother used to write. It was signed *Your friend, Mrs. Martinelli.*

Bobby Wheeler couldn't believe what he was reading. Your great escape? This Mrs. Martinelli had actually *encouraged* Prudence to leave him? Bobby had remembered Prudence talking about the lady, who had been her babysitter and piano teacher, too. But this letter— these were the words of an instigator. An accomplice!

He read the letter a second time before slowly turning it over. There, on the back, was a handwritten score with those famous lines, known all over the world. An earworm before anyone had ever heard of the term. Oh my *god,* thought Bobby. The Pep Soda jingle! It'd been right under his nose the whole time. Prudence was a liar and a cheat. The great solo artist had a partner—at the very least—yet she had taken credit for this jingle and who knows what else?!

He turned off Debussy and double-tapped on Molly Hatchet, "Flirtin' with Disaster." Great fucking song. He turned the volume way up. He tried to jump up on his coffee table but needed the aid of his ottoman as a boost.

He played air guitar, rocking back and forth like a king. He whipped his head up and down, working himself into a sweat. Roaring out the lyrics, he imagined being up on a stage surrounded by his bandmates. The crowd went crazy. This was the persona he'd arm himself with. Rock god.

The song finished, Bobby Wheeler jumped off the coffee table (but lost his balance and fell against the recliner). He wiped his brow, took a bow, and picked up the letter, which he carefully slid back into its envelope.

Once more, he could feel his luck changing.

"See you soon, Peanut."

CHAPTER FIVE

Battaglia

Prudence had been about to take a bath. What else could she do when her husband was in London and she had screwed up the thermostat so that it was stuck at an uncomfortable 59 degrees. She had selected her records and poured in her bath salts. The water was at the perfect temperature. That's when the doorbell rang.

Prudence ignored it. Once a bath was started, it was an inconvenience to stop. But the bell rang a second time, and then a third.

"Oh, dear," Prudence said as she shivered in her summer pajamas. Annoyed, she donned her full-length mink and descended the stairs.

There was something familiar about the man at the front door. Arizona was full of balding men in cargo shorts and bright golf shirts. But this one . . . Prudence studied the triangular face, the pointed chin, the funnel-shaped nose that looked like it had been broken once or twice. She had seen this person before. Had he gone to Juilliard with her? Was he once a neighbor?

Looking into his eyes, those churning swirls of amber and brown, Prudence had an incredible urge to slam the door. She should have, too, because her gentle existence was about to be disrupted.

"Good morning," she said.

It was three in the afternoon.

"Morning, Peanut. Still eccentric as ever, I see."

Peanut? Oh, no.

"Bobby?"

"Ta-da."

"What are *you* doing here?"

He gave her a patient smile. "Aren't you going to ask me in?"

"No."

"It's hot out here, Peanut."

"If my Stuart catches you here, he'll kill you." Prudence wished she'd said "my husband."

Bobby knew she was alone. He'd been watching the house the last twenty-four hours, which wasn't easy to do in the heat. The day before, he watched a man put a suitcase in the trunk of a late-model Jaguar and drive off. He bit down his lip. Her Stuart. She had never referred to him as Her Bobby.

"Stuart, huh? What's he do, run a bank or something?"

"As a matter of fact, yes."

Bobby shifted his weight and chewed his gum and lamented the fact that he was very inept at managing money. "He sounds boring."

"To each his own," Prudence said.

"I'm out in the Bay Area," he said with a nod. "Looking into getting into some start-ups. You know—stock options, percentages, that kind of thing."

"Good for you."

This was not the reaction he sought. Somehow, Plan A, extorting money from Prudence to pay his debts, had skidded into Plan B, trying to win her back. Because Bobby Wheeler had a cart-before-the-horse mentality whenever he attempted to execute any sort of plan. "Yeah, looking into getting out of the car business, you know."

Prudence didn't know. And didn't care. She wanted him gone.

"*Any*way, wanna go get some coffee?"

"What? No."

"Why not?"

Prudence started to shut the large iron door. "I'm married, Bobby. Happily."

He quickly backed up to Plan A. "Wait! I have something for you."

"I don't want anything from you."

"Yes, you do. Same thing you wanted the night you left me."

"My Joan Armatrading album?"

He held up the battered box haphazardly strapped with duct tape. "Your music!"

"You came all this way to give me back my music. After all this time?"

"Yep." He had a look in his eye. She remembered that look. She didn't like it.

"You needn't have bothered. I've replaced it."

He shook his head slowly. "Not this you haven't." He couldn't wait to see her face when he showed her the letter. "I'll just carry this box inside for you."

"No, leave it."

"It's heavy, P."

"I'm very strong."

His tone turned mocking. "Really, since when? You never lifted a thing because you were always so worried about your stupid hands."

Prudence was getting angry. "You're letting all the hot air into my house. I'm shutting the door."

He knew that once that door was shut she would not open it again. "How about let's go for a drive? Get ice cream like we used to."

"Are you high? I'm not going anywhere with you."

"Well, I'm not leaving until we talk."

"Mind the rattler under that sage bush, then. He likes to sun himself not more than three feet back from where you're standing."

Was she putting him on? Bobby Wheeler couldn't tell, but since he didn't like snakes he got right to the point. He set down the battered box and pulled an envelope from his pocket.

"Remember this, Peanut?"

"I can't read it, I don't have my glasses."

"Here," he said, pulling a pair of readers from his pocket.

"Can I see that paper, please?"

"See with your eyes, not with your hands."

She rolled her eyes and leaned in. He watched her blue-green irises move back and forth. It took her a while to recognize it for what it was: the original manuscript to Pep Soda, her very first commercial jingle, the one she won the Clio for. She still made money from it.

Prudence handed the glasses back. "You try to sell this on eBay and I'll have you arrested. It's not yours."

Bobby Wheeler's face hardened. "Turns out, it's not yours, either."

"What are you talking about?"

Bobby Wheeler flipped the manuscript over to the handwritten note.

"A letter from my piano teacher. So what?" Prudence said. "She wasn't your biggest fan, by the way."

"More than a letter, I'd say." He read it aloud, "'Use this jingle for your great escape. You have such talent.'"

Prudence froze.

Sometimes when you have lived with a lie for thirty years, you come to think of it as truth. This was the case with Prudence. She had backed into her short marriage to Bobby Wheeler after all that nasty business with her grandmother. All the tantrums, and the beatings, the endless humiliation and the eventual running away. It had been a terrible time. Prudence had survived the only way she could, by repressing those awful memories.

Including how she came to acquire the Pep Soda jingle.

Prudence absorbed Bobby Wheeler's words, the buried memory making its way to the surface, until her mouth opened to release a gasp—she was not the author of the jingle! And if she was not the author of the jingle, then her worst fear had been realized: She was an imposter.

She felt hot and clammy. She became light-headed, as if someone had shot a blast of helium through her ear. Mrs. Wintour whimpered, for she knew her mistress was in distress.

"Felt like I'd won the lottery when I found this," Bobby Wheeler said, snapping his gum. "Looks like the prodigy's a fraud."

"I think I'm going to throw up."

"Now, now . . . we can work something out," Bobby Wheeler said.

Prudence thought of Stuart finding out she was a fraud and the color drained from her face.

"Peanut, sit down. You're not well."

There were two elaborate armchairs in the foyer. Bobby Wheeler guided her to one and sat across from her in the other.

"What do you want?" she whispered.

Plan B: "You."

"I'll slit my throat first," she said, not in a whisper.

Back to Plan A: "I need some money."

"Absolutely not."

"I don't want nearly as much as you'd be sued for in back royalties. Once Mrs. Martinelli's heirs find out who really wrote that jingle . . ."

Prudence put her head in her hands. "Oh, god."

Bobby Wheeler shifted his weight, his large body casting a dark shadow over Prudence. "I just have a few bills to pay, Peanut."

A few bills.

Prudence knew that once Bobby got what he wanted, he would only want more. There would be no end to this. And there was no way to pay him without explaining everything to Stuart.

But if Prudence did not give Bobby the money, he could expose her. Her commercials played all over TV and radio. Websites sold collectibles from her prodigy days, like the plastic reproductions of her four-year-old hands and a series of beginner piano books. It wouldn't matter that Prudence had written every other jingle herself, the world was full of assholes who would come crawling out of the woodwork looking to sue.

"How much?" she asked.

Bobby Wheeler smiled. He remembered that if you wanted a puppy, you should ask your parents for a pony. When they said no to the pony, you'd settle for a puppy. "I'd like a million dollars. Cash."

"*What?* I don't have a million dollars cash."

He surveyed the domed ceiling and sparkly chandeliers.

"I think you do, Peanut."

"We don't keep millions of dollars stuffed in a drawer, you idiot. It's all invested."

Bobby did not like when Prudence called him names. "I'll settle for five hundred thousand."

"Five hundred thousand? Why wouldn't you just follow through on your start-ups and your stock options and what have you? All those companies you're *looking into* in the Bay Area."

Again, Bobby Wheeler never thought things through all the way. He began to stammer. "Well, I've, I've had some . . ."

"Forget it!"

"I'm not leaving until we work something out. Remember, I'm the one with the letter." He looked around and, patting the armrests of his chair, said, "Look at us, Peanut, we're like the king and queen on our thrones."

Bobby Wheeler was not her king. "You either hand that letter over to me now or I will destroy it."

"Destroy it? While it's in my pocket? That would be a neat trick. I'd like to see it."

She shot up out of the chair and marched out her front door into the one-hundred-degree heat, her fur coat flapping like a cape.

Bobby Wheeler watched her. "Now what the hell is she up to?"

CHAPTER SIX

Una Fantasia

The morning before Bobby Wheeler tried to extort money from his ex-wife, Tamara Quigley sat at the head of the table in the Quail Mountain conference room, unzipped her brand-new $300 leather Coach portfolio, and extracted a legal pad. It was Tamara's first day as president of the Quail Mountain Homeowners Association. Actually, it was her first day working outside the home since getting married more than twenty years ago.

Tamara had been a stay-at-home mom. Her dream of flitting across the stage in toe shoes and tutus long abandoned, she had given her youth to raising their son, running a household, and keeping to a strict budget. Now that Tommy was grown (though twenty and still at home), she was ready for what was next. Next being a life among the privileged people of Quail Mountain.

"I now call this meeting to order." Tamara had always wanted to say that. "Let's start with lot violations then move on to building permits."

To Tamara's immediate left sat Carl Weston, one of two Quail Mountain residents who served on the HOA board in exchange for a small honorarium. A former insurance salesman who spent most of his days golfing, Carl toured the development in his Buick, on the lookout for even the slightest infraction.

"Lot 15 consistently keeps their garbage dumpster on the street twenty-four hours after trash pickup. CC&Rs, Section 2.1, state, and I quote, 'that all garbage receptacles shall be hidden from street view no more than eight hours after garbage collection.' End quote."

"Have they been issued a warning?" Tamara asked.

"Three times too many, thanks to our last president."

"Is that right?" Tamara said.

"Technically, residents only get one warning. If unheeded, they're fined. If unpaid, we have the power to put a lien on the house."

Tamara smiled at this efficient reporting. But then Carl, who was in this job primarily for the gossip, spent the next fifteen minutes updating the board on Lot 15's imminent divorce.

Tamara steered him back on track. "All right, let's issue Lot 15 one more warning. If they don't respond, fine them."

"They've had multiple notices," Carl said. "Why don't we just fine them now?"

It wasn't that Tamara didn't want to issue the fine. She was dying to use the embossed letterhead she had splurged on:

Tamara Quigley
PRESIDENT
Quail Mountain Homeowners Association

But her instincts told her to use a softer approach until the residents got used to her.

"Not yet. For now, we'll let them know there's a new sheriff in town. Next?"

"Does anyone want that last bagel?" asked a slight young man. His thick mop of hair was wet from the shower, his collared dress shirt a size too large.

Tamara frowned. "Jesse, if you want another bagel, go ahead and take it." Jesse O'Neal was Tamara's assistant, her only direct report. Like his boss, Jesse was not a resident of Quail Mountain. He lived in Tempe near the campus of Arizona State University, where he had, until recently, been a student. At twenty-two years old, and having changed his major no less than five times, he was unable to complete any sort of degree. Jesse had been the sole applicant for the newly created position, which had been posted on the university's website under the heading of "Career Ladder."

Carl continued. "Lot 20 planted a bougainvillea bush. It's in violation of Section 9.0, LANDSCAPE DESIGN."

"Ooh, I heard the wife got a second DUI," said Claire Bialosky. A childless fiftysomething and the former artistic director of the local theater, Claire joined the HOA for something to do after being fired for mounting an overbudgeted, undersold production of *South Pacific*. The last straw had been her ill-advised decision to cover the stage with three thousand pounds of white sand, which resulted in a stage collapse during an encore performance of "There Is Nothing Like a Dame."

"We'll issue them a warning, too." Another opportunity to use the new letterhead!

Wow, that felt good. Tamara was amazed she even got the job in the first place. A posh property management company out of Scottsdale had posted the opening on Indeed. Tamara was thrilled when she landed an interview. She spent days preparing, pressing Tommy to conduct faux interviews so she could practice. She bought a blue power suit that showed off her best feature: her hair—the penny red of her youth had oxidized to the color of walnut shells. What Tamara didn't know was that nobody else had wanted the job.

She had been embarrassed earlier that morning when the guards wouldn't let her pass through the elaborate front gate that was fashioned in the shape of a sprawling palo verde tree.

"Badge," one said.

"Oh, uh, they were going to give it to me today."

"Name."

"Tamara Quigley, president of the HOA," she said proudly.

Wordlessly, he turned from her and made an indeterminable number of phone calls. Finally, the gate opened as if Moses had parted the Red Sea.

"You're only doing your job," she said to the sentries, even though they hadn't apologized. "We all have a part to play in maintaining the grandeur of this magnificent development!"

Tamara may have had more in common with the guards than she did with the residents of Quail Mountain, where houses ranged from a modest one million dollars to a decidedly immodest five million. They had wine rooms, massage rooms, and panic rooms. They had teams of house cleaners and armies of landscapers. Tamara Quigley did not have teams of this or armies of that. But starting today, she had as much right to roam the streets of Quail Mountain as did its residents.

Carl wasted no time proceeding to the next violator. "Lot 22 keeps hanging swimsuits and towels to dry on the gate by the pool."

"And?"

"CC&Rs prohibit outdoor hanging of laundry. Wet swimsuits included."

A self-admitted neat freak, even Tamara had been known to hang her son's swim trunks on their pool fence rather than have them drip all over the bathroom floor. But Tamara did not live in Quail Mountain. She worked at Quail Mountain and she had a job to do.

"Has she had a verbal warning?"

"Plenty of verbal warnings. Lot 22 is a repeat offender."

"That won't do."

"It's not only the towels. You name it, she's done it. And she writes 'Return to Sender' on all violations sent by post. Residents pay a thousand dollars a month in fees, and it's our job to enforce the rules."

The letterhead was turning out to be a wise investment. "What's the address, Carl?"

"10534 Pricklypoppy Lane. Stuart and Prudence Childs."

Tamara copied the address down on her legal pad.

"She's that piano player, you know," Carl said in a tattling tone.

"Pianist," Claire corrected. "She was a child prodigy back in the day. A massive talent."

"Wait," said Tamara. "You don't mean Prudence Paddington, do you?"

"She's Prudence Childs now."

The pen dropped from Tamara's fingers.

"It was so sad when she quit performing," Claire said with a sigh. "What a waste."

"Don't feel too bad for her," Carl said. "She made plenty of money in advertising, from what I hear."

"That's right!" said Claire. "She wrote that jingle to Pep Soda. That detergent commercial, too." Then Claire sang, "I am *NEET* because I've got dirt *beat,* and the smell so, so *sweet.*" The room was filled with music, as she had a big voice, having performed many a show tune onstage.

"Great, now I'm going to have that thing in my head for the rest of the day," grumped Carl.

The neurons in Tamara Quigley's brain were firing at a high rate. "I think I may have heard the name," she said stiffly.

"That girl was everywhere in the seventies," Claire said, unaware of the change in Tamara's tone. "She was on all those talk shows for playing Mozart sonatas. I don't know about you, but I was listening to Donny Osmond at that age."

"She lives here now?" Jesse asked. He had never met anyone remotely famous.

"She sure does," Claire said. "I tried to get her to play the piano for some of our musicals but she never returned my calls."

"I say we issue a steeper fine this time," Carl said. "She ought to have the money to pay for it."

The board then looked to their president.

"I'll do you one better," said Tamara Quigley. "I'll visit her in person."

CHAPTER SEVEN

Yesterday

Alexei Petrov had not been a child prodigy. His skill came from hours and hours of hard work. His mother liked to tell people this because it spoke of her son's immense discipline and sacrifice to the craft. (Not to mention the many sacrifices she herself had made.) Before perfecting this boast, Tatiana had told people that her husband commanded one of the highest salaries in the Soviet Union. For a prominent physicist like Nikolai Petrov, such things were possible. Then the Cold War thawed and Russia was plunged into turmoil. Science budgets dried up. Careers derailed. That's when a desperate Nikolai accepted an offer to relocate to Beijing to assist with China's rocket program. Since Tatiana was a schoolteacher who was not likely to assist with China's rocket program, she stayed behind.

The new bride was forced to move from their spacious flat to a cramped unit in a drab gray complex. She continued to teach, but sometimes went without a paycheck for months at a time. Tatiana had survived by borrowing money from family and friends, the few that had anything to spare. Still, there was no meat and little bread, only long lines outside the market that gave way to empty shelves inside. Teenage prostitutes wandered Moscow's streets. Abandoned children filled its orphanages.

As Tatiana Petrova watched her country disintegrate, a quiet panic brewed inside her. She took up smoking and cultivated odd little rituals. Like getting out of bed—five, six, seven times a night—to make sure the door was locked. Or washing pots and pans several times before putting them back in the cupboard. Or arranging canned goods according to color and lining up pencils according to size. These repetitive behaviors offered Tatiana a reprieve from her angst, a brief feeling of control.

The reprieve may have been temporary, but the behaviors became permanent. When an unremarkable job with an oil company allowed Nikolai to return to Moscow, he was shocked to see the changes in his wife. She had become moody and demanding. When did she get so thin?

"Please hang your shirts properly," she'd say, standing in front of the wardrobe, fussing over hangers, leaving precisely a half-inch space between each one.

"Wash your hands," she'd say when he'd arrive home each evening, followed by "Did you lock the door?"

"Who can live this way?" he would complain.

Not long after Nikolai returned, Tatiana became pregnant. Along with joy came terror. Now she really had something to lose. Despite her husband's current reassurances—it will be fine, my *rodnaya*—Tatiana's fears worked their way into her pregnancy. She was convinced that the slightest cramp or moment of fatigue meant she would lose her baby. But Alexei Petrov arrived into the world screaming, a nearly ten-pound infant who, when held to his mother's chest, had reached up a tiny hand and stroked her cheek as if he could sense her perpetual unease.

Alexei exhibited the same intelligence and inclinations as his father. Both liked puzzles and chess, both brought a methodical approach to any task. He also exhibited some of the compulsive traits of his mother, like alphabetizing his books and lining his toys up on their shelf, precisely spaced apart. He'd constantly readjust them as if someone had moved them in his absence.

Tatiana Petrova feared idleness. She believed that an unstructured day brought trouble. That's why she enrolled her son in formal piano instruction at the age of six. Alexei learned the patterns of scales and how to count the beats in a measure. It wasn't long before he could play phrases of music over and over until it was second nature. Most young children didn't have the patience for that sort of repetition, but Alexei thrived on it. Tatiana was thrilled, which made the boy work even harder. Day after day, he would sit on the piano bench, swinging his legs as he arranged his music. Alexei found solace in the structure of music, in its mathematical connections and consistency. The piano gave him purpose but not passion, a distinction his mother failed to notice. For passion to flourish, the child needed a space all his own to explore the feelings that bloomed inside him while he played, where his heart could roam.

That would never happen.

When he was eight, Alexei was practicing four hours a day—an hour before school, two hours after, and one before bed. When he did not want to practice, Tatiana would goad him. "It makes me sad you can't play that waltz as well as Galina. You can tell she practices more than you." Then she'd light a cigarette, feigning disinterest until he sat down at the piano.

Tatiana was the embodiment of a Janus mask, one side happy, the other side sad. If she was unhappy, it was because Alexei hadn't memorized his chord progressions. If she was happy, it was because he played a minuet flawlessly. She demanded his empathy as he craved her attention. Her worries became Alexei's worries—*Don't worry, Mama, I'll check the locks again*. A claustrophobic pact formed between them.

Each afternoon, when he sat down at the piano, Alexei would watch from his window as a group of boys walked in the direction of the park, playfully shoving one another while bouncing a ball. He longed to be included.

"Please, Mama, just once may I join them?"

"But where will they be in ten years?" his mother would say over his shoulder. "Keep practicing, Alyosha."

It was no use complaining to his father. Nikolai found the idea of confronting his wife impossible. Maybe it was his residual guilt for having abandoned his young bride during the five worst years of her life that prevented him from standing up for his son.

The more Alexei practiced, the less he hung out with other kids. The less he hung out with other kids, the more unsure he felt around them. He was awkward around his classmates, rarely participating in their conversations for fear he would say something stupid, prompting them to laugh at him. But sitting before the piano? A mistake could be corrected, a Bach minuet honed to precision. This was where he was in control.

Before long, Alexei was accepted by the Moscow State Conservatory, where Tchaikovsky had once taught. He won his first competition at ten years old. Soon, he was winning against older kids who had more training. He was well-suited for piano competitions since judges typically favored precision over personal expression.

In the summer of 2010, an instructor from the conservatory approached Tatiana Petrova. "Alexei has so much potential. If you want him to develop as a pianist, you have to get him out of Russia."

"But Russia is the home of Rachmaninoff, Prokofiev, Stravinsky!"

The instructor shook his head. "The minister of culture believes art should serve the state. Only mediocre artists are willing to promote that cause. Alexei will have no meaningful career if he stays here."

Tatiana Petrova listened. Her husband had once been needed by the government and then discarded. That would not happen to her son. Alexei's destiny flashed before her like a burning white light.

The conservatory in Paris was one of the best in the world. Thousands applied every year, but few were admitted. To Alexei, the thought of beating those odds was overwhelming. His mother was not overwhelmed. She was determined.

Poor Alexei; not for the first time he wished he had a sibling to share the weight of Tatiana's expectations, someone else to count on. Someone to confide in. Or at least someone to dilute his mother's focus.

He spent an intense year preparing for the audition. He practiced for hours on end, which left him with sore wrists, stiff fingers, and forearms as tight as rubber bands. Some mornings, he'd wake up with a yearning to work in a bottling plant. To watch bottles run through a conveyor belt, every day the same, no pressure. To sleep until noon on days he didn't work. To play music purely for enjoyment. Then he'd hear the creak of his mother's footsteps in the hall, the whistling of the kettle in the kitchen. There would be porridge and tea and an hour of scales before school. If he complained, she'd cry and tell him he didn't appreciate her. Alexei learned to absorb his mother's demands.

The preparation paid off. He was accepted into the Conservatoire de Paris at the astonishing age of sixteen. But when Tatiana Petrova went to the embassy to apply for three visas, the man behind the desk told her there was a two-year wait. They didn't have two years. Alexei had been admitted to the Conservatoire for the coming fall, and they would not hold his place. Well, the man told her, maybe something could be worked out.

And the first of many pieces of a Faustian bargain were quietly shuffled into place.

CHAPTER EIGHT

Summer of Love

From the minute she was born, Prudence could see, hear, and feel music. It coursed through her body like a current, finding its charge in some mystical, soulful place. Music made her fingertips tingle, made her squeeze her toes to a beat only she could hear. Prudence constantly drummed her fingers. She did this against tabletops, books, the wheel of a car, the head of a cat. The drumming was sharp and rhythmic. Even her dreams were wired, everything from Bach to Gershwin to a Coca-Cola commercial. If there was some sort of phenomenon in her DNA, some credence to the debate of nature over nurture, it was this.

But talent is nothing without the circumstances to nurture it. Or perhaps exploit it. Had the particular events of Prudence's childhood not unfolded the way they did, the music might have stayed at the ends of her fingertips, never making its way into the world.

It started with a rooming house.

Adeline Martinelli's rooming house in Boulder, Colorado, was an unassuming place, a communal dwelling where a nice old widow rented out rooms to stay ahead of the bills. The old Victorian was located on the edge of the university's campus where, on the night of February 15, 1968, two college freshmen met at an antiwar demonstration. It was the night that one serenaded the other with Bob

Dylan songs on an old guitar, the night that—nine months later—led to the birth of a six-and-a-half-pound baby girl. "We'll name her Prudence," said the teenaged parents, enamored with the Beatles song that had just been released.

Babies were prohibited in dorm rooms, as were illicit drugs, hot plates, and members of the opposite sex. But babies were much harder to hide than any of that other contraband, so the teenagers were forced to rent a room in Mrs. Martinelli's boardinghouse.

They held on to their dreams of changing the world, even though the Summer of Love was over and the Vietnam War was raging and the sexual revolution was getting some really bad press. The young parents spent a good deal of time giving passionate speeches in their political science classes and marching in antiwar demonstrations down Twenty-eighth Street. Very little time was spent changing diapers or preparing bottles, however, which was why Prudence was often left in the care of Mrs. Martinelli.

In addition to running the rooming house, Mrs. Martinelli was also the neighborhood piano teacher. She was very busy because, in the sixties, every parent wanted their child to learn how to play. A child who could play classical music was a child from a good home, one of refinement, tradition, and culture. One with enough money to pay for lessons. Her first student arrived at seven in the morning, the last left at seven in the evening, with a lapse between nine and two when the children were in school. This went on six days a week, days wherein young Prudence amused herself in a playpen next to the piano.

Often, Mrs. Martinelli held the toddler on her lap while counting out measures to her students. "*One* ee and a *two* ee and a *three* ee and a . . ." When a child rehearsed four measures of Toccata in C Major over and over until he nailed it, those four measures also implanted themselves in baby Prudence's gray matter.

One evening, when Prudence was three, she climbed atop the piano bench and hummed a tune she had heard all morning. And then, with one pudgy finger on the keyboard, she picked out Johannes Brahms op. 49, no. 4 in the key of E-flat major—otherwise known as "Brahms' Lullaby." She played it all the way through flaw-lessly before asking for her nightly glass of milk.

At last, the chubby fingers had released the jumble of notes that collected like steam under the lid of a pot. Prudence could already sense that the piano's sound was the end product, that the music started in her soul and made its way up to her mind, rising like a vapor until it seeped out into the world through her fingers when she placed them on the keys, creating a vast new world for her to explore.

Mrs. Martinelli knew what Prudence had inside her, and she nur-tured this gift the way an oyster forms a pearl from a grain of sand. This little one was unlike her other students, ordinary boys and girls who needed structure and discipline to work at music on a daily basis. Children who were cajoled into practicing with promises of a cookie. Prudence required something quite different. She needed permission to let what was inside come out.

Music carried Prudence through the uncertainties of her child-hood. Her first thought every morning was playing piano in order to set free what had built up in her during the night. Still in her paja-mas, she'd climb onto the bench and, kneeling before the keyboard, would coax out complex phrases of music, her tiny body rocking to an internal rhythm.

Alas, when she turned five, her parents' union, which was never formalized by marriage, crumbled. Prudence's mother joined a cult in Bolinas, California; her father fled to a commune in upstate New York. So a call was made to the maternal grandmother who lived in Longmont, fifteen miles outside of Boulder. It was this steely woman who puffed resentfully up the steps of the rooming house to find Mrs. Martinelli clutching the frightened child to her breast.

Yet another mess she'd have to clean up for her irresponsible daughter and that goddamn communist she'd taken up with. Mr. Paddington had died the year before and now she was expected to raise a grandchild on her own. With what money?

Having grown up in the Great Depression, Granny Paddington knew how hard a life without money could be. She had taken piano lessons as a child and had dreamed of attending a great music college where she would be taught by the best instructors. Her talent recognized, her promise nurtured, she would perform throughout the great concert halls of the country. Maybe even Europe. She imagined a grand future, one where the spotlight would be fully trained on her. But it was not to be.

Not long after the stock market crash, her middle-class parents had gone from being financially stable to being financially embarrassed to being financially distressed. With that distress, the music lessons were discontinued. At the age of fourteen, Granny Paddington was forced to trade in her piano for a steam iron. Every day after school she went to work in a sweltering laundry where she pressed men's dress shirts and folded them carefully into brown paper. With each passing year, her chances of becoming a concert pianist grew smaller and smaller, until, like so many of her generation, her dreams were scrapped altogether.

Granny Paddington may have been forced to let go of her dream, but her desire to be defined by something other than the monotony of ironing and the harsh gray of poverty could not be crushed. She eventually married, because that's what women did. She wed an unassuming man recently discharged from the service who sold vacuums door-to-door. The postwar boom brought a rise to the suburbs and all the new homes had wall-to-wall carpeting. Vacuum sales were steady and reliable. As was her unimaginative husband.

The Paddingtons had a child and bought a nice little house in a nice little neighborhood where there were coffee klatches and poker nights and children's birthday parties. They bought a shiny new Steinway that Mr. Paddington had argued they had neither the money nor the space for. But his wife got her way—as usual—and an entire year's worth of vacuum commissions went toward financing a six-foot, eleven-inch, Model B, grand Steinway in ebony finish.

Granny Paddington vowed she'd give her daughter everything she never had. As a result, Prudence's mother was overindulged. Spoiled. She grew up to be selfish and irresponsible. The first in the family to go to college, and how was this gift put to use? By getting pregnant and dropping out, that's how.

The grandmother had failed as a pianist and as a parent, her dream of greatness yet to be realized. Now this.

Mrs. Martinelli stood by her small charge, two suitcases beside them. The smaller one contained three dresses, a pair of red school shoes, and a stuffed lamb. The larger one held piano music.

Granny Paddington peered inside Prudence's luggage. "What am I to do with all this?"

To which Mrs. Martinelli replied, "It belongs to the child."

"Chopin? Beethoven? Mozart?"

"She has a gift."

"She can't possibly . . ."

"She is a phenomenon."

A thin smile took over Granny Paddington's face. She remembered a remark her husband had made when talking about their wayward daughter. "Maybe it skips a generation," he had said, referring to her lack of talent, or perhaps discipline.

Maybe it did.

If Granny Paddington had possessed a natural talent—one that, tragically, had not been sufficiently cultivated—perhaps it had been passed along to this small replica. The child did look a little like her, after all. Surely the resemblance would not stop there.

But if Prudence did indeed inherit the same natural potential, it would have to be managed. There would be no spoiling or overindulging this time around. Granny Paddington would follow in the footsteps of her parents. A paddling to the bottom and a rapping of the knuckles would get the job done. Spare the rod and spoil the child. She had learned that lesson the hard way with her aimless, entitled daughter.

Granny Paddington would not spoil this child or this chance. This was what she had been waiting for since those dreary days pressing the steam iron back and forth. This was Granny Paddington's new beginning. She wasn't going to waste it.

CHAPTER NINE

Tiny Dancer

Tamara Quigley studied herself in front of the mirror once again. She had put a lot of thought into her outfit, a teal wrap dress that accentuated her slender waist and complemented her rust-colored hair. Today she would visit Prudence Childs under the guise of asking her to bring her wet towels into the house. This reunion would be like returning to your childhood room to face the monsters under the bed.

That's what she told herself.

Tamara Quigley had been crafting a scenario, one where she would tell Prudence about the HOA citation. "I know it seems silly," she would say, "but there have been complaints." The two women would laugh and Tamara, citing her power as president, would offer to "take care of it." Prudence would thank her and promise not to hang swimsuits out on the back gate anymore. Wait, no, first she'd ask Tamara into her house, which looked, from the outside anyway, like something out of *Architectural Digest*. Prudence would offer her tea and tell Tamara she had the loveliest hair. *We've met before,* Tamara would say. And Prudence would say, *Wonderful, where?*

That's when Tamara would recount "the Incident."

Tamara Quigley pulled up to 10534 Pricklypoppy Lane as Prudence dragged a garden hose into her house. "That's odd," Tamara said.

She clutched her new portfolio containing the citation and clicked up the walk, the anticipation of a new friendship like the scent of wet paint in an old room.

Tamara arrived at the threshold of the marble foyer just in time to see Prudence aiming a hose at someone as if squaring off for a duel. Little drops of water dripped onto the marble floor.

"I will give you exactly three seconds to hand over that letter before I soak you to kingdom come and the note along with it."

"Peanut, just . . ."

"One, two . . . three." Prudence squeezed the trigger and a pressurized blast of water hit the man square in the chest.

"Oh my," Tamara gasped.

Prudence spun around. "Now, who are you?" Prudence was in a foul mood as she was being blackmailed by her ex-husband. Since Tamara was not in the know about such blackmail, Prudence's reaction caught Tamara off guard. She had not expected this. She had rehearsed the scene in her mind so many times that she automatically opened her portfolio and presented the HOA citation on the letterhead that bore her name and title. "I'm Tamara Quigley, president of the Quail Mountain HOA."

This was not an auspicious beginning, given Prudence's history with the HOA. "For god's sake, what do you people want now?"

Poor Tamara Quigley. She was always colliding with Prudence on the wrong damn day.

IN THE SUMMER of 1982, Prudence had just completed a European tour. She was thirteen years old and wanted to spend the remainder of the summer doing teenage girl things like meeting friends at the mall and experimenting with lip gloss. But a fancy arts camp in northern Michigan thought it would be great publicity to have "the Prodigy" play the music for its annual ballet recital. Granny Paddington thought so, too. Jet-lagged and exhausted, Prudence had only two days to rehearse the new pieces.

When Prudence and her grandmother arrived at the rustic property on a sweltering Thursday afternoon, Tamara, then a nine-year-old first-time camper, was waiting for them. The counselors had warned the young campers that the Prodigy would need space in the beginning. This extraordinary girl had a grueling schedule and had just flown in from London. London! Home of the Royal Ballet, where Tamara's idol Margot Fonteyn had made history. It was all too exciting.

Tamara watched from a distance as Prudence and an older woman were escorted to a private cabin that was outfitted with two metal-framed beds and a worn upright piano for practice. For the next thirty-six hours, Tamara spent every free moment she had sitting cross-legged on the grass outside the wooden bunk, hoping for an audience.

Tamara was proud to have gained a place at this camp. It was a prestigious, audition-only institute that provided a rare opportunity for her to escape small-town life and the apathy that gripped her parents. If she could prove herself here, it might open doors for her. The camp's annual recital was regularly attended by talent agents who booked performers for Broadway shows. Every year, a few kids were snatched up by scouts for the best ballet companies in the country.

This was Tamara's big chance.

She dedicated her whole summer to practicing assiduously, almost obsessively. When she rose up in her pointe shoes, her instep arched like a banana. Her arms, when she danced, oscillated like ribbons in a breeze. She was rewarded for her efforts with a coveted solo in the final recital, performing a specially choreographed routine to the "Theme from Swan Lake." Prudence would accompany her on the piano.

Tamara never did catch a glimpse of Prudence as she perched outside the private cabin, but come Saturday morning, there she was, sitting in front of the glossy Yamaha in the recital hall. Everyone took their places onstage and Prudence played the campers through several hours of rehearsal without a break. It was nearly eleven o'clock when the dance master called to everyone to take five.

This was Tamara's moment.

While the other children stretched and adjusted their toe shoes, she took a deep breath and dashed up beside the piano. After introducing herself in a shaky voice, she told Prudence that she, too, was working to make it all the way to London. Prudence couldn't imagine why any kid would want to be as miserable as she was. She'd gladly trade places with the little ballerina. Prudence thought she was being helpful when she replied, *You don't want this life, it's not for you.*

The comment seared Tamara Quigley with the intensity of a branding iron, for what she had heard was *You can't have this life, it's not for you.* Prudence was surely comparing Tamara to the dancers she had seen in London and had judged Tamara defective.

The little ballerina wanted nothing more than to prove the Prodigy wrong.

With the recital only a few hours away, Tamara set her intention for success. She was ready, and at the appointed time, when the curtain drew back from the stage, Tamara felt the magic of her own power. But midway through the piece, an exhausted Prudence flubbed a measure of notes, which caused Tamara to miss a step. Prudence quickly recovered, but Tamara could not. Flustered, the carefully practiced routine drained from her mind and she ran off the stage in shame. Prudence had sabotaged her chances on purpose. Tamara was sure of it.

None of the scouts approached her after the recital, nor did any of the talent agents press their business cards into her mother's waiting hand. For months, Tamara refused to discuss what had happened, and in the years that followed she coached her family to refer to this epic disappointment only as "the Incident." But it was clear to Tamara that Prudence was responsible for the moment when her hopes were dashed, when her life was separated into Before and After.

—

THIRTY-FIVE YEARS LATER, Tamara Quigley once again stood before the world-famous piano prodigy. Other people might have moved on, having convinced themselves it wasn't meant to be. Not Tamara. All these years later, she still craved recognition and validation. Or maybe some acknowledgment of the wrong that had been done to her. In her mind, if she could be friends with Prudence, she'd be accepted into that rarified world of immense talent. Maybe not on Prudence's level, but after a lifetime of laundry and PTO meetings, to be a mere acquaintance would suffice. When she rehearsed the moment in her mind—for Tamara was always rehearsing—she would remind Prudence of the Incident. Prudence would be horrified at her thirteen-year-old self. *How awful I was!* she would say, which would give Tamara the opportunity to wave her hand and say, *Oh, come on, we were just kids*. Prudence, touched by Tamara's graciousness, would invite her to lunch. They'd meet at an outdoor café where women wore white linen and drank white wine and gossiped into the afternoon. There, the new friends would talk about dance and music. Prudence would open up to Tamara about the loneliness of the creative soul. *If only I had had someone like you to confide in when I was young, how much better life would have been.*

But she wasn't counting on Bobby Wheeler.

Tamara should have let the HOA matter drop. She should have said she'd return at a better time. But she looked around at the heavy glass windows and the marble floor and the sparkly chandelier and thought, *This should've been me.*

"You're in violation of the CC&Rs."

"In violation of what?"

"Neighborhood rules. Section five, point six A, *No hanging of laundry to dry outdoors.*"

"I don't hang laundry outdoors."

Tamara was aware how stupid she was going to sound, but she had started something and, clearly, this was an opportunity to put the former prodigy in her place. "Swimsuits on the back gate. You can't hang things on the gate. If you don't comply, we'll have to fine you."

A beat went by while Prudence absorbed this. "Is this a joke?"

Taking advantage of this fortunate distraction, Bobby Wheeler made a move toward the door. Prudence wheeled back around but before she could give him another blast, he snatched up Mrs. Wintour and held her as a shield. "Careful, Peanut, you might hit your dog."

"Give her to me!"

"Just want to get into my car, okay?"

He backed out the door with the little dog, Prudence close behind lugging the hose, and Tamara shoring up the end. They got to the end of the flagstone walk, where a very audible exchange took place.

"Don't you dare get into that car, Bobby!"

"Watch me!"

"GIVE ME MY DOG, YOU MONSTER!"

The noise drew neighbors from their houses, shielding their eyes from the sun and trying to figure out what the hell was going on.

Only after Bobby Wheeler slid behind the wheel of his rented Chevy Aveo and started the engine did he release the little dog. Mrs. Wintour ran down the walk, and back into the cool of the house, as Bobby drove off.

"Dammit!" Prudence was furious that Bobby Wheeler got away.

"Enough of this, Ms. Childs," Tamara tsked. "I need you to focus." She held up the letterhead bearing her name and title and those damn violations. "I'm going to leave this with you, and I'll expect you to call me at my . . ." But the world-famous pianist blasted the paper with water. She then dropped the hose and strode back into her house and slammed the large iron doors signaling that today's business was complete.

The neighbors chuckled and shook their heads and took one last look at Tamara Quigley before going back into their houses. Tamara, fully humiliated, hopped back into her Escalade. Her silk dress was water damaged. Her beautiful leather portfolio was water damaged. And thanks to the scene on the sidewalk in full view of God and everyone, her reputation was damaged.

From the time it took Tamara to drive back to the gated entrance of the Quail Mountain development, her embarrassment turned to white-hot rage. She had no other choice, she reasoned, but to go back to the board and report on this aberrant behavior.

Prudence Childs was going to pay.

CHAPTER TEN

Flight of the Bumblebee

The threat of exposure was serious business. The matter of five hundred thousand dollars was also serious business. Prudence was going to have to find a way to pay Bobby off, and she was going to have to do it quickly. Stuart would be back from London in a week. Which meant she had just seven days to end this nonsense with her former husband and a lifetime to keep the transaction secret from her current one.

This was really going to push back the start of her book club.

Prudence dropped her fur coat to the floor, where Mrs. Wintour promptly curled up on it and fell asleep. Prudence paced back and forth in front of the Steinway. Then she circled the Steinway. Then she marinated a plan.

Because here's the thing: Steinways are the only pianos that appreciate in value. All other pianos are like cars in that their value drops the moment you drive them off the lot. Not a Steinway. Especially not *this* Steinway. Prudence had been photographed many times at this piano. There was the cover of *TIME* when she was six, dressed in a plaid jumper and perched on top like a little doll. The *New York Times* arts section ran the gamut of covers from a smiling pink-cheeked child to a cheerless and gangly adolescent, the ever-present piano remaining unchanged. Her *People* magazine covers—

from the first, *Little Miss Big Bucks!*, to the last, *Child Star Burn Out*—all featured her sitting at this piano.

Prudence went into the Sewing Room and fired up her computer. Searching for Steinway auctions, she came to a link: "Auctions Near Me." Lo and behold, Steinway Hall, the Steinway dealership in North Scottsdale, had an event scheduled for Thursday. Today was Tuesday! Bravo, she could go down there and square it all away. *Fin.* This whole ugly business would be over. It was almost as if fate had intervened. She'd sell the piano and pay off Bobby Wheeler. Then, she'd hire a lawyer to draw up a gag order stating if Bobby Wheeler decided to blab to the world about his knowledge of the Pep Soda jingle, he'd have to give the money back. Maybe he'd even have to pay a penalty. That would keep him away.

But what to tell Stuart? Prudence did not like keeping secrets from her husband. She made a mental tally of the facts:

1. Stuart would never suspect she needed a large sum of money to pay off a blackmailing ex-husband he did not know existed.
2. Stuart was not attached to the piano and therefore would not miss it.
3. Stuart did not really care about the piano, only Prudence's happiness.
4. Selling the piano and paying off Bobby Wheeler would make Prudence happy.
5. Selling the piano would also solve her problem of having to view this monument of failure on a daily basis.

"There!" she said to Mrs. Wintour. "What could possibly go wrong?"

STEINWAY HALL WAS located next door to the North Scottsdale Mercedes-Benz showroom. Both buildings have floor-to-ceiling windows displaying their luxury wares, be it peak performance sedans or glossy pianos. Both contain salesmen in expensive suits who try to sell merchandise for just a little more than the customer wants to pay.

The Mercedes dealership was experiencing a healthy sales quarter, for Scottsdale is very much a car town due to its lack of inclement weather and its abundant supply of wealth. Steinway Hall, however, had been in a slump—spending eighty grand on something you could drive outpaced spending eighty grand on something you had no idea how to play. In the last six months, there had been countless marketing meetings on how to increase sales and publicity. The store was in danger of closing, and the best way to increase traffic was to hold an auction of rare Steinways.

There was a sale in progress when Prudence visited the showroom. A salesman was sitting at a $56,000 Model M playing a Haydn sonata. Beside him was a woman and beside her a young girl about twelve. The salesman stopped playing and said, "Now this particular model is a starter piano that I think would be wonderful for your daughter here."

The woman turned to her daughter and said, "What do you think, darling?"

"I told you, I don't want to take lessons," the daughter replied.

"Please, honey. I would've killed for this opportunity at your age."

But the young girl did not care about her mother's lack of opportunities. She went back to staring into her phone.

The other salesman on the floor had been brought out from Steinway headquarters in New York to boost sales in the Scottsdale showroom. When he saw Prudence walk through the door that afternoon, he calculated his pitch. It hadn't taken him long to figure out that women in North Scottsdale bought Steinways like they bought paintings: as art for the front room. A Steinway grand denoted culture, much like a painting. It didn't matter if you could play it or not.

The salesman glided up to Prudence. "Good afternoon," he said. "May I help you find something?"

Now Prudence knew quite a bit about playing pianos but not

much about selling them. She couldn't show all her cards yet. "I'd like to see a piano."

"Grand or upright?"

"Grand. Do you sell them used?"

"I'd recommend a new one."

"I'm not interested in a new piano."

The salesman recalculated his approach like a navigation app recalculates a route. "Very good. We have some wonderful preowned instruments. It really depends on what you'll use the piano for."

"Oh, I'm not planning on playing it," she answered.

Bingo. The piano was for show.

"Well, this one," he said, eyeing her and sitting down at a gorgeous $75,000, six-foot-two, Mahogany Model A, "was handcrafted here in the USA, all wood construction, completely rebuilt by Steinway & Sons in New York. Isn't it beautiful?"

"Rebuilt?"

"Oh, yes. We rebuild all our used pianos."

Prudence hadn't counted on that.

"Listen to the way it sounds," the salesman said. He knew what he would do next, worked every time—he'd play Elton John's "Don't Let the Sun Go Down on Me." He could play a handful of pop tunes and the first movement of "Für Elise." To the untrained ear, he sounded terrific.

"Ah, listen to that," he said. "It's never too late to learn, you know."

But Prudence was not listening to his playing. She was too busy thinking. "How much does it cost to rebuild a Steinway?" she asked.

He stopped playing. Because he couldn't play and talk at the same time. "Depends."

"On what?"

"The age, the wear, the condition of the sounding board—this is the sounding board," he said, pointing into the open lid. "The damper pedals . . . these are the damper pedals," he said pointing to the ground, "built with premium wool and maple heads for endurance."

He wanted to turn up the gas a bit, really impress his customer with his piano knowledge. "Now," he said, "this is a *very* special piano because of its action."

"Really," Prudence said, somewhat bored.

"Yes, you see the action is the soul of the piano, each has its own, much like a fingerprint. Of course, only people who've played many pianos would ever care about the action."

"Huh."

"Here, let me show you. Put your fingers on the keys and thump around a bit. Doesn't matter if you can't play, you'll notice its sound."

He rose from the bench and Prudence took his place. She certainly was going to thump around a bit.

She looked up at the salesman and smiled.

He smiled back.

She took a deep breath and lowered her head and closed her eyes and launched into "Bumble Boogie," a fiery jazz version of "Flight of the Bumblebee." At a bouncy 180 beats a minute, it was a good song to test out the action on a piano. Her hands attacked the upper end of the keyboard, her fingers a blur to the human eye. The lower end growled with a boogie-woogie swing.

All around the showroom, eyebrows rose and mouths parted. A tech who'd been oiling a damper pedal stopped and craned his neck. The showroom manager stepped out of his office.

"Wow!" said the young girl, looking up from her phone. Prudence winked at her. In that very moment, the young girl's life was altered. She would not go on to date the boy who sold edibles to middle-school children. She would not go on to steal final exams from the teachers' lounge. She would not stay out past her curfew drinking at field parties in the desert. She would, from this point forward, be consumed with the desire to create music—to feel it, understand it, and inhabit it. To live it.

Prudence finished the song by dragging her fingers over the keys, creating a sound like the oceanic roar of a swarm of bees. The showroom was silent.

"The damper pedal sticks," Prudence said.

There may have been several million dollars' worth of pianos in that showroom, but Prudence's performance transcended commerce. It was art. Ephemeral yet resonating.

The young girl squealed. "I want to play like *that*!" she said.

Prudence wanted to squeal, too. For something had changed for her. The music still lived inside her. Could she prove herself to be a true artist, someone who played from instinct? Rather than a manufactured child star, someone who played to expectation?

The odds were stacked against her. She had lost decades of real practice, decades of learning and honing and studying technique. To once again become a world-renowned pianist at the age of forty-eight would take a miracle akin to raising the dead. Then she thought of Bobby Wheeler, who might as well have been raised from the dead, and she hated him all over again. He was going to ruin her life a second time.

"Now that you've blown the roof off the place," the salesman said, "this piano has your name written all over it."

Prudence shook her head. "I'm not here to buy a piano."

"Oh?"

"I'd like to sell one at your auction on Thursday."

She pulled from a Chanel tote bag the 1976 *LIFE* magazine where, at eight years old, she was sitting at her Steinway playing something (she couldn't remember what), dressed all in pink. The president of the United States and the first lady, Gerald and Betty Ford, stood over her, a look of wonder on their faces. Its headline read, PRODIGY PLAYS HER WAY TO THE WHITE HOUSE AND BEYOND. Her toothless smile and her curly pigtails belied the slaps and ten-hour days at the keyboard.

The salesman from New York was now very excited. A promotion back in New York was a given now. Not only was this exactly the publicity they needed for the "Rare Steinways" auction, the ace up their sleeve walked right in the door with it.

"Would it have to be rebuilt?"

"I'm sure we can work something out."

CHAPTER ELEVEN

Entr'Acte

The very morning Prudence had blasted Bobby Wheeler with the hose, Pierre Millet stood in the threshold of his 1927 bungalow having an all-too-familiar conversation.

"But how do you know it's too soon?" The woman wasn't asking so much as she was challenging.

"I've been doing this for sixty years," Pierre Millet said.

"Then you should know a little genius when you see one."

Here we go again. After six decades of piano lessons, Pierre Millet had not known one little genius. He could not say the same for stage mothers.

"There's no way to tell at three years old," he told her.

"What about Mozart?"

Pierre Millet looked down at the towheaded toddler, whose chin was shiny with drool, a red plastic truck clutched in his tiny hand. Pierre Millet wanted the woman to leave. He wanted to shut his front door to keep the cool air in. He wanted to keep the hot air—and this woman—from invading his home. "What about him?"

"I read on the internet that Mozart had an incredible ability to communicate emotion. Martin does this all the time." She gave her son a slight push forward. "Go on, Martin, tell Mr. Millet how excited you are about music."

The little boy stood silent, chewing on his plastic truck.

Which was fine with Pierre Millet. He didn't want to hear how Martin had split the atom. He wanted his lunch of boiled eggs and pickled beets. Then he would take his nap. He felt tired, these days. Very tired. Low blood pressure, his doctor had said as he upped his medication. The medication didn't seem to help. Not as much as a nap, anyway. An hour after lunch and he was good to teach his lesson at three o'clock. And the one at four o'clock, and the one at five.

He pretended to listen as Martin's mother reeled off all her son's accomplishments. Pierre Millet didn't know her name, but he knew her type—and countless others like her.

After teaching piano for more than a half century, he concluded that the parents who wanted their children to learn music fell into one of three categories. This woman was a member of the first. She stood on a mountain of expectations, a slope so high no one but her could scale it. Her child's accomplishments were her accomplishments. If her child placed first in a piano competition (and boy, he'd better) or mastered Beethoven's *Appassionata,* it was because, under tight supervision, he had practiced for hours on end.

Acceptance to Oberlin College and Conservatory? Who do you think filled out that application and arranged the interview?

The second group was nearly as bad. These free-range parents took the opposite approach, paying Pierre Millet $75 an hour to expose their children to music. But exposure without expectation was worthless, and since there were never any expectations— practice was too much of an effort, for the parents as well as the kids—there was never any improvement. Music should be a joy, they said. Not a chore. Pierre Millet had spent too much of his life trying to convince these more lenient parents that the brain cannot learn music unless the fingers and mind work together every day for at least twenty minutes. Children in this group would never know the joy that comes from honest work and earned accomplishment.

Then there was the third group. It was a small circle, but a rewarding one. These parents raised children who turned music into a lifelong passion. The secret to this was simple: thirty minutes of practice a day. If the parents did not punish or threaten, the thirty minutes would grow to an hour. After a few more years, it would grow to two. Pierre Millet had seen this firsthand.

"Mastery of the piano requires discipline. Your child is too young."

The woman stood firm on her mountain and took out her checkbook. "I will double your hourly fee."

Pierre Millet did not need the money. In addition to giving lessons, he performed almost nightly at cocktail parties and holiday parties and dinner parties around the Valley. Skilled piano players were in high demand by those with means who liked to entertain. At eighty years old, he was busier than ever.

Pierre Millet shook his head. "Take him home and let him play in the sandbox."

"Play is a waste."

"Far from it," he said. "Play fuels the imagination, which develops creativity, which is the most important element of musicianship. When he turns six, bring him back and we will see."

"Six?!"

He may as well have said forty. "Fine," she snapped, "I'll find another teacher." She pulled her son up by the arm and clopped down the walk of 17 Willetta Drive, the little boy bouncing behind her.

CHAPTER TWELVE

Ode to Joy

Around the same time Prudence left Steinway, showrunner Les Strom was returning to his Burbank office after a lunch with the network brass. The big dogs wanted a real contender for the October 27 episode of *Alexei Petrov's Dueling Piano Wars!* Someone who was or had once been famous but also had skills on par with Alexei's. They wanted this someone in forty-eight hours so they could promote the hell out of the show. Forty-eight hours!

"What about Harry Connick, Jr.?" Les Strom suggested.

Under contract with *American Idol*.

"Condoleezza Rice?"

Security would be an absolute nightmare. Besides, Condi isn't *that* kind of performer. Think *Dancing with the Stars*, Les. They always have some former football player or washed-up child star. You know, like all those actors from 1970s-era sitcoms? They're popping up all over the place these days.

"Yeah, but any idiot can learn to dance."

We're confident you'll find someone. A million dollars is a good incentive.

"Right," said Les. "But you need Alexei to win. You've made that clear enough, which means this real contender you want isn't actually going to get that million-dollar check. They're going to have to agree to throw the competition before they even step foot in the studio. Now tell me, gentlemen, who is going to sign on for that?"

They don't have to sign on, said the brass.

"Wait . . . you're saying we rig it?" Their silence meant *yes*. "You can't rig a televised contest, not if it involves intellectual knowledge or skill. If you haven't heard of a little thing called the Federal Communications Act, perhaps you saw that movie *Quiz Show*?"

The brass sipped their $15 iced teas and stared at their $40 lamb burgers. Alexei has to win, Les. He's the main attraction. Season 2 won't work with a loser host. Oh, and another thing.

"Yes?"

You're going to have to talk to our star, tell him there'll be a slight change in the program.

"Change?" Like Alexei, Les Strom had grown suspicious of the word.

We're thinking that, instead of three categories of classical music, we combine classical with romantic, make contemporary the second, and pop or rock the third.

"Alexei doesn't play rock."

Well, they said, this is what market research is telling us. If we want to grow the audience, we need to switch up the format. Get more kids to watch. It shouldn't be that hard, Les. You'll find a way. We have faith.

Les did not have faith. Back at his desk, with the hot breath of the network on his neck, Les Strom knew that if he did not find a human unicorn, he would soon be driving last year's Tesla.

He opened his laptop, muttered "fuck" several times, and entered the most basic search terms into Google.

With two index fingers he typed "child star." Several mug shots appeared. Next he typed "child" and "piano" and "prodigy." Up came recent videos of small children sitting before enormous pianos. "Famous pianists" returned a list of mostly dead men—Glenn Gould, Mozart, Horowitz, Beethoven, for cryin' out loud.

"Oh, for fuck's sake." He then tried "former" and "prodigy."

Jackpot!

A headline jumped out at him: FORMER MUSICAL PRODIGY SET TO AUCTION OFF ICONIC PIANO IN SCOTTSDALE.

Holy shit.

Twenty-four hours later, Les Strom had landed at Phoenix Sky Harbor Airport.

"4725 North Scottsdale Road," he told the Uber driver.

PRUDENCE'S STEINWAY DID not have to be rebuilt. According to the Steinway technician, that would have been like touching up the *Mona Lisa*. So, per the auction agreement, she would return to the store on Thursday evening at seven o'clock and play a medley of her famed commercial jingles.

Prudence did not want to play at the auction. It was somewhere in the middle of a very long list of things she did not want to do. However, having been told that a personal appearance would drive up the price of the piano, she figured that if she gave Bobby Wheeler a little more than he expected, maybe (*maybe*) he'd leave her alone.

After Prudence played, the bidding would start. After that, she would arrange a transaction with Bobby Wheeler.

The texts with Bobby went something like this:

Prudence: I'll ping you with a meeting place on Friday and give you a cashier's check for the piano's worth.

Bobby Wheeler: Looking 4ward to it, Peanut!

Prudence: Fuck you.

STEINWAY HALL WAS packed. Two hundred people were milling about as if they were waiting to view a rare solar eclipse, instead of a former prodigy. Few had any intention of bidding on the famous piano. Fewer still had the means.

The six-foot, eleven-inch, Model B, grand Steinway in ebony finish sat on the stage in the concert area. It gleamed under a spotlight, the only distraction a framed and very official placard that read: "Do not play or touch piano."

Next to the piano was a podium with a wooden gavel and an array of pamphlets.

Steinway & Sons Model B Grand

- Opening Bid: $50,000
- Length: 6'11" Width: 58" Weight: 760 pounds
- Sitka Spruce soundboard and ribs
- Satin Ebony Finish
- Manufacturing date: 1952

Former piano prodigy Prudence Childs was just five years old when she performed her first concert on this piano. She made her debut in London at age six with a full orchestra. By the time she was eight, the musical sensation toured extensively through Europe, Asia, South America, and the United States. She has performed for presidents and royalty alike.

Ms. Childs enjoyed a successful career as a commercial composer. Her most notable work includes Pep Soda, Neet Washing Detergent, Double Bubble Dish Soap, Flush 'N Clean Toilet Bowl Cleaner, Flash Brite Toothpaste.

In addition to the people in shorts and flip-flops (they weren't allowed their stupid water bottles), there were journalists and photographers and cameramen from the local news. There was a wealthy man in a tailored suit and Hermès wingtips. There was also Pierre Millet.

Only one person was missing.

Prudence Childs was sitting before the large mirror in her *en suite,* the vanity scattered with flotsam—tubes of lipstick, pots of face cream, crystal perfume bottles. She had been thinking since Tuesday that maybe, just maybe, she could become a serious performer once again. It would be a lot of hard work. That didn't deter her. She wanted to prove that she understood the music in ways that even she couldn't comprehend. It was inside her, sewn into her like the lining of a coat. But tonight, she heard the tobacco edges around Granny Paddington's voice. *I'm the one who made you. You'll never be anything now that I'm gone.*

What that meant, to *be anything,* was something Prudence had carried with her into adulthood. She took the words out in her darker moments, turning them over like a kaleidoscope, trying to put the broken pieces back together. Their power had waned through the years. In part, thanks to Stuart. Early in their marriage he had comforted his wife in her periods of doubt and insecurity. When Prudence repeated the ugly words spoken to her as a child, he would reassure her. "You're not *anything*? Darling, don't you know that you are *everything*?"

She had never known a love like that, what one good person could give to another. She needed him in all the right ways. It had been enough. For years it had been enough.

Until now.

LES STROM WASN'T milling about inside. He was milling about outside in front of a parking spot that said, RESERVED FOR PRUDENCE CHILDS. He planned to corner Prudence, to make his pitch before she could even step foot in the building. But Les Strom had not taken into account the Arizona heat. It was nearly sundown, and the temperature outside was hovering over a hundred degrees with a breeze so hot it felt as if someone was holding a hair dryer to his face. Les Strom could not believe anyone would actually choose to live in this circle of hell. "Repent, people!" he shouted and shook his fist at the sky.

As if on cue, one of the network executives texted him, casually wondering if he had found a suitable pianist. Translation: Return to Los Angeles without a viable contender and you will be replaced as showrunner. In Hollywood, lightning rarely strikes twice. That'd be it for Les Strom. He was midtext when a horn blared, declaring the arrival of a late-model Porsche. Down came the driver's-side window. "Excuse me, you're in my spot and I'm late!"

Les Strom jumped to the side and the Porsche zipped into place. Out popped Prudence in a ruffled blouse looking like Mozart incarnate. (Had Mozart worn sunglasses, bright red lipstick, and diamond earrings.) Energy radiated from this woman like heat from the pavement. Les Strom had been in television long enough to know there was a certain presence about people who had incredible gifts. Prudence Childs had it.

"Are you Ms. Childs?"

"I am."

"Can I talk to you?"

"You are talking to me."

"Yes, well, I mean, can I—"

"Sorry, I'm in a terrible rush." With that, she blazed toward the building without looking back.

Les Strom's career might have ended right there had he not noticed the large ruffles flopping at her wrists.

"Madam, wait! Your cuffs are undone!"

Prudence stopped so abruptly, Les Strom nearly toppled into her. She examined her sleeves. "Drat. There's always something."

Les Strom unclipped his cuff links and, pinching one of Prudence's ruffled cuffs, launched into his spiel. "Ms. Childs, I've come from Burbank, California."

"For this stupid auction?"

He slid the tiny silver rod through the buttonhole and flipped it in place. "I'm not here for the stupid auction . . . I mean, for the piano. I'm here for you."

"I'm not for sale, only the piano."

"No, no." He grabbed her other arm. "I've got an offer for you."

"I don't have time."

Neither did Les Strom, whose phone was chiming with another text. "Listen to me, Ms. Childs, listen . . . do you want a chance to perform on television?"

"Nope."

"Don't you want to reintroduce yourself to the world?"

"Nope."

"But I have this TV show . . ."

"Sorry."

"You don't even know what it is . . ."

"I don't watch television. I read. Well, next week I will."

Les Strom must have been in the heat too long. No one preferred reading over fame.

"Let me start again. I am a television producer." At that, he produced his card. Prudence studied it while he reeled off a list of TV shows she had never heard of. *The Dogs of Central Park, L.A. Waitress,* and something about a man who lived in a tree with a forty-year-old cockatoo. Then he launched into great detail about *Alexei Petrov's Dueling Piano Wars!* He used words like *competition* and *suspense. Cliff-hanger!* Words that Prudence did not want to hear.

Never once did he mention anything about art.

"I simply can't be on your show," Prudence repeated. "I'm going to start a book club."

Les Strom wondered what grade of pot Prudence Childs was smoking. Or whether, possibly, she had banged her head on something very hard. Perhaps she had fallen off her piano bench.

"I'm giving you a special opportunity," he said.

"I've had enough special opportunities, thank you very much."

Oh, Jesus, mother of God. "Don't you want a second chance at fame?"

"No, thank you," she said over her shoulder, making her way to the showroom. "Once was ee*enough.*"

Les Strom resorted to manipulation. It wasn't the first time. It sure wouldn't be the last. "You might as well auction off your legacy along with your piano."

Prudence stopped, her back to him.

Les Strom continued. "I know all about you."

"Oh?"

"You were a phenomenon. The brightest star in the sky. A wunderkind. Then you disappeared."

"All good things must come to an end."

Unemployment loomed. Les Strom was going to have to play dirty. "Another child star who crashed and burned. What a shame. Whatever happened to Baby Jane, you know?"

Oh, how Prudence wanted a different ending than what she was about to get. Like in music, when you played through a piece the first time and were instructed to repeat it. The ending is different, more grand and resonant than the first. A second ending.

Prudence smiled. What a lovely thought. Too bad it was interrupted by Granny Paddington's voice.

You will never . . .

"I'm sorry, Les, our business here is finished."

IT WAS TEN after seven. While the manager of Steinway Hall was in a state of near apoplexy—"Where is that woman?!"—Pierre Millet was waiting patiently in the front row. He had not come to buy the piano, only to hear Prudence Childs. He'd seen her perform many years ago at New York's Metropolitan Opera House. She was but nine years old, yet he'd never heard a child play the way she did. Yes, she played with great precision and timing but that came from hours of practice. What did not come from hours of practice was the maturity with which she played. At nine years old, she seemed to understand the complex emotions of her pieces. It was something that could not be taught, only learned through years of wading through the messy and uneven business of life. But with Prudence, it was instinctive. When he heard her play Beethoven's *Ode to Joy* that evening, he was astonished. She had pulled off one of the most complex emotions to convey in music: an exalted contentedness.

He wanted to see Prudence play as an adult now. He was curious to see how the talent had cured through the years. He longed to be inspired by her once again.

Pierre Millet did not look eighty. Some said it was all that music that kept him so youthful. He still enjoyed performing. He still got a rush from turning an audience on to Robert Schumann and Dave Brubeck. He was still very much in demand. But he was not young. He was not even middle-aged. His body said as much. His wrists became inflamed when he practiced too long and his back ached from hours at the bench. His fingers might feel the years but the music kept his mind young.

At fifteen minutes after seven, the manager of Steinway Hall approached him.

"Pierre Millet, the very person I was looking for."

"Oh?"

"Yes, see, we've hit a snag."

"Ah, that's too bad."

"It is. The piano is very special." Pierre knew that by the way the manager said "special" he meant "expensive."

"I was wondering if you could play it before we start the bidding. You see, the owner of the instrument has not shown up."

"Happy to," Pierre Millet said. "One thousand dollars."

"A thousand dollars?"

"That's my rate."

The manager was in the business of making money, not spending it. But his hands were tied. People were getting restless. Reporters were checking their watches. New York was waiting. "Fine."

The manager took to the podium. "Folks, please forgive the late start."

A woman stood. She wore a thick silver necklace around her neck. "Where is Prudence?"

"She was unavoidably detained. However, in the interest of your time, we'll start without her."

A groan swelled from the packed hall.

The showroom manager pressed on. "We are very lucky to have with us here tonight the venerable Pierre Millet. He has been a Valley fixture for the last fifty years and he's generously agreed to play something from his vast repertoire."

Pierre Millet began the slow descent into George Gershwin's

Rhapsody in Blue, a piece he had performed a million times. He teased out the first notes, playing slowly, building an energy toward the anticipated climax. *Rhapsody* was a powerful piece, but it was never like this. He felt as if the piano itself was helping to build the song's momentum, like a gust of wind to a sail. It was magnificent. Magical. The audience was entranced and so was he. When he played the final measures, notes rained throughout the room like a musical waterfall.

Pierre Millet was not known for superlatives, but he bowed before the crowd and said, "This is the finest piano I have ever played."

Prudence arrived at the doorway to the concert hall just as the music was trailing off.

"I guess that's that. I'm too late," she said. "It wasn't meant to be."

Les Strom placed his hand on her back and said softly into her ear, "Such a shame you won't be able to play it one last time."

"That *is* a shame, isn't it?"

"We did go through the bother of the cuff links."

"We did, didn't we?"

If there's one thing a producer knows, it's how to seize the moment. Les Strom opened the door and practically pushed Prudence through the threshold. "Look who I found!" he said.

The showroom manager froze. The entire room turned its attention to the door.

"Hello, everyone," Prudence said with a shy but triumphant smile. For Prudence, too, knew how to seize the moment.

The audience cheered. People in their T-shirts and flip-flops held up their phones for pictures. Journalists scribbled, photographers clicked, television cameras whirled.

"Play the jingles!" came the cries. "Play the jingles, Prudence!"

Prudence climbed the stage and sat before her piano.

"Play the jingles!"

So she played all her famous commercial jingles and the audience sang the lyrics. *I am NEET because I got dirt BEAT!* And, *Double Bubble, that dirt's in trouble!* After each song, they clapped. But the clapping annoyed Prudence. Somewhere under her shell, a memory was making its way to the surface. The *clap, clap, clap* became a *clink, clink, clink* and the room grew very cold.

Prudence was a little girl. Her father was pulling her down the sidewalk in a red wagon. Women in bright dresses and silver shoes danced in the street and behind them came a marching band. The air smelled of caramel corn and hot dogs and something close to happiness. Prudence and her father came to the end of the sidewalk where a crowd had gathered. An old man churned a hand organ and beside him, in a red suit and little red cap, a tiny monkey held two miniature cymbals the size of silver dollars. "Make him dance!" the crowd cried. "Make him dance!" The organ-grinder played the music and the monkey danced and clashed his little cymbals. The people laughed and threw money into a bowl. *Clink.*

"Daddy," Prudence squealed, "I want a coin!"

Her father refused. "There is no beauty in being exploited," he said. Then he pulled the wagon on down the sidewalk.

A year passed and Prudence's parents were long gone. It was December and she was sitting not in a cute little wagon, but before an enormous piano in a department store. Prudence wore an itchy taffeta dress—a bright Christmas red—and tight black shoes. She was stationed between women's wigs and the perfume counter. It should have been the enticing scent of perfume that stayed with her, but it was the synthetic smell of the acrylic wigs. Nasty and pretend was how she thought of it. And Granny Paddington, in her shiny leather boots and a rabbit fur coat. She smelled of something that Prudence couldn't find words for. All she knew was that it made her feel sad and alone.

A crowd had gathered.

"Play 'Jingle Bells'!" they cried.

An obedient child, Prudence played "Jingle Bells." The crowd laughed and threw coins into a jar.

Clink. Clink. Clink.

Prudence shook her head at the parallel memory. The Steinway crowd clapped and chanted and sang to commercial jingles, songs

Prudence wrote to sell laundry detergent. The music sounded tinny, the piano taunted her.

Clink, clink, clink.

When she had played all her songs, the showroom manager announced it was time to start the bidding. But Prudence did not get up from the bench.

"Ms. Childs?" the showroom manager said.

Prudence caressed the keys. *Show them you can play.*

"Shall we begin the auction now, Ms. Childs?"

Not yet, thought Prudence. *Not yet.* She began the first movement of Erik Satie's *Trois Gymnopédies*. It was a slow, maneuvering waltz that swelled with feeling and long-buried memories. It was gentle and sad, hopeful yet solemn. This dissonance had a hypnotic effect on its audience. The showroom manager forgot he was standing in front of a podium because he'd begun thinking about taking up painting again. Les Strom had the urge to read a novel instead of draft contracts. Pierre Millet thought of taking a boyish swing at composing, a gift to himself for his eighty-first birthday. It did not matter if you were seated in the first row or the last, the music reached everyone, inspiring them to run out into the world, to grab hold of something beautiful and drink it in as soon as they could.

When Prudence finished, the applause contrasted greatly with the jingle applause. It was slower, deeper, thoughtful. Earned.

A gentleman sitting in the third row squeezed the handle of his paddle. He was very wealthy. He collected expensive paintings and vintage cars, and he had come to the auction to buy something famous. But hearing the piano's sound, hearing Prudence play *Gymnopédies,* he was suddenly tired of collecting. It seemed monotonous. Empty. He did not want to simply acquire the piano. He wanted to master it, to create instead of merely consume.

He was prepared to be the highest bidder.

But the piano's magic had also reached Prudence. When she played *Gymnopédies,* the *clink* sound did not echo in her head. She stood and bowed. She grabbed a pamphlet and took her seat in the special chair near her piano.

The showroom manager began the auction. "The opening bid will be $50,000. Do I hear $51,000?" He nodded and said, "We have $51,000. Do I hear $52,000?"

Prudence tried to distract herself by reading the pamphlet. But the words *successful commercial composer* and *Flush 'N Clean Toilet Bowl Cleaner* jumped out at her. *Well, there it is in black and white*, Prudence thought. *I'm no artist.*

Her hands curled into fists as if she were getting ready for a fight. Because she was thinking about how one day soon she would die and she would remember this. How she had sealed her fate by selling her piano.

But she was very much alive right now.

"We're at $60,000. Do I hear 62?"

The wealthy gentleman who was tired of collecting lifted his paddle at $70,000.

Another at $75,000.

The wealthy man countered at $80,000. For he had to have this piano.

"$85,000!"

"$90,000!"

The wealthy man's paddle went up a final time. "$95,000!"

There were no other bids. The showroom manager raised the gavel and Prudence shot up from her chair. "$100,000!"

The room roared in confusion.

"You're the seller!" the showroom manager protested. "You can't drive up the price!"

"I want a second ending!"

"A what?"

But the wealthy man was determined. "$120,000!"

"Folks, I'm the auctioneer!" said the showroom manager.

"$125,000!" Prudence said.

"$150,000!" the wealthy man said.

The showroom manager said, meekly, "Do I hear $160,000?"

Prudence held up her hand (because she didn't have a little plastic paddle). "$160,000!"

The wealthy man did not raise his paddle again. The showroom manager banged the hammer. "Sold!"

That's how Prudence bought back her own piano. Along with "Buyer's Premium" (the agreed upon 15 percent of the hammer price), and the "Commission Fee" (that the showroom manager would collect for holding the auction), and the thousand-dollar movers' tab to have the six-foot, eleven-inch, Model B, grand Steinway in ebony finish moved back and reassembled in the marble foyer of 10534 Pricklypoppy Lane.

Prudence signed the contracts to *Alexei Petrov's Dueling Piano Wars!* right there on the lid of her famous piano while the camera shutters clicked and the entertainment reporters scribbled onto little notepads, already drafting the headlines in their heads.

Les Strom wanted the publicity. The showroom manager wanted the publicity. The salesmen on the floor wanted the publicity.

Prudence handed the pen back to Les Strom just as her phone chimed with a text: See you tomorrow, Peanut.

CHAPTER THIRTEEN

Stayin' Alive

McDowell Mountain Regional Park sits on the edge of the desert, twenty-four miles from Scottsdale. Here, the brittlebush and sage give way to jagged rocks. Ocotillo sprout from the desert floor like green-gold fountains and groups of ancient saguaros stand together like men on street corners. Off the main road there is a small playground with picnic tables and swing sets. Children are warned not to wander, for the desert floor is lined with all sorts of cacti that do not feel good when you touch them. Not to mention scorpions the size of your hand that skitter under the rocks. And, of course, rattlesnakes.

In the cooler months, the park is busy with mountain bikers and hikers and campers. From April to October, the twenty-two-thousand-acre park is empty. Hiking and biking and camping are dangerous in triple-digit heat, and those who do not respect the heat of the desert are in for a rude awakening. Not a summer goes by without the fire department having to rescue hikers, often by helicopter. At best, they're merely dehydrated. But every year, there's at least one rescue that turns into recovery, meaning death.

—

PRUDENCE GOT INTO her red Porsche and drove toward the park. With each mile, the sprawl of Scottsdale crumbled away. First the strip malls and the gas stations and then the fast-food restaurants and the golf courses, until it was just saguaros and brittlebush and open space and the hot, unrelenting sun.

Bobby Wheeler was running the air at full blast in his rented Chevrolet Aveo. He rolled down his window when Prudence pulled up alongside him. In his hand was an extralarge Jamba Juice. "I'm not getting out of my car. It's way too hot. Why don't you get in?"

A wave of hesitation washed over Prudence. But it was already 110 and the sun was high and in the short amount of time her window was open, enough heat had filled the little car that she'd started to sweat. Prudence got into Bobby Wheeler's royal blue rental.

"Hi, Peanut."

"Shut up."

He took a long pull of his smoothie. "I hate to bother you about finances."

"Well, you are."

"I'm in a real jam here and . . ."

"Then you shouldn't be drinking $12 milkshakes."

Bobby Wheeler shrugged. "It's not a milkshake. It's an Aloha Pineapple Smoothie." He held it out to her. "Wanna try it?"

"No, those things are pure sugar."

Bobby Wheeler shook his head. "That's not what Katie told me."

"Who?"

"The girl who works at Jamba. Katie said it has nine grams of protein." He took another slurp. "I'm on a health kick. Turning over a new leaf."

"A new leaf? One that includes blackmailing ex-wives?"

Bobby Wheeler shifted his large body in his small seat.

"Why do you need so much money anyway?" Prudence pressed. "Do you have a drug problem or something?"

No, Bobby Wheeler did not have a drug problem. He didn't have a gambling problem either. Bobby Wheeler had a lonely-hearts problem. This girl, Candy, had messaged him through the Heart-2-Hearts dating site. She was gorgeous and liked fast cars. He was in over his head. No way was he going to tell Prudence about Candy.

"Just give me the check and I'll be out of your life forever."

"Oh, right, that."

"What?"

"I don't have a check for you."

"Why not?"

"I didn't sell my piano."

Bobby Wheeler sat squished in his seat, processing this piece of information. "Why?" It was the only question he could think of.

"Because I decided not to start my book club."

"You're not making any sense," he said. Then added, "As usual."

"I make perfect sense."

"I'm about to lose my condo," Bobby Wheeler said.

"That's really not my problem."

"But I've got nowhere to go."

"I know where you can go. I'd love to tell you."

Bobby Wheeler had two speeds: daft and dark. Fourth grader or serial killer. The gears were switching at the moment Prudence threatened to tell him to go to hell.

He stared out the front windshield, shaking his head slowly.

"Don't make me do this. Don't make me tell Mrs. Martinelli's daughter, Karen, that you're worth millions because of her mother."

Prudence narrowed her eyes. "How do you know about Karen Martinelli?"

"PeekYou."

"Peek who?"

"PeekYou. It's a people search engine. You find people on there. For forty bucks I found out that Mrs. Martinelli has a daughter in Boulder, Colorado. Divorced with three kids. Her mom was a piano teacher, her father a postman, both deceased. Didn't really have much to pass on to her . . . except jingle royalties. But she never got them."

Prudence adjusted the vent on the air-conditioning. "She was rescuing me from *you. Elle m'a sauvée.*"

"What does that mean?"

"It means you're an idiot."

"Whatever. Nobody cares about me. They only care about you."

Bobby Wheeler cared only about Bobby Wheeler.

"All that fuss they made over your piano. Think how much fuss they'll make when they find out you're a fraud."

"I'm not a fraud."

"You are. I can prove you are." Prudence and Bobby never knew each other as adults. They picked up right where they left off, bickering like they were teenagers.

"Well, I'm going to prove I'm *not*."

"How're you going to do that?"

The little gatekeepers in Prudence's head started to bang on the glass windows: *Do not tell him anything more.* But pride and anger got the better of her and she did not listen to the little gatekeepers. "I'm going to be on television."

"You?"

"Me. A television producer approached me. I'm going to play my piano on TV. That's why I couldn't sell it. I'll be needing it."

The moon in Bobby Wheeler's orbit eclipsed the sun and his face showed total darkness. *Why,* he wondered, *does everything always work out for* her?

"You've done a very bad thing, Peanut."

Upon hearing the change in Bobby Wheeler's voice, Prudence grabbed the door handle. A loud *CLICK* told her she was too late. "Going somewhere?"

"I want to get back into my car."

"Bye-bye, car, we're going for a drive."

Bobby Wheeler didn't know exactly what he was doing, but as was his way—act first, think later—he made a move. He threw the car into gear and punched the gas. They jutted forward and then he slammed on the brakes. "Put your seat belt on, please."

Bobby Wheeler then sped off down a mountain bike trail, but it was very hot out. There would be no mountain bikers today.

"I have nowhere to go, Peanut," he said over and over.

Prudence slipped her phone out of her dress pocket but they were too far out for service. They got a full two miles through the brush when Bobby Wheeler slammed on the brakes. The temperature on the dashboard read 112 degrees.

"I will drive you back to your car once you agree to give me the money."

"Nope."

"I can sit here all day."

"Me, too." Prudence crossed her arms over her chest.

They probably would have sat there all day, those two. They were both that stubborn. The Chevy Aveo, however, was not that stubborn. It was not about to hang out in the triple-digit heat waiting for these two to get their shit together. Parked in the middle of the cholla and buckhorn and the sage, the car died. The hum of the motor was replaced by a ringing silence.

"What just happened?" Prudence said.

"I don't know." Bobby Wheeler turned the key. There was a stuttering *tktktktktk,* but the engine would not turn over. He tried a second time. And a third. "I think the battery died."

"Oh, perfect," Prudence said.

The air-conditioned air began to dissipate. Prudence pushed the button to roll down her window but the window would not move. Bobby Wheeler tried his window, which also would not move.

"I'm getting out of this car before it turns into an oven," Prudence said, yanking the door handle. But the door wouldn't open. She tried a second time, and a third.

"Oh, this isn't good," Bobby Wheeler said.

"What the hell is going on?"

"The alternator must've given out."

"What's that?"

"It charges the battery when the car's running. But if it failed, we drained the battery sitting here."

"What about the windows? The locks?"

"Computerized. They need the battery. It's the brain of the car." He shook his head. "Newer models are all so overengineered."

Prudence's irritation turned to panic. "Are you saying we're trapped?"

"There should be a mechanism somewhere that overrides the locks." Bobby Wheeler ran his hand under the dash and the driver's seat, but found nothing. "Huh."

The temperature inside the car began to climb. Slowly at first. Then not so slowly. Within a minute, it was 120 degrees. In a few minutes more it would reach 130. Prudence's breathing was heavy, the hot air passing through her lungs like thick oil. A sweat stain flourished on Bobby Wheeler's shirt. His eyes were puffy and red, his face dripped with perspiration.

"I'm going to break a window," Prudence said. "Or we'll be dead in fifteen minutes."

"Better find something hard," he said weakly. "These windows are tempered. They won't shatter easily."

His head was bobbing as if he were falling asleep.

Prudence looked in the glove compartment but found only the manual. She looked under the seats but found only fast-food wrappers and empty Coke cans.

At some point, soon, heatstroke would set in. All those thoughts of death Prudence had been having over the past month seemed stupid now that she was actually facing death. She did not want to die next to Bobby Wheeler in a stupid rental car.

"Till death do us part, Peanut."

CHAPTER FOURTEEN

Birth, School, Work, Death

At the same time Prudence was locked inside Bobby Wheeler's car fighting for her life, Alexei Petrov was taking a break. He sat outside on the terrace of his hillside home and read a short story by Chekhov while he ate a prepared lunch of braised chicken, steamed asparagus, and brown rice. Alexei was not expected (or permitted) to cook his own food. Tatiana had purchased a subscription meal-plan service designed for elite athletes. Every week, seven lunches and seven dinners customized by Tatiana on her laptop in Paris were delivered to Alexei's house in L.A.

Alexei's parents had returned to France at the beginning of the summer, just as his television show was getting off the ground. He was living alone for the first time in his life. But this newfound independence was a façade. Tatiana Petrova still called the shots even though she was a good five thousand miles away.

Alexei's schedule in Los Angeles was dictated by his mother and run with the precision of a Swiss watch. He woke at five every morning and ran three miles on the treadmill. After a light breakfast of porridge and black tea, Alexei took an eight-minute shower. He shaved, brushed his teeth, trimmed his nails, and was at his piano no later than 7:00 A.M., where he warmed up for thirty minutes.

From 7:30 until 10:30, Alexei Petrov worked on a single piece of music, breaking it down measure by measure. Each measure had to be perfected before he moved on to the next measure. To achieve this perfection, he would play a single measure over and over up to twenty times. Sometimes more.

At 10:30, his technical coach arrived and they worked for an hour. At 11:30, Alexei Petrov took a twenty-minute lunch break. After lunch, he was at the piano for another three hours.

From 3:00 to 4:00, on alternate days, he had several tutors, all hired and paid for by Tatiana: a poet who helped him with his English, a novelist who helped him with his writing, and a painter who schooled him in fine arts. All of them were supposed to give Alexei Petrov a heightened sense of artistic emotion in the music he played.

From 4:00 to 6:00, he worked on memorization and assembling programs for any upcoming performance. On the day of the braised chicken lunch and the Chekhov story, these two hours were spent preparing for the October episode of *Alexei Petrov's Dueling Piano Wars!*, which would air in exactly eight weeks.

After all those hours of practice, he'd take a bath in Epsom salts, where he'd drink white wine, study musical scores, and listen to Bach. Once he was finished with his wine and his Bach and his scores, he would have his dinner. No later than 9:00 each evening, he'd brush his teeth, apply nighttime face products, and rub cream into the cuticles of his very long fingers.

Alexei Petrov did not have time for serious relationships. He did not have time for pets (he was severely allergic to cats anyway). He did not do his own laundry. He did not clean his own house. He did not pay his own bills.

The rigid structure of Alexei's days left little room for loneliness. He often told himself that success required an unrelenting commitment to his craft. And if he ever woke up in the morning feeling tired and burned-out, he would remind himself of all the sacrifices his parents had made for him.

They had quit their jobs, given up their pensions, and left their friends and families to begin new lives in France after Alexei was accepted to the Conservatoire de Paris. Nikolai and Tatiana Petrov had organized everything around their child. They did this without questioning their own needs or taking a single look back. It had been difficult for Nikolai. He thrived on research and lab work, but now he had to content himself with an assistant professorship at the Sorbonne, teaching introductory physics to undergraduates.

But their selflessness paid off. The Conservatoire had molded Alexei into a mesmerizing performer. After graduation, he played Radio France, London's Wigmore Hall, and Carnegie Hall. He was a soloist with the New York Philharmonic and the Boston Symphony Orchestra.

It had all led him to Los Angeles. At the end of the previous year, Alexei and his parents were invited to L.A. for the first time. It was supposed to be a short-term stay, just long enough to fulfill a recording contract with Sony Classical as part of his prize for winning the Van Cliburn International Piano Competition. But Tatiana, who served as Alexei's de facto manager, took the opportunity to meet with all the big talent agencies in town. As she had hoped, she struck gold. Less than two months after arriving in California, she received a telephone call from a showrunner who wanted Alexei to host a television program.

"A competition show," she told Alexei, "like *The Voice*."

Alexei Petrov was not a fan of these shows. Most of the contestants seemed to care more about fame than music. Besides, he did not want to host anything or even extend his stay in L.A. He wanted to complete his recording obligations and return to Paris.

"I'd rather not, actually," he told her.

But Tatiana would not be dissuaded. "There's not a concert pianist alive who wouldn't kill for an opportunity like this. This is your chance to earn a fortune."

Arguing with her would be useless. Alexei simply agreed to do the show and willed it to fail.

But the opposite happened. The show had exceeded everyone's wildest expectations, including his own. And until his audience latched on to the next big thing, the young and beautiful host of *Alexei Petrov's Dueling Piano Wars!* was stuck in limbo, in Los Angeles, living the same day over and over again.

CHAPTER FIFTEEN

Layla

Prudence thought of how Stuart would take the news of her death. How confused he'd be that she was found dead in a car with a man he had never heard of. How betrayed he'd feel on top of all his grief. She was angry at herself. Angry that she didn't go to him first with this Bobby Wheeler nonsense. He'd have known what to do. He always did. Stuart would never sit in a hot car with a $12 milkshake. He would never try to blackmail his ex-wife. He would never even *have* an ex-wife.

What a mess.

Stuart would know that Prudence died with secrets. The mystery would haunt him for the rest of his life. All those happy, perfect years together, an illusion.

FORMER PRODIGY DEAD AT 48, TRAPPED IN RENTED BLUE CHEVY AVEO WITH EX-HUSBAND AND AN ALOHA PINEAPPLE SMOOTHIE.

If I get out of this, I will tell him everything.

Prudence's head throbbed. Her heart raced and her breath quickened. She was moments away from having a heatstroke. She could hear Bobby Wheeler's labored breathing.

She did not want to look at him because she wanted to die with the images of Becca and Tess and Stuart and Mrs. Wintour in her head. She leaned back in the seat and closed her eyes and envisioned their faces. She remembered the first time she met Stuart. How handsome he was in his blue suit. She was in the height of her jingle-writing days and had been making a lot of money. Her bank, after telling her it wasn't a good idea to keep a quarter million dollars in a checking account, had assigned her a wealth manager for high-net-worth clients. That's how they met, in a conference room, Stuart explaining how to diversify her portfolio with index funds. "They're low risk, with high potential, and they're very little work. You, uh, don't seem the type to check the S&P every day . . ."

He was surprised when she said, "Sold." And then invited him to the opening of the Warhol exhibit down at the Whitney that started in an hour.

"You want some time to think about it?" he asked.

"Nope." Maybe she was distracted by his beautiful brown eyes. Or his thick, neatly trimmed hair—he looked like a Kennedy! Or maybe because she knew, immediately, that this was someone she could trust.

She was sad just thinking of it. Fucking Bobby Wheeler.

Prudence tried to remain calm in the face of her certain death. This was the moment she had feared since she dropped Becca off at college.

She'd been waiting her whole life for a chance to finally prove herself. Not just to the world. But to Prudence Childs, who woke up every single morning with music playing in her head. She could not die a semiobscure jingle writer.

Fuck this, Prudence thought. *My life is worth fighting for!*

"Actually, I think I will have sip of your stupid smoothie," Prudence said. "You, too. We need to hydrate."

"What's the use? We're going to die in here."

"I'm not going to let us die in here. I'm going to break a window."

"With what, your hands? You'll never play again."

"If we don't get out of here, I won't live to play again, you idiot." Prudence took a sip of the smoothie and thought for a moment. She looked at the passenger window. If she used her shoulder, surely it would break before the window did. She would have to use her feet. She was wearing leather over-the-knee boots, with heels the shape of golf tees. This could work.

Prudence climbed over the seats and into the back. She lay flat and placed both feet on the window. With all her might, she kicked. Nothing.

"Harder," Bobby said.

Prudence braced herself with her arms and kicked again. With each kick, she thought of her grandmother. Of the manipulation and control. Of all that she took from Prudence. Here was her chance to get it back and more. She thought of Stuart, and Becca, and Tess. No way was she giving in. She was a fighter. She kicked with the same fierce determination she used to master Beethoven's insanely difficult sonata, *Appassionata*. She had fought so much of her life and here she was fighting again, not with her hands but her feet.

She grasped the front seat with one hand for leverage.

She kicked the window harder and harder. Over and over, using up the last bit of air in her lungs. She was suffocating. *Bam, bam, bam!* Finally, there was the crash of breaking glass. All at once, fresh air flooded the vehicle. Prudence took a deep breath and crawled out the window, back to life.

Once Prudence was a good two miles from Bobby Wheeler's car, she got out her cell phone and called 911. When Rural Metro asked what her emergency was, she told them there was a man, no, a "living tragedy," in a disabled royal blue Chevy Aveo approximately two miles off the Pemberton bike trail in McDowell Mountain Regional Park. "You might want to check on him," she said.

CHAPTER SIXTEEN

What's New, Pussycat?

London had been soggy and Stuart Childs was tired. He was tired of all the work travel. He was tired of making small talk at meetings and researching hedge funds. He missed the warm swimming pool and the large kitchen stocked with cold beer and four different kinds of salsa. He missed his dog and the dry heat.

Most of all he missed his wife. Her eyes were still large and green despite the soft crinkles that were beginning to form around them. The way they'd light up so easily at little things like an unexpected bloom on a cactus. Through those green eyes, the world was filled with a million hidden wonders he was not otherwise privy to.

There was nobody like Prudence. She maintained a childlike sense of curiosity that Stuart adored. "Did you know horses have a special skeleton that allows them to sleep standing up?" she would say. Or "I wonder what Picasso's dreams were like?" He admired her independence, how she would go see a foreign film by herself because everyone else complained about subtitles. Or spend weekday mornings at the Biltmore Hotel to study the art deco architecture that so fascinated her. She'd meet him for drinks after work and he was always late because of a last-minute call. She'd be sitting at the bar waiting for him, sipping a martini and reading a book, not at all bothered. She was spontaneous. Interesting. Different. Up until recently, she was a hell of a lot of fun.

He didn't like taking off while she was in the midst of a midlife crisis. Especially since he was having a midlife crisis of his own. It wasn't as big as Prudence's. He didn't sleep until noon or take long baths. He didn't brood on the chaise by the pool all day. But each morning he started the day with a quiet despair, a nameless unease.

Stuart was becoming increasingly dissatisfied with life.

Once he had loved his job. Researching securities and watching his clients' portfolios grow had excited him. But wealth management was changing. Would-be investors relied less and less on a banker to pick stocks and more and more on computer-generated programs. It made him feel obsolete, like a candlemaker or a bowling pin setter.

Stuart wanted to make something besides money now. He wanted to retire. They had plenty of investments and he knew how lucky he was. But he didn't feel lucky. He felt weary. Stuck. He, too, had a dream. It had oddly resurfaced with the reappearance of Prudence's piano. As a child, Stuart had a reoccurring dream that he could fly. The dream took on many forms, but the most frequent one was where he had a bicycle that, when he pedaled fast enough, would take off into flight. The dream was always the same: He'd pedal furiously down his street then take off and fly above the rooftops, a cross between Mary Poppins and ET.

Years later, when he was at Yale, he'd had a roommate whose father was a pilot. One weekend, when the roommate took Stuart home for a visit, the father took them up in his small plane. He showed Stuart how to fly, even asked if he wanted to have a try at the controls.

Did he ever.

The feel of the throttle in his hands, the thrum in his chest while they soared through the air . . . it was everything Stuart had dreamed about and more. There was a peacefulness in the sky, a beauty that land couldn't match.

Stuart yearned for the tranquility that sitting behind the controls offered. It wasn't the same being a passenger. Especially not on this trip. The journey from Heathrow to JFK was fine, but the flight to Phoenix was fully booked, which meant he had to check his carry-on. He took his seat only to be evacuated from the plane ten minutes later because of mechanical problems. Once seated at the gate, he realized that his wallet was in his jacket pocket. Which was in his carry-on bag. Which was checked.

The layover lasted three hours. Three hours in which he could have been sitting at the bar with a burger and a beer, only he couldn't because he didn't have any money or cards. For three long hours he watched other people sit at the bar and order burgers and sip beer.

When he was finally able to reboard the plane to Phoenix, he tried to catch up on his sleep. But sitting in his row was a young woman, wearing a neck pillow and leopard-skin leggings, who kept getting up to use the restroom. Stuart offered his aisle seat, but no thank you, she preferred the window.

A burly man with thick glasses and a beard like a lumberjack sat between them. He requested that Stuart turn his air off because he had a sinus infection. Then the young woman sitting in the window seat told the man sitting in the middle seat about her incredibly fucked-up childhood. After two hours of that, the man with the sinus infection spent the next two hours telling the young woman about *his* incredibly fucked-up childhood.

If only Stuart had headphones. But they were in his carry-on bag. So for four hours, he listened to their stories until the man invited the woman to this megachurch he belonged to in Phoenix. Presumably for people with fucked-up childhoods.

Stuart's childhood had not been at all fucked-up.

Stuart came from a happy family. He'd grown up in a suburb of Houston. His father worked for NASA and his mother was a journalist. Stuart played baseball and assembled airplanes from little kits made of balsa wood. He and his sister spent summer afternoons drinking Tang and watching *I Dream of Jeannie* reruns because it was a show about an astronaut who worked for NASA and when

his father came home from work, they'd recount episodes at the dinner table to make his father laugh. Stuart had an ant farm and his
sister had a Barbie collection. They shared the chemistry kit. They
played cards after dinner and picnicked in the park.

They were nice people, Stuart's family. He still called them every
Sunday afternoon.

NINETEEN HOURS AFTER he'd left his hotel room in London, Stuart
walked through the front door. His head was a block of wood. His
back was stiff and his legs were cramped. He dropped his bag and
stood in the marble foyer, which for some reason felt empty.

Stuart couldn't figure out what was missing.

"Honey, I'm home!" he announced.

"Welcome back, my darling."

She stood before him gulping down a glass of water. Her dress
was torn and her suede boots were splotched with a red dust. Her
tousled bob was wilted like a thirsty plant.

"Good god, you look like you've been in a fight! What in the
world happened?"

"Would you like a drink?" Prudence asked.

"No."

"I'd take the offer if I were you."

"Fine."

Stuart, Prudence, and Mrs. Wintour filed into the great room,
where the ten-foot-tall windows butted together giving a nearly
seamless view of Scottsdale. It was evening now, and the setting sun
lit up the clouds like the embers of a fire. Prudence made a drink and
handed it to Stuart.

"You're not having one?" he asked.

"I need to hydrate."

Stuart watched as she took another slug of water. And another.
"What the hell is going on?"

"You should sit down."

He lowered himself into a club chair.

"Cheers," Prudence said, raising her glass.

"Get to it."

"So, my piano."

That triggered Stuart's memory. "That's what's missing! Wait, where is it?"

"I tried to sell it."

"You *what*?"

She told him all about the auction, except for the very last bit. Actually, the very last *two* bits.

"Why?" he asked her in disbelief.

"I needed the money."

"Why?" he asked her again in disbelief.

"Well, first things first. Happily, I once again own the piano."

"Post-auction."

"Yes!"

Stuart shook his head as if he were trying to get water out of his ears. He then took a sip of his drink and tried to envision the best-case scenario. Because you never knew with Prudence.

"You canceled the auction."

"No, I didn't cancel it."

Stuart tried to envision the second-best-case scenario. "No one bid on the piano?"

"Actually, there were several bids."

Stuart shifted in his chair and tried to envision the third-best-case scenario—and the most improbable. "Their bids fell through due to lack of funds." He was a banker, after all.

Prudence shook her head.

"I outbid everyone."

"You *what*!"

" 'Fraid so."

Prudence did not have a head for finances. "Why?"

"I need it now. See, there was this guy in the parking lot."

"What guy?"

"The one who approached me in the parking lot about being on TV."

"A reporter?"

"No, a television producer. From L.A."

"A guy from L.A. just walked up to you in the parking lot of Steinway Hall?"

"Right? Crazy. See, he produces reality shows."

"Like—?"

"I don't know. Something about dogs and hockey moms. Oh, *L.A. Waitress*. I remember that one."

"A man convinced you not to sell your piano so that you could be on *L.A. Waitress*?"

"No, no, no, *Alexei Petrov's Dueling Piano Wars!* It's a competition show like *American Idol*."

Stuart took a moment to absorb what he'd just heard. None of it sounded plausible. "We have to verify he's a legit producer before we move ahead."

"Too late."

"Define 'too late.' "

"I agreed."

"In what form did this agreement take place?"

"A contractual form."

Stuart leaned forward. "You signed a contract?"

"Actually, three. A release permitting the network to broadcast my performance, a waiver not to sue anyone involved with the show for any reason, and a confidentiality agreement to not talk publicly about the program or anyone associated with the program for any reason."

Stuart stared at his wife, trying to process that last statement.

She said, "Would you like another drink?"

"Do I need one?"

"Perhaps. There's more."

He handed her his glass and looked out the window. The sun had set and the neighborhood lights sprinkled below them like spilled sugar. He could not reconcile the fact that his wife thought an appearance on some ridiculous television show was going to solve this business of feeling old and useless. He had just about had it up to here. His wife was anything but old and useless. Hadn't he turned cartwheels to convince her otherwise?

"There are some things about my past," she said, handing him a fresh drink. "Things you don't know."

"Like?"

"You might change your mind about me."

Stuart gave Prudence a tight smile. "Well, I am beginning to feel a bit furious with you as this conversation progresses. But I don't think I could ever change my mind about you."

Prudence stroked Mrs. Wintour. "It's amazing, isn't it, that we've known each other so intimately for a quarter of a century and there are still things we don't know about each other?"

"I believe you know everything there is to know about me."

In an effort to stall, Prudence asked, "Who was your first kiss? I don't know that!"

"It's best forgotten."

"Nonsense, everyone should remember their first kiss."

"Julie St. John, seventh grade, spin the bottle in her parents' basement."

"I'm jealous."

"She had braces and wore T-shirts with kittens on them."

"I'm still jealous."

"Good. Yours?"

"Rob Lowe."

"Get out!"

"Seriously."

"I'm in*sanely* jealous."

"He was an early admirer."

"What other tidbits have you got?"

"When you're not home, I listen to Burt Bacharach songs."

"That's not so bad."

Prudence ripped the Band-Aid off. "Oh, and I was married once before."

Stuart's smile did not falter. "To Rob Lowe?"

"No, darling."

"Who? *When?*"

Prudence told Stuart the whole sordid story, from *once upon a time* to *not so happily ever after.* She told him about dropping out of Juilliard, working at Disc World, and marrying Bobby Wheeler.

"Why, Prudence? Why didn't you tell me?"

"Because I was a fool and I still can't think about it without wanting to smash things."

"But I'm your husband. One of them, anyway."

"Officially, you're my only husband. I had the marriage annulled and then went back to Juilliard and graduated."

"It worked out then?" Stuart wanted to be supportive, but he wasn't sure what that meant in a case like this.

"There's more."

"Darling, we haven't enough booze for more."

Prudence told him about Mrs. Martinelli and the Pep Soda manuscript. She told him about how Bobby Wheeler was blackmailing her into paying off his debts. Finally, she arrived at *Alexei Petrov's Dueling Piano Wars!*

"I made Google News," she told him.

Stuart did recall flipping through the headlines on his phone while waiting at the baggage carousel, but then his phone died because his charger had been in his carry-on, which he had not been allowed to carry on.

He tried to absorb it all. Then he said, "How did your dress get torn?"

"Oh, I almost forgot!"

"There's more?"

Stuart was wrong. There was enough booze for more.

"Long story, short . . ." She told him everything, from the Aloha Pineapple Smoothie to kicking out the car window.

How could he have not known these things about his wife? He was sitting before a virtual stranger.

Prudence shrugged. "At any rate, Bobby is a dangerous person. *Un véritable bâtard.*"

Stuart felt as if he had little bits of broken glass in his throat.

"Bobby? *Bobby?* What kind of a person goes by the name of Bobby after the age of fifteen?"

"Pretty much sums him up there."

Stuart shot out of his chair. Because he had an epiphany about the reality of marriage. Her mistakes were now *his* mistakes, their pasts entwined like a double helix. There was no running away, here.

"We'll have to pay him!"

"Never."

"This is no time to be self-righteous, Prudence. You took credit for someone else's work and profited. He's got the proof."

"I know him. He'll just demand more and more. If you give a mouse a cookie, he's going to want a glass of milk. And if you give him a glass of milk . . . The girls couldn't get enough of that book, remember?"

Stuart knelt at her dusty feet and rested the palms of his hands on her torn dress. "That commercial has played for over thirty years, you know how much in royalties that is? The Martinelli heirs, if they sue, could take everything."

"They could."

"We've got kids in college who depend on us. I'm fifty-two years old, Prudence. It's too late for me to start over."

Stuart wanted to retire. Learn to fly. Explore new places with his wife rather than face down another thirty years of traveling back and forth to London because they got their asses sued off. No way was this worth it. They would pay this man.

He got up from his knees. "This idiot wants a half million dollars?"

"Every idiot wants a half million dollars. But I'm not giving it to him."

"You're not thinking this through, Prudence."

"I'm telling you, it won't be the end of it, Stuart. He'll keep coming back for . . ."

"We've got to take that chance! If we don't, there might not be anything left for him to want—*we'll be wiped out*. We're looking at fraud, here. *Fraud*. You could face prison time if convicted."

"Oh, dear." She began to pace the marble floors as if to temper her growing panic. "Okay, okay, well, I guess we pay him then."

"We're not that liquid. Most of our earnings are invested. Unless you want to rob from the college fund—that would take all of it."

Prudence stopped pacing at once and said, through gritted teeth, "I'd rather go to jail than ruin my children's future. What else is there?"

"We'd have to sell our stocks at a loss. There's our retirement account. But if we pull money out of it before we're sixty, we'll have to pay tens of thousands of dollars in penalties and taxes."

"Really?"

Stuart, as it was his job, was very good at crunching numbers on the spot. "Well, if we need a half million dollars . . ." He looked at the ceiling and calculated a number so large, Prudence gasped, "Good lord, what would we live off of?"

Normally, she would find discussions about taxes and retirement accounts and liquid assets painfully boring. However, in her current circumstances, she was very much present for this. Impending disaster has a way of bringing even the most remote genius back into the here and now.

"What about the house?" she asked. "Can't we pull some equity out of it?"

"Not on the mortgage we've got. The bank wouldn't give us another dime. We'd have to sell it. Fast. Likely for less than it's worth."

The gravity of the situation hit at full impact. Prudence collapsed onto the club chair and stared out the enormous great room windows. Night had fallen and the pool glowed phosphorescently. The outside lights were switching on, illuminating the flame-colored bougainvillea, the stately palo verde trees, and the blooms on the lantana. The best memories of Prudence's life had all happened under this roof. "Oh, Stuart, our beautiful home."

Stuart nodded. "You're going to have to win that competition and pay him off. If not, we'll either get sucked into a very high-profile lawsuit or lose this house."

Prudence saw that her husband looked very tired. It was not the kind of tired you get when you stay up late watching television. It was the kind of tired you get when you diffuse bombs in airports so everyone won't get blown to bits. Stuart looked older.

Prudence had tears in her eyes and the weight of a sob in her chest. "We are not going to lose our home to Bobby Wheeler."

Stuart stood before her. "Losing that competition is not an option. You have to win. And I think you can. Are you up for it?"

"Stepping up has been in my subconscious for decades. I'm tired of people standing in my way when it comes to my music, making me feel like I'm not a real talent, that I'm nothing. It's time to banish those voices in my head, including my own."

"First thing in the morning," he said, "I'm taking out a restraining order on this maniac."

Prudence knew a restraining order would have no impact on Bobby Wheeler. He'd be back. She would have to be ready this time.

The pressure was on now in a way it had never been before. But, in this moment, Stuart needed a show of strength and reassurance from Prudence. "There's no need for that, my love," she said. "I have a gift. And it might just set us free."

CHAPTER SEVENTEEN

La Folle Journée

Twenty-one-year-old Prudence Paddington walked down Ninth Avenue in New York. She turned left onto Fifty-seventh Street and continued until she came to an old soot-stained building. Chunks of concrete were missing from the steps and a pair of gargoyles glared at her from above. The lobby was dim and smelled of mildew and stale cigarette smoke.

These were the offices of an esteemed psychoanalyst?

Prudence pulled a scrap of paper from her pocket and, having studied the address, ran her finger down the directory. Dr. Otto Schneider, Room 12, Floor 7. This was the place, all right. She wondered why one of the most sought-after therapists in the city would choose to practice out of such a dump. Then again, she wondered about a lot of things.

Prudence knew nothing of psychoanalysis, except what she had looked up in an old textbook titled *The Study of Human Behavior.* Freud, Jung, and Adler were men with blinding white hair and trim beards who studied your dreams. You lie down on a couch and stare at the ceiling and talk about anything, *anything* that comes to mind—free association.

It was her Juilliard mentor and chamber instructor, Dr. Helen

Chen, who had urged Prudence to log a few sessions with the therapist. Graduation was six months away and Dr. Chen worried that Prudence was unraveling. The young pianist had always been hard on herself, but lately her internal struggles were creeping to the surface. She had grown alarmingly thin and increasingly disheveled—she'd wear the same shirt days in a row and seemed to subsist entirely on Pop-Tarts and Marlboro Reds. Whenever she flubbed a note she would claw at her arms as if developing a rash.

"My dear," Dr. Chen said after rehearsal one day. "I think it's time to get some help."

It had been three years since Prudence had run away from Bobby Wheeler, landing back in her grandmother's house, penniless and with a very large piano in tow. At that time, Prudence was devastated at having to start back at square one. But Granny Paddington was thrilled. Assuming they were back in business, she pressed Prudence to rehearse a new program. She even bought her a pink taffeta dress that looked like something a child would wear to a birthday party.

Having lived with Bobby Wheeler and his impossible mother, Prudence had learned a thing or two about sticking up for herself. Or so she thought until she balked at the taffeta dress Granny held up before her.

Prudence scoffed. "No way I'm wearing that."

Granny's eyes flashed with anger. "You giving me lip?"

"I'm not going to dress like a baby."

Granny flung the dress onto Prudence's bed and snarled, "Say goodbye to your precious records." She grabbed a thick stack of albums off the stereo console and made her way out the door.

"No, stop! I'll wear it, I'll wear it."

Prudence had to end this toxic duet with her grandmother if she had any hope of survival. She saw promise in Mrs. Martinelli's eight-bar melody, certain it would provide her with the intended means of flight. If she decided to use it, that is.

Lovely Mrs. Martinelli. Prudence's first piano teacher was the only adult who really cared for her. Mrs. Martinelli understood that it took a special type of nurturing to develop a true talent, one that calls for sensitivity, compassion, and unending support. Adeline Martinelli had wept as her sweet little girl was carted away. When she looked in the grandmother's face, she saw a selfish determination all too common in parents of gifted children. Her worst fears for Prudence were about to come true.

When Granny Paddington took over, Mrs. Martinelli was lost to Prudence forever.

Some misguided slice of Prudence's brain thought maybe she could reason with Granny, explain why she should return to New York. Maybe then the two of them could declare a truce. Maybe Granny would be proud of Prudence's desire for independence. She might even offer the encouragement and approval Prudence always craved.

On a chilly November evening, not long after she had fled Bobby's garage, Prudence sought out her grandmother, who was sitting on the porch in a wicker rocking chair, wrapped in the rabbit fur coat, her ever-present pack of Newports nestled beside the ceramic ashtray.

"I've been thinking about going back to Juilliard," Prudence said. She issued this statement casually, in a way that she hoped suggested a tone of *oh, by the way*, when in fact she was petrified.

Granny Paddington ignored her and lit a cigarette. A dog barked somewhere in the distance.

Finally, she turned to her granddaughter and said, "That's a terrible idea."

"Why?" asked Prudence. "You were the one who wanted me to go to college in the first place."

"That was before I discovered what kind of musician you really are," she said slowly.

"What kind of musician I really am?" Prudence spoke slowly, aware of the minefield that she was entering.

"You are not quite the talent we've made you out to be."

Prudence felt as if she had been slapped. Which was exactly what her grandmother had wanted her to feel. "What's that supposed to mean?"

"You had some early skills, I admit. But let's face it, you've only gotten where you are today because I pushed and molded you."

"Maybe." Prudence lifted her chin higher and said, "But maybe, with the right teachers, I could become great on my own."

"That's an interesting theory," Granny said, smirking. She turned and gave Prudence her full attention now. She paused, like a cat about to pounce. "Who encouraged you, who spent countless hours, tackling the Chopin prelude that got you into Juilliard in the first place?"

"You."

"You know how hard that piece is? How impressive it sounds when it's perfect? I got you to do that. You wanted to play that tired Mozart sonata. They would've laughed you right out onto the street had you auditioned with that. I know what you do best, don't you realize that?"

"I don't know."

"Oh, and your phrasing . . . ha!"

"What about my phrasing? They say I'm a natural."

"A natural—they pumped you up with so much hot air. That was all me, me teaching you to have a sense of direction when you play a piece. Me pointing out how to lift notes, how to pause without screwing up the rhythm. Me! You used to play like a damn robot, spitting out the melody without thinking. It took years of practice to nail the phrasing. Do you think you'd have the same stamina to practice hours a day without me?"

"I don't know."

"You're goddamn right, you don't know. An hour tops, that's all that you're good for."

"I guess."

"You *guess*? Stop guessing and start thinking. Was I with you when you went to Juilliard?"

"No."

"No! If you could truly do it on your own, wouldn't you have grown into something even more brilliant at Juilliard?"

"Maybe."

"Maybe? I don't think so," Granny scoffed. "You didn't grow into anything, did you?"

"No," said Prudence. She could hear her voice becoming more and more uneven, ready to crumble.

"What happened instead?"

Prudence didn't respond.

"*Answer me!*" Granny barked. "*What* happened?"

Prudence let out a wobbly "I choked."

"Correct." Granny Paddington exhaled a fat cylinder of smoke. "You choked like an amateur."

"But I'm not—" Prudence didn't know what she could say that would possibly make a difference to Granny Paddington. Worse, she didn't know what she could say that would make a difference to herself.

"Face it, Prudence. You're no artist. Not in the way that you like to imagine yourself. You're a convincing phony with a good coach. Do you want everyone in New York to realize you're a fraud?"

Tears slid down Prudence's cheeks. "No."

"No, you don't. Good. Let's just continue what we've started. We'll tour, record, and otherwise establish your legacy in a controlled environment." Granny Paddington crushed her cigarette in the ashtray, grabbed her pack of Newports, and stood. "Now there's a good girl. Go to bed."

Prudence was catatonic with despair. She couldn't imagine going back to the old days, Granny calling all the shots, dictating the day's schedule, what Prudence ate, how long she slept, what she wore, who she spoke to. Prudence turned their conversation over and over in her mind until the despair hardened into resolve. There had to be something better out there. Prudence woke up early one morning, stole the jar of spare change from Granny's dresser, and ran down the street to the Texaco station, where she locked herself in a phone booth.

"Dr. Chen," she cried, almost breathless. "I want to come back to Juilliard."

She fed the phone more quarters and told Dr. Chen about Granny Paddington. All of it. From withholding her dinner to the four in the morning practice sessions to the pittance of a weekly allowance she got, hardly enough to buy a movie ticket, let alone a bus ticket out.

Dr. Chen was horrified, but not entirely surprised. She had always questioned why such a seasoned performer was so fragile in the classroom, how Prudence never felt comfortable asking for help on a piece. Juilliard was an environment that fostered learning and growth. Making mistakes was part of that. Prudence seemed to not know what to do with that freedom. Now Dr. Chen knew why.

A brilliant musician with strong instincts, Dr. Chen also had a solid sense of right and wrong. She had to help this gifted student. The kind of talent Prudence had didn't come along every day, even at Juilliard. Prudence didn't have the money for tuition, and it was very unlikely that she could secure a scholarship so late in the semester, but Dr. Chen wouldn't let that stop the girl from returning.

"Come back, Prudence. We'll find a way to keep you here."

"But how?" Prudence asked.

"You let me worry about that," Dr. Chen replied.

And worry about it she did. Getting Prudence back in class wasn't so hard. But stalling the bursar was. Dr. Chen was running out of excuses and running out of time. Until one fortuitous day she passed by Prudence's studio and heard her playing a simple but clever little song.

"What's that you're playing, Prudence?" It certainly wasn't Bach.

Prudence had Mrs. Martinelli's letter on the stand. "Just a fun little tune I've been messing around with. Um, I was thinking of submitting it to an ad agency, like as a jingle."

That was what Mrs. Martinelli wanted her to do, anyway.

Dr. Chen thought for a moment. "I think I can help you with that."

"Really?"

"Yes, I've stayed in touch with a former student of mine who recently started a new advertising agency, Higgins McCann. I'll give Randall a call and we'll go from there."

There was no time to waste. The next day, Dr. Chen phoned her former student. "I need a favor." She then explained the situation and who Prudence was and asked if maybe he'd consider scheduling an appointment where Prudence could play her jingle.

"Sure, Dr. Chen. We've just landed an account, Pep Soda. It's a new kind of cola we're trying to market. If she can put some words to her melody, I'll see her on Friday morning around ten."

Prudence showed up that Friday morning and played Randall Higgins the jingle on the Yamaha in his office. The hook grabbed him immediately. The indelible little tune had already cemented itself in his head, an advertising home run. "Is this the first jingle you've written?"

Prudence paused, wanting to give Mrs. Martinelli credit. But then she'd have to go back home, back to Granny, where the nightmare would resume. Besides, didn't Mrs. Martinelli give it to her?

"Yes, sir, this is my first jingle."

It was exactly what Pep Soda needed to establish itself with consumers. He scooped up the prodigy's song on the spot, offering Prudence a contract and an advance check against royalties. "Ms. Paddington, you've written the best advertising hook I've ever heard in my entire career. A good ad can run two, maybe three years. Give you a bit of a cushion."

What a cushion it turned out to be. The jingle was an instantaneous hit and Prudence received a healthy amount of royalties over the next few months, enough that she could officially reenroll in Juilliard.

Granny Paddington was furious that her golden goose had skipped town, and as a final punishment, she denied entry to the moving service Prudence hired to ship the Steinway to Manhattan. Instead, Mrs. Paddington sent her granddaughter a postcard: *If you don't return home immediately, I'll sell your piano.*

Prudence sent a postcard right back: *Tell it good fucking riddance for me.*

Higgins McCann tapped Prudence for more jingles and Prudence came up with ditties for dish soap, shampoo, toothpaste, and hamburger chains. Catchy tunes seemed to come to her with the swiftness of a sneeze. "You have a real talent for this," Randall Higgins said multiple times. Though none of her compositions became as big as Pep Soda, Prudence had more money than ever before. Her own money.

She also had more confidence. Safe in the twin cocoons of school and the advertising agency, Prudence was happy in her work. She felt accomplished. For the first time in years, she was able to relax.

But as graduation neared, a top-rated talent manager, who remembered Prudence from her prodigy years, began leaving messages on her answering machine and the façade began to crumble. The talent manager wanted her to record and tour again. "Won't it be wonderful to see your name in lights once more! You'll be even *bigger* this time! Give me a ring back, dear." But Prudence wasn't at all certain that she could.

Deep down, she believed that she was her grandmother's creation, a doughy lump poured into a tray and baked. She wasn't a prodigy. She was a sham. Wasn't there evidence of this when she chose the simple, more playful pieces that spoke to her—like Prokofiev's *Musiques d'enfants*—each time she was asked to perform in class, while her classmates always opted for the demanding technical beasts? They had ambition and nerve. She had a gimmick.

"What is worrying you, dear?" asked Dr. Chen one morning after presiding over a rehearsal of Prudence's chamber group. The group was preparing Chopin's Prelude in E Minor for a concert, but the drumming melancholy in Prudence's left hand flooded the room with such anguish the cellist broke down in tears. The session ended early and the other students fled.

"I'm not a true artist," Prudence confessed to Dr. Chen. "My talent is only average. At best, I'm a worker bee. At worst, I'm a hack!"

"I don't think a worker bee is the worst thing. In fact, I think it's quite admirable. But a *hack*? I hardly think so."

"Well, what do you think?" Prudence really wanted to know.

"I think you're focusing on the wrong question. Who cares what you are if your music touches people? If you create feeling, if you elicit a response, then you create art."

Dr. Chen had seen this kind of existential crisis many times before, especially in students who grew up under the crushing expectations of stage parents.

"Prudence," she said, "I believe you are a true artist. But the only thing that matters is what you believe. Would you be willing to talk to someone about this problem?"

"I'm talking to you right now."

"I meant a therapist, Prudence. I know a good doctor, someone who can help you deal with your anxiety. He's renowned for treating performers like you. You can tell him anything."

THAT'S HOW PRUDENCE came to be in the dim lobby of the old medical building on Fifty-seventh Street. She pushed the elevator button for the seventh floor, but as the doors started to close, an arm shot between them and in stepped a distinguished-looking man in a tweed suit.

"Sorry," he said. "This elevator takes forever. I don't want to be late for my next patient. Floor seven, please."

To Prudence, he looked exactly like the men in *The Study of Human Behavior*. He had cottony hair, a close-cropped beard, and wore round little glasses. His eyes were kind and his voice soft. And he was going to the seventh floor.

How embarrassing, to be sharing the elevator with your very own psychoanalyst.

The cables creaked and the elevator began its ascent. But after a few seconds, it yanked to a stop so abruptly that Prudence lost her balance.

"Not again," groaned the man in the tweed suit.

"Again?" Prudence deplored confined spaces.

"Don't be frightened," the man said, as Prudence proceeded to smash a random assortment of buttons. "Probably just another

blown fuse. Push the red button . . . just once. It'll alert maintenance." His voice was soothing and Prudence did as she was told.
The button made a loud buzz. A voice crackled through a little metal
speaker assuring them maintenance was on the way.

With that bit of business settled, the man in the tweed suit turned
to Prudence.

"What brings you here today, young lady?"

Prudence thought this odd, starting her session in an elevator.
But she went with it.

"Well, Doctor, I need to know if I am one or not."

"One what?"

"A true artist."

He gave Prudence a quizzical look.

"I mean, just because I'm famous doesn't mean I have any real
talent. Just because I've entertained the queen doesn't mean I'm the
real thing."

"Have you really entertained the queen?"

"Oh, several times. But only because Granny was such a task-
master."

The man in tweed smiled. "I doubt that's the reason," he said
softly.

"What do you mean?"

"There's only so far one person can push another. For instance,
my dad wanted me to be a professional athlete, but you don't see me
playing for the Yankees, do you?"

"I wouldn't know," said Prudence. "I don't watch sports."

"It doesn't matter. What I mean is, if the gift wasn't in you to
begin with, no amount of discipline could put it there."

"Ha! You don't know my grandmother." Then it all came out
with such force it was as if someone had pulled a string in Prudence's back like a talking doll. "At the beginning, Granny would
snap me with a wooden spoon whenever I made a mistake. A missed
sharp, wham! Sluggish eighth notes, wham! If she got really frustrated, she'd haul me off the bench by my arm and shove me into the

hall closet and keep me there in the dark while she smoked a cigarette and paced the floor."

"No wonder you hate small spaces," said the doctor.

"*Right?*" agreed Prudence. "The mind games were the worst. I
was about ten when I had to prepare Gavotte in G Major for a performance. But I kept stumbling over the arrangement. Well, when
we were rehearsing one day, Granny, real calm, said, 'Let's see how
good you really are.' I played it slowly. Granny said, 'Faster, this is
allegro. Keep up with my tempo.' And she kept time hitting the
spoon against the bench, right next to my leg. It was too fast, and of
course I made a mistake—it's not an easy piece. I tensed up, waiting
for that smack. But nothing came. I made more mistakes and each
time I waited. Nothing. The anticipation was unnerving. What was
she waiting for? I couldn't concentrate, her tapping that spoon, and
I was completely butchering Gavotte. I thought, 'Well, I'm in for it
now. Once I finish, it'll be a terrible beating.' When I got to the end
of the song . . ."

Prudence paused and looked at the floor. The man in the tweed
suit was aghast. "Go on, by the time you got to the end of the song?"

You can tell him anything.

Prudence's eyes stayed on the floor. "When I got to the end of the
song . . . I was so upset, I wet myself. It was humiliating. But you can
bet I got Gavotte as polished as silver after that."

"That's awful, the abuse you endured . . . it's horrifying."

"Or maybe it was necessary for someone of average talent like
me? The problem is, I'm graduating soon and I'm supposed to go
back to performing. But I get terribly anxious thinking about what
it will take to get on that stage again."

"One thing is clear," said the doctor. "You can never go back to
your grandmother. Even if that means you'll never play in front of
an audience again. She's too dangerous."

"Yes, yes, she is." It hit her then: What kind of idiot would subject themselves to that kind of abuse? Prudence sighed and leaned
against the mirrored wall of the elevator. "But are you saying I

should quit everything to do with music? I've been writing commercial jingles for an advertising agency and it's going very well. For some reason, I can see catchy tunes like other people can see animals in the clouds."

"Can you really? Well, if I were you, I'd try that for a while longer. There's no shame in doing work that comes easily to you. You probably should—"

The buzzer cut the doctor off before he could finish making his suggestion: that she take steps to process the trauma of her abuse before going back to performing. The elevator jerked into motion and began its short descent back to the lobby.

"Oh, thank goodness," Prudence breathed, relieved that escape was imminent. She also felt the anvil of expectation lifted, if only for the moment. The question had been answered: stick to writing commercial jingles. "I can't thank you enough," she said. "I know what I have to do now."

The doors opened and Prudence wanted nothing more than to get out of that elevator as quickly as possible.

"Well, good luck," he said. "I'm rooting for you."

As the elevator ascended again, the man in the tweed suit lamented he hadn't thought to recommend the excellent therapist who rented space on his floor. Silently wishing the poor girl the bright future she deserved, he unlocked the door to his office. The nameplate read: DR. THOMAS MILLER, PODIATRIST.

CHAPTER EIGHTEEN

It's Only Rock and Roll

Alexei Petrov did not take calls after seven. The only exception would be made for his parents in an emergency or when Alexei refused a direction and Tatiana had to intervene. (Which she, Tatiana, would consider an emergency.) Barring a crisis or an accident, Alexei's parents called on the same days at the same times: Monday, Wednesday, Friday, and Saturday, noon Pacific Standard Time. So why was his phone ringing now?

"Alexei speaking."

"Alexei, Les Strom. How are you, kid?"

"Fine, thank you. And yourself?"

"Great. Just back from Phoenix. Jesus, Phoenix is hot. I'm surprised it doesn't dry up and blow away in a big, brown puff of dust."

"How can I help you, Lester?" Alexei sat on the vintage art deco chair his mother had bought and curled his long fingers under his chin. He did not want to hear about Les's trip to Phoenix. He wanted to take his bath and eat his dinner. He wanted to get this call over with so that he could salvage the rest of the evening.

"Get this, kid. I signed a contender."

"Marvelous. Who?"

"Prudence Childs."

"Never heard of her."

"Don't you ever watch TV?"

Alexei Petrov may have been a television star, but he did not have time for television. "Is she an actress?"

"Nope, she's a pianist."

"What does this have to do with television?"

"Commercial jingles. She used to write commercial jingles. Pep Soda? NEET Washing Detergent? You know, *I am NEET because I've got dirt beat . . .*"

Alexei couldn't help himself. He picked up the rest of the ditty, "*and the smell so, so sweet . . .*"

"Listen to you. I told you we'd turn you into an all-American boy." Alexei rolled his eyes as Les Strom continued. "Anyway, google her. She was a child prodigy and very famous. Huge, promising career."

"What happened?"

"Well, like you, she played the White House a couple of times. The difference is, she played when she was six and when you played, you were—what, twenty?"

Alexei Petrov understood what had happened to the career of this Prudence Childs. Had his career not been carefully monitored, had all pitfalls not been avoided, he would be like this now-washed-up contender. Alexei's instructors warned his parents against early touring. Young musicians needed the chance to learn and develop out of the spotlight. It was vital to both the craft and the psyche.

"She's the perfect opponent," Les Strom said. "You've got her beat, of course. But she'll put on quite a show."

Alexei Petrov leaned back in the art deco chair and smiled. Perhaps this wouldn't be so bad.

"Aannnnd . . . here's the other little, tiny thing . . . Alexei."

There was a catch to Les Strom's voice, an oh-by-the-way catch that meant this "other little, tiny thing" wasn't going to be a little, tiny thing at all.

"What's that, Les?"

"Listen, the network execs want to spice up the format. They think we can attract a wider audience for this round if we add something new."

"Oh?" Alexei imagined dancing dogs in tutus or men in sequined underwear jumping through flaming hoops.

Les had already cleared the network's ideas with Prudence. Pop music? No problem. But Alexei wasn't the *no problem* type.

"Yeah, see, they want to showcase a contrast between classical music and, say, pop or rock."

"I have no previous training with rock music."

"You can learn."

"You said I would make Beethoven sexy again. You said that's why you put my name in the title of the show."

"Look, don't sweat this. You're a pro."

Alexei Petrov shifted in the art deco chair and the leather groaned under his weight. "I do sweat this. It was not part of our original agreement."

"Alexei, you *got* this. Seriously? It's pop music."

For all of Alexei's illustrious musical education, he had not been widely exposed to contemporary music or Billboard hits. He'd heard of Adele and Beyoncé but that was about it.

"You're telling me this eight weeks out? I can't learn an entire new discipline in two months."

"Listen, Alexei, that's the deal, that's what the network wants. The last song has to be one that ends with a bang, you know? This is the word from on high and it is *not* negotiable."

AFTER HANGING UP with Les, Alexei Petrov skipped his bath of Epsom salts and his wine and his musical scores. Instead, he went into his den and turned on his computer and googled "greatest rock-and-roll songs of all time."

There was a very lengthy list, not one with a piano at center stage. They all needed a guitar and a drum kit. After some research, he pulled up YouTube and searched for a supposedly famous rock star named Buddy Holly. Up came a video of a band wearing matching cardigans and bad wigs who called themselves Weezer and sang a very bizarre song about the Buddy Holly guy. It was ridiculously repetitive. Next he entered "Lyin' Eyes" by the Eagles and found a concert from 1977. Up on the stage stood four guitarists and behind them a drummer and to the side, a keyboard. A piano arrangement of this song would sound like elevator music. It would be terrible. The texture of the song came from its guitars and its harmonizing and the twang of Don Henley's vocals.

He then clicked on a grainy black-and-white video, "My Generation," by the Who. The tune seemed simple enough. But there was a driving energy to the song that Alexei Petrov could not imagine replicating. Plus, the musicians seemed angry; at the end of the song they heaved their guitars like clubs and destroyed everything on the stage.

He threaded through many videos and listened to many songs. He needed one that centered on the piano. One that did not need its vocals. It was midnight before he found one that knocked him off his feet: "Great Balls of Fire" by Jerry Lee Lewis. The song was electric. There seemed to be fire in the pianist's fingertips and in his heart. When the video ended, Alexei Petrov watched it again. And again. And again. Jerry Lee Lewis played the piano with his fists and even his feet. He slid under the piano and climbed over the top of it.

Alexei Petrov was twenty-two years old and a roaring success. He believed this success had come because he followed the rules. From the time he could play a note, his entire existence was carefully planned and watched over and debated. But popular music seemed to require a completely different approach, one that was full of anger and rebellion and hell-raising.

He was pretty sure that the Who did not get their mother's approval to kick over the drum kit or jam a guitar neck into an amplifier. It was more than having to learn "Great Balls of Fire" or trying to avoid getting dusted by a prodigy-turned-housewife on live TV.

No, the real problem was that Alexei suspected he was constitutionally incapable of that level of abandon.

Alexei Petrov downloaded the sheet music to "Great Balls of Fire." It looked simple on paper. He put the music on his Steinway Salon Grand Model A and played the notes exactly as they were displayed.

He did not sound like Jerry Lee Lewis. He sounded as if he had taken a hit of Vicodin. Like something you'd hear in a grocery store while trying to decide what brand of peanut butter you wanted.

He would need help. But his technical instructor was a serious German who wore a tweed blazer and solved logic puzzles in his free time. Fortunately, this was L.A. and you couldn't swing a bag of dead cats and not hit someone trying to break into the music scene. He knew a guy who booked studio musicians. He would call this guy and he would hire a studio musician to help him. A rock musician. Because if he failed, he would look like a total fool up there. And everything he and his parents had sacrificed would be wasted.

CHAPTER NINETEEN

Tempo di Mezzo

Every Sunday afternoon, Prudence and Stuart sat in the great room and telephoned their daughters. Tess was first, at two o'clock. Becca was next, at four. If Prudence and Stuart tried to call their daughters on any day other than Sunday, the call would go to voicemail and the child in question would text (hours later) to explain that academic matters had kept her from answering: Sorry, was in class. Was taking a test. In a study session.

However, if Tess or Becca ever called their parents on a day other than the agreed-upon Sunday—which was rare—it was safe to assume she was calling about matters of the financial persuasion. Matters that demanded immediate attention. Seventy-five dollars for lab fees. Seventy-five dollars for a lost bus pass. Seventy-five dollars for an art history book. The requests were always in increments of $75, an amount Stuart and Prudence understood to be "rounded up."

It was a Sunday, eight weeks before the show, when Prudence gave her daughters the big news. Each had pretty much the same reaction.

What do you mean, *television*? they asked.

"I'm going to perform on a TV show."

What *kind* of show?

"A competition show, *Alexei Petrov's Dueling Piano Wars!*"

They did not watch competition shows on television now that they were in college. They were beyond such frivolous pastimes. Never mind that their high school years had been consumed with *American Idol* and *The Bachelor.* The girls now favored more intellectual pursuits such as drinking cheap beer and discussing Nietzsche.

To Tess and Becca, competition shows conjured up images of acerbic celebrity judges and thirsty young vocalists belting out Adele. Their mother had once been an accomplished concert pianist. Why in the world would she agree to take part in such mediocrity?

Prudence should not have expected more. Her children knew her only as the mom who could play "Circle of Life" on the spinet in the Sewing Room, not as the young pianist who performed *Pathétique* at Carnegie Hall with a sixty-piece orchestra.

Well, good luck, Mom, they said. I'm sure you'll kill it.

And that was that.

PRUDENCE HAD SEVEN weeks to prepare. Seven weeks of scales and finger exercises. Seven weeks of Mozart and Chopin and Liszt. Seven weeks of self-doubt.

When her alarm went off at 7:00 that first morning, Prudence thought it was the middle of the night, as she had developed the habit of sleeping until noon. She forced herself out of bed. Action, she told herself, was the antidote to uncertainty.

Within an hour, Mrs. Wintour had been walked, the houseplants watered, and the breakfast dishes cleared. Lined up on the music stand were *Schmitt, Volume 434, Op. 16: Preparatory Exercises for the Piano* and *Hanon, Volume 925, The Virtuoso Pianist, Sixty Exercises for the Piano* and *Bach Volume 13, Well-Tempered Clavier* and *Chopin, Volume 34, Preludes for the Piano.*

And a metronome.

Prudence opened *Schmitt* and read the notation: *Repeat each exercise ten or twenty times. Gradually increase tempo to build up finger strength and flexibility.*

"Okay," she said to Mrs. Wintour, who was curled up by her feet. "Let's do this!"

Setting the metronome to eighty-four beats a minute, she began.

Three measures in, she stopped.

"I should turn off my phone."

Mornings were terrible with calls. The pool company, the termite inspector, the veterinarian's office reminding her of Mrs. Wintour's annual appointment.

Powering off her phone, she began.

Four measures in, she stopped.

"What if Tess or Becca need to get hold of me? They're always forgetting the Uber password. What if someone forces them into the back of a van and—"

Powering up her phone, she began again.

Five measures in, she stopped.

Maybe more coffee? She poured herself another cup. And noticed a pile of unfolded towels. Well. She folded the towels and put them away in the linen closet. That's when she saw that the disaster of a closet was in need of an immediate tidy.

Prudence accomplished a great many things over the next four hours. She rearranged the glasses in the China cabinet, polished a pair of alligator pumps, and alphabetized her sheet music. But not one full finger exercise. When the hall clock chimed twelve, she hadn't accomplished one full anything.

"Noon! It can't be. Enough of this procrastinating!" Mrs. Wintour gave out a little woof. "For Chrissake, when I was eight, I could sit for two solid hours before even getting up to pee. If I could do it then, I can do it now."

She went back to her piano and completed four exercises. She would have completed five, but at 12:26 she was close to collapsing from hunger. That's what she told herself.

The plate of cold chicken from the refrigerator was just the thing.

So was the bath.

So was the nap.

Prudence woke with a start. When she saw it was almost four

o'clock, panic set in. A panic that was further activated by the stark reality that soon she could be homeless. Or in prison. Adding to this anxiety was the YouTube video she had pulled up of Alexei Petrov playing Tchaikovsky's Piano Concerto no. 1 in B-flat Minor.

He was pretty good. Actually, he was better than pretty good. He was great.

Granny Paddington's voice wended its way into Prudence's ears like a tendril of smoke. *That's what you get for wasting your best years on throwaway music. It's too late for you now.*

"Nonsense!" Prudence shouted, prompting Mrs. Wintour's tiny head to pop up.

Prudence set Chopin's Prelude, op. 28, no. 18, on the stand. "I used to play this in my sleep. This will get me going."

It was no use. She tried to play, but all she saw was Alexei Petrov's brilliant performance at Rome's 21st Premio Piano Competition. He was refreshing. Dynamic. No wonder. He was twenty-two. He hadn't spent his life washing breakfast dishes and composing jingles about mouthwash.

Prudence's fingers would not put the notes together the way her mind wanted. She started the piece again. Again, she could not play it with the precision it demanded. She took a pencil and wrote out the counts to each measure and began again. The notes came out mechanical and stilted. The harder she tried, the louder the voices of failure.

When six-year-old Prudence was preparing for a concert, Granny Paddington told her how Mozart had traveled from royal court to royal court. "He was only five, this kid, and he received gifts of diamonds and gold," she had taunted.

"I've received gifts," young Prudence said.

"Stuffed animals and ribbons. A few hundred dollars. Big deal."

Prudence had thought it was a big deal.

Granny Paddington continued. "You're a year older than that boy, but you're nowhere near as accomplished as he was. If he was here, he would play circles around you." Prudence imagined a train track going round and round as she performed. "You are lazy and spoiled. You are going to lose your gift and no one will come see you." Prudence had been confused. She didn't understand that a gift of gold was different from the gift of talent. But if talent was a gift, why did she have to work so hard to keep it?

Back then Prudence had feared an empty concert hall. Now she feared a packed television studio.

Why hadn't she just started that book club? Nothing to do but read until lunchtime. Then book club night with appetizers and drinks and chats about story and character. There would be no expectations. No scales. No pressure. No lawsuits or blackmailing ex-husbands.

She leaned down and scratched Mrs. Wintour behind the ear. "What did I get myself into, love?" Mrs. Wintour licked Prudence's cheek and Prudence scooped her into her arms and said, "You're so lucky you're a dog."

Prudence was going to fail in front of millions of people. And for what? An ill-advised decision years ago to break into advertising? Prudence was almost fifty years old. Aside from plagiarizing a commercial jingle, she had lived an honest existence. She had worked hard, raised two wonderful children, and had a wonderful husband. Why was she still haunted by her childhood? Why was she still haunted by that damn piano?

She banged the keys with her fists.

"I should have sold you when I had the chance!"

STUART FOUND PRUDENCE under her piano when he returned home that evening. Seeing his wife curled into the fetal position, he surmised (incorrectly) that she was exhausted from practicing all day.

"Hello down there," he said to her.

"Hello," she said quietly.

Stuart asked if Prudence needed a drink and she said no. When he asked if perhaps she'd like a pillow, she said, no, she was good. What she really needed was a hammer and would he be a dear and collect one for her? Certainly, he told her and he went into the laundry room cabinet and retrieved one. Unfurling her fingers, Prudence placed her hands, palm side flat on the marble, and asked if he would smash her fingers.

"It's the only way out of this," she told him.

"Breaking bones?"

Prudence thought for a moment. "You're right, could you tie my hands to the stove and then turn it on?"

"Certainly not."

"Burns heal. Eventually. Maybe."

"You're being dramatic. And sadistic."

"You don't understand, I've made a terrible mistake!"

"How so?"

"I'm nowhere as good as I thought I was."

"You're just coming to this realization?"

"*Oui.*"

"And you think you can get out of this now?"

"I have to."

This conversation came at the end of Stuart's very long day of work on top of worrying himself sick about his finances and the fact that he would be enduring eleven-hour flights to London until his hair turned white and his teeth fell out. Why was he the one trying to cheer *her* up?

"Darling, if you put a hammer in my hands, I would only be tempted to smash your head instead of your fingers."

"What an awful thing to say."

"Well, I said it."

Prudence crawled out from under her piano and stood before Stuart. "Well, it wasn't very nice."

"Neither is being charged with fraud, Prudence."

"But I *am* a fraud. I can't do this, Stuart."

"Yes, you can. We need that prize money. We're facing bankruptcy—or worse—if they find out you didn't write that jingle. The lawyers alone will cost us this house if Bobby Wheeler doesn't take it first."

Prudence shook her head. "No, I want out."

"The only way out is for you to win."

"You do realize I'm no longer the precocious prodigy whose name alone could draw people in."

Oh, he realized that, all right. He then touched a nerve he did not know was raw. "No, you're not. You are a middle-aged woman. You will have to prove yourself now. Wasn't that originally the point of all this?"

A middle-aged woman. This was the new identity Prudence had been fighting off ever since that afternoon on the pool deck when she realized the second half of her life would be spent dealing with things that she didn't properly deal with in the first half. She felt old and inadequate. And the fear and the anxiety and the day's frustration rose to the surface like bubbles in soda.

If only Prudence had told her husband she was afraid. That she was only human after all, not the goddess everyone made her out to be. If she had told him this, he would've held her. He would have been the strong one in that moment. He would've taken in her demons so she could vanquish them.

But fear wasn't something Prudence could admit, so she retreated to childhood.

"Oooo," she screamed. "I *hate* you!"

To her surprise, he said, "I hate you right back!"

To his surprise, she said, "I want a divorce!"

The biggest surprise to both of them came when Stuart said, "Fine!"

Prudence and Stuart were inexperienced fighters. Not that they didn't have disagreements—Stuart checking sports scores on his phone during dinner, Prudence forgetting to empty the dishwasher. But the reappearance of the piano changed the game. There had been a shift. This was new territory. No matter how strong a marriage, there are times when it is quite fragile. Stuart and Prudence could feel their twenty-two-year bond undergoing some sort of test. And this scared the shit out of both of them.

They regressed to the type of behavior reserved for young new-lyweds learning how to argue.

"That's a terrible thing to say!" Prudence said.

"And keeping secrets is a terrible thing to do!"

Prudence threw up her arms. "Oh, here we go, *here* we go, my *se*crets!"

"For twenty-one years I was under the impression I was your only husband."

"Well, technically, you are. I mean, the marriage was annulled."

"You're going to try and wheedle your way out of this on a technicality?"

Prudence stamped her foot. "All right then, I'm sorry!"

"Could you say that with a little less petulance?"

"Nope."

"Humph."

Prudence stomped off to her study, announced that she would remain there for the rest of the evening, and slammed the door. Only to open it ten seconds later to let in Mrs. Wintour, who was scratching and whining for her distraught mistress. She opened it ten minutes later to remind Stuart she did not want to be bothered. She opened it ten minutes after that to listen for Stuart's footsteps. There were none.

Around nine o'clock, Prudence opened the door and heard the football game from the master bedroom. It made her angry that he was watching football. Then it made her sad.

Maybe he truly did not love her.

Who could blame him? She was a cheat and a liar.

Prudence shut the door and lay down on the couch in the Sewing Room and cried. Prudence felt things deeply and had an enormous imagination. This made for an interesting combination. It was why she could play music the way she did. She could feel emotion in every note a hundred times more intensely than the average person. And in her overloaded and heartbroken mind, she came up with a plan. She would pack her bags and go away in the morning. Like to a hotel. For a little while. Until she and Stuart could work out the terms of the divorce. No reason he had to be embroiled in all her troubles. If she ended up getting sued, at least *he'd* be free.

Stuart could get married again. He could be even happier. Prudence would have to go far away, though, because she wouldn't be able to bear seeing her Stuart so happy with someone else. She would go where she wouldn't be recognized. Like to a damp cottage on the coast of Spain, forced to live a simple life with what little money she had left.

She'd die alone.

What about the kids!

Would they come visit her in Spain?

Not at first. At first they'd be very angry once they found out she'd been married to Bobby Wheeler and that she'd not really written the Pep Soda jingle. Poor girls. They would never think of their mother the same way. They would question everything now. They would have to go to therapy. Stuart's new wife, some insanely wealthy, younger, gorgeous client of his, would see to it. Prudence felt shame imagining how her girls would react. She loved them so much. Of course they'd want to spend all their school vacations with Stuart and his rich young wife who didn't steal or lie about things.

Prudence lay awake on her little couch in her study. In all the years she and Stuart lived in this house, they had never not slept in the same bed together. She was sad now imagining such loneliness in her old age. This is how she would die, alone, having accomplished nothing.

Who would fix the toilet when it overflowed in her little cottage on the coast of Spain? Who would do her taxes? Update her phone?

She felt a great weight in her chest and she rose and sat at her little spinet and played Rachmaninoff's *Rhapsody on a Theme of Paganini, Variation 18.*

Sometime around four in the morning, she drifted off to an uneasy sleep with all those terrible thoughts marinating in her head. She woke the next morning to Mrs. Wintour whining to be let out.

It was nearly ten o'clock. Prudence went upstairs but Stuart had already left for work. He had not said goodbye. He had not kissed her cheek like he usually did each morning. He had not paused to tell her he loved her.

"*C'est fini*," she said and then Prudence wept again. "I will never love another. I shall pack at once."

CHAPTER TWENTY

Bel Canto

Stuart had slept a deep and dreamless sleep. He woke refreshed and with a new perspective. How quickly they had both blown it all out of proportion. That's the problem with words—once they were out there, you couldn't put them back. Stuart, when he wasn't consumed with thoughts of bankruptcy and the welfare of his children and working fifty years longer than he'd planned, was an even-keeled guy who rarely went off the rails.

What Prudence didn't know was that before Stuart fell into that deep and dreamless sleep he had tiptoed down the stairs with the thought of coaxing his wife into bed. He traveled so much and spent so many nights without her—years without her—he now realized how it had affected their marriage. How the lack of daily conversation had turned them into roommates. The two of them had become like houseplants growing at different rates, one now needing repotting before the other or else it would wilt and die.

He did not want that for Prudence. He was very, very sorry for what he'd said to her.

Further, Stuart was most certainly not thinking about divorcing his wife; he was not thinking about marrying anyone else; and the very last thing he would have wanted was for Prudence to slip off to a small cottage on the coast of Spain without him.

He stood by the door to the Sewing Room and listened to her play Rachmaninoff's *Rhapsody on a Theme of Paganini, Variation 18*. He was seized with a nameless emotion, a longing for something. The song, although he was certain he'd never heard it in his life, was nostalgic and familiar and sad and wonderful at the same time. He leaned his head against the door and closed his eyes and saw himself as a small child in the backyard. The grass was impossibly green and, in his child's mind, it was an enormous space that stretched as far as he could run. There were lilac bushes fat with purple blooms and rows of bright geraniums that dotted flowerbeds like gumballs. There was the smell of burgers grilling and the sound of ice clinking in glasses. His mother chased him in a game of tag and when she caught him, he fell to the soft grass and she tickled him and held him and kissed him and called him her little boy. He could smell his father's pipe smoke and his mother's flowery perfume. He recalled his father's striped ties and his mother's creamy pearls. He wanted to talk to them now. *Remember the tulips in the backyard and warm nights we'd run barefoot across the grass? Please live forever.*

He wouldn't have recalled such a wonderful moment had he not heard Prudence play. This was the power of her incredible gift, the retrieval of memory. He had never heard Alexei Petrov play. He was likely quite good. He was likely very good. But Stuart could not imagine how anyone could relay this depth of emotion. Maybe his ear was not a trained one. But he couldn't imagine a live television audience of fourteen million people with fourteen million pairs of trained ears.

She had a chance. A good one. Why didn't he support her instead of unleashing all his frustrations on her? The pressure she must be under.

Tomorrow, they would talk.

They would fix this, together.

Stuart stood outside the door of the Sewing Room and cried. He did not want the music to stop. So he did not disturb her. He climbed quietly back up the stairs with strains of Rachmaninoff at his back.

He got into bed and closed his eyes. In the morning, he would tell her what he had heard. He would tell her he believed in her.

But his wife slept very little that night. While that might be good for the poetry of her music, it wasn't so good for decision-making. Stuart did not know that in the morning, after he'd left for work, Prudence would pack a bag and make a reservation at a hotel. And that she had been looking into little seaside cottages on the coast of Spain. And that she'd googled divorce lawyers. It might all sound extreme and rash and not well thought out to anyone else. But Prudence was in crisis and she tended to think in extremes anyway.

On that very afternoon as Stuart sat at his desk and labored over high-net-worth individuals, Prudence sent Les Strom a text: Sorry, change of plans. Quitting the show and moving to Spain.

She then gathered her things, juggling a small bag, a stack of records, and her portable turntable. Mrs. Wintour was under one arm and a stack of sheet music under the other. Prudence never left on a trip without her music. When she grabbed her watch off the bathroom sink, she inadvertently dropped her phone in the toilet. She said a bad word so loud Mrs. Wintour jumped from Prudence's arms and hid under the bed.

If Stuart had known any of these things, it would've saved him a lot of heartache.

CHAPTER TWENTY-ONE

Wrecking Ball

The nightclub district in Old Town Scottsdale is where the young and hip drink pink martinis and seek ephemeral lovers, where art galleries sell $20,000 oil paintings alongside souvenir shops selling $5 paperweights. It's here that modern nightclubs with flashing lights and glowing dance floors face off against faux Wild West bars stuffed with tourists. To say nothing of the Hotel Valley Ho.

A desert escape. That's what everyone calls the hotel now. Indeed, that's how it began. Built in 1956, it was a splendid example of midcentury architecture with its concrete pillars, thick glass walls, and abstract balustrades. It was the first hotel in Scottsdale to have air-conditioning. It was also the first hotel to have a parking lot, allowing guests to come and go in their own cars—discretion and all that.

This made it an ideal getaway for film stars who knew Hollywood paparazzi wouldn't follow them all the way to Scottsdale. Newlyweds Natalie Wood and Robert Wagner held their wedding reception at the Hotel Valley Ho. Marilyn Monroe was a frequent fixture by the pool. And Janet Leigh and Tony Curtis could be seen having drinks on their balcony in the evening. It is the sort of hotel that shares its secrets with no one.

Then came the 1970s, when the hotel underwent an odd renovation. Save for a few Queen albums and maybe *Star Wars,* little that was good came from the seventies. Certainly, little that was good came for the Hotel Valley Ho. Some nameless person or group of people—that was more likely, for a disaster of these proportions could only come from a committee—decided that foil wallpaper and plaid sofas were in order. The terrazzo floors were covered in flagstone and the arrowhead pillars were covered with mirrors. And brown, brown, brown, from carpet to drapes. Drained of its charm, the hotel aged like milk. In 2004, it was scheduled for the wrecking ball.

It would have been a rubble of concrete had nostalgia not intervened. Letters were written, campaigns were organized, and the hotel was restored back to its original glamour. Hotel Valley Ho became an icon of midcentury architecture. Once again, celebrity sightings such as Tom Brady and Beyoncé were written up in gossip columns. Lively pool parties were plastered all over Instagram. Famous chefs were employed in its kitchen, serving up everything from steak tartare to grilled Portuguese octopus.

The Hotel Valley Ho got a second chance. It was even more magnificent the second time around.

It was here that Prudence, lost and heartbroken and ready for the wrecking ball herself, pulled up to the entrance in her little red Porsche. The bellhop unloaded her suitcase, a stack of sheet music, a stack of record albums, a portable turntable, and a ceramic mixing bowl containing uncooked rice and a soggy smartphone.

With Mrs. Wintour tucked under her arm, Prudence approached the front desk and sighed before she said, "We'd like a room for two, please."

"Of course. Two adults?"

She held up Mrs. Wintour. "The two of us."

"That's one adult . . . and your little dog?"

One adult? That hit Prudence hard: room for one, table for one, a seat for one at the theater. One, the loneliest number. "I guess I'll have to get used to that," she said.

"How many nights?"

"I don't know. I hadn't thought that through."

The front desk clerk was used to seeing glamorous people in despair. "Why don't we see where we're at tomorrow, hmm?"

"Good idea."

She handed Prudence a plastic door key. The bellhop led her through the famous lobby, past the bright orange couches and glass-tiled walls, where guests in white robes were coming from the spa and couples in cool evening clothes held hands on their way to dinner. He led her outside into the magnificent gardens. All around the pool, guests laughed and drank cocktails with umbrellas in them. Happy, carefree people, people who hadn't been made to perform as children or who were being blackmailed by their ex-husbands. Whose phones were not submerged in rice.

Finally, the trio arrived at Room 3, Building 6, Floor 1. When the door was opened, Prudence gasped with delight. The room was so sleek and modern it was like something out of the *Jetsons*. It had teal curtains and a terrazzo-tiled bar. A retro-style mirror in the shape of a sunburst hung above the bed. A wall entirely of glass gave a sweeping view of the desert. And in the middle of the room was a large, round soaking tub!

The bellhop unloaded the suitcase and the music and the records and the portable turntable and the bowl of rice.

"Enjoy your stay, Ms. Childs."

"That wasn't part of the plan," she replied.

"What wasn't?"

"To enjoy myself." Because she had many things to be sad about and she intended to be sad.

"Oh," said the bellhop. "Well, just in case, happy hour in the Zuzu lounge starts at five P.M. The pianist will play until seven."

"Oh, delightful, a pianist?"

"Pierre Millet. He was friends with Jimmy Durante back in the day when Mr. Durante was a guest at the hotel. He'd come down and play the piano in the middle of the night for guests who couldn't sleep."

"Pierre Millet?"

"Jimmy Durante. Once the hotel was renovated, we got Mr. Millet to come in a few nights a week. He's a big draw, not something to be missed."

The bellhop left and Prudence threw herself onto the large bed. A wave of loneliness washed over her. She missed Stuart badly. She wanted him with her. But her marriage was over now and she would be forced to move to Spain, where there would be no Stuart to tell her that she was everything.

Her ex-husband was going to expose her as a fraud!

She would be a no-show on *Alexei Petrov's Dueling Piano Wars!*

She was about to be sued to kingdom come!

But all around her the room beckoned to be explored and enjoyed.

Prudence sat up. "I'm going to have to make the best of things," she said to Mrs. Wintour. "Look at that tub. I must take a bath."

CHAPTER TWENTY-TWO

Great Balls of Fire

Alexei Petrov wondered if he had made some mistake. He looked down at the tired street, with its ragged palm trees and crumbling sidewalks. Then he looked up at the bungalow with its peeling paint and mismatched chairs scattered across the front porch. The lawn was neither dead nor alive. Surely this was not the home of the once-famous pop star.

Fearing his fingers might get broken or his wallet stolen or his car vandalized, Alexei got back behind the wheel of his Mercedes. He would get out of this neighborhood. He'd go back home. Home was safe.

And then what?

He would be right back where he started. Worse, he might fade into Bolivian.

Alexei Petrov got out of his car and forced himself to walk all the way to the front door. He took one last look at his Mercedes-Benz and hoped he had the right insurance for theft or vandalism.

Then, because he had only seven weeks to learn "Great Balls of Fire," he rang the front bell.

At the trill of the bell an enormous mastiff bounded up to the pocked screen and barked so loud that the porch shook. Alexei did an about-face and headed toward the car, but he was stopped by a simple question.

"Can I help you?" a voice called from the house.

Alexei turned and saw a tall man wearing a batik shirt and worn jeans. He did not recognize the face of the man he had seen on You-Tube, the man who had played for thousands of screaming girls. That man did not have on silver-framed eyeglasses.

"Are you Mr. Puente?"

"Call me Gabe."

"Gabe, I'm Alexei Petrov, the pianist. We spoke earlier?"

"Oh, I know who you are," Gabe Puente said with a laugh. "Who doesn't?" He stepped aside for Alexei to enter, but a low growl like the sound of an idling motorbike came from the mastiff. Alexei hesitated.

"Hey, don't worry about Duke. Loves music. Can always tell a musician. Seriously, it's freaky."

Alexei Petrov crossed the threshold and the enormous mastiff rose on his hind legs to put his paws on Alexei's shoulders. Alexei thought he'd die of a heart attack right there in the entryway of this beaten-down old house.

"Duke, get the fuck down," Gabe Puente said.

Duke got the fuck down and Gabe led Alexei through the tiny house, followed closely by Duke.

The bungalow's curtains were faded and the furniture worn and soft. One wall was covered in shelves and loaded with record albums. Another held books. There was an enormous floor-to-ceiling abstract oil painting that exploded with color. Alexei stood before it and gazed at it because good art radiated possibility, pushed him to think beyond his own limits. The house was not grand like Alexei's, but there was a comfort and ease to the place.

They came to a room crammed with computer screens and guitars and an electronic keyboard and a drum kit. Tapestries hung from the wall and on the floor was a large Persian rug, so worn the threads were visible. Tucked in a corner was an enormous upright grand that looked as if it had an earlier life in a saloon.

Why, Alexei wondered, were there so many large things in such a small house?

Alexei sat on a desk chair. Duke, who looked close to two hundred pounds, did not sit at Alexei's feet, he sat *on* Alexei's feet and got fur all over Alexei's black gaberdine trousers.

"Can you tell me a little bit about your training?" Alexei asked.

Gabe was not put off by the question. He knew about Alexei's education at the Conservatoire de Paris, all the prestigious piano competitions he'd won, his performance at Carnegie Hall, and his late-night talk-show appearances.

"I can read music. Does that work?"

Gabriel Puente was thirty-five years old and a California native. After graduating from Torrance High School in the year 2000, where he'd been part of every musical program the public schools could fund back then, he attended the Los Angeles College of Music on scholarship. At the time, he cared only about making it in the music business. The world had not yet broken his heart.

After a year of college, Gabe got his big break. His band, Bounce, had been on the L.A. club circuit and it all happened like a fairy tale. There was a record executive in the audience one night at the Viper Room. The record executive heard the band. The band got a recording deal and went into the studio and produced an album. On that album, the single "Grit" climbed to number ten on the billboard charts. Bounce went on tour, opening for Matchbox Twenty. They were just nineteen, for fuck's sake. Their next single, "Take Me," hit number one. Someone, probably a record exec or some manager, told them to expect the album to go gold. Gabe dropped out of the Los Angeles College of Music because where he was going he would not need a degree.

Gabe—full of musical knowledge but not quite worldly knowledge—saw his future laid out like new carpet. The first thing he did was buy a shiny car. And some leather boots. And some leather pants. And a leather jacket to match the pants. There were drugs. *Rolling Stone* articles. Girls. More girls. So many girls. And girls' moms. Free everything, too. Free drinks. Free food. Free clothes. Free cocaine. There were backstage passes. They met Radiohead and Green Day and The Strokes.

Everyone told Gabe how talented he was. They stuffed his ego the way you stuff a Thanksgiving turkey. Gabe got a bunch of new tattoos. After the new tattoos came new vices. Gabe soon had as many vices as he had tattoos because, Christ, he was a rock star.

The little tiny voice in the back of his head told him he had not earned any of it. But with his pockets fat and his head fatter, Gabe didn't listen. He threw television sets out windows and drove cars into swimming pools. He spent all his money. He bought fast motorcycles and a racehorse he never saw. What he didn't spend he lent to anyone who asked. Because there was going to be more money. Much more.

Then it ended.

All at once.

There was no second album. No more concerts. Bounce couldn't get arrested at a state fair let alone perform at one. The album did not go gold. Why not? Who knows. Bounce joined the ranks of one-hit wonders. The car got repossessed. The girls left and took their moms with them. A drug dealer, a landlord, and an ex-girlfriend were after him.

Gabe went to rehab. He was no longer a rock star. He was a cliché. Once he got over himself and all his vices, he remembered who he was.

That's when he became a studio musician and focused on the music.

That's when an artist was born.

Now in the tired little house with the peeling paint and the huge dog and the old piano and the remnants of a once-glorious past, two men were about to embark on a strange and fascinating collaboration, one that would make Alexei Petrov doubt everything he ever learned in his carefully managed life.

"All right, brother, what can I help you with?" Gabe asked.

Alexei Petrov took the music out of his leather satchel. "I've got to learn how to play this song."

Gabe looked over the sheet music. "Great arrangement. Someone of your caliber should be able to pull this off."

"That's the problem. My caliber. I can't make it sound the way it's supposed to." Alexei sat at the old piano and played through the piece.

He played with great precision and order. But there was no fire and very little smoke. Gabe listened and when Alexei finished, he motioned for Alexei to move. "Yeah, no. Here, I'll show you."

The first chords hit the strings like spats of gunfire. Everything in the room shot to life and as Gabe sang, the lyrics rose from some unseen place inside him. Even the piano appeared to rock to and fro. Duke, who'd repositioned himself back on Alexei's feet, howled— whether in appreciation or participation, Alexei wasn't sure. All he knew was that anything in the room that was even remotely alive—a plant, a spider, a mouse, the mold in the shower—was moving to the boogie-woogie beat.

Lord, what a sound that piano made. It wasn't even a Steinway.

When Gabe finished, it was so quiet Alexei's ears rang and he felt something he'd not felt before in all his years of being a highly trained pianist: envy. Gabe did not even need the sheet music. It lived somewhere inside him. Alexei's ear was not trained for this. Neither was his soul.

"And that, dude, is why they called Jerry Lee Lewis *the Killer.*"

"The Killer," Alexei repeated.

"Here's the deal," Gabe said, "it's four-four time but you gotta really make this thing swing. There's just three chords in the whole song. You've got to put yourself into it or else it's going to sound like a fucking lullaby, okay?"

He had played a fucking lullaby.

Alexei Petrov usually performed as a soloist. When he performed with symphonies for various competitions and performances, there were many rehearsals. But Gabe Puente, unlike Alexei Petrov, made his living as a studio musician. Studio time is expensive and no one wants to pay for rehearsals. You just go in and play, get out. Gabe, in this peeling old house on this worn street, was a better piano player than Alexei Petrov. At least that's what Alexei Petrov thought.

"All right, try it again at 156 beats a minute."

Alexei Petrov sat at the old piano. He put the music back on the stand and played the song again. Duke did not howl, the room did not shake, and the plant leaned toward the sun as if to escape. Alexei wanted to get back into his Mercedes and drive away. Maybe over a cliff. He waited for Gabe to tell him that he didn't have what it took to get people jumping out of their seats.

But Gabe did not say this. "Dude, this thing is supposed to be messy. You don't need to be precise with every single note."

"But that's part of my training."

"Forget your training."

Alexei was not used to this kind of direction. He stood and collected the music.

"Where you going?"

"I can't do this."

Alexei carefully put the music back into his satchel and took out an invoice and a business card with his parents' Paris address and his address in L.A. and said, "Thank you for trying. Please send the top copy of the invoice to the Paris address."

Gabe scratched Duke's head and said, "No, man, there's no charge."

"I insist."

Gabe stroked Duke's ears. "Don't think I don't know what's in your head."

"I'm sorry?"

"The great pianist cannot fail."

"I'm not giving up if that's what you are thinking."

"I don't think you're giving up. I think you plan *around* giving up. I think *you* think if you sit at your keyboard and work hard enough, and hire the right people, then it will happen."

Alexei secured the strap on his shoulder. "I have to find a different song, something that's closer to my style."

"Dude, *this* is the song. It's ready for a whole new generation to appreciate it. Isn't that what your show does best?"

Alexei shook his head. "There isn't enough time . . ."

Gabe disagreed. "Hey, if you insist on paying me, then I insist you give it fifteen more minutes. Then you're free to go." Alexei was convinced that another fifteen minutes would accomplish absolutely nothing. "Come on, man. You know how many championship basketball games have turned around in fifteen minutes?"

"I have no idea. I don't watch the basketball."

"We'll have to go to a game sometime. But for now, let's say we give the Killer another try."

Alexei fingered the strap. He wanted this. He wanted to master a song that epitomized everything he wasn't, a song that wasn't three hundred fucking years old. He studied that decrepit piano, the hairline cracks in the keys, the brass finish worn from the pedals, the wood scraped and gashed as if it had been moved around too many times. Its humble looks masked the explosive energy it could produce.

"I think I know what the problem is," Gabe said. "Come on, sit down."

Alexei sat down. He put the music back on the stand, but Gabe leaned over and snatched it and ripped it in half.

Alexei Petrov felt adrenaline flush through him like lake water. "Why did you do that?"

"Because *that* is the problem. The intensity comes from you. Not the music. You're too focused on the notes. Bang on the piano."

"What?"

"Bang on it."

Alexei stared at the yellowed keys and played a series of staccato notes.

"I believe the direction was to *bang* on the piano. That's the easiest thing, little kids do it better than you. I want you to bang on this fucking piano like a little kid would."

Alexei slapped the keyboard.

"That's it?" asked Gabe. "That's all you've got?"

Alexei shrugged.

Gabe leaned in. "What makes you angry?"

"When my car doesn't start."

"Nope, that makes you annoyed. Let's try again: *Who* makes you angry?"

"I don't let people get to me."

"Maybe you should."

"It consumes my energy."

"Energy comes from feeling things. You got a girlfriend?"

Touchy subject. "No."

"A boyfriend? A fucking roommate?"

"Nope."

"You got family?"

"My parents live in Paris."

"You talk to them?"

"Four times a week on scheduled days."

Gabe paced across the small room once and back. Duke watched him and then rested his head on Alexei Petrov's satchel. "So you're alone?"

"Entirely by choice."

Gabe suspected this was bullshit. "You like it?"

Alexei bristled. "It's hard to have a balanced life in this business, with all the travel and preparation and pressure. It's the way it has to be for now."

"Life is messy, bro. It never gets easier, just lonelier."

Gabe sensed a thread of pain locked somewhere inside Alexei. The man could play. He was no robot. Gabe was going to get that pain to the surface. "I want you to picture something, okay?"

"Okay."

"Close your eyes."

Alexei Petrov did not want to close his eyes. "Can't I leave them open?"

"No, live dangerously."

Alexei closed his eyes.

"Have you ever had something taken away from you?"

"Sure."

"Like?"

"I bought a pair of Rollerblades once when we lived in Paris. My parents found out and took them away. They were afraid I'd break my arm."

"Did that make you angry?"

"I moved on."

"So that's it, Alexei? A pair of Rollerblades?" Gabe Puente was going to crack this egg.

"What does this have to do with the music?"

"Everything. Music is expression. I want you to think of a time when you really wanted something and it was taken away from you. Stolen."

Alexei took a labored breath. He shook his head. He rubbed the piano keys. He pursed his lips. "There was a girl."

"Ah."

"A violinist."

"Where is she?"

"Paris."

"Did you love her?"

Alexei nodded.

Gabe waited.

Duke snored.

Gabe whispered, "You left her behind?"

Alexei shook his head. "There was no other way."

"You sure?"

Alexei squirmed. The armor had been nicked. "It doesn't matter anymore."

"It doesn't?"

"She is with someone else now." He felt like his mouth was full of staples.

"And you're okay with that."

No, he wasn't okay with that. *No, he wasn't fucking okay with that.* The anger had now found its way to the nick and was gnawing through, making a hole. He tried to hold it in, reassure himself he had done the right thing for the right reasons. "My parents gave up everything for me so I could be here."

"This isn't about your parents. This is about *you,* about what *you're* feeling."

But those lines had long been blurred.

Alexei lifted his hands and brought them down hard on the keys, so hard the room shook and Duke's head snapped up. "I don't want to tell you anything more!"

"Don't tell me, tell the piano!"

Alexei banged on it. Then again. And again. Beads of sweat collected on his forehead. He asked Gabe if he could open a window but Gabe said no because he wanted Alexei to be uncomfortable and sad and miserable. Alexei wanted to play something, but he could not think of anything that would match what he was feeling. Gabe told him to keep banging and Alexei asked for the torn sheet music but instead Gabe called out the chords, "G, A flat, A! G, A flat, A! G, A flat, A!" Over and over and over.

It went this way for well over an hour as the chords Gabe kept calling out took their shape and began to construct their own rhythm and it seeped into Alexei Petrov's brain like oil and he learned it in under an hour without ever looking at the music.

Three years of trying to forget her. Down the drain.

CHAPTER TWENTY-THREE

Piano Man

It was hard to be depressed in a luxurious suite with lush gardens and an enormous bathtub. Yet, as the afternoon wore on, as the bright and cheerful colors of the room's décor began to fade, Prudence felt her spirits wilt along with her surroundings. Once again, she was sad. She had convinced herself that Stuart did not love her anymore, that he did not give her absence a single thought.

The reality was much to the contrary. But the imagination of a genius can be very powerful. Especially a genius whose phone is drying in a bowl of rice and has missed fifteen frantic text messages from her husband.

While Prudence was soaking and drinking and listening to Coltrane, Stuart, unaware of his wife's new digs and the unfortunate phone mishap, had called her three times. Maybe it was four. He texted several more times, too. *She's still angry with me, I'll leave work early and take her to dinner.*

He told his receptionist he would be out for the rest of the day and drove home to 10534 Pricklypoppy Lane. But Prudence was not there. Neither was Mrs. Wintour. Neither was the stack of sheet music. He tore through the house in a panic because Prudence always took her music when she planned to be gone for more than one day.

Prudence knew none of this as she stood before the mirror in a white minidress and silver sandals. She adjusted her dangly earrings, finished her drink, and applied her lipstick.

"Oh, my dear friend," she said to Mrs. Wintour, who was splayed out on the large hotel bed, tiny paws pointed at the ceiling. "How lucky you are not to know the travails of life."

She rubbed Mrs. Wintour's upturned belly. "Now then, my darling, I won't be long. You have all the comforts of a queen in here. *Ma reine.*"

After she changed the record to Puccini—Mrs. Wintour was fond of *Madame Butterfly*—and hung the Do Not Disturb placard on the door, Prudence slipped down the hall and through the gardens and into the Hotel Valley Ho bar, which looked as if it'd been lifted from a James Bond film.

It was precisely five P.M. when Prudence deposited herself on the bar stool nearest the piano. The iconic Pierre Millet was already planted before the Baldwin BP178 Grand near Prudence's elbow and he was playing one of her very favorite songs, "Dream a Little Dream." She was so taken with the music that the bartender had to ask three times if she wanted a drink.

At ten minutes after five, a large group of hotel guests, all dressed in University of Washington football shirts, gathered in the bar and ordered drinks. They were very loud and not just because they had been drinking poolside all afternoon. They were very loud because they were on their way to a football game at Arizona State and thought it would be fun to try to outdrink one another while telling bad jokes.

Prudence could hear the bad jokes. She could not hear the music.

She approached a man who seemed to be the leader of the group as he was trying to arrange a fleet of Ubers.

"Excuse me, sir?"

"Yes?"

"Can you ask your friends to quiet down?"

"Excuse me?"

"They're too loud and I can't hear the piano."

"It's a *bar*."

"But I can't hear the music."

"So?"

"Don't you like the music?"

"Sure, we like the music."

"Then why aren't you listening?"

"We didn't come here to listen to the music."

"Well, I did."

"Okay, well good for you. I came to see my friends and I want you to go away now."

Then he turned his back on Prudence and the other purple-shirted people around him laughed as if he'd told another bad joke.

This made Prudence angry. She had no patience for people who did not appreciate music. This had happened before but Stuart usually accompanied his wife and kept her out of stupid arguments.

However, Stuart was not in the bar at the Hotel Valley Ho. He was at home calling everyone he knew, looking for his wife.

Prudence walked over to the piano and said to Pierre Millet, "Your playing is marvelous."

"Thank you." He was absolutely flattered because, of course, he knew who she was.

"I have a request."

"What would the great Prudence Childs like to hear?"

"Something fast and loud."

Pierre Millet laughed. "It's happy hour. We're background music."

"There's no such thing as background music."

"True enough."

"Those people wearing purple shirts are talking over your piano playing. It's like hanging a Monet over the toilet. I should call the manager over."

"Maybe we should just think of another song. You're a pianist, you choose."

"I don't play anymore."

"Oh? When did you stop?"

"This morning."

"Sounds a bit abrupt."

"Yes, well, I'm moving to Spain and starting a book club."

Pierre Millet smiled. Only last week he had watched her bid on her own piano. He had read about her upcoming stint on *Alexei Petrov's Dueling Piano Wars!* He had many questions he wanted to ask her. But first he had to pee. "I gotta go check on my horse, okay?"

"Okay."

"Don't go away."

"I won't."

When Pierre Millet left for the men's room, the leader of the purple-shirted people said to Prudence loudly, because he was drunk, "Hey, hall monitor! Are we allowed to talk now? The music's over."

Everyone laughed.

Someone asked the bartender if they could turn up the sound to the Notre Dame game. That's when Prudence, who did not want to listen to the Notre Dame game, sat down at the Baldwin BP178 Grand and played the opening measures to "Piano Man." The purple-shirted people stopped talking so loudly. They stopped telling bad jokes and watching the Notre Dame game. They leaned in. Because "Piano Man" played live on the piano is a song everyone likes. Especially when drunk.

The purple-shirted people surrounded the piano and sang about bar life and broken dreams and when the song ended, they stuffed money in Pierre Millet's tip jar and bought Prudence a drink because she was such a brilliant musician.

"Another song!" someone shouted.

So Prudence played "Mr. Bojangles." Because when people hear "Mr. Bojangles" after a long afternoon of sitting around the pool and knocking back bottles of Corona, they get weepy and think about sweet old men and dogs they once loved. When it came time for the chorus, everyone joined in. They were so moved by "Mr.

Bojangles" that some of them started to cry and they, these purple-shirted people, were hugging one another and saying how much they loved everyone.

They thought they were quite good singers, too. They also thought Prudence was the best piano player they'd ever heard, even though they had no idea how famous she'd been.

"You really should think about a career in music," a man in plaid shorts told her.

At any rate, things were getting a bit sappy for a bar, so Prudence lifted the mood and played the jingle to Pep Soda. Well, now then, when you're good and oiled up, famous commercial jingles are quite a bit of fun. It wasn't just the purple-shirted people around the piano now. Others were drifting in. Some sang, all were amused. When Prudence finished with Pep Soda, she played the NEET Washing Detergent jingle. Everyone was having so much fun, they almost did not hear the leader of the purple-shirted people announce that their Ubers were here and they had to leave.

They hugged Prudence and stuffed more money into the tip jar and told her how fabulous she was. Some were still singing about Pep Soda and dead pets as they trickled out to their waiting cars. Pierre Millet shook the tip jar. "You certainly know how to earn your keep. You might want to rethink that book club."

"Oh, no, I've settled on it."

"Can I buy you dinner?" He needed to figure out what the hell was going on.

"Thank you, but I'm exhausted. I didn't get a lot of sleep last night."

"You're really going to Spain?"

"I have to."

Pierre Millet had been in the piano playing business for over sixty years. He didn't believe prodigies existed. People loved to romanticize talent. As if it came from some sort of piano god. He'd thought if he'd been able to actually meet Mozart he'd see him struggle like the rest. That Mozart, at birth, did not crawl out of some black velvet bag of magic.

But tonight, his long-held belief changed. There was a quality to Prudence's playing, the presence, the intensity, even the molecules that surrounded her seemed to crackle. At last the sixty-year-old question had been answered: Prodigies were born, not created.

People with that kind of talent didn't just quit. The mind of a genius is fragile. Something must've happened.

"I think you ought to reconsider," he said.

"About dinner?"

"About Spain, my dear."

"Oh, right. I did consider Mexico, but I don't think it's far enough away."

"Why are you running from this? Didn't you see them tonight, how much they got from the music? You touched something in them."

"They did seem pretty happy, didn't they?"

"You gave them a joy they won't soon forget. You can create something that lasts. You have that power, Prudence."

She looked around the half-empty bar. Energy resonated in the air like the scent of sulfur after fireworks. Something, indeed, had happened tonight. She could feel the music buzz inside her. Prudence realized many things just then. She wasn't likely to die anytime soon. Turning fifty was not the end of the world. Moreover, there was something she very much wanted to do that did not involve starting a book club or leaving the country.

The decision clicked in her head like a key turning in a lock. "That settles it."

"Settles what?"

"I can't go to Spain."

"Marvelous, what changed your mind?"

"The music."

By EIGHT THAT night, the number of people looking for Prudence Childs totaled three: Stuart Childs, Les Strom, and the leader of the purple-shirt brigade, who wanted to invite Prudence to play the piano and make everyone cry again.

The number of phone calls fielded by the Scottsdale Police Department was seven: Stuart Childs called four times and Les Strom three. Stuart even broke down and called Prudence's mother, who had left the cult in Bolinas and was now a born-again Christian in Seattle. She did not know where Prudence was but said she'd pray for her.

Stuart wondered if maybe Prudence's crazy ex-husband had kidnapped her for ransom. Les Strom thought she might have left for Spain (although, Prudence, who remembered her Herb Alpert and the Tijuana Brass records, had forgotten her passport).

The parks were searched, the libraries rummaged, the art museums combed, the airport explored, the bouncers at Old Town nightclubs questioned, and the bookstore on Ninetieth Street and Shea scoured. Also alerted were the *Arizona Republic* and its parent company, *USA Today*. Social media was on high alert.

Prudence Childs had disappeared.

CHAPTER TWENTY-FOUR

Hello, I Love You Won't You Tell Me Your Name?

Alexei Petrov wanted to disappear. Two years at the Conservatoire and he was crushed by the heavy burden of expectation.

One particularly grueling morning, he had been in his vocal accompaniment course with a vocalist who was performing "Quando M'en Vo' Soletta," an aria from *La Bohème*. Alexei loathed these accompaniment sessions as vocalists took liberties with the music, which Alexei thought unnecessary.

She had such power in her voice, the vocalist. She stood next to the piano as solid as marble. Her posture erect, feet shoulder-width apart, arms outstretched as if to pull someone into her grasp. Midway through the aria, she stopped singing and threw up her arms. "You play like a donkey!" she snapped at Alexei.

"This is Puccini," the instructor said to him. "It is about passion! Desire!"

Puccini. Passion. Desire.

"Okay, right. We can start from the beginning," Alexei said. But the vocalist stopped singing and, in the same spot, threw up her arms. But this time when she snapped at Alexei she did not call him a donkey. She called him an ass.

The instructor pointed to the notation above the measure that was causing all the fuss. He said, patiently, "*Quasi ritardando,* hold back a little. Make us feel Musetta's *desire* for Marcello, her *yearning* for him. You are rushing. This is the gravitas of the opera. Picture slowly stretching a rubber band, slowly increasing the tension, Alexei. *Quasi ritardando.*"

Yearning. Desire. Tension.

"Got it."

They began again. The same thing happened—again. The sequence was repeated several times, the instructor's patience gradually dissolving into exasperation. When they finally came to the finale of the aria, the instructor said, "Alexei, what does *morendo* mean?"

"It means fade awa—"

"IT MEANS THAT YOU PLAY IT AS IF YOU ARE DYING! AS IF LIFE IS LEAVING YOUR BODY! AS IF YOU ARE DEPARTING FROM EARTH!"

BY THE TIME class ended, Alexei thought his head would explode. He needed quiet. He needed fresh air. He needed to be as far away from the campus as possible. Far from the vocalist and the music and the aching and the desire and all the yearning. He did not want to be called a donkey. Or an ass. Or any other sort of animal.

He slipped outside and walked through the Parc de la Villette and strode along the Canal de l'Ourcq. As he passed one of the red metal follies that lined the canal, he came to a complete stop, for he was, at that moment, overtaken by an internal windstorm.

Mia Khouri was also walking along the Canal de l'Ourcq, but she was headed in the opposite direction. Cradling a violin case like a bouquet of long-stemmed roses, she proceeded at a clipped pace toward the Conservatoire. Maybe it was her hair that first caught his attention. It was the color of liquid sunshine, the strands so transparent they nearly glowed. Or maybe it was her smile, so bright he swore flowers bloomed in her wake. From that first glimpse Alexei's heart pounded and ached all at once. He thought about this girl for the rest of the day. He thought about her petal-pink lips and the way she walked and even how she held that violin case.

The next day, he returned to the exact same spot along the Canal at the exact same time. He would speak to her then. Surely, that would break the spell. *Are you a student at the Conservatoire? Oh? I am, too.* It would be best to keep the questions simple since his experience with the opposite sex was limited. He had only just started to talk to the serious girls in his chamber group, where discussions usually centered on sedate matters such as the accidentals in a Bach fugue.

It was when Alexei ventured beyond the staid conversational borders of music that things went awry. For instance: the humiliating exchange with the American cellist. He'd see her in the quad between his morning classes. She had perfect teeth and wide, chestnut-colored eyes. She wore leather riding boots that looked expensive, with a slight scuff to telegraph that she was above any sort of vanity. At first, they'd just catch each other's eyes—she noticed him, too! The eye-catching eventually led to short nods. The nods graduated to coy smiles. The coy smiles grew bolder, flirtier.

Until one morning she said, "Hey, how are you?"

Inadvertently, he translated his response directly from Russian with "I'm normal, thank you."

The laugh that burst from those perfect teeth seemed to hit him right in the stomach. "I think you mean fine? Or maybe you didn't?"

It was the sort of encounter that took on a life of its own. Alexei, and his questionable "normalness" became fodder for a joke among a clique of kids, some going so far as to refer to him as *Norman*. He avoided eye contact with girls in the quad after that.

But the morning he first laid eyes on the girl with the golden hair changed everything. The yearning and the longing was giving way to another feeling, one of loneliness. Not the kind he had as a child. This was a new kind of loneliness, one he couldn't entirely explain, only that he felt the rest of his days would be empty without her.

Sure enough, she appeared along the Canal in the spot where he first saw her, striding toward campus at the same hour as the day before. She was eating a plum with one hand and holding the violin case with the other, a leather book bag slung over her shoulder. She approached . . . and the words he wanted to say to her dissolved on his tongue like a tablet. She passed right by.

The next day Alexei took up his spot again. Obviously, she was a music student like him. They would have many things in common and he was making this too complicated. He would speak to her and that was that. But when he saw her again the following day, something unexpected happened. She looked up at him and smiled! He felt as if someone had microwaved his heart. This unexpected sensation rendered him mute once again. The moment passed before he could ask her course of discipline or even say hello.

He vowed to say something the next time he saw her. Only now there was a problem. These missed moments began to build inside him so that he was overthinking the simplest of interactions and how they could lead to the worst possible outcomes. He could not shake the feeling that he'd screw it all up.

The image of her consumed him. As if Chopin had turned a prelude into a woman. The beauty, the nonchalant ease of her walk, the flow of her hair.

One evening, at dinner, his mother said, "Alyosha, you've not even touched your dumplings. You must eat."

"I am not hungry." He played with his fork, twirling it over and over between his long fingers.

"Are you unwell?"

He shook his head and went to his piano, where he played some dark and somber music. Once finished, he dragged himself to bed, fully clothed.

Tatiana looked at her husband. "He must've contracted some sort of virus. I will call the doctor." This illness, whatever it was, must be treated immediately. Alexei could not afford to fall behind.

"There is no need to call the doctor," said Nikolai Petrov.

"How do you know?" she asked him.

"It is not that kind of sick."

"Well, then, what kind?"

"Lovesick."

Tatiana Petrova folded her arms and leaned back in her chair. "That's ridiculous."

"There's someone, I am certain."

It is a strange thing to fall in love like that. Alexei Petrov knew nothing about Mia Khouri. He had not even seen her eyes because she always wore a pair of tortoiseshell Ray-Bans. And yet, she had hijacked all his senses.

Alexei could neither approach this girl nor stop this torturous routine. Then, after a week of mooning about, an extraordinary thing happened. She dropped her scarf on the ground and did not notice. Alexei Petrov was sure this was fate. He picked up the scarf and ran after her.

"*Mademoiselle!*" he said.

Nothing. His heart pounded like a fist on a door.

He repeated himself, "*Mademoiselle,* your scarf!"

She did not turn around. He drew back, the scarf clutched in his hand, convinced he was too dull for such an exquisite person. Yet, he could not let the moment go. He took the biggest risk of his life and caught up with her. With a shaking hand, he tapped her shoulder.

She turned and looked at him for two torturous seconds, waiting. He could not speak, so he held the scarf up. She then removed an earbud. An earbud! She had not heard him. He felt the temperature in the air rise several degrees.

She said, "Oh, *merci.*"

He stood there because he forgot how to respond when someone tells you *thank you*.

"I would've been very upset if I'd lost this scarf," she said. "Someone very special gave it to me."

He was immediately jealous of this special someone. How was he to know that Mia's special someone was a former tutor, an eighty-five-year-old woman who lived in Vienna and who got around using a cane.

Mia Khouri smiled and it pulled him in like a thousand magnets. "I owe you a coffee," she said. "Are you free?"

He wasn't free. Not at all. He had a musical theory course in fifteen minutes and then a practice session with another pianist where they were playing a duet from Mozart's *A Little Night Music*. But he did not want to sit through music theory and he did not want to practice the duet. He wanted to learn about Mia Khouri.

He said, "I have the rest of the afternoon free."

For the first time in his life, Alexei cut class and went to a bistro, where he learned Mia was nineteen, a few months younger than him. And that she had caramel-colored eyes that were cut like crystals. She was a violinist from Beirut. Her mother had played the oboe in the Lebanese Philharmonic Orchestra. Her father was a filmmaker and video artist who had a series at the Tate Modern exploring buildings abandoned following Lebanon's civil war. She had attended the Cannes and Sundance film festivals with him.

Mia told Alexei that once she graduated from the Conservatoire, she planned to audition for several orchestras, from Salzburg to Johannesburg. She wanted to become a conductor.

"What do you do when you're not practicing?" she asked.

"I play chess." He did not tell her that he usually played with his dad.

He sounded terribly boring.

To his surprise, she said, "I've always wanted to learn how to play chess. Can you teach me?"

The next day, at lunch, he nervously waited for her in the square, the sky gray and threatening rain. His coat pocket held an orange, the weight of it multiplying by the second. Surely, she had changed her mind. It was just as well with the rain coming. He was busy studying the clouds when someone whispered, "*Bonjour*" into his ear, the tickling of it radiating through him. Her champagne-colored hair was bright against the nickel-colored sky. He lifted the orange from his pocket and held it out to her.

They went to a park and sat at a table. Little nips of green were

starting to push out from the ends of the Paulownia trees. After arranging the chess pieces on the board, Alexei showed her how to
move them. Every time his fingers brushed hers, he felt an electric
current shoot down to his toes.

She overused her pawns, underused her queen, and could not get
the hang of how the rooks worked. He let her beat him—twice.

"I'm in awe of your chess skills," she said. It was the first time
anyone saw something in him beyond music.

Alexei Petrov was never able to break the spell she had over him.
It was impossible in a city that encouraged romance in every corner.

She showed him how to use Snapchat. Now he was privy to the
minutiae of her day and every time his phone lit up with a snap, his
heart would light up, too. The first time he kissed her, lights exploded in his head. Bastille Day times a million. They went to the
opera, *La Traviata*, and both cried in the final scene.

They'd walked down to the shops after class, arms linked and
passing a baguette back and forth. They talked about instructors
and classes and music and ensemble performances. He loved the
intimacy of sharing food and the freedom to vent about the tedium
of their days. The Conservatoire was such a competitive environment that true friendships were rare.

She could draw things out of him as if bending a light wave to
see all its colors. These were things he had never shared. Not because they were scandalous, but because they seemed so prosaic.
Like his recurring dream of drowning. And his fondness for vintage
books.

Mia told Alexei about how her parents, when they were children,
lived in beautiful apartments, ate at elegant restaurants, and attended ballets. She told him how that all changed during Beirut's
endless civil war. They had lost everything.

He told her about his parents, how his father was once a prestigious scientist. How his parents had also lived in an elegant
apartment—in the same neighborhood as Mikhail Gorbachev—and
how, after the Soviet Union collapsed, his father moved to China
and his mother moved to a concrete building that often lacked heat.

These seismic shifts in their family histories became a bond between them.

They'd sneak off to her apartment and climb into her bed. When she touched him, it was like someone had snipped a cord in his head, a paradox of feeling powerless over his limbs and truly free at the same time.

His playing improved. He was experiencing life, experiencing what Chopin, Rachmaninoff, and Debussy set music to. He no longer looked out the window to watch other kids play. He was on the other side of that glass now. The weeks slipped by in that halcyon bliss of first love.

It took most students four years to get a degree at the Conservatoire, but Alexei Petrov was on track to do it in three. Because he'd only been sixteen when he'd been accepted, Alexei started off younger than his classmates, had always lived with his parents, and was perpetually overscheduled. Now, graduation loomed like a cloud ready to burst. There would be lots of travel in the next year, a series of tours and piano competitions that would take place in seven different countries on four different continents.

Meanwhile, Mia would be at the Conservatoire for another three years. He could not bear the thought of being separated from her by an entire ocean.

A month before graduation, Alexei said to his mother, "I think I want to stay in school and go for a master's."

"And do what with that?" she asked.

Alexei shrugged. "Teach."

Tatiana Petrova grabbed a cigarette and tapped the end on the pack. Her son could not be a professor. Their three-year visas would expire in one month. To renew them, she had spent the better part of the year putting together an exacting touring schedule. Invitations from symphonies had already been accepted. Applications for competitions already completed. Dates for solo performances already scheduled. Alexei would have maximum exposure in multiple countries, a summer of music festivals from Switzerland to Vail.

"Papa is teaching. I could get another student visa and we could stay in Paris," Alexei said.

She knew why he wanted to stay. And it wasn't to teach.

Tatiana Petrova took a long drag of her cigarette and exhaled. "Alyosha, Papa was only allowed to teach here because you were not yet an adult. But now you are an adult and in order to stay, you have to prove you have important work. I have to demonstrate I work for *you*, that I manage your career. Don't you see? You must tour. Or else we go back."

Alexei saw the dilemma. If his student visa was renewed, his parents wouldn't need to be in Paris anymore. They'd be sent home to Moscow, where they would once again have to start a life all over from nothing.

Well, he told his mother, he and Mia could have a long-distance relationship.

"Oh, Alyosha," Tatiana said. She smoothed his hair from his eyes and cupped his chin in her palm. "I've been there. I promise you, my love, it changes things, that kind of distance. The two of you are much too young to make such promises."

"So maybe she can come with us."

"Maybe. But you must think of *her*," his mother told him. "She'd have to give up her spot at the Conservatoire if she traveled with you. Do you really want to ask this girl to give up her dreams to follow a boy?" She shook her head.

Alexei had seen this when he traveled to competitions, boyfriends and girlfriends carrying the bags and staying in the background. His life on the road would not consist of sightseeing and lounging but of practicing and preparing. Mia would only end up resenting him in the end. His mother was right.

Sensing that she had won, Tatiana stamped out her cigarette in the ashtray and said, "It is best to think of your parents now. As we have always thought of you. If you are too distracted and can't deliver what is expected of you . . . we will *all* have to go back to Russia."

—

FIVE MONTHS AFTER the breakup and just as he was about to go onstage with the Cleveland Orchestra, Alexei saw Mia's Snapchat story, the one with her new boyfriend. He had truly lost her. He was surprised the audience could not hear his heart cracking over the music.

He unfollowed her on all social media.

For a long time, Alexei Petrov could not forget. His heart felt as if it were filled with concrete. He bought a bottle of her perfume, Shalimar, and kept it in his suitcase. When he sniffed it, a memory of her burst to life like a freshly lit match, breaking his heart all over again. He resigned himself to the reality that he would have to live the rest of his life in unbearable pain. He debated the merits of a lobotomy. A disruption of the frontal lobes. All his feelings for Mia would disintegrate. How wonderful, he thought, to go through the rest of life as a slow-moving, unfeeling mass of human tissue.

To alleviate this misery, he gradually shut off his emotions and lived just above the surface of his life, a flat place where lovers remained nameless, friendships remained at a distance, and technique became more important than feeling the music in his heart.

For three years, he circled the globe. He played to crowds and saw new cities. He ate strange food and met even stranger people. He grew an inch and gained some needed pounds. His brows thickened and his eyes darkened and his chest widened. He now wore his suits instead of his suits wearing him.

A very different Alexei Petrov emerged. One who appeared unbreakable and untouchable. The real Alexei Petrov, the one who was once loved by Mia Khouri, had disappeared.

CHAPTER TWENTY-FIVE

The Rite of Spring

Stuart was glued to his phone waiting for a call alerting him of Prudence's whereabouts so it was hard to miss the text from Tess: OMG, Dad!!!!!! Mom's playing piano in a bar & the tweet has gone viral!!!!! Check Twitter!!

He had two immediate reactions to this text. The first was relief that Prudence was not locked in some dark basement, chained to a torn mattress, Bobby Wheeler dripping hot wax onto her chest.

The second was frustration: He did not have a Twitter account.

Stuart texted Tess: Call me immediately!!! Because his children had the annoying habit of never answering their phone, preferring to text instead.

Tess complied.

"Hey, Da . . ."

"Where in the hell is this bar!" he barked.

"Dad, chill. It looks like she's having a lot of fun. It's on TikTok, too, a longer version of it. Wow, I didn't know Mom could play like that. Cool."

This also bugged him: Why was she in a bar without him while he was worried sick that her extortionist-psycho-maniac of an ex-husband had kidnapped her?

He followed Tess's direction to *chill*. He took a few deep breaths before proceeding.

"Tess, my dear, did this Twitter thing say where the bar was located?"

"No, but the TikTok post did. She's in the Hotel Valley Ho. Why aren't *you* there with her?"

This was followed by a few more deep breaths. Then, "Good question."

PRUDENCE WAS UNAWARE of anything that was not taking place beyond the confines of the hotel bar. It wasn't until she saw Stuart rush toward her, accompanied by a couple of Scottsdale police officers and hotel staff, that she realized something was wrong. "What in the world?"

"Oh, thank god you're okay," he said.

"Of course I'm okay."

He stopped to catch his breath, then said, "Don't ever do that again."

The words tumbled around in Prudence's mind. Did he mean, don't threaten divorce with a subsequent move to Spain? Or don't leave my phone in a bag of rice for eighteen hours? Maybe, don't check into the Hotel Valley Ho without leaving some sort of note on the kitchen counter?

"Don't ever leave me," Stuart clarified.

Prudence felt a pull on her heart, the kind that reminds you of the history you have with someone, the kind that tells you there will never be another.

From their first meeting, Prudence knew that Stuart would be an unwavering constant in her life. Who knows what accounts for such insight in a single moment. But it happens. And she had been right. Because here he was, standing right by her, even after the last eight hours of absolute nonsense.

Prudence focused on the terrazzo floor. "I need you to . . ."

"Tell me," Stuart said. He looked around at the little group and added, "Us, rather."

She looked up at him. "I need you to believe in me. And I'm . . ."

"You're what?"

"I'm scared."

"Oh, Prudence. Why didn't you tell me?"

"I don't know, I guess I thought you wouldn't understand."

"Okay, so what if I don't understand?"

Prudence looked helplessly into his eyes.

He took her hands in his. "You would have to explain it to me. That's all. Like you have to explain to me why you never put the cap back on the toothpaste. Or the juice. Or the milk. Don't ever stop talking to me. I love you."

"I love you, too."

He pulled her into him and kissed the top of her head. "I believe in you. More than anything I've ever believed in my life." He held her tight in his arms.

The little group that had gathered was a big group now, full of hotel guests, bar hoppers tipped off by the viral posts, a crime reporter for the *Arizona Republic,* and more than one purple-shirted football fan. They applauded, all except Pierre Millet. He handed Prudence his card. "Let's get you ready for television."

CHAPTER TWENTY-SIX

Comptine d'un Autre Été, l'Après-Midi

Les Strom could not believe his luck. His status as Studio Big Shot had been sealed. The phone in his office rang off the hook. The publicity department, thanks to this little stunt at the Hotel Valley Ho, wanted to speed up TV ads for *Alexei Petrov's Dueling Piano Wars!*

After the headline on the splash page of USweekly.com (mistakenly) read: MISSING PIANO PRODIGY SLATED FOR REALITY SHOW COMPETITION FOUND ALIVE, the network marketing machine churned to life with headlines of its own. Promoted ads on Twitter ran old clips of young Prudence playing on *The Merv Griffin Show* alongside outtakes of *Alexei Petrov's Dueling Piano Wars!* City buses, plastered with Alexei's face, read, "Meet His Match!" and subway walls were emblazoned with "Who Will Be the October Surprise!" Two evenings later, Alexei Petrov walked down Sunset Boulevard, where he saw a large billboard, his face six stories tall.

He hurried home to practice "Great Balls of Fire."

STUART WAS HAPPY to get his wife back. He wasn't so happy about Pierre Millet's $10,000 fee.

"I mean . . ."

"Mr. Millet is very good at what he does," Prudence said. "I'll need his expertise. I've a lot of catching up to do."

"Sure, yeah, but it's so much . . . money."

"Spending $10,000 to win a million. Seems like a good investment to me."

"I mean, if you look at it that way."

"Would you rather I lose to Alexei Petrov? After the lawyers get done with us, we'll have to move into a studio apartment by the bus station."

Since they both knew that losing to Alexei Petrov meant losing to Bobby Wheeler, nothing more was said.

Prudence would meet with Pierre Millet every weekday morning at nine o'clock when his young pupils were in school and he did not have to perform. Usually he practiced at this hour, but he couldn't turn down the opportunity of working with the great Prudence Childs. Prodigies come along but once in a lifetime, after all.

First things first: Assemble her repertoire.

CENTRAL MUSIC OPENED its doors in 1953 because someone had to provide music to all those baby boomers. Located in a strip mall and crammed between a delicatessen and a cigar shop, the store is small in scale but large in purpose. Shelves of music stretch from the front of the store to the back. So much music that the violins and guitars and clarinets hang from a ceiling covered in sheet music. Whatever song you desire to create on whatever instrument you play, Central Music is the first step in making that dream a reality. Of course, you can get anything online. But why would you?

Being surrounded by all that music is intoxicating.

Pierre Millet was perusing the shelves, selecting sheet music and placing it in a basket that was about to overflow.

"Mr. Millet, it's only an hour show," Prudence said when she saw the basket.

"It'll work in your favor to be overprepared. Even though there's only three categories, and you have some in your repertoire already, you should prepare nine pieces, three for each category. Sight-read these and pick some new ones that resonate with you."

There was a small upright piano in the middle of the store where many a musician had played arrangements, hoping to find just the right one.

Pierre Millet gestured toward the piano. "All right, let's try these out."

Prudence did not move.

"What's wrong?" he asked.

Picking performance music was new territory for Prudence. It may seem like a small thing to the non-piano-playing, nonprodigy crowd raised in loving homes with loving parents. But Prudence had never been allowed to choose her own music. She was taught to play any piece that was set before her and to play that piece flawlessly. Her grandmother chose everything, usually very showy and highly technical. Prudence, when she dared to voice an opinion, preferred deeper, more thoughtful pieces. Anyone could play those, Granny Paddington said, encouraging Prudence to question not just her talent, but her taste.

On the upside, Prudence was a fantastic sight reader.

Now she looked at the thick stack Pierre Millet placed on the spinet and was immediately overwhelmed.

"Can't you pick for me?" she asked.

"Of course not."

"But you know what you're doing. I don't."

"Who says you don't know what you're doing? You're the interpreter. You're the one who has to feel it. That will be paramount to your performance."

All Prudence felt was incompetence. "I don't trust myself."

"If you don't trust yourself to pick your music, then you don't trust your gift."

She let out a theatrical sigh. Her gift. Not that again.

"Pick one piece and we'll go from there."

"Just one?"

Pierre Millet nodded and Prudence walked toward the little

piano as if she were walking toward a guillotine. She thumbed through the music before pulling *Six Ecossaises* by Beethoven.

"Well?" she said, after running through it.

"I get more emotional washing my socks."

Prudence snatched the piece from the stand. "I told you, I'm awful about picking my own stuff."

"Just because it's Beethoven doesn't mean it's going to work for you. You're putting too much faith in him and not enough in yourself."

"He's got a better track record than me."

Pierre Millet shook his head. "Prudence, everything you need is already inside you."

But she did not know how to get to these things that were inside her. She groaned and pulled another piece, an obscure jazz piece titled "Holiday in Spain," driving through it with an intense rhythm, as much as the little piano could handle. Technically, she mastered it, but it lacked a good bit of fire. Pierre Millet felt he was being put to some sort of test. It was as if she were a child who wanted him to intervene. Take the reins. But he would not. No growth comes from that. He would have to tread carefully here.

"How did it feel when you played that piece?" he asked her.

Prudence shrugged. "Like I was solving a math problem."

"An apt analogy."

He let her absorb what he'd said.

Since Prudence could be very stubborn, they sat there for a long time. Time they didn't have much of. They would have to decide on the repertoire today in order to perfect and polish.

They sat so long, Pierre Millet began to question himself. Maybe he'd been wrong. But choosing for her went against every instinct he had. The only way this internal door deep inside her would open back up—a door Pierre imagined had been slammed shut decades ago—would be if she unlocked it herself.

Finally, Prudence said, "I don't know what I'm looking for in any particular song."

"A connection to it," he told her.

She flipped through the basket again and pulled out a piece, studied the notes, slipped it back in, and went to the next. Then the next, and the next, and the next. He willed himself into silence, but he was getting hungry for his lunch.

"What if the connection I have is wrong? What if I make a mockery out of the piece?" she asked.

"Embrace your emotions, Prudence. Composers are tortured souls. That's why we like them."

Prudence stared intently down at whatever was on top in the basket. Pierre Millet could not see it. He remained silent, the only sound the rumble in his empty stomach.

Finally, she pulled out George Gershwin's "Summertime."

"This," she said.

"A good song but widely performed. You'll have to set yourself apart."

"By some connection."

"Yes."

"It's the opening song to *Porgy and Bess*. Clara sings it to her baby as a lullaby. It was originally a lullaby."

"Of course. And you have children."

But it wasn't her children she was thinking of.

She placed her hands on the keys and hesitated. Pierre Millet wondered if he'd pass out from hunger.

But then Prudence played "Summertime" on that unremarkable little piano. Under fluorescent lights. To the din of cars on the street. The dusty scent of so much sheet music lingering in the air. And in that banal setting, Pierre Millet got chills as if there were an army of frost-footed spiders crawling up his back. Prudence had allowed herself to yearn for her mother. To be cared for, protected, and loved. A mother who made soup when Prudence was sick. Who tightly held her hand as they crossed a street together. Who gathered her in her arms when she shivered in the cold. A love so unconditional and pure, she would give her life for her child.

"That was gorgeous," Pierre Millet said when she finished.

"If you call overt suffering something to be admired," Prudence said.

"God loves the poets more than the saints, Prudence. To suffer is human. To turn it into art is extraordinary."

She had found her first piece.

CHAPTER TWENTY-SEVEN

The Impossible Dream

Discovering her genius was like slowly unwrapping a gift. First the ribbon, then the paper, then the box, all the while anticipating the treasure inside. Prudence understood that the gift could only be accessed through practice. That didn't bother her. What bothered her was the looming specter of Granny Paddington, a maleficent figure who appeared whenever Prudence approached the keyboard.

Pierre Millet had his work cut out for him.

The next morning, promptly at nine, teacher and student met in the living room of the Willetta Drive bungalow, in which two full-sized Steinways—a six-foot-two Model A and a five-foot-seven-inch Model M—took up residence.

"The next six weeks will be a test of endurance," said Pierre. "Not only musically, but physically. Stay healthy."

"Got it."

"You're going to ache after eight to ten hours at the keyboard. Fingers should get a daily soak in Epsom salts. Forearms, too; you'll feel the tightness there first. Since you can't afford to take one day off practicing, we want to avoid any sort of inflammation."

"Ah, self-care. Now that's refreshing. When I was a child, I went to bed with bruises at night."

Pierre Millet scowled. "Every single tiger mom should be put in a cage."

"Let's start a movement."

"When children pursue perfection to please adults, the result is a submissive child. And how can one project confidence in a piece of music if they've been taught never to express themselves?"

AT ELEVEN O'CLOCK, when the lesson was over, Pierre Millet said, "Don't try to go for eight hours today. You'll lose your focus. Attention span is learned. Increase each day by thirty minutes. I usually tell my students ten minutes, but we're working against the clock here."

He pulled out a spreadsheet on which everything had been planned to the hour, from finger exercises to sonatas. Each day, something more was added. "You should feel some sense of achievement every day. There will be many moments when you'll feel frustration, and that's normal. But if you also feel progress, that will carry you. If you break it down into bits, you can master anything."

For the next four days, Prudence dedicated herself to Pierre Millet's schedule. It wasn't easy. She didn't like it. But she did it.

On the fifth day something happened.

Prudence lost track of time. One hour turned into two. Two into three. Monday she was late for her dentist appointment. Wednesday she forgot to eat her lunch. By the end of the week, she was so immersed in her practicing that she'd logged six hours in one day, the most she'd sat at the piano in over thirty years.

Stuart left for London that next Monday. He'd be gone six nights. For the first time, Prudence was looking forward to having space. She planned to go to bed early and get a full night's sleep so that she would be ready to drive through the long practice day.

The problem was, she was so excited about devoting a full day to practice, she couldn't sleep. Her mind kept ruminating on the themes of *The Nutcracker Suite* and how she could incorporate them into her playing.

Prudence had gotten into bed promptly at nine o'clock and thought about the day ahead. The anticipation wound inside her like the gears of a clock. She tried counting sheep. When that didn't work, she tried counting sheep backward. When that didn't work, she named all fifty states. And then all their capitals. Still, notes danced in her head.

After three hours of this, Prudence threw the sheet back and yelled, "Oh for god's sake, I might as well play the goddamn song!"

So at half past midnight, she padded down the curved staircase, followed by Mrs. Wintour. (There is, after all, no more willing companion than a dog.)

On the piano was the spreadsheet where Pierre Millet had scales and finger exercises tailored to each song. Since "Pas de Deux" was written in the key of G, she was to play three octaves of the G scale five times, once at 87 beats per minute on the metronome and again at 108 beats, and three times in contrary motion, as well as finger exercises 21 and 25 in *Hanon*. The warm-up took forty-five minutes.

"Pas de Deux" was next. It was a daunting piece. If only she could work through the fingering, her mind would be at ease and she would get back in the large bed and sleep a sound sleep. The opening measures sounded as if she were picking up the notes by the fistful and throwing them against the wall in a huge splat.

Prudence banged her forehead on the keyboard in frustration and the piano roared back at her. She collapsed onto it and buried her head in her arms. She couldn't do it. Alexei Petrov would win the competition and Prudence would lose her house. The wonderful life that she and Stuart had built together would vanish, the music having betrayed her.

Mrs. Wintour, sensing her mistress's distress, poked her little nose into Prudence's leg and gave her a tender look. It was just a moment, but it was enough to know she had lost her sight, only thinking of what she had to lose and not what she had already gained. Hadn't there been subtle triumphs the past few days, the music making its way back to her in a way she hadn't thought possible? And she recalled what Pierre Millet told her: *If you break it down into bits, you can master anything.*

Prudence played each measure very slowly. First, only with her right hand, which was the melody, until it was perfect. Then came her left—the accompaniment—until it, too, was perfect. She did this over and over, hands separately, until the gray matter in her brain physically molded to the pattern. Then she put her hands together and played those same measures over and over. Until, at once, the notes revealed themselves to her. Hearing their beauty, feeling their shape in her fingers, Prudence let out a gasp.

The last thing she wanted to do was go back to bed now. She was not at all sleepy and she continued to practice for hours. Sometime around seven in the morning, she felt a delightful ache in her back. She got into the bath and soaked and listened to records until it was time to go to her lesson with Pierre Millet. Then, since there were no children at home and her husband was away, the rest of the day was hers. Well earned. She grabbed her little dog and got into bed and slept.

The next night was the same.

And the next and the next. In the quiet of the night, Prudence felt free. She counted measures out loud. Sometimes shouted them. Sometimes she sang and sometimes she danced. It was liberating to seek perfection merely for the music's beauty.

Prudence slept all day and played all night. And the music began to form in her soul the way wet plaster bonds to limestone with the permanence of a fresco.

IN HER SOLITUDE, Prudence could play through instinct. She went to her piano each evening and left it each morning not with a feeling of dread and panic, but with accomplishment and wonder. How beautifully the triplets rolled off her fingers in the piece from *La Bohème*. The staggering contrast of tenderness and boldness in "Pas de Deux." She could finally hear herself play and this made her happy.

These daily victories were insignificant compared to winning a televised competition, but she had begun to realize something else. When her grandmother beat her, Prudence did not care about the music, only her grandmother's approval. The better Prudence played, the happier her grandmother became. Life was pleasant, if just for that moment. But of course, the happiness didn't last. Prudence had to please her grandmother or she would be hit with the dreaded wooden spoon.

It had never been about the music.

Until now.

When the practicing went well, the rest of Prudence's day went well. True passion makes the mundane sweet and the minutiae vibrant and enjoyable. Like hearing about Tess's philosophy class. Or drinking tea from a pretty cup and cuddling with Mrs. Wintour. Prudence had long ago embraced the ordinary. But the satisfaction she got from playing a piece well had shown her just how extraordinary the ordinary could be.

She felt a certain power in knowing she could master a piece of music without being slapped or berated. Although the hours of practicing combined with the dry desert air made the tips of her fingers crack, the feeling of doom that had been swirling inside her like a black dye had dissipated. When she played her piano, she was ageless and immortal.

By the end of that week, Prudence was practicing eight hours a day.

Then it all came to a screeching halt.

CHAPTER TWENTY-EIGHT

Classical Gas

Here is a thing that happened about fifteen years ago on Pricklypoppy Lane. A wealthy widow lived across the street from Prudence. One summer, when the desert got too hot, she went away for the month of July, as widows do. When she returned in August, someone had broken into her house. All her jewelry, gone. The necklaces were never recovered, nor were the earrings, rings, or bracelets. "Wear your jewelry every day," the widow had told Prudence. "That's what it's for, not to be stored away."

Prudence took this advice to heart. She had a large amount of jewelry, thanks to Stuart's largesse, which she kept in a velvet-lined case that stood on the lingerie island in her dressing room. (Except for the emerald ring, which remained in the cutlery drawer.) The drawers and compartments were always ajar because every morning, while in her pajamas, Prudence plucked several pieces to wear for the day.

This particular morning, Prudence wore an enormous sapphire ring on one hand and an emerald-cut ruby ring on the other. Her wrists were adorned with gold and silver bangles. All this sparkle kept her interested while playing an hour's worth of scales and finger exercises. It distracted her, too, because she had practiced too long now and was going to be late for her lesson with Pierre. She skipped up the staircase for a quick shower. That's when the door-bell rang. Followed by the door knocker. Followed by a very loud rap on the large iron door.

"Ms. Childs, I know you're in there. I heard you playing your piano."

Prudence's first thought was that maybe Bobby Wheeler had sent someone over to serve her with papers. Damn. Just when everything was going so well. She crept down the stairs and cracked opened the door and on the other side stood Tamara Quigley in a heavy tweed suit that seemed too heavy for the hot weather.

Tamara, upon seeing Prudence in cool linen pajamas with pretty blue piping, felt ridiculously overdressed.

"Ms. Childs, I've got a matter to discuss with you."

This HOA person again. "I'm just on my way out."

Tamara gave the slightest hint of a smile. "In your pajamas?"

Prudence flustered. "Well . . ."

"What beautiful rings. How *fun*, wearing them with pa*jam*as."

Prudence glanced at her hands and frowned.

Tamara continued. "Won't take a second. A little neighborhood issue."

"Burglaries again?"

"No, no more burglaries. Actually," and she lowered her voice, "this is about you."

"Me?"

"I'm afraid so."

"Sorry, the last time we met was so chaotic. I apologize for that, by the way. Could you please tell me your name again?"

Dismissed once again by the great Prudence Childs. "I'm Tamara Quigley, president of the HOA. I'm here to make sure all our residents get treated fairly. Not everyone has the privileges of fame."

Tamara could detect vulnerability in another person like a heat-seeking missile. Sensing Prudence's discomfort—it was "privilege" and "fame" that provoked a teensy reaction—she sought to press her advantage.

"May I come in?" Tamara asked.

"I have somewhere important to be."

"Ms. Childs, this is important, too. Well, it's important to your neighbors."

Prudence was unaware of any issues with the neighbors. Mainly because there weren't any. That didn't stop Tamara Quigley from stepping over the threshold and bathing the foyer with her heavy perfume. Prudence was late for her lesson and Pierre Millet was a stickler for promptness. Still, Prudence did not want to seem insensitive and ill-mannered. "I assure you, I care about my neighbors."

"Of course you do," cooed Tamara.

"The thing is . . . no one's said anything to me . . ."

"I know, no one has confronted *you*. They've come to me. And I'm sorry to tell you that some of them are quite upset." She was not sorry at all.

"Oh dear."

"Which is why I'm here to sort this out. To be honest, I have more important things to do, so I'd really like your cooperation."

Prudence felt silly, frivolous even. "How can I help?"

"There's been piano music coming from this house during the night."

"And?"

"We've had a number of complaints."

This was a lie. Tamara had been spying on Prudence day and night, parking her Escalade a block away and waiting for misbehavior. Hearing the overnight practicing, she had what she needed.

"Complaints? From whom?"

"These grievances have been shared with me in confidence. I have to respect that. I'm sure you understand." Prudence nodded, a testament to her understanding. "I would have liked to let the residents work this out for themselves . . . *your*selves. I had actually suggested that at first . . . but these people . . ." Tamara tapped a manicured nail atop the lid of Prudence's enormous piano. "To tell you the truth, they're a little intimidated."

"Intimidated?"

This was not welcome news for Prudence. She did not like disturbing her neighbors. Nor did she like intimidating them. But she needed the nighttime sessions. It was the most creative time of her day and it was paying off. She could not lose this competition; the stakes were too high. Everything was riding on it.

Tamara pulled a packet out of her portfolio. "You do have your copy of the CC&Rs?" she said as if it were the most important document in the world.

"CC&Rs?"

"The Covenants, Conditions & Restrictions. You've read through them, correct?"

Prudence shook her head. "I can't say I have."

With a sigh, Tamara opened up a tabbed page and read aloud. "The covenant defines 'nuisances' as anything that could interfere with the quiet enjoyment of the homeowners. In practical terms, garish Christmas light displays that attract traffic, excessive noise from backyard barbecues. And loud music. All stated in the CC&Rs."

Tamara's heavy perfume was giving Prudence a headache. "I'll try to keep it down," Prudence said.

"Mmmmmmm," said Tamara, running her eyes over Prudence's jewels with the intensity of a burglar. "I'm sorry, but the individuals who've confided in me just want to get a good night's sleep."

"I understand," Prudence said, deflated. "I appreciate you feeling comfortable enough to tell me."

Tamara Quigley, her agenda now complete, moved toward the door. It was then she saw Tess's and Becca's graduation portraits hanging on the wall. It was the first time she thought of Prudence as a mother. The thought had never occurred to her before.

"My children," Prudence said. "They're away at college."

Tamara said, almost without her own permission, "I'll bet you miss them."

"Terribly. I'm so much more aware of how old I really am now. Two kids grown and out of the house?! It all hit me at once. Do you have children?"

Tamara paused, reluctant to share. But there is a universal connection parents have with each other, and it happens instantaneously.

"I have a son. He's twenty." She smiled as if to apologize. "He's still at home. Can't figure out what he wants to do. It's a worry."

"Every parent has their worries," Prudence said. "You're not alone."

"I suppose. I just wish I could help him somehow."

"Oh, I think all they really need is for us to believe in them. That's our most powerful tool as parents."

Tamara smiled. When her son was ten, the neighborhood kids teased him because his bike had training wheels. One day, Tamara took the training wheels off.

"Get on," she told her son and held the bike by the seat.

"But I'll fall," he said.

"Then I'll catch you," she told him. She held the seat and ran while he pedaled. When she let go, he fell. She picked him up and kissed him. He fell again and again and cried in frustration. But Tamara could feel herself holding the bike less and less. "Don't give up," she told him. "You're almost there." He didn't believe her.

When he fell again, he walked toward the house in defeat. "I told you I couldn't do it," he complained.

"Yes, you can," she said. "You are five minutes away from learning to ride this bike, I promise." True to her word, in five minutes Tommy was riding that bike and feeling the joy of sailing down the street.

Tamara brought herself back to the present. "Your children," she said, "they study music?"

"Oh, no."

This surprised Tamara Quigley. "That would be a tough thing to live up to, I guess."

"They were just very interested in sports."

"Oh, sure."

"They take after their father."

"Wonderful."

Prudence remembered when it wasn't so wonderful. When they were very young, Tess and Becca worshipped their mother. They'd follow her from room to room, always wanting to be near her, arguing as to whose turn it was to sit on her lap when they watched television. They'd play dress-up in her clothes and sit at the spinet in the Sewing Room and pretend they were famous concert pianists. Prudence even bought a candelabra to set on top. When each one turned ten, Prudence enrolled them in lessons, thrilled they were learning music under much more supportive circumstances. Then, when each turned fourteen, it was like the clock struck midnight and the spell ended. Prudence, it seemed, could do nothing right and the piano became the focus of their teenage rebellion. Tessa refused to practice, saying piano "wasn't her thing." Becca followed suit two years later. The rebellion ended once adolescence did, but they never did return to the piano.

Prudence was sensitive about their indifference to music. "I wish I would've pushed them a bit more, but I didn't want them to resent me. You're right, it is a tough thing to live up to."

"I'll bet."

"I paid a steep price for it, too. I did not have a childhood. I didn't want that for my children."

Now there it was, a moment in which the past was laid bare, a moment that could have ended this one-sided feud. Here was the epiphany that Tamara so desperately needed. That Prudence had not been out to destroy anyone, that her childhood was far from the fairy tale Tamara believed it to be. The connection they just shared— the universal bond of parenthood—could have gracefully diffused the tension. The matter of nighttime practicing could have been dropped entirely.

Alas, Tamara refused to quit while she was ahead. "I used to be a dancer. *Swan Lake* was my favorite."

"Tchaikovsky's wonderful." Prudence slipped behind the keyboard and played the opening bars to the "Theme from Swan Lake." Tamara was standing near the harp of the Model B. The music entered into her on short bursts of air and found that special place where her dream lay dormant. Once again, she could hear the soft click of her pointe shoes on the wood floor, feel the powerful momentum of swirling across the stage in a flurry of chaînes turns.

This was not music. It was the discordant remnant of a dead dream. One that Prudence had demolished.

Like a record needle scratching the vinyl, it was as if the last five pleasant minutes had never happened.

"So, Ms. Childs," Tamara said, "do I have your word that we'll have no more of the nighttime disturbances?"

Prudence was thrown by the change of tone. "Surely we can work out some sort of compromise."

"Look, this is very serious. One of the complaints has come from a woman—one of your neighbors on this very street, in fact—who tells me your practicing is preventing her from sleeping. This same woman has confided in me that she suffers from serious health issues. She needs her rest. Please, have some compassion."

The clock in the hall chimed the half hour. Prudence didn't have time to change. She grabbed her sheet music and her little dog and her purse and her car keys.

"I'm so very sorry, Mrs. Quigley, I appreciate the gravity of this situation, but I have to go now," Prudence said. "Perhaps we can talk more later?"

She opened the door to show Tamara out. "Is that your car in the driveway?"

With an air of satisfaction, Tamara said the Escalade was indeed her car.

"You're blocking me in."

Prudence opened the garage and hopped into the little Porsche. The Escalade looked cumbersome next to the sleek little sports car. Not to mention that, dressed in her crisp pajamas and magnificent jewels, Prudence was effortlessly chic.

A fresh spark of anger struck Tamara as she watched the Prodigy speed down Pricklypoppy Lane. She made a note to have Prudence cited for driving 35 in a 25 zone.

CHAPTER TWENTY-NINE

Next to You (Outlandos d'Amour)

Alexei Petrov tried to rip through "Great Balls of Fire" for the millionth time. He pictured himself playing it onstage like Lang Lang, his childhood hero, who had once performed live with Metallica. Heavy metal was about as far away from classical music as you could get, but Lang Lang's rolling glissandos and heavy chords complemented Metallica's blistering guitar licks and amplified them. That was the goal. But each time Alexei tried to replicate that energy, it sounded labored and mechanical.

Alexei had a different memory of Lang Lang, one he tried hard to suppress.

He had taken Mia to Lang Lang's recital at the Palace of Versailles, where the pianist was filming a music video to promote a new album recorded in the Opéra Bastille. It was a rare performance, invitation only.

"How can I get into that concert?" Alexei asked Professor Lavigne. The professor, who taught conducting and had conducted symphonies all over Europe, was well known for his connections. "I will do anything."

"Anything?"

Anything turned out to be a fill-in accompanist for the senior

women's choir at a small Catholic church in the 15th arrondisse-
ment every Sunday for the month of April.

It had been worth it.

There they were, Mia and Alexei, side by side in that incredible
room of ancient mirrors, glass chandeliers, and priceless paintings.
Lang Lang was nothing short of magical and they sat a mere twenty
feet away. Mia couldn't take her eyes off Lang Lang's spellbinding
performance and Alexei couldn't take his eyes off Mia. And while
everyone in the room could not believe their luck at getting to witness such an intimate performance by the world-renowned pianist,
Alexei could not believe his luck at getting to sit beside the girl of his
dreams.

They held hands and listened to Chopin's Scherzo no. 1, the
notes winding up and down the keyboard as if powered by knots of
lust. They were two musicians feeling the music together, listening to
the melody fight itself, alternating between madness and despair,
complacency and contentment.

They listened not side by side, but as one.

Alexei shoved the memory back to where it had stayed dormant
for so long.

It had taken years for him to dispose of all reminders of Mia
Khouri. No photographs or cards or letters remained. The bottle of
Shalimar was long gone, left in a hotel room in Singapore. He even
gave away the vintage copy of Voltaire's *Candide* that she'd presented to him on his birthday.

Alexei had also kept his promise to himself and had not snooped
on her social media for a good twelve months. He hadn't seen her
post how happy she was and who she was with and what she was
wearing. Or eating. Or drinking. He wouldn't let that fuck with him
again.

He had to focus now.

He had to get this right.

He had to work up the anger he felt that day at Gabe's house
when he nearly blew the walls out and he had to do it without sum-

moning up memories of Mia. Relying on her shadow to fuel him
was too dangerous.

He didn't need a shadow. He needed a white-hot light.

Turning back to YouTube, to Lang Lang and Metallica, Alexei
added himself to the 1.4 million views.

There was Lang Lang in his starched shirt and sparkly tux, eyes
closed to absorb the music, then open to absorb the energy of the
crowd. The band played and the camera panned between Kirk Ham-
mett on lead guitar and Lang Lang on a Steinway Model D Concert
Grand. The first few minutes were almost polite, as if the musicians
were getting acquainted. Then came a wild explosion of sound and
light, the pianist and the rockers doing their thing, each nudging the
other to a better, bigger performance.

It was huge. It was magnificent. It was beyond him.

The pressure was intolerable. If Alexei did not get this right,
there would be a fall from grace. He would no longer be a social
media sensation. Or a celebrated television icon. He would still be
young, but already washed-up. A has-been, that's what he would be.
He could see the YouTube comments now.

> My grandmother has more balls playing Balls.
> Props to his contender who managed not to burst out
>   laughing.
> Alexei's playing sounds a lot better with the volume off!

He had to focus on winning this competition. Not just for him, but
for his parents, who had given him everything, had given up everything so he could have this opportunity. Alexei had to trust his mother.
She had a Midas touch. Through sheer force of will she had brought
the family to prominence a second time following his father's infa-
mous fall. Their lives were so much better than they were in Russia.

He attacked the song once more; still he could not overcome his
years of training. He wanted to access a wild carelessness, but all he
could find was precision.

Time was running out. Alexei had been at it all day and was completely off his game—and his schedule. Only five more weeks to go and he had other pieces to work on besides this.

Alexei Petrov had to loosen up and a glass of white wine wasn't going to do it. He needed a beer. Maybe a few beers. The more Alexei Petrov thought about it, the more he was convinced that booze would help.

A great idea occurred to him: The daytime hours would be used to practice the technical pieces that demanded fussiness and exactitude. At night, he would drink beer and play "Balls of Fire," which demanded a looser, fiercer approach.

He rose from his Steinway Salon Grand Model A and grabbed his wallet and donned his jacket and walked to the upscale liquor store in his upscale neighborhood. There were so many different kinds of beer. He did not know much about beer except that Americans couldn't seem to get enough of it.

He stood before a glass case filled with ales and lagers and malts and stouts, each in a different colored bottle. He decided on a case of Stella Artois because it was French. It also cost $30 and Alexei Petrov thought this was a very good deal.

It wasn't until he had gotten home and loaded all the beer in his refrigerator that he realized he could not just twist the cap off and thus returned to the liquor store and was sold a $10 bottle opener.

There is nothing like the first sip of a crisp, cold beer and Alexei Petrov was an instant convert. He turned on some Dizzy Gillespie and drank a couple of bottles. When he felt loose, he sat before the Steinway Salon Grand Model A and began again on "Great Balls of Fire."

It was flat. The stuff you hear when you're put on hold while scheduling a dentist appointment. It wasn't about precision. It was about inhibition.

He thought about calling Gabe. Maybe Gabe could come over. Gabe could pump him up again.

He should've called Gabe. Gabe would've explained that the alcohol was not giving Alexei anything he didn't already have. Gabe Puente knew of such matters and that would've been the end of Alexei Petrov's experiment.

But Alexei did not call Gabe.

Alexei went out.

CHAPTER THIRTY

Peter and the Wolf

 Tamara Quigley called the weekly meeting of the HOA board to order.

"New business," she barked.

The agenda was jam-packed. Many important items demanded Tamara's attention, like the reassessment of the yearly fees and the scheduling of the annual holiday brunch. There was the task of re-negotiating the landscaping contract and approving recent building permits. Too bad Tamara Quigley was not focused on a single one of them.

She pushed aside a stack of papers. "We have a problem," she declared. "Prudence Childs is purposely disturbing the peace."

"And you know that how?" asked Carl.

Tamara shrugged her shoulders ever so slightly. "It was brought to my attention by someone who has suffered a great deal."

"Oh, no," Claire said. "Who?"

"I can't name names," Tamara Quigley said with authority. "We're not doing that. Everybody got that?"

Everybody nodded to show that they had indeed got that. Even though they spent a good amount of time gossiping about whose kid was in drug rehab, who was having an affair, and who had an eye job.

Tamara continued. "Ms. Childs plays her piano all through the night and it's disturbing her neighbors."

This was a lie. Tamara had observed Prudence practicing over several nights, but she wasn't able to hear a single note until she left her car and crept right up next to the house.

"Ah, I bet she's rehearsing for that TV show. The one with the dreamy host . . ."

Tamara Quigley's face darkened. "She's going to be on TV?"

"It's all over the internet. She's going to be on *Alexei Petrov's Dueling Piano Wars!*"

Aha! That's why Prudence had been practicing so much. She was planning to come out of retirement.

"I can't believe you got to hear her play in person!" Claire sighed. "Tell us what she's like, Tamara."

Tamara Quigley rearranged the stack of building permits in front of her. She loved being the center of attention. Nothing pleased her more than being asked for her opinion. And yet, she was being asked for her opinion *of Prudence Childs*. Tamara proceeded with caution. "She's a little strange, I'd say." She held back, wanting to hook her audience. "I've met her twice now, and I've only ever seen her in pajamas."

"All day long?" said Jesse O'Neal, impressed. "Must be nice."

"It's inappropriate," snapped Tamara. "Self-indulgent. Especially when you consider that she also wears a great deal of jewelry at the same time. I'm surprised she could even lift her fingers, they were so weighed down with diamonds."

"In her pajamas?" Claire asked. "How decadent!"

"Look," Tamara continued, "it's important not to get starstruck here. Ms. Childs and her husband have an obligation to uphold the rules. I don't care how famous she is, her neighbors can't continue to have their sleep disturbed. We're going to have to impose strict limits on her practice hours."

"Can we do that?" asked Claire.

"What happens if she doesn't follow the rules?" asked Jesse. "Seems like she never has before."

"We may have to hire a lawyer."

"Is that really necessary?" asked Claire.

"It is really necessary!" shouted Tamara, her fair cheeks turning the slightest shade of pink.

The room went quiet.

Tamara Quigley composed herself. "I'm sorry. This is an urgent matter, in my view. If you must know, I'm very worried about the homeowner who complained. She's got some medical issues and needs her sleep. I can't allow this person's health to be compromised on our watch. I mean, we could get . . . sued . . . you know, if . . . if anything should happen to this person."

Oh, what a tangled web we weave.

But it was working, this elaborate lie. Tamara could sense the room turning her way.

"Oh, dear," said Claire. Carl nodded.

"Maybe we can come up with a surveillance schedule," said Jesse O'Neal. "You know, keep tabs on her."

Tamara's face brightened. "That's a really great idea, Jesse. Maybe you could take the nighttime shift? That's the most important one."

Tamara Quigley needed someone else to do her dirty work for a while. All visitors in and out of Quail Mountain were logged and scrutinized. She didn't want to raise suspicions by lurking around after dark too often. Being a suspicious person herself, Tamara was attuned to the suspicions of others.

AND SO IT was that for the next few nights, Jesse O'Neal took up his duties outside 10534 Pricklypoppy Lane. To sweeten the deal, Mrs. Quigley had given him $300 out of HOA funds (which was quickly eaten up by groceries and gas). He even had a uniform that identified him as a person of authority, a black mesh polo, embroidered in red on the left breast with the words *Quail Mountain Home Owners Association: Board Member.* Jesse O'Neal sat in his car and waited for the piano music to start, all the while thinking of himself as something of a hero. Wasn't this more significant than pursuing a college degree?

Tamara, meanwhile, took up her evening duties with her husband and son. After the dinner was eaten and the kitchen cleared, she sat up reading in her small, wood-paneled den. She didn't read her self-help book, nor did she read the latest selection from the Book of the Month. Powering on her tablet, she scrolled the gossip sites and the music sites and the fan sites and wherever else she could find information on the big episode of *Alexei Petrov's Dueling Piano Wars!*

Tamara smirked when she saw Prudence referred to as the Comeback Kid. *Some kid,* she thought. She felt a little smug when she read of the age difference between Alexei and Prudence. *She's got four years on me,* Tamara realized. *And she looks every one of them.* But when she learned that the winner of the duel would win a cash prize of a million dollars and a ton of exposure—and fame!—her demeanor changed.

Once again Tamara Quigley was consumed by white-hot rage.

CHAPTER THIRTY-ONE

Heard It in a Love Song

Stuart returned from London, exhausted. The trips were becoming more and more draining. Yet there was always that moment when the plane left the ground, when he was lifted above the clouds, the aircraft ascending into the boundless blue sky, that he felt a profound sense of weightlessness and joy. Sealed off from the world, he was free from its demands. If only for a little while.

Still, the trips were grueling and it was taking him longer and longer to get over his jet lag. Which was working out fine, since Prudence was always at her piano during the wee hours.

His wife's sleeping habits had undergone a dramatic change in his absence. Prudence didn't sleep eight straight hours. She catnapped throughout the day and night, Mrs. Wintour tucked into her side. Sometimes they slept on the chaise lounge by the pool and sometimes it was the couch in the Sewing Room. Sometimes it was the cushions atop the viewing deck and sometimes, because she missed her husband and wanted to be near him, she'd curl up on the leather sectional in his study while he worked.

Stuart noticed a difference in her playing, too. The music had taken on a dimension that he could not put into words. He was fascinated by the way she could produce such sound from a completely inanimate object. Because when she wasn't sitting before it, the piano was as alive as a stone. One afternoon, when Prudence was napping, he sat at her piano and pressed a key hoping for some magnificent sound. That didn't happen. He had pressed a single key and it made a single sound. It was an equation. When he tried pressing multiple keys—for that's what Prudence did—it sounded as if he'd thrown the piano out the window.

Stuart could not read a note. Could she teach him? It could be a way to be together. It could be fun.

That evening, he sat beside Prudence on the piano bench and kissed her cheek.

"Hello, darling," she said.

"My love."

"Are you tired of all this?"

"Hardly."

She smiled and he said, "Teach me."

Prudence was taken aback. Stuart had never expressed an interest before. She was thrilled that he wanted to know more about music, it meant he wanted to know more about her. "Oh, I'd love to."

Prudence could read music before she knew the entire alphabet. She could read music before she could read books. And she knew all her scales before the age of five. Teaching Stuart to read music would be much like trying to describe an ocean to someone who's never seen it.

"See this note?" she said pointing at some music.

"Yes." To Stuart, it looked like an egg lying on its side.

"That is called a whole note and it's worth four beats."

"What's that mean?"

"It means you hold it down and count to four."

She placed his right index finger on middle C and Stuart counted to four much the same way someone would count the change in their pocket. He kept his finger on the key when he finished as if he expected the note to silence itself.

"Lift your finger up," she said.

"Oh."

"Try it again."

Stuart tried it again. And because he did not remove his finger when he finished counting, Prudence shook her head. She could not believe that he did not understand this.

There were many things Stuart did not understand. As Prudence tried to explain them, unknowingly she overwhelmed him with explanations of scales and chords and flats and sharps. He could not distinguish between minor and major—*Minor makes a sad sound, can't you hear that?*

No, he could not hear that.

After twenty minutes, Stuart's head began to hurt. "How can you play the music so quickly and not have to think about all that each time?"

Prudence shrugged. "But that's the thing. It's not about thinking. It's about feeling. Maybe we should try learning a song."

"Better make it an easy one."

"Doesn't get easier than 'Twinkle, Twinkle, Little Star.' Watch my hands, okay?"

With one hand, which seemingly never moved, Prudence played the child's tune. Then she placed his hand on the keys and told him to sing the song and use his ears and that his fingers would find the notes.

"Promise?" he asked.

"Promise," she said.

Stuart sang "Twinkle, Twinkle, Little Star," but the tune that came from his lips did not match the tune that came from the piano.

Stuart was a college graduate. He could do a great many things. Like strategic acquisitions and portfolio management. He could calculate profit margins and interest rates in his head! Very important people relied on him. He could work on multiple pitches at once.

But he could not play "Twinkle, Twinkle, Little Star."

His brain could not grasp basic music. And for another twenty minutes, he tried and tried until his sanity was hanging by a thread. This had not turned into the fun marriage-bonding activity that he had planned. Stuart chose to believe his wife possessed a mystical power and left it at that.

He rose from the piano and said, "I'm going to go up to bed now. If I ever attempt this again, I want you to go into the garage and find the heaviest shovel, the *heaviest*, and whack me over the head with it."

Mrs. Wintour looked at her mistress and tilted her little head.

"*Je vois ce que tu veux dire*," Prudence said to her. "I see what you mean."

She grabbed Stuart's hand. "Sit by me, my love."

Stuart was frustrated. He did not want to sit back down. Prudence then began to play a love song. Their love song. The one she had played for him on the little spinet when they first met.

She played it so sweetly and simply yet there was such mysterious strength behind the notes: *I will always love you.* He sat down next to her again and closed his eyes. He remembered when Prudence first played it for him, she told him Dolly Parton originally wrote the song and Elvis wanted to record it but never did. It sounded so different from the Whitney Houston version. More subtle. This, for some reason, affected him more.

His dream, once again, rose to the surface. "Can I tell you something?"

"Of course," she said, as the song switched keys from F to G, the melody switching gears, taking it a notch higher and intensifying the sentiment.

Stuart kissed his wife's bare shoulder and listened for a bit, then said, "Never mind."

"Oh, you'd better tell me now."

A long moment followed. It was just the music, the melody celestially swirling up above the staff line now.

"What do you think of me taking flying lessons?"

"Like to fly a plane?"

"Yes, I've always wanted to. Ever since I was a kid."

"Really? I never knew that."

"Do you think that's ridiculous?"

She stopped playing and turned toward him. "Absolutely not! I think it's wonderful."

"You do?" He held her hand and played with her long and sturdy fingers.

"I do, my love."

"There's a flight school nearby, at the Scottsdale Airpark. There's a beginner program and, I don't know. It feels so good to tell you that. I felt like it was, you know . . ."

"What?"

"Silly."

She touched the tip of her nose to his and said, "Everyone thinks their dreams are silly. That's why so few go after them."

They stayed like that for a few moments. Then Stuart said, "Let's go to bed."

Prudence didn't want to practice anymore that night. She wanted to go upstairs with Stuart and hear all about his dream.

CHAPTER THIRTY-TWO

A Taste of Honey

 Alexei Petrov walked down Olive Avenue in his black chinos and his black collared shirt, his black calfskin shoes shiny with polish.

Walking into the Park Bar and Grill, he was told by the waitress that it was Manic Monday, which meant half price on draft beers and bottles of wine. The waitress flirted with Alexei Petrov because he was gorgeous and his beautiful sable-colored hair had just the right amount of pomade. Also because he looked very familiar. But this was L.A. and famous people were always popping up in the most pedestrian of places. There were three young women at a table next to him. The one with blue hair kept looking at him.

Alexei ordered a bottle of beer and a pulled pork sandwich. He felt loose and that felt good. The drinking had relieved the pressure he was under, though his brain was oblivious to just how temporary this fix would be.

Alexei talked to a group of men watching *Monday Night Football*. They bought each other shots of tequila and chased them with beer. Around 11:00 P.M. PST, when it was already Tuesday morning in Paris, he called his mother and told her things he'd wanted to tell her for many years.

He liked feeling loose.

Then, ignoring the voice in his head blaring in Dolby surround sound, he looked at Mia's Instagram. Sure enough, there she was with some guy, a different one from the last time he had checked twelve months and eight days ago. Dewy-eyed, the two of them held hands as if they'd just vowed to spend the rest of their lives together. They looked like they should be in a jewelry ad.

Devastated, he drunk-dialed his beloved violinist, and when she didn't answer, he sent a rambling text that, if it had been edited down to four words, would be: I still love you. He held his breath for her response.

To which she said, Go to bed.

He felt like a bottle drained of its contents.

The next text went to Gabe: I QUITE!!!! In which he misspelled "quit."

CHAPTER THIRTY-THREE

Linus and Lucy

 An hour had gone by since Tamara Quigley received the last text from Jesse O'Neal. It was one in the morning and the tiniest grain of worry was beginning to take root.

Ultimately, she was responsible for him. Or for whatever happened to him. And he wasn't very bright.

She tapped out another text: What is going on? Please reply.

Nothing. She checked his location: 10534 Pricklypoppy Lane.

If he would just text back, she could get a few hours of sleep. But another hour passed without a reply. Now his phone was marked "offline." Maybe someone spotted him lurking and called the police.

She ought to drive out there and make sure Jesse was safe, but she was dressed in flannel pjs and her hair was gathered in a large plastic clip. Prudence Childs might swan around in her pajamas, but not Tamara. She took a few tentative steps up to the bedroom to change into street clothes, but there was that squeak in the floorboards and she'd wake her husband, who would ask where she was going. He'd probably call the police on her himself.

No, she'd have to sneak out in her pajamas.

—

THE GATEKEEPER GAVE Tamara a suspicious look that she tried to ignore. How was he to know she wasn't on official HOA business? Pulling up to 10534 Pricklypoppy Lane, Tamara could see a light on upstairs. The rest of the house was dark, though. Only the moonlight gave Tamara any visibility. She got out of the car. Where was that kid?

"Jesse," she whispered.

Nothing.

She looked into the window of the foyer. The piano was illuminated by the moonlight, and for a minute, Tamara was mesmerized by the sight and did not move.

Then she heard something.

"Jesse?"

More rustling in the bushes. Tamara gripped her phone.

"Who's there?"

The bushes moved and a hushed voice that was clearly not Jesse O'Neal's answered back. "Who are you?"

"I'm with the HOA. Identify yourself."

The shadow of a large man was illuminated on the grass.

"What are you doing here in the middle of the night?" Bobby Wheeler asked.

"Official HOA business."

Bobby Wheeler took in Tamara's attire. "Don't look like any official business to me."

Tamara Quigley was good at thinking fast on her feet. "The gatekeepers know I'm here. And they know exactly why I'm here."

That last part was a lie.

"Now, who are you and why are *you* here?"

Bobby Wheeler was not skilled at thinking fast on his feet, which was why he told Tamara Quigley something he shouldn't have, something that would greatly complicate Prudence's life.

"I'm her husband."

"Nonsense."

"Her first husband."

Tamara tilted her head. "I was not aware that Ms. Childs was previously married."

"*I'm* the one who should be living in this house. Not him."

"Is that so?"

Bobby Wheeler really should've stopped talking right then and there. Both he and Tamara wanted something from Prudence. But what they wanted were separate and incompatible things.

Bobby wanted money and Tamara wanted—well, what exactly?

"She owes me a lot of cash," said Bobby. "And not just me."

"Who else does she owe?"

"The Martinellis."

"Who are the Martinellis?"

"You don't need to know. But I'm telling you, she stole millions from them."

Tamara paused. The story didn't seem right. How could Prudence Childs steal millions of dollars and not get caught? She was something of a public figure. A relatively visible person.

"How exactly did she do this?" asked Tamara. "A Ponzi scheme? Did she rob a bank?"

"Prudence? Rob a bank? My Peanut wouldn't be able to point a gun at an amusement arcade." Bobby Wheeler shook his head and chuckled.

"Then how, for fuck's sake?" hissed Tamara. "How does a former child star steal millions of dollars in plain sight?"

This whole strange conversation was happening, quite literally, under Prudence's nose. You'd think all the heated back-and-forth might reach its way up to the master bedroom. But Stuart and Prudence were too deep into a postcoital slumber to notice Mrs. Wintour lift her little head and give a pint-size growl.

Too bad. Because Bobby Wheeler was about to tell Tamara Quigley the most damaging thing of all. That Prudence Childs was not the rightful author of the Pep Soda jingle.

"Oh, please," said Tamara. "I don't believe a word of this."

"I got proof."

Bobby then told her all about the letter from Mrs. Martinelli, which prompted Tamara Quigley's mind to form a plan. There was physical proof Prudence Childs was a fraud? She, Tamara, had to get ahold of that letter. She wasn't sure how, but fraud? This was big. Surely she could use it to ruin Prudence. When Tamara Quigley spoke next, her tone had sweetened considerably.

"My heart goes out to you, Mr. Wheeler. It must sting to see Prudence living in this enormous house, without a care in the world, when you know the truth."

"It's not fair," he whispered.

"It certainly isn't," said Tamara, looking at him from the corner of her eye. "Especially now that she's on track to win a million more from that television show."

"Talk about unfair."

All was quiet for a few moments, except for the wind rattling the pods in the palo verde trees. Suddenly, Tamara perked up.

"Hey, if you really do have proof that she lied about writing that music, like you say. Well . . . then I'm sure the producers of the TV show would be interested in that . . ."

Before Bobby could ask Tamara to explain, they heard the whir of a golf cart behind them. They turned to see a man in a khaki uniform and a matching cap that said QUAIL MOUNTAIN SECURITY. The guard pulled alongside Tamara and Bobby, giving each a curious look. "Can I help you with something, Ms. Quigley?"

"Thanks, Derek, but we're good," said Tamara, with surprising equanimity. "You might have heard about the issues we're having this year with the javelina eating up all the landscaping? Well, Mr. Wheeler here is a javelina expert and since they're nocturnal, he can only diagnose the problem and create a remediation plan at night."

"Good enough, ma'am. You all be careful, though. We saw a pack of coyotes earlier."

"We're just finishing up anyway." Tamara turned to Bobby and handed him her HOA card. "Please email me and we'll find a time to meet and discuss your proposal. Don't forget to bring the documentation we discussed, okay?"

"Yeah, okay," Bobby Wheeler said, catching on a few beats behind.

Tamara leaned in and squeezed Bobby Wheeler's hand. "I know exactly how to help you," she whispered.

Finally, someone on his side.

THE NEXT MORNING, after a sleepless night cursing Prudence and worrying about her missing employee, Tamara Quigley began to plot. She had an idea that would trick Bobby Wheeler into giving her that letter. It would take a little finesse. The man was no genius, but he wasn't a total fool either. He had been reluctant to reveal too much information when they'd stumbled upon each other the night before. Still, if she played it right, she'd be able to fool Bobby into helping her ruin Prudence for good. But first, she needed to make sure Jesse wasn't lying somewhere dead in a ditch.

CHAPTER THIRTY-FOUR

Runnin' Down a Dream

It was September 26, less than five weeks until the showdown. The opening bars of Beethoven's Fifth Symphony, *ta-ta-ta-TAAA*, the most famous in Western music, filled the marble foyer on 10534 Pricklypoppy Lane.

No one heard the large glass door from the pool deck slide open and click back shut. No one heard the footsteps go up the back staircase and through the hallway overhead—footsteps that paused to take in the violence of the chords. Then, as if to imitate the fragile melody that followed, the footsteps softly continued to the master bedroom and into Prudence's dressing room, where, atop the island that housed her lingerie and stockings, sat the large alligator jewelry box.

No one heard the intruder gasp at the contents spilled across the counter winking and glowing like the stellar remnants of a tiny galaxy, or at the rows of rings lined up like candy. The gilded bracelets and gold chains. The TAG Heuer watch. The ropes of pearls and the diamond-studded chokers. There were drawers and drawers of earrings. Sapphires, rubies, emeralds, each in their own tiny compartment. At once, the little drawers were hastily pushed in, the necklace wings secured, and the lid clicked shut. No one heard the heavy alligator case being lifted by its handle and removed from the island.

What they heard was the boom it made as it fell. Mrs. Wintour let out a short bark and Prudence's fingers froze. Two little drawers had slipped from the case, and Prudence caught the distinct sound of the gemstone studs scattering like broken glass across the marble floor above her head.

The footsteps thumped, thumped, thumped to the back staircase. Mrs. Wintour took off like a shot, and all eight pounds of her cornered the perpetrator on the landing with loud and incessant barking, as small dogs often think they are very large dogs.

With her heart beating like a helicopter blade, Prudence crawled into the kitchen on her hands and knees, grabbed her cell phone from her purse, dialed 911, and whispered her emergency.

She peeked over the counter and saw a young man holding her jewelry box. The young man saw Prudence, too, and he made a dash for it. Prudence had no intention of confronting a burglar. But Mrs. Wintour was at his heels, nipping his ankles.

"Ouch!" he cried. "Ouch, ouch, ouch!" Because Mrs. Wintour, even though she had little teeth, had very sharp teeth. He went for the large glass pool door from which he entered. But he couldn't manage the glass door's opening mechanism while holding the jewelry box so he turned around to set the jewelry box on the dining table and inadvertently tripped over Mrs. Wintour, as little dogs have a knack for getting underfoot. Prudence picked up a dining room chair, ready to whack him in the head.

"Don't hit me! I don't have health insurance!"

The burglar lay on the floor, Mrs. Wintour an inch from his face growling as if there were a little motor in her throat. Prudence thought he looked incredibly young and extremely frightened. He was also wearing a shirt that said *Quail Mountain Home Owners Association: Board Member.*

"Who robs a house wearing a shirt that identifies the organization they work for?" she asked.

Jesse O'Neal looked down at the shirt he forgot he'd been wearing. The night before, he had slipped around the backside of the house to escape from whoever was in the bushes. He hid under a blanket on the chaise lounge and turned off his phone because Tamara Quigley kept texting. Lulled to sleep by the sound of filtering pool water, he woke with a start as he remembered his dilemma. He did not have any recording of Prudence playing the piano in the night. He could not record her playing in the daylight hours because they did not need footage of her playing in the daylight hours. He did not have the money to return the HOA funds Tamara had given him. And he could not return to Tamara Quigley without either the recording or the money.

Hence his decision to lift the jewelry he'd heard so much about.

"The police are on their way," Prudence said.

"Oh, no," Jesse said.

"The contents of that jewelry box would amount to grand larceny. You might as well have robbed a bank."

A burst of air came from Jesse O'Neal's lungs. "My parents are going to kill me."

He rose to his feet and put his hands up surrender style.

Prudence lowered the chair. "What were you planning on doing with all this? You weren't going to wear it, were you?"

Jesse O'Neal shook his head. "No." But his reply was weak and uncertain and his no sounded very, very small, like, "no."

"Were you going to sell it?"

"I guess."

"To whom and for how much?"

"I'm not sure."

Prudence picked up her jewelry box. "You have to hold it by the bottom, like a bag of groceries." And she set it on the dining table and opened one of the little drawers and took out a gold bracelet with a large garnet faceted at the clasp. The beauty of the bracelet was in its understated simplicity.

Prudence held it up to Jesse and said, "How much do you think this is worth?"

Jesse shrugged. "A hundred dollars?"

"A thousand." Prudence dropped the bracelet back into its place. "If you were smart, you would've taken only the bracelet and probably would've gotten away with it. It would've been *months* before I even noticed. How is it that someone as inept as you is breaking and entering?"

"I guess I'm not very smart."

"I didn't say you weren't smart. I said you were inept."

He was terribly young. Prudence, having raised two teenagers, was used to young people doing dumb things. Like the time Tess ate an eraser on a dare and was hospitalized for two days. Like the time Becca stole a $2 Frisbee from Walgreens and had to do twenty hours of community service.

Jesse O'Neal looked at his feet. "I didn't come here to steal your jewelry. Not at first."

"Why did you come then?"

Jesse O'Neal did not know what to say.

"Answer," she said.

"I'm not supposed to tell you."

"You'll have to tell the police. May as well start with me."

Jesse O'Neal confessed. It didn't take much. "I was on a stakeout," he said.

"A what?"

"Stakeout."

"Where?"

"Here." He pointed at the floor.

Prudence narrowed her eyes and tilted her head as if she had not heard him properly. "Here, as in *my* house?"

Jesse O'Neal's head bobbed up and down. "They want to get you in trouble."

"They who?" Prudence asked and Jesse O'Neal pointed to the writing on his shirt. "The HOA?"

"You're not supposed to play your piano at night. It's against the rules and you said you won't stop. Mrs. Quigley paid me to get the evidence."

"I see," said Prudence, recalling the uncomfortable details of her meeting the day before. "Can you tell me which of the neighbors made the complaints? I could try to talk to them myself."

"Mrs. Quigley wouldn't say who was doing the complaining. But she convinced everyone on the board that you're a serious community problem. She also said that . . . oh, never mind."

"Tell me."

But Jesse O'Neal could not tell Prudence what Tamara said. Because it was hurtful and mean. "I can't say it."

"Why not?"

"It's not a nice thing."

"Out with it."

"She said you're only playing in the dead of night because you can't face the fact you're a has-been and that you'll probably make a fool out of yourself on TV."

This silly insult stung Prudence Childs more than it should have. Her will to conquer the day drained away. The words had a familiar ring to them. They had the slap of Granny Paddington in them.

Did this Mrs. Quigley have a point?

Was Prudence about to look like a fool in front of fourteen million people?

She sat on a dining chair and put her head in her hands.

Jesse O'Neal was confused. He did not understand why the words of a woman Ms. Childs did not even know affected her so greatly. "I think you're really good," he offered.

"Do you?"

"I do! I heard you play when I was robbing you," said Jesse. "You're seriously amazing."

He could not believe Prudence Childs did not know this herself. He could not believe she could not hear it herself.

"Hey, Mrs. Childs? Maybe, before the cops get here, could you play me a song?"

Prudence shrugged. "Why not?"

Prudence played "Somewhere Over the Rainbow," because that was a song Tess used to love.

Jesse O'Neal leaned on the piano. His mind went back many years. He thought of the little metal cars scattered across the floor of his childhood room. He had a plastic racetrack with an elaborate mechanism that shot the cars through loops and chutes. He remembered eating French toast for breakfast and apple slices after school. He remembered the soft white curls of Snowflake, his toy poodle.

Jesse began to weep out of shame. He did not want to participate in stakeouts anymore. He did not want to drift through his life not having a passion. He certainly didn't care about this dumb HOA job. It was nothing more than a tyrannical mini fiefdom, a magnet for emotionally constipated people like Mrs. Quigley. He did not want to be like her. But he did not want to go back to school, either. College wasn't for him. At least not for now. He wanted to do something but he could not name it.

"Why are you crying?" she asked.

"I don't know."

"The song makes you sad?"

"My life makes me sad."

"You should stop breaking into houses then."

"That would be a good start. It's probably not the best way to pay my rent, I'm four months behind. I just don't know what I want to do. I'm not good at anything."

"Everyone is good at something."

"Not me."

"You can think of something."

He shrugged. "I guess I'm good at shuffling cards."

"There you go. That's something."

"It's pretty impractical."

"So are dreams, but we need them." Prudence thought for a second and then said, "You need a dream."

"I don't have any dreams. It's part of the problem."

"Everyone has a dream."

"Not me."

"Did you ever read Steinbeck's *Of Mice and Men*?"

"Only the SparkNotes."

Prudence leaned against her piano and said, "It was about these two farmhands. They had nothing in the world except the clothes on their backs. They went from ranch to ranch for work. What money they made, they'd blow it all. Then they'd move on to the next ranch. It was the same thing every time and it was a very lonely existence. But they kept on."

"That's depressing."

"What makes them do it, right? What powers them to get out of bed every day when their lives are so monotonous and hopeless?"

Jesse slowly shook his head. His mouth was open.

"It was because they had a dream," Prudence said.

"What dream?" Jesse asked.

"Of owning a farm. They talked every day about getting a little piece of land and what they would grow and what animals they'd raise. And Lenny just wanted to tend the rabbits."

"Rabbits? That doesn't seem exciting."

"But that was *his* dream. It got him out of bed every day."

"I don't get it."

"It was the *power* of the dream and not the reality of it. Even the most jaded people in the most hopeless environments need dreams." Prudence stopped to take in her own words. Her life had changed in the last six weeks. It had purpose and meaning beyond her children. Would she go back to the way life was, the old things that made her happy?

No.

A police car pulled up outside.

"Your ride's here," Prudence said.

They watched two police officers walk up the stone walk. Jesse O'Neal wanted to think about a dream. He'd have plenty of time, too, because he was going to jail.

"Goodbye, Ms. Childs. Thanks for everything!"

"You're welcome." She saw a little spark in his eyes that was not there before. She hoped that he, too, would have some clarity now.

Prudence watched as an officer handcuffed Jesse O'Neal, read him his Miranda rights, and guided him into the back seat of the patrol car. Then, with a bit of sleuthing and a few phone calls, Prudence hired a lawyer for the boy—a lawyer who promised that, under the circumstances and with a few weeks to work the system, she could probably have Jesse's sentence reduced to probation and time served as long as the rest of his record was clean.

After that, Prudence did a bit more sleuthing and made a few more phone calls and paid off the back rent on Jesse's apartment. Then she paid the next six months, too. Because dreams can take a little time to get organized.

CHAPTER THIRTY-FIVE

Traümerei

 "You were *arrested*?" Tamara Quigley felt a mix of relief and anger.

"Yep."

"For *what*?" She figured one of the neighbors must have spotted him prowling outside Prudence Childs's house.

"Robbery," Jesse O'Neal told her.

How to make sense of such a statement?

"*Attempted* robbery," he corrected.

"Whom did you *attempt* to rob?"

"Mrs. Childs."

"Dear god. *What* did you attempt to rob?"

"Her jewelry."

Tamara had seen Prudence Childs's jewelry. This was not petty theft. Grand larceny was more like it.

Tamara paced her Saltillo tiled floors.

She did not want to lose her temper.

She could not afford to lose her temper.

"I need you to bail me out," Jesse O'Neal said. "If you do, I promise I won't tell the police you sent me over there."

Fuck.

"Who caught you?"

"Ms. Childs."

"Fuck."

"She was nice about it, Mrs. Quigley. Really nice."

"Fuck!"

FIRST THING TAMARA Quigley said to Jesse when they got into the Escalade was "You're fired."

"I figured."

"I want the $300 I gave you from the HOA funds and the additional $500 I had to come up with for your bail."

"Okay, but I need a job and you just fired me."

Tamara pulled her Escalade over on the shoulder of the very busy 202 Freeway so quick and so hard that the red dust of the desert rose up, surrounding the vehicle like smoke. Reeling from the frustration that her own son did not yet have a job, that she had never realized her dream of becoming a dancer, that Prudence Childs was going to be on television, had nicer pajamas, beautiful jewelry, a useful husband, and two bright children who were *away* at college, Tamara Quigley screamed at the top of her lungs, "Get *another* job!"

A semitruck blew past so fast the Escalade shook.

Jesse O'Neal shrunk down in his seat. He could understand why Mrs. Quigley was upset, but he could not understand why she was so filled with rage. It wasn't as if she was his mother. And, boy, he was not looking forward to that conversation, the one where he would tell his parents what he had done.

Mrs. Quigley sat with her hands gripping the steering wheel. "You are truly a useless human being."

Jesse thought about his conversation with Ms. Childs. "I am not useless," he said. "I can shuffle cards."

"What?"

"I'm good at shuffling cards."

Tamara narrowed her eyes in disbelief. Perhaps Jesse O'Neal had been dropped on his head as a baby. And as a teenager. And as an adult. "Who cares that you can shuffle cards?"

"Ms. Childs."

Tamara shook her head. "Why would she care about that?"

"*Right?* But she said everyone was good at something and everyone needs a dream, their own dream, one they . . ."

"She talked to you about dreams while you were stealing her jewelry?"

"She did. Then she played the piano for me and it was really inspiring and it made me want to . . ."

"I can't hear this right now."

"But she . . ."

"Shut *up,* Jesse."

Jesse O'Neal paused for a second. Then he stuck his hand in the lion's mouth. "Ohmygodyou'rejealous!"

Anger radiated from Tamara Quigley like heat rising from the pavement. She shoved the Escalade into park and trained her fiery eyes onto Jesse. "Take that shirt off," she growled in a voice that, to Jesse, sounded just like Darth Vader's.

"But I don't have another one."

"Take it off. *Right now.*"

"Can we wait . . ."

Tamara Quigley growled, "I gave you a chance, a job . . . some *money* and you screwed it up!"

It all made sense now. There was a clarity of sorts on the shoulder of the 202. Jesse O'Neal no longer cared about what Tamara Quigley thought of him. He wasn't a loser. He was good at something and this gave him hope. If a poor ranch hand could get out of bed every morning with the dream of one day tending rabbits, Jesse O'Neal could subsist on his dream, too. He could make it happen.

He took the shirt off. "Here." Jesse could hear the piano music in his head. It changed something in him and Tamara saw it.

She settled down as if someone had snapped off a switch. "You've made a mockery of our organization."

Normally, Jesse O'Neal would admit to being a fuckup. He would admit to being careless and unmotivated and unfocused. Not anymore. "I did not," he said.

"Yes, you did. Because you're a moron."

"I'm just inept at robbery." Because that's what Ms. Childs told him.

"You're inept at everything!"

Jesse O'Neal chanted the riposte in his head, *I'm rubber you're glue, your words bounce off me and stick to you.* It was evident to him now that Tamara Quigley thought herself useless and inept. It was coming to him so quickly.

For the first time in his young life, he could see clearly.

He thought about his dream. He was good at shuffling cards. He had a thing for casinos. The dinging bells and the flashing lights. That once inside, you could not distinguish day from night, or Tuesday from Saturday. He lost track of time when he played card games.

Isn't that what everyone wanted? To be absorbed by their day?

He wanted to be a blackjack dealer. He loved interacting with other players at a small table where no one else mattered if only for just that hand. This is what he wanted to do. He would be very good because he was good with cards. He would get through this mess. He had hope.

They rode in silence the rest of the way, Tamara Quigley fuming, Jesse O'Neal dreaming.

She dropped the shirtless Jesse O'Neal off at his apartment complex and he got out of the car and just stood there.

She rolled her window down. "What now?"

"I was just curious, Mrs. Quigley: What are you good at?"

Tamara floored the Escalade and left Jesse, quite literally, in the dust.

CHAPTER THIRTY-SIX

Train in Vain

Alexei Petrov was horribly sick. He wanted to stay in bed but his stomach would not cooperate, so he made his way to the toilet and threw up. For a brief moment, all was right with the world. Then he stood and his head felt as if it were full of rocks. He lay on the cool tiles of the bathroom, which, oddly, he found preferable to his mattress. He didn't know how long he stayed there, but he did know that his head was likely to crack open if he attempted to stand.

How did he get so sick from a few beers?

Then he remembered—kind of—the tequila shots he had with his new *Monday Night Football* buddies.

He had gone to bed very late last night (this morning?) without brushing his teeth or using his face products or rubbing cream into his cuticles. His calfskin loafers were scuffed and his arms and chest were covered in ink.

That girl, the pretty one with blue hair, she had drawn on him with a pen. She said she was an artist. She knew who Alexei was. A groupie.

The drawings were very good, too.

A phone number with "Call me!" was scribbled across his navel. This made him smile until he thought about the gas station nachos. He promised himself he would not, for the rest of his life, ever eat nachos again. Or drink tequila poppers. Or beer.

Alexei was way off his schedule now.

By this time of the morning he should have completed his scales and finger warm-ups and been well into drilling his pieces.

Panic set in.

He had not worked on his program for the last several days because he was playing "Great Balls of Fire" like elevator music.

His technical coach would be by in thirty minutes to work on the Tchaikovsky piece, but canceling this late would mean paying for the $250 lesson, which was billed directly to his mother, along with feedback on how the lesson went. After an indeterminate amount of time on the bathroom floor, Alexei crawled back to his bed.

That's when he noticed the small gray cat curled up inside his clothes hamper.

Where did that come from?

The small gray cat looked up at him and stretched languidly before settling back into the comfort of some socks.

Alexei did not remember acquiring the cat.

Alexei could not have acquired the cat, as he was severely allergic to cats!

Did it belong to the blue-haired girl?

The cat had to be returned before he had a fatal reaction. He knew he would have a fatal reaction because when he was very young his mother had told him that if he were to pet a cat, his throat would close up and he would die. It would happen instantaneously, this fatal reaction.

No, he could not touch the cat. Someone would have to remove it for him. He retrieved his phone from his bureau and saw multiple texts from his parents in Paris. He had a thin memory of calling his mother and accusing her of some very horrible things before hanging up on her, which at the time had felt like some sort of release. Like he could run down the block like the wind. Now he could barely stand.

He reviewed the texts, which had evolved from anger to panic to fear.

What the hell is wrong with you!

Then: Call back and apologize at once.

And: This is your father, Alexei. I implore you.

And then: Alexei, please call, we are very worried.

He saw, too, that he had texted Mia.

Had he lost his goddamn mind?

ALEXEI PETROV HAD been indulged as an only child. But he had not been allowed the luxury of adolescence. If he ever expressed anger toward Tatiana, she would burst into tears, effectively extinguishing the spark. Alexei had his own cell phone at the age of ten, was allowed his first sip of champagne at twelve, and was attending operas unchaperoned at the age of fourteen. But he had not been allowed the period of teenage rebellion that would help him separate himself from his parents, so he could not find out who he was and make his own mistakes. Without his own mistakes he could not make his own decisions, decisions that would allow him to grow up and away. Claim his independence.

Which was just how Tatiana wanted it.

Alexei Petrov, dressed only in his underwear and with writing scrawled all over him, did not know who he was. He did not understand what he was feeling toward his mother. He was confused as to why he had been so angry. He loved his parents and they loved him.

So, why did he say such dreadful things?

How did he fuck everything up in a mere twelve hours?

He had to fix it. He had to fix it *now*.

His first call would be to the girl with the blue hair because maybe she could tell him where the cat had come from and could return it to its home before he had some sort of attack and died.

He looked at his navel area and dialed the number.

"Hello?" It was a man's voice.

Alexei Petrov could not remember the girl's name. "Um, with whom am I speaking?"

"*With whom am I speaking?* You're speaking to me, that's who."

"May I please talk to the young lady with blue hair." The line was quiet for a long time, so long, in fact, that Alexei Petrov thought he'd been disconnected. "Hello?"

The voice barked right back at him. "What do you want?"

Did the girl with the blue hair have a boyfriend? Why would she write "Call me" on his abdomen? Now he remembered, the blue-haired girl took him to a club with loud music. They danced and she kissed him and he kissed her back. They did this for hours, dancing and kissing. When they left the club, they stopped at a gas station and got nachos and a six-pack of beer. They came back here and had sex in Alexei's bed.

"Are you her boyfriend?"

"I'm her husband, asshole."

Alexei Petrov hung up the phone, because the guy on the other end sounded like he could really kick Alexei's ass.

He steadied himself against his bureau, willing the call to his parents to go more smoothly. He would apologize. He would promise never to drink again. He would tell them he was very sorry and was working very hard and would be very successful. He would have a second and even bigger season of *Alexei Petrov's Dueling Piano Wars!*

They would be so proud.

It was his father who answered. "What the hell is wrong with you?" he snapped.

"I know, I'm sorry."

"Why would you say such ugly things to your mother?"

Alexei Petrov could not remember exactly what ugly things he said because he'd been drinking.

Which was the next admonishment. "Obviously, you were drinking quite a bit."

"I am under a lot of pressure."

Hearing the weariness in his son's voice, Alexei's father searched for the words to encourage him. What followed was a rambling monologue that Alexei could not focus on. His head and his stomach were at war with each other and formulating any sort of response, even something as benign as "sure" or "I see what you mean," took a tremendous effort.

He rested his aching head on the cool surface of the bureau and closed his eyes while his father spoke. He meant well, his father. He always did. But Alexei was preoccupied with keeping his stomach lining intact and did not hear the words that were being said to him. Nor did he hear the little gray cat jump up next to him. But when he felt something very soft and warm nuzzle his ink-smeared arm, he jumped back. His heart thumped up through his throat, his throat that was about to close up and restrict his breathing.

Nothing happened.

The little gray cat let out a little gray mew. Alexei tested his breathing. He filled his lungs with air and exhaled.

Nothing.

Maybe death would come more slowly. He took another deep breath. And another. Nothing. In fact, he felt better, taking in all that air. Alexei ran his fingers through the little gray cat's fur and she nuzzled him again. She was incredibly soft. He petted her again and again and he felt happy. Instead of instantaneous death, he'd fallen in love. The little gray cat was on his side. Alexei could feel it in his heart.

Had it been a lie all along, this allergy story? A lie to keep him from wanting a pet, to keep him focused on one thing and one thing only?

The little gray cat perched on the dresser. Her tail swung to and fro and she knocked over a framed photo of Alexei playing in a recital when he was a student at the Conservatoire. He was wearing a black tuxedo and sitting before a Bösendorfer Model 280, the best piano in the world. His arms were spread across its keyboard and his eyes were closed in concentration. He was sixteen. He remembered feeling petrified because he could not make one mistake that evening. Studying the photo, Alexei realized that there had not been a day in his life when he did not feel that kind of pressure.

All at once, he saw things differently.

He did not see a young man with opportunity. He saw a boy who had taken on the burden of his mother's happiness, a child who had been responsible for reversing the misfortune she had experienced in her own life.

Looking at that photograph, he saw a child held captive in a silver frame.

A child who had been lied to.

Alexei Petrov had been told that he wanted to be the best pianist in the world.

But that was not what he wanted.

"I quit," he said to his father.

"Quit what?" his father replied.

"The show."

It had taken a blue-haired girl and a little gray cat and some gas station nachos for Alexei to realize that what he wanted was his independence. The words—*I quit*—would give it to him.

He repeated those words to make sure he was heard. "That's it, I quit."

He was heard, all right.

Alexei's father handed off the phone. "Alyosha."

"Mother."

"Alyosha, you are not thinking straight."

"I cannot handle the pressure right now. I need some space."

"Space from what?"

"You."

Tatiana would have to be careful now. "I understand you are under pressure. But you will not have this chance again."

"I'll figure something out."

"Alyosha, I am here to protect you." She measured her words a teaspoon at a time. "They will eat you alive without me."

Alexei knew plenty of Americans his age who were not eaten alive on a daily basis. Who could do many things without their parents. He envied their freedom.

"We just want what's best for *you,* Alyosha," she told him.

"The best thing for *me* right now is to figure out what I want on my own. I want access to my bank accounts."

"You have no idea how to manage money."

"I'll learn."

"Are you mad? What has gotten into you?"

"I want to enjoy my life while I'm still young. To not have everything planned out to the minute." Because the night before, Alexei had a little taste of freedom. To go back to the way things were would be like trying to put salt back into its shaker without removing the lid.

"Maybe you need a holiday. We can work that out."

"A *holiday*? All I've done is work. I need more than a holiday."

"Papa and I will fly out and we'll spend a weekend somewhere. How about Carmel? I hear it's beautiful this time of year."

"I am old enough to go on a holiday without my parents. I want to take six months off. And I can well afford it."

The little gray cat let out a mew.

Tatiana let out a deep sigh. "No, actually, you can't."

"I can't what?"

The doorbell rang. It was Alexei's instructor. Too bad Alexei was in his underwear and his sable-colored hair had a finger-in-the-light-socket look.

"Alyosha, you have to do this show."

Beneath her stern voice was the slightest timbre of panic.

The doorbell rang again. It was very, very quiet.

"I can hear the doorbell," she said. "It sounds like it is time for your morning lesson. We can talk about this later."

"No," he said sternly. "Now."

"You're broke."

Silence. And in that short but vast space of time, moments that people often describe as the world coming to a stop, Alexei remembered a Leonard Bernstein quote: *Silence in the right places can be the most electrifying thing in music.*

"I'm broke?"

"There is no money."

"This is a joke."

"No."

Alexei Petrov, phone tightly clutched in his hand, jaw clenched, felt as if his entire body had been freeze-dried. "How can that be? You couldn't possibly have spent it all."

"I needed to keep you free from them. I needed to buy them off."

Free? Now that was ironic. "Free from whom?"

Tatiana spoke slowly and deliberately when she finally replied.

"When you were accepted into the Conservatoire," she began, "the officials at the Russian embassy refused to grant us the visas we needed unless I paid them. I had no money, so I gave them promises. About what we could pay in the future."

"You bribed them with my earnings? Then bet on the margin?" He had been a fool, a work mule who never looked up from his feedbag.

"Every time you play a new venue, make a new record, get a new endorsement, they find me and threaten to call us back home. Every time we need to renew or adjust the terms of our visas, they want more, Alyosha. They always want more."

"But surely you've paid enough at this point?"

"Do you know what it takes for a Russian to get a work visa to the United States?" Tatiana asked. She was pleading now. "You know how many plates I had to keep spinning to make that happen?"

"How could I, when you kept it all from me?"

"We need those endorsements, my darling. You have to do the show and you have to win. Everything you collect from advertisements this year will go to the embassy officials."

"And after that, Mother? Do I continue this way forever?"

"Not at all! If the show is renewed, you can prove that you have long-term employment in the United States and that you are supporting your family. The network will negotiate your visa renewal in the spring, not me. You will be able to bank whatever you earn from the second season of *Piano Wars!* as well as future earnings."

He was trapped. Not only did he have to do the show, he had to win. There were long beats of dead air as Tatiana waited for her son to speak. But he didn't speak, so Tatiana had to fill the space. It was in that space that Alexei learned how the remainder of his earnings had been poorly managed. The rent on his ridiculously large, L.A.-based home was $12,000 a month. And she had filled it with expensive furnishings and art, things Alexei did not want or need yet were all part of the image Tatiana was trying to create. The excessive staff she'd hired—like the Japanese chef, the manicurist, and the masseuse—must have cost a fortune. The poet probably made more money working for Alexei than anything he had ever published.

"You ruined me," he said, when he could finally find the words. "I do not play for pleasure anymore. All these years you pretended you were making sacrifices for me when the truth was that I was the one giving up *everything* for you and Papa. You never even had the courage to tell me."

"Oh, please," she said. "Would you rather work in a coal mine?"

Anger cracked inside him like lightning. "Maybe I would! At least I would enjoy the music!"

He hung up and kicked the fancy art deco chair. Then he upended the coffee table and a crystal bowl shattered on the travertine floor. Who knows how much the fuck that stupid bowl had cost him.

Alexei stood in front of the large window, where the view of L.A. was smudged with pollution as if someone had tried to erase the skyline with a dirty eraser. He hated the piano just then. Look at all it had taken from him, and there was nothing to show for it. He wanted to put his fist through the glass. Maim himself and destroy his future because he could not control it now. He squeezed his hand into a ball and drew back his elbow.

"Alexei!" His instructor pounded on the door. "*Alexei,* are you okay in there?"

He snapped back into his reality. He lowered his arm and unclenched his fist.

"Alexei!"

He looked at his hands. He had been born with perfect fingers. They were long and muscular and could do anything the piano demanded. It took years of work to accomplish that. He could not destroy them. They were all he had left. No, he would take control of his situation. He answered the door and, with less than five weeks before the Big Episode, promptly fired his technical coach.

He spent the rest of the morning petting the little gray cat and firing everyone his mother had hired. He fired the poet, the novelist, and the painter who was also a sculptor. He gave his landlord notice. He took the paintings off the wall, the ones he paid for but did not choose.

It was surprisingly liberating.

He did not feel the anxiety of disappointing his mother. Because *his* fate was hanging in the balance. Win or go back to Russia. Master "Great Balls of Fire" or lose. Winning meant sponsorships, more seasons, and real money. And money meant independence. And not just from his parents. The bigger he got, the bigger the show got. The bigger the show got, there was no way the network was going to let those fuckers in Russia screw with his visa. Win at all costs.

Over the next several days, Alexei would eventually realize he had no idea how to cook, clean, or do his laundry. He would nearly burn down his hillside house when he started a grease fire on the stove. A few of his cashmere sweaters would shrink to the size of doll clothes.

He would eventually learn that browning ground lamb should be done at a lower temperature. That washing a pair of black pants with a white T-shirt did not turn out well. The lesson about reds and whites would take another month.

He would go on to put up several "Lost Cat" posters around the neighborhood and when no one claimed the little gray cat, he happily bought a cat bed for which he paid $101.99. The cat did not sleep in this bed once, preferring Alexei's hamper, Alexei's chest, and the bathroom sink.

Alexei Petrov's newfound independence would get a little overwhelming with just four weeks to go before the biggest moment of his career. But each time he felt his courage slipping, he pictured his mother. He pictured her shaking her head, saying, *You can't do this without me.*

He needed to show her he could. He would not fail.

But before he learned all these things, that same morning, after he hung up on his parents and fired his technical instructor, there was a loud pounding at the door again. Alexei froze. He wondered if it was the blue-haired girl's husband. He wondered if the husband had found out they had slept together. And that he had his cat. Alexei Petrov picked up a fireplace poker and walked cautiously to the door.

CHAPTER THIRTY-SEVEN

My Ever-Changing Moods

 Pierre Millet advised Prudence to start small. To Prudence, "small" meant a few hundred people. In her youth, she had played for thousands. She told him as much.

"And how long has it been since you last performed a concert?"

Prudence pretended to think about the answer, when in fact she knew to the day. "Twenty-nine years," she said.

"As I said, you start small," Pierre Millet said. "Very small."

"Like a church service?"

"Smaller."

"A cocktail party?"

"Smaller."

"A bar lounge."

"Smaller."

"A café."

Pierre Millet shook his head. "Like almost-no-one small."

"That leaves Mrs. Wintour in my foyer."

"But in public."

"But to no one."

"Correct."

Prudence tilted her head in thought. "Where do you find no one in public?"

Pierre Millet cleared his throat. "In the waiting room of the Mayo Clinic is a Steinway," he told her.

"A *hospital*?"

"There are never more than one or two people sitting there. Most pass through on the way to the elevator bank. It'll be perfect and the piano is terrific. I've played it."

Prudence thought this was very silly indeed.

Pierre Millet knew different.

This was not the same as playing in a hotel bar to drunk patrons waiting for an Uber. Not the same as performing as a child where part of the wonder was her young age. Pierre Millet knew Prudence would internalize that heightened expectation, would feel that she had something to prove. She would have to address any possible inhibitions before her televised performance.

"Remember," he told her, "people there will have a lot on their minds. A lot of worries. Pick your music accordingly."

"Okay. Got it." Prudence only agreed to humor Pierre Millet.

"Give it an hour tomorrow morning before our lesson," he told her.

"An hour tomorrow morning before our lesson," she answered smugly.

That's why, on Monday, October 2, at eight in the morning, Prudence Childs strode through the enormous lobby of the Mayo Clinic dressed in silk paisley pants, a silk paisley top, and the day's allotment of jewelry.

It was an atrium that stretched five stories up to a glass ceiling, so that if you took the elevator to any floor, you could lean over the balcony and view the lobby below. Pierre Millet had been right. The club chairs were arranged in groups of four, but apart from an elderly woman reading *People* magazine near the administration desk, the lobby was empty.

At 8:12 A.M., while Stuart was taking his first flying lesson, Prudence sat before the Steinway Model B, Classic Grand in ebony fin-ish and played Beethoven's *Moonlight Sonata.*

At 8:22 A.M., she was in her Porsche, speeding down the 101 toward 17 Willetta Drive.

What a disaster it had been. She hoped Stuart's morning had been better.

"BUT YOU PLAYED the piece, no?" Pierre Millet asked, as they sat in the parlor of his tiny bungalow. He was eating his breakfast of but-tered toast and sliced peach.

"It started out well," Prudence told him. "The piano was quite lovely."

"Then what?"

"I got halfway through the first movement."

"And?"

"A man sat down next to the piano."

"Wonderful."

"He was listening!"

"Good."

"But it was awful. *Je ne me suis pas bien amusée!*"

"Why?"

"I blanked for the first time in my life! I couldn't remember one more note. I've been playing this song for forty years. When I was eight, I played it for a thousand people. But today, there was just this one very nice gentleman . . . listening, and I started . . . sweating and, and shaking and then . . ."

"You started again?"

Prudence shook her head. "I ran."

"No!"

"Yes!"

"Go back!"

"Never!" She stood and paced and waved her hands around. "I'm finished! *Je suis ruinée!*"

"*Au contraire.*"

Prudence stopped pacing and, in a very dramatic fashion, drew a big breath. "I'm too old, Mr. Millet," she said.

"I'm older. By decades." Pierre Millet was not having any of this. Every artist, no matter how talented, has their own insecurities. He would not let Prudence give in to hers. "I played a cocktail party last night. If I'm not too old, no one is."

"But I'm not the same person I used to be when I was eight."

"Good. Beethoven did not intend for an eight-year-old to play such a moody song. No matter how well you played it back then, your life experiences will have added another dimension."

Prudence thought Pierre Millet was not listening to her. "I can't get up on a stage anymore. I've no confidence."

Pierre Millet dropped his napkin onto his empty plate. He leaned back on his couch and said, "No, you've grown into your pieces. You've entered Beethoven's head. Once you feel what he meant, it's intense."

"I did, I felt . . ."

"Exposed?"

"Absolutely."

"Vulnerable?"

"Incredibly."

"Excellent."

Prudence shook her head. "The song was too beautiful. Just one man listening and he turned to me as if he were bathing in the glow of a candle. It was unnerving."

Pierre Millet nodded. "As opposed to the thousands you've played for. Now the listener was close. That made him real to you. And you, too, have become real in a way you couldn't as a child. Now the music is as real as the man sitting next to you."

"Oh, dear."

"Don't you see how powerful you are? You are not a spectacle anymore, Prudence. You are able to interpret one of the greatest pieces of music ever composed. *That* is the gift."

"How will I play before thousands?"

"Van Cliburn said that you must try and reach the person sitting in the very last row. Go back to the Mayo. If not for the sake of the competition, then for those who need what you can give."

Prudence dropped to the couch opposite Pierre Millet. "I'm not sure I can go back."

"Oh, but you must. Tomorrow, if possible. And whatever you do, don't run away again."

"Why?"

"Tell me what happened when you ran back to your car."

"I stopped shaking . . . and I felt better."

"Exactly! You rewarded yourself for escaping something terrifying. You felt calm. That feeling helped reinforce the idea that your response to the perceived trauma was reasonable. Incorrect, of course. But if you keep deceiving your brain in this way, you'll be too afraid to play in public at all."

Prudence did not need to develop a phobia four weeks before she was due to play on television to fourteen million people. She thought about Bobby Wheeler just then and his demand for money. If she lost, how would Stuart ever retire? How would the six-foot, eleven-inch, Model B Grand fit into a tiny apartment? Surely, she and Stuart would have to share a closet. They'd fight over hangers. And shelf space.

She needed to win.

She would not run.

THE VERY NEXT day, Prudence returned to the waiting room at the Mayo Clinic wearing a gray turtleneck, black leggings, and simple ballet flats. No jewelry.

She stood in the entrance and stared at the piano across the empty lobby. The atrium felt taller and wider and brighter than it had the day before. Her heart galloped like the hooves of a horse. She felt as if her very life was in danger.

Pierre Millet was right—if she ran now, she would never come back. But just as she was readying herself, she heard Granny Paddington's voice: *They will laugh at you now.*

Prudence froze.

A woman from the administration desk looked up. "Are you okay?"

"I can't be sure."

The woman walked over and took Prudence by the elbow and led her to a nearby couch.

"Do you need a doctor?" the woman asked.

"I think I just need a minute," Prudence said.

The woman, who had sat behind the administration desk for many years, had seen all sorts of things. "Sit as long as you'd like." She left and returned with a paper cone filled with water and went back to her desk.

It was that small bit of kindness that saved Prudence from a full-blown case of stage fright.

She rose from the couch and walked to the piano. Sitting down, she took a breath and began Chopin's Prelude in E Minor. The first measures clanked together like keys jangling on a chain. But soon the notes flowed together in a stream.

Then a terrible thing happened!

The man from the day before returned.

He sat on the couch near the piano and folded his hands in his lap and tilted his head and listened.

Adrenaline flushed through Prudence's body. The notes started to leave her mind. She made a mistake. And another. Flustered, she stopped.

She waited for the building to explode.

But the building did not explode. The man on the couch continued to sit. The phones at the administration desk continued to ring. The elevators continued to ding at the elevator bank. The atrium did not cave in. The piano bench did not collapse. No one laughed. No one taunted. The world did not stop.

Instead, it bloomed with freedom.

Prudence began Chopin's op. 28, no. 4, again. This time she closed her eyes and allowed herself to feel the quiet desperation in the song. She imagined a one-way conversation, one of trying to convince a lover to return. To not see how life could be lived beyond the lover's absence. Intensity streamed through her fingers.

When she finished, the man on the couch said, "You know, don't you?"

"What's that, dear?" she asked.

"How it feels to slowly lose them. How powerless we are." His wife of thirty-six years was in Room 403. He could not save her. "That it is better to have loved. It is always better to have loved."

The music did not offer an escape to the man in the waiting room nor did it offer hope. The music underscored the beauty of what he had experienced.

That was all. And that was everything.

CHAPTER THIRTY-EIGHT

Crocodile Rock

There was a second pounding on Alexei Petrov's door. It was louder this time. Alexei gripped the fireplace poker that he had never once used to stoke a fire, because he didn't know how. "Who's there?"

"KGB! Open up!"

"Who?"

"Dude, it's Gabe, open the fucking door." Alexei opened the door and Gabe glanced at the fireplace poker in Alexei's hand. "Whoa, I'm here to help."

Alexei stepped aside to let Gabe enter. "Sorry, my life is falling apart. How did you know where I lived?"

"You gave me your card, remember? I figured you were at the L.A. address and not the Paris one. Why do you look like you need to be pushed through a car wash?"

"You will not believe what I got up to last night," Alexei groaned.

"It'd take you years and you still wouldn't catch up with me."

"I got very drunk."

"Big deal."

"I called my parents."

"And?"

"I think I told them I hated them. I've never said something like that to them before."

Gabe righted the fancy art deco coffee table and sat on the fancy art deco chair and put his feet up. "You're not exactly making history there. Generations of teenagers have said that to their parents at one time or another."

Alexei continued. "Worse, I texted my old girlfriend."

"Uh-oh."

"I'm still in love with her."

"What'd you tell her?"

"That I was still in love with her."

"What'd she say?"

"She told me to go to bed." Alexei handed Gabe the fireplace poker. "Just plunge this into my heart. Please. Do it now."

A smile crept across Gabe Puente's face. "I actually find that endearing, you drunk-dialing your girl."

"She's not my girl. She's someone else's, thanks to my mother."

"At least you're a romantic when you get polluted. Did I tell you about the night I drank a fifth of Jack Daniel's, snorted a gram of coke, popped some uppers, got up onstage, ripped off all my clothes, and got into a fistfight with my drummer?"

It took Alexei Petrov a moment to run through the visual. "In front of an audience?"

"Yep. Not a onetime occurrence, either, buddy."

"Really?"

"Well, there were variations."

Alexei Petrov closed his eyes and let out a long sigh as if he'd been holding his breath for an entire week. "I told my parents that I was not going to do the show. That I quit."

"Come on, you're not quitting over this fucking Jerry Lee Lewis song."

"I will make the biggest fool out of myself on live television."

"Dude, have you ever seen *American Idol*?"

Alexei ignored this. "Here is the thing, I *can't* quit. You want to know why? I'm broke. My parents spent *all* my money."

"I spent all my money, too. It happens, we're human."

"Did you spend it paying off corrupt individuals?"

"Just my drug dealers."

"It seems I've been paying off the Russian government."

"Man, are you shitting me?"

"I am not shitting you," Alexei said. "And get your feet off the coffee table, it has to go back. If I quit, I will not be just broke, I will be deported back to Russia. If I don't win, I'm twisted."

"Screwed. You'll be screwed. And no, you're not. I've got a plan." Gabe swung his feet onto the floor and slapped his thighs with his palms. "Go take a long, hot shower. And wash off all those hiero-glyphics."

Alexei reexamined his arms.

"Shower, nap, and meet me back at my place at six," Gabe said.

"I can't. I've got to practice the Killer."

"Do *not* practice 'Great Balls of Fire' today. Repetition won't help. This isn't Tchaikovsky, man." He stood up to leave.

"I don't have the money to pay you."

"You don't have to. We're hitting the club scene."

"I'm not sure clubbing with you is such a great idea."

"I didn't say we were going to drink."

"Then what are we doing?"

"Gonna let you be human, buddy. It's not the shit you did that you regret, it's the shit you *didn't* do."

Gabe Puente left and Alexei Petrov did the one thing Gabe told him not to do. He sat down at the piano to run through "Great Balls of Fire," because he was a perfectionist. But the little gray cat jumped up on the piano and walked across the keyboard. The keys made a soft tinkling sound as she padded her way to Alexei's fingers. He picked her up and held her to his face and he said to her, "Okay, my little sun. I will do what I am told."

At six o'clock, Alexei Petrov was in Gabe Puente's tiny studio along with the big dog, the old piano, and two takeout burritos.

Alexei was dressed in a creamy button-down shirt, jeans, and a black blazer. His beautiful hair had a carelessly tousled look.

"You sure clean up well. Nice threads," Gabe said. He then tossed some sheet music in Alexei's lap.

Alexei sifted through the stack. "What are we doing?"

"We're going to get you used to working without a net."

"Who is Annette?"

"No, a *net*—tonight, you're just going to play. No judges, no television cameras." Gabe paused and then added, "No parents . . ."

"I would need at least a day to run through this stuff."

"No, you don't. You've got to be careful covering pop songs with a piano. Spontaneity counts. We don't want some easy-listening stuff. Total snore fest."

"Then what are we doing?"

"You'll have the sheet music as backup, but just memorize the key and then riff off it. Didn't you have some sort of improv training in your fancy French school?"

"I did, but I am not very practiced at it."

"Then let's get practiced at it. You don't have to fly solo. I'll be lead guitar and vocals. All you need is to wait for my cue, and then jump in."

"Where will all this be happening?"

Gabe was known to start a fair amount of their conversations with "There's this guy I know." Because this was L.A., and Gabe Puente had been a pop star and he was a studio musician, he seemed to have a never-ending stream of connections. Of guys he knew.

"There's this guy I know, he runs a very small club down in West Hollywood. Well, it's more like a little tavern. Drink specials, live music on weekends. Got a piano in the corner. Not a big-ass Steinway like you're used to but you'll dig it, it's got a great sound."

Alexei wasn't so sure about this. The kind of people who show up to a place for the drink specials were not the sort who listened to Mozart. Besides, there was a good chance people would recognize him. Alexei Petrov never played anything to a crowd that wasn't absolutely polished.

Gabe read his mind. "Look, man, I've played in absolute toilets, this is a nice place. Anyway, the name of the game is not precision, comrade."

"Then what would you call this game?"

"Blowing the Motherfucking Roof Off the Dump."

"I don't think I will be good at this game."

"Would you trust me for once? I've done this a million times. Baby steps. Place holds about thirty people. Tonight's Tuesday, there'll probably be eight people, okay? And, Jesus, you're so pretty, you could go up there and play polka music and they'd adore you."

They ran through about ten songs a lot quicker than Alexei would've liked. They ate their burritos, took Duke for a quick walk, and piled into the black Mercedes.

THE MUSIC SHOP had an all-brick interior except behind the bar, which was floor-to-ceiling shelves of every kind of liquor you could imagine, enough bottles to get a small country intoxicated. Alexei thought Gabe was talking in hyperbole when he said the place held about thirty people. But the place physically could not hold more than thirty people. That evening, oddly enough, there were eight people scattered around at the few high-top tables and the bar.

The two musicians walked in and The Guy Gabe Knew was standing behind the bar. "Hey, Bill."

"Gabe." They high-fived each other.

"You mind if we play a few tunes in the back?"

"Be my guest."

"This is my friend Alexei."

Bill the bartender got wide-eyed at the sight of Alexei. He wiped his hands on his apron and nervously shook Alexei's hand. "Hey, wow, Alexei *Petrov*. Oh, man, walks right into my bar. My wife loves your show."

"Thank you. That is very kind."

Gabe said, "A Diet Coke for me and a Corona for Baryshnikov, here."

"You got it."

The two of them went to the back. Gabe tuned his guitar and Alexei played a couple of warm-up scales to get a feel for the piano.

"Ready?"

"Maybe I could just watch you tonight."

Gabe fiddled with his guitar strap. "You know what Hemingway said about bullfighters?"

"Nope."

"Nobody ever lives their lives all the way up, except bullfighters."

"I don't know what that means."

"They face death every time they go out there. If you face your worst fear, you're able to live more fully."

Alexei looked at the small crowd. "I keep picturing them walking out."

"Live like a bullfighter, man. We're gonna start with some Van Morrison. G major, follow me with chords."

There was no need for a microphone in such a little place. Even if it hadn't been such a little place, Gabe had a voice that didn't need a microphone. He started with "Someone Like You." Gabe played the melody on his guitar and Alexei quickly figured out the accompanying chords. Bricks make decent acoustics and the music sounded good.

Patrons swiveled around on their barstools. Some swayed to the music. Some sang along. Since Gabe, and not Alexei, was the center of attention, Alexei was comfortable enough to be creative. He added a few flourishes to the chords and played with the dynamics. And yet, without the safety net of hours of practice, Alexei Petrov was waiting for the other shoe to drop. He was still playing cautiously. The fearlessness of a bullfighter eluded him.

When they finished their first song, Gabe said, "Since no one left, we're going to take it up a notch."

"Oh, god, can't we just . . ."

"Brubeck's 'Take Five,' E-flat minor. I'll start us off. Watch me for cues."

Gabe plucked out the famous, foot-tapping chords until Alexei was able to find his way on the piano and they jammed. Alexei was surprised how lost he got in the music. His fingers seemed to know exactly what to do. The song was a perfect marriage of guitar and piano.

Soon everyone knew who the two musicians were. Photos were taken and posted and immediately got thousands of likes and shares. People off the street came trickling in. By the time they got to Harry Chapin's "Cat's in the Cradle," it was standing room only.

About midway through their hastily assembled set, Gabe played a romping blues solo. "Time to show off, you," he said. "Let's give them some Mozart."

Alexei's dark eyes widened. "You have got to be kidding."

"You don't know 'Rondo Alla Turca'?"

"Of course."

"I'll play the boogie-woogie bass line and you do the Amadeus stuff in the treble clef."

"Impossible."

"We'll alternate the keys from A major to C major, from precision in the treble clef to swing in the bass clef. If it doesn't work, we play something else."

Turned out that it worked. Because Alexei Petrov's specialty was Mozart and Gabe Puente's specialty was anything he felt like.

THAT'S HOW IT started. The two of them would just show up in the evening. Sometimes it was a Tuesday. Sometimes it was a Friday. Sometimes it was a bar. And sometimes it was in the lobby of a hotel. Once they went to the south terminal of LAX and drew an enormous crowd. The clips were all over Twitter, Instagram, and YouTube. All these guys Gabe knew, they came in the form of drummers, bass players, saxophonists, and vocalists. Whoever was up for an impromptu gig. The showstopper was a medley—Gabe's idea, of course—of the best piano riffs in rock. Eric Clapton's "Layla," Queen's "Bohemian Rhapsody," Madness's "Our House," Boomtown Rats' "Why I Don't Like Mondays," Vanessa Carlton's "A Thousand Miles," and ELO's "Evil Woman." Alexei could play them all. (He practiced this medley daily like a madman.)

Gabe Puente was amazed at Alexei Petrov's razor-sharp precision. Alexei Petrov was in awe of Gabe Puente's fearlessness. What each admired in the other began to imbed itself so that Gabe became a more exacting player and Alexei did not perseverate on the occasional flub.

There was only one song Alexei Petrov didn't and wouldn't play on those nights: "Great Balls of Fire."

CHAPTER THIRTY-NINE

The Entertainer

"You're early."

Prudence stepped inside the Willetta Drive bungalow. She was wearing jeans and a white silk shirt with ropes of pearls around her neck. But Pierre Millet's eye was drawn to her feet, on which she wore a pair of flame-red loafers.

"*Je regrette,*" she said.

Oh, dear, what now. "Let me finish this email to the Ocean Club," Pierre said. "I have to confirm some performance dates. Then we'll begin. Five minutes. If that."

"Take your time." Prudence spoke with such heaviness that the room sank along with her. She sat down at the Model M and began noodling around on the keyboard.

He studied her for a moment. "You okay?" He worried that something had happened on her return to the Mayo Clinic, but he didn't want to press.

Prudence shrugged and Pierre Millet went into his little office off the kitchen. Soon, "The Girl from Ipanema" was flowing out from the Model M.

But the tone changed by the time his computer had booted up. Now Prudence was playing a simple bass line over and over. He peeked around the doorframe and saw a flame-red loafer keeping beat. The bass line sounded familiar, but Pierre Millet couldn't place it. Who knew with Prudence? She was a walking jukebox and could summon whatever tune she wanted.

The chords on the Model M took on a palpable intensity. The right hand kicked in with the melody, which took on the shape of a Kinks song. Simple at first, but as the notes grew, they flourished, spawned more notes that grew into a frenzy as if any second she would lose control.

A scene from *Fantasia* came to Pierre Millet's mind. He half expected to see broomsticks racing around the piano, frantically carrying buckets of water. He went back into the front room to watch. The toe of a flame-red loafer was planted into the carpet and the heel bounced in cut time. Prudence was completely lost in the song, like it was leading her somewhere. The more absorbed she was, the more flourish the melody took on, and the more she banged out the bass line. He imagined the neural pathways in her brain lighting up like streetlights, showing her the way.

He forgot all about what he was supposed to be doing.

She looked up at him. "Did you get your email sent?" Whatever agitation she brought inside had burned off through her fingers.

"I was distracted."

"Sorry."

"You want to tell me what's going on?" he asked.

She took a dramatic breath worthy of Norma Desmond in *Sunset Boulevard*. "I have a confession."

"Okay."

"I'm not the author of the Pep Soda jingle."

"Really?" It was all he could think to say.

"Really. I'll probably get sued up the ying-yang if it gets out."

Part of him, a large part of him, did not believe this was true. He just heard her turn a Kinks song on its head. And the Kinks had done a pretty good job of turning the song on its head in the first place. He knew what Prudence was capable of, and it was way beyond any frivolous soda pop jingle.

Prudence got up and continued pacing. Still wearing the sunglasses. "When I die, Mr. Millet, there won't be a scrap of me left. I think about that all the time."

"Did you want to be known for the commercial jingle?"

"That's just it."

"What is?"

"Scott Joplin."

"What about him?"

"What do you think of when you think of Scott Joplin?"

"Most famous ragtime composer who ever lived," Pierre Millet said. "Everyone knows 'Maple Leaf Rag.' "

"It was a highly successful, highly commercial piece. But at the end of his life, it was art he was after. He was succumbing to dementia, a result of syphilis that had long gone untreated. Terrible thing. So he worked as fast as he could to finish his opera before his mind was completely gone. *Treemonisha*—that's the name of the opera—was everything to him. It was genius. Ahead of his time, as was he. I get it. That compulsion. That urgency. This morning, I avoided the trash trucks in my neighborhood because I didn't want one to hit my little car accidentally."

"Death is around every corner, Prudence."

"It's a mindset. You know you have something in you that needs to get out. Mozart, Puccini, Tchaikovsky. They all died working on something that was *nearly* finished. Okay, well maybe Tchaikovsky finished his sixth symphony, but he died nine days after its premiere. You get to a certain age and you realize death is inevitable. It becomes your biggest motivator. If I pull this off, Mr. Millet, you can shoot me the next morning and I'd die happy. This is my *Treemonisha,* this silly little show."

Pierre Millet smiled. "Yes," he said. "I think I understand."

CHAPTER FORTY

Once Upon a Dream

Tamara Quigley was born three weeks prematurely, four days before Halloween. Her mother—who already had two boys and had not planned on getting pregnant a third time—was sitting at her sewing machine, where she was fashioning costumes for her sons, aged seven and nine, when she went into labor. The costumes were never completed, and the brothers resented the football-shaped bundle who had ruined their trick-or-treating.

Because she was a preemie, Tamara Quigley stayed in the hospital for three weeks. Tamara's mom was forty, the birth was difficult, and she was exhausted. Mrs. Quigley resented having to change diapers at her age. To make matters worse, Mr. Quigley was not sure he loved Mrs. Quigley anymore. He resented Tamara's birth and the feeling that he was even more stuck in his marriage than before.

It was under this cloud of resentment that Tamara Quigley took her place in the world.

But she was a beautiful baby who smiled easily. She had red hair the color of new pennies, soft little ringlets that curled around her head. She had large blue eyes and a round face and freckles sprinkled across the bridge of her nose.

She grew to love ruffled dresses and plastic barrettes in the shape of bows. She had a Minnie Mouse wristwatch with a red leather band that she wound every morning.

But her favorite thing in the world was her music box. Each evening before her bath, Tamara turned the little brass key and unlatched the lid and a ballerina in a pink tutu popped up and spun to the music of *Swan Lake*. Then Tamara would twirl and leap around her pink room. She loved ballerinas.

But her brothers, who had absorbed the stress of the adults in the household, were cruel to their much younger sister.

They put spiders in her bed and squirted shaving cream in her shoes. They liked to hide the little brass key from the music box so that Tamara could not watch the ballerina spin. When the little brass key had been lost for good, Tamara used a wrench to wind her beloved toy.

The boys also liked to tell Tamara she'd been an accident. Not wanted at all. When she cried, they called her a baby. When she told on them, they called her a tattletale. Mrs. Quigley did not intervene. Her heart was as tough as an orange peel. She told Tamara teasing was good for the character, as one must develop a thick skin to navigate life.

By the time Tamara Quigley turned six, she did not smile as easily anymore.

But she continued to love ballet, and she began to take lessons at the local studio. Tamara was not tall, nor did she have long arms. But she could twist and stretch them as if they were made of elastic. Her legs were short but they were strong and she could jump very high. She had a low center of gravity and could spin effortlessly from one end of the room to the other.

Tamara dreamt of becoming a professional dancer. Her parents did not encourage her, but neither did they object when she won a scholarship to an arts camp in Michigan the year she turned nine. It was cheaper than shelling out for ballet classes all summer, they told themselves.

And young Tamara Quigley excelled at camp. She had passion

and skill, and one fed the other into a perpetual cycle of growth, and even bliss.

Unfortunately, that cycle was disrupted by "the Incident." After Tamara met Prudence Paddington, after the wildly misinterpreted comment, the flubbed solo, and the disinterest from the scouts and talent agents, Tamara no longer believed in her skills as a dancer. Since she no longer believed in her skills, she did not love dancing as much. She quit, which disappointed her parents. The money they had spent. They would not make the same mistake again.

The light inside Tamara had gone out. She was no longer vulnerable to her brothers so she was no longer ridiculed. This was the thick skin her mother told her she must have.

But a thick skin is terrible for art—and for empathy.

Although Tamara moved on, the disappointment of her past was never too far from her psyche.

This damaged woman was the Tamara Quigley who, thirty-five years after her fateful meeting with Prudence, rendezvoused with Bobby Wheeler on a bench at Fountain Park. She had a plan.

CHAPTER FORTY-ONE

Fantasia in D Minor

Fountain Park was exactly the sort of idyllic spot you might see in a commercial for allergy medication. Children were whooshing down yellow slides and gliding around on bright scooters. A young family tore chunks from a baguette to feed the ducks. Couples walked dogs around the lake, chatting amicably. Not to mention the fountain itself. People came from all over the world to see this miracle of engineering, which, every hour on the hour, shot a spectacularly giant plume of water six hundred feet into the air. It was, as anyone from the area would tell you, one of the world's tallest man-made fountains.

But Tamara did not notice the fountain when it roared to life at precisely four o'clock that afternoon. She did not notice the way it teased the sky. She did not notice the children or the slides or the scooters. Or the ducks. She was preoccupied with her plan. And how, with Bobby Wheeler's help, she would expose Prudence as a fraud. Like Woodward and Bernstein, those reporters who took Nixon down.

Tamara was a justice warrior. A punctual one at that.

Bobby Wheeler, however, was late.

When he finally showed up at 4:15, he plopped his large body on the park bench next to Tamara.

"Everything okay?" she asked.

"I don't know," he said. "I guess I'm not sure about taking this public."

"Listen, she's a plagiarist. She's gotten away with it for *years*."

"I guess." Plagiarism sounded despicable when Tamara talked about it. Bobby Wheeler didn't think it was the worst moral failing.

"You guess? People shouldn't get credit for something they didn't actually do."

Bobby Wheeler chewed his gum and watched a toddler toss far too much bread to the ducks. Then he said, "Maybe this isn't the right way." It had started out as something between Bobby and Prudence. Something that would help him get out of the hole he had dug for himself, with a bit of comeuppance for Prudence on the side. Now that this Tamara was involved he worried that it was getting away from him. Things had a habit of getting away from Bobby Wheeler.

"You'd be doing the network a favor."

"How?" He didn't think to ask the bigger question, which was why he, Bobby Wheeler, would want to do a favor for a television network.

"Hang on, I'm about to explain. But if you're saying you don't need the money anymore, let's just forget it."

"I do, though," he said. "I'm in debt. Really in debt."

"Child support?"

Bobby Wheeler didn't want to reveal the reason he was broke to Tamara. It was too embarrassing. "No, I don't have kids."

"Hmm, well, whatever it is, I'm sure it's not *your* fault."

"No! It wasn't my fault." Finally, someone who understood.

"You can tell me, you know. Maybe I can help."

Bobby Wheeler shrugged. "It's stupid."

"We've all done stupid things."

He slid a finger under his sunglasses and rubbed his eye. He was tired of keeping this inside him. "There was this girl, Candy; she'd messaged me through the Heart-2-Hearts dating site."

"Oh?" Tamara adjusted her tennis visor.

"She was pretty, you know? In the photo she sent me, she was sitting in a 1973 Chevy Corvette. The '73 L82 model? I mean, I thought, a girl into vintage 'vettes?"

"Sure. Who wouldn't be drawn to a pretty girl in a classic car?"

"She liked baseball, too."

"Seems like you two had a lot in common."

"We did! I mean, I thought we did."

"Don't tell me she broke it off with you." Tamara's tone was heavy with sympathy.

"Let's just say, she was after something more," Bobby Wheeler said.

She peered at him, her thick red hair obscuring everything except the bill of her visor. "Oh, no. Like what?"

Bobby Wheeler tugged on the hem of his shorts. "Cash. She always needed some. She told me she'd pay me back. Never did and now I'm about to lose my condo."

Tamara had to suppress a smile. (A smirk, actually.) He was exactly where she needed him—in deep and vulnerable. "Listen, you won't have to worry about money after this. You'll have plenty."

Bobby Wheeler nodded. He didn't tell her the rest. He didn't tell her that, in the end, he hadn't wanted to let the relationship go, even though he knew something about Candy didn't add up.

At first, she was just someone to talk to. After meeting on the dating site, they started exchanging messages. She said she lived in Texas but was often traveling. Because she was a model. Could she come see him in the Bay Area? he'd asked. That'd be difficult, she told him. Because she was always going in the *other* direction. Like to New York. And Paris. And Milan. But someday. Someday soon.

They kept messaging and Bobby Wheeler asked if she liked baseball and she said she loved baseball so they watched games together online. The more time passed, the less Bobby Wheeler felt lonesome. Candy was nice. He did wonder at first whether the photo was real. But the longer things went on, and the more photos she sent, the more he looked forward to their chat sessions. And the more he paired the face with the person on the other end. Bobby Wheeler fell in love, in the online sense of love. It was easy.

Fantasy and imagination in full force.

It wasn't until week three that she asked for money. Five hundred dollars for a plane ticket because she had a modeling gig in Paris and wouldn't get paid right away and there was some sort of problem with her credit card. Okay, sure, Bobby Wheeler had $500 to help her out.

He loved her. Or he needed her—it was getting hard to tell the difference. And she needed more and more money. There was the hotel room in Milan, the rent back home in Dallas, new pictures for her modeling portfolio. She'd pay him back when she got her modeling checks, she promised.

Bobby Wheeler didn't have that much money to begin with and soon he had drained his savings. That's when he started using the company credit card to wire the payments. It was just a loan, he told himself. Fraudulent invoices for brake pads. And alternators. And shocks. Bobby Wheeler did not like to think of himself as a bad person. He justified the thefts. Vantage had put a freeze on raises and his salary hadn't gone up in over two years. So this thieving took the place of a much-deserved raise. Besides, it wasn't like he was stealing from an actual person. He never would've done that.

Anyway, it got out of control.

When he tried to sell a 2017 Camaro that had belonged to Vantage Car Rental, he altered the VIN number and was caught. Of course, he got fired. Lucky for Bobby, Vantage declined to press charges. Attorney fees and time spent to successfully prosecute their former employee didn't seem worth it. It would be best to just fire him and try to get the money back.

Candy ditched Bobby when he told her. Fast. According to the FBI, who got involved after Vantage Car Rental contacted them in hopes of retrieving their money, "Candy" was actually a group of guys running a fraud ring out of Nigeria.

Bobby Wheeler now had exactly three weeks to make his first payment to Vantage Rental Car if he wanted to stay out of jail.

"How soon could I get the cash?" he asked Tamara.

This would be a delicate process. Tamara would have to time it just right. She didn't trust the media—it was too easy for stories to get buried in the news cycle. She wanted Prudence to experience a sweep of humiliation on national television the night of the competition. Just like Tamara had thirty-five years ago at the doomed ballet recital.

Proportion didn't seem to matter to Tamara. She made no distinction between a summer camp and national television. That was always one of her problems. Everything was too important.

"I'm working on it. I just need the original Pep Soda manuscript with the handwritten note on the back," she said.

"What will you do with it?"

"I have the perfect connection to help us pull this off."

"What kind of connection?"

It was at this point that Tamara spun the lie that Bobby Wheeler would not unravel until it was too late. "I have a sorority sister I'm in contact with. She works for the network that produces *Alexei Petrov's Dueling Piano Wars!*"

"Really?"

"Yep. You know the prize is a *million* dollars." Tamara Quigley emphasized "million," knowing that's what Bobby Wheeler's brain would process above all else.

"You sure it's that much?"

"Check the website, it's all on there."

"But how would we get the money?"

"You want to keep this quiet, right?"

"Definitely."

"My sorority sister can get me backstage right before the show."

"But that's all the way at the end of October, and I have to pay off my debt before Halloween," said Bobby. "Why can't we do it now?"

"Timing is everything. The more the network has invested in the show, the more they have to lose. No one is going to want this to get out minutes before showtime. I'll simply show the letter to one of the network executives backstage. I'll tell them that if the prize money isn't handed over to you, I'll give the manuscript to the press and expose their main attraction as a fraud. They'll have no choice—not unless they want to turn their biggest night of television for the year into a sham."

Tamara Quigley was well aware that this plan had more holes than a roll of Life Savers. But Bobby Wheeler was too focused on how he was going to get Vantage their money.

A million dollars sounded pretty good to Bobby Wheeler. "You're going to a lot of trouble. You sure it's okay if I only pay you ten percent?"

"*Please*. It's fine," Tamara said. "I'm most interested in justice."

"If you say so," said Bobby with a shrug.

"So we're agreed?" asked Tamara. "You'll give me the manuscript, and I'll fly out to L.A. the Thursday before the special?"

"Wait, I thought we were a team. I want to come, too."

She hadn't counted on this. "I really think it would be better if I went alone. All I need is your banking information so they can wire you the money."

"But why can't I come? If I'm with you, they can just hand me a check."

She had no intention of taking Bobby Wheeler with her. Once she got what she wanted, she would no longer need him. "I'm worried Prudence might catch you backstage. I mean, if she sees you anywhere near that competition, you know . . . she'd . . . she'd think you were up to something. Right? The plan would be ruined. So you really can't be there. It's too risky."

This Tamara was pretty bossy. Bobby Wheeler did not like bossy people. His mom had been bossy. That's why Prudence left him, because of his bossy mom.

He could feel himself losing control of the situation. "This is Prudence's document."

"What? You're not having second thoughts, are you?"

"No."

The truth was, Bobby Wheeler was having second, third, and fourth thoughts. "Maybe if she bought it back from me?"

"You tried that."

"Maybe if she knew we were going to go public with this—"

"No! You can't tell her anything about what we're planning. Don't be dumb, Mr. Wheeler."

Tamara had a lot to learn about Bobby Wheeler. Like how quickly his insides could turn from pink to black.

Tamara did not pick up on the slight change in her accomplice's tone. "You're not thinking this thing through," she said.

He raised his voice to the first notch. "I am too thinking this through." He said this loud enough that an elderly couple walking their beagle momentarily stopped their conversation and looked up.

"Shhhhhhh!" hissed Tamara.

Bobby Wheeler stood, covering Tamara in his shadow, and his voice went up to the second notch. "Don't order me around!"

The anger in his eyes flared like the cherry of a cigarette. At last, Tamara realized what she was dealing with. "Okay, okay, lower your voice," she said. "Look, of course you're not stupid."

Bobby Wheeler relaxed his shoulders. He looked around at the couples walking their dogs. He looked around at the couples in the café drinking an afternoon glass of wine. And he looked around at the couples with children who fed the ducks.

Why couldn't he be part of a couple?

While Bobby Wheeler thought about what he didn't have, Tamara Quigley was processing his potential for violence. She understood that if the scales tipped a little too far in either direction, the whole thing would topple. She only had three weeks until the special aired.

"You're right, you should fly out with me. We're a team. How about this . . . since you're short on cash, I'll buy the plane ticket for you."

"That would help me out a lot, Ms. Quigley."

"Happy to do it. Now just to make sure we're all good here, I'll need the manuscript."

"Why?"

Tamara had to think fast. "Where are you staying while you're in town, a hotel?"

"Motel. Desert Vista Motor Lodge."

"The residential motel?" It was notorious for its monthly rent-ers, the type who didn't sign apartment leases because they couldn't afford the up-front costs like security deposits and first and last month's rent.

"It's all I could afford."

"Think about it, Mr. Wheeler. As of now, that manuscript is worth a million dollars. You think it's safe to leave a million dollars in a motel room?"

It wasn't a very nice place, the motor lodge. Bobby Wheeler thought about how men hung out in the parking lot at night by their trucks and smoked cigarettes and drank beer and smashed bottles on the ground. How, anytime he left to go somewhere, he could feel someone watching him as he locked his room. "I could keep it in my bag, which I always have with me."

"All it would take is one careless moment, like leaving it in a restaurant or on the seat of your car . . . a million dollars." Again, she peered at him from under the bill of her visor. "I have a safe in my house," she lied. "It's where I keep birth certificates and other official documents in case of a fire. The manuscript would be very secure in there."

He chewed on the inside of his cheek and took out a clear plastic folder. Bobby Wheeler removed the envelope from the folder to show Tamara Quigley the postmark. "See that, November 14, 1986. And here," he said, "here's the letter. On the back is the jingle."

Tamara Quigley read the letter, keeping it in the plastic so as not to damage it. She turned it over and studied the iconic score. History in her hands. She carefully slid the plastic folder into her handbag. Then she smiled as she exhaled and said, "Okay, here's the plan."

CHAPTER FORTY-TWO

In Through the Out Door

Alexei's new living room was different in every way from the old one. The old living room had beautiful travertine floors and exquisite area rugs and damask curtains. Floor-to-ceiling windows that looked out onto the twinkling lights of Los Angeles. Oil paintings and bronze sculptures and a very cool art deco coffee table.

This new living room had brown carpet that smelled of cigarette smoke, vertical blinds that were bent and broken, windows that looked out onto a neighbor's broken and battered fence. There was no artwork in this living room, no fancy art deco coffee table. In the new living room, there were two plastic chairs Alexei found out back on the crumbling patio as well as a brown sofa and two end tables left by the previous owner.

The movers, who had packed up the Model A in the old living room, looked around the new living room and wondered *Why?* Then they got down to work, assembling the Steinway on the worn and soiled carpet. Alexei thought the piano was somehow shinier and glossier and more spectacular in the middle of all the chaos and wear. All the movers could think was how it about took up the entire room.

"Good luck, mate!" one of them called as they gathered up their equipment and left.

"Thanks, mate!" Alexei called back. He felt a solidarity with the workingman, a sort of scruffy independence prompted by his new surroundings. Alexei Petrov looked at the little gray cat nestled on the ugly couch and smiled.

He was finally free to hang whatever he wanted on the walls. Free to stock the fridge with whatever he wanted. Free to keep to his hours. At twenty-two years old, Alexei was finally in control.

With all the packing and the moving, and the club playing, he had been way off his regular practice schedule. He was on his own now. He could not afford the instructors. No afternoon massages. No meals of figs and salmon. No analytical sessions with the novelist who was also a poet.

But he had his teapot. And his cat. And his piano.

He also had some beer in the fridge. However, the beer was strictly an end-of-the-day thing now, to be consumed in reasonable quantities and not all in one sitting or chased by tequila shots and a belly full of gas station nachos.

And when he won the competition and got his TV deal and his line of tuxedos, he would, once again, have money for luxuries. He would never again ask his parents for money. He would prove to them that he could succeed without their micromanagement.

With this in mind, Alexei Petrov settled down at the Model A. He released the pendulum on the metronome and began warming up with finger exercises and scales. Every so often he looked over at the little gray cat.

This was all going to work out!

He had not yet finished his B-flat major scale when there was a knock at his door. He ignored it, as Alexei hated to be interrupted while practicing.

Another round of knocking. Again this was ignored and the B-flat major scale continued.

The knocking then turned to pounding. Alexei Petrov turned off the metronome and opened his door and there stood a gentleman in his underwear.

"Sir, what is it I can help you with?" Alexei asked.

"You can shut the fuck up," the gentleman in his underwear said.

"Excuse me?"

"The music. It's rattling the windows and it has to stop."

"I'm practicing. I'm a pianist."

"Yeah? Look, buddy, we have a joint wall, you and I, and we've got to get a few things straight. I work the graveyard shift at Paddy Cakes."

"Where?"

"Paddy Cakes? The bakery? I'm a baker."

"You make cakes?"

"I make bread." The gentleman in the underwear folded his arms in front of his chest and said, "I go to work at eleven at night and I finish at seven in the morning. That means I sleep in the day and I don't wanna hear you pounding on that thing while I'm trying to rest."

"But I'm a pianist."

"And I told you, I'm a baker. I have to work at night, so everyone can have their bread in the morning."

Never in his life had Alexei Petrov had his practice hours restricted. This was the one thing he hadn't counted on: neighbors. At his old house, he did not have neighbors. But now he did. And it was a problem. "When can I practice?"

"Do I look like your mother? Figure it out, man. Just don't do it when I'm sleeping."

"When do you sleep?"

"From nine in the morning until five at night."

"Those are precisely the hours I practice," Alexei Petrov said.

The baker's eyes blew up to the size of nickels. "That is definitely not gonna work."

"Well, we have to figure something out because I must practice."

"*You* figure something out. I'm going back to bed."

CHAPTER FORTY-THREE

Baby Elephant Walk

Alexei stood in his new living room and tried not to panic.

Maybe he could do some exercises quietly by pressing the soft pedal. He went back to the Model A and started in on *Hanon*'s #35 when he heard a pounding on the wall, followed by a muffled, "Don't make me come back there, man. I'm not gonna be so nice this time!"

"Fuck," Alexei muttered.

He picked up the little gray cat. "Where can one find a piano not in use at nine thirty on a Thursday morning? Where, my little sun? Where?"

She nuzzled and purred and licked his nose and it hit Alexei Petrov so quickly he gave 100 percent credit to the little gray cat. "A church!"

He googled churches in his area and found a Baptist one a few streets away. Packing his satchel with his music and his travel metronome, he kissed his cat and got into his Mercedes.

The Calvary Baptist Church was a redbrick structure, an enormous white steeple pitched on its roof. Alexei entered and saw, adjacent to the sacristy, a small office in which an elderly woman sat stuffing envelopes. She wore a name tag with "Margaret" printed across the front.

"Good morning, Margaret," Alexei said.

"Good morning, dear."

"My name is Alexei Petrov."

"Hello, Alexei. My name is Margaret Paisley." She always forgot about her name tag. "How can I help you?"

"I am a pianist and I was wondering if there was a piano in the building I could use for a practice session?"

Margaret pulled a wadded tissue from her sleeve and wiped her nose. "There's one in the basement," she said. "It's the Sunday school piano."

A basement, excellent. Privacy at last.

"Ah, very good. I've got a performance coming up and I need to prepare."

Alexei did not tell Margaret how long he needed to practice. He would cross that bridge when he got to it.

"You are welcome to it, young man."

Alexei wanted to drop to the floor and kiss Margaret Paisley's feet in gratitude. He thanked her over and over and she directed him to the basement and he thanked her some more.

This was all going to work out!

THE PIANO WAS an ancient Wurlitzer upright and in terrible shape. It was horribly out of tune, the action was shot, and someone—presumably a child—had used a crayon to write the letters to the alphabet across the ivory keys. When they ran out of letters, they started on numbers.

It was a far and distant cry from the Steinway Salon Grand Model A in Alexei's current living room. But that didn't matter. He could not afford to spend his morning looking for another piano. This would have to do until he figured something else out. He took the music and his travel metronome from his satchel, then placed them on the stand.

Again, he began his *Hanon* finger exercises.

Again, he was interrupted.

"What're you doing playing Mrs. Weatherby's piano?" asked a child with bed head and a runny nose.

"Who?"

"My Sunday school teacher, Mrs. Weatherby. She won't let anyone touch the piano."

From the looks of things, Alexei could understand such a rule. "I'm only borrowing it."

"But no one's supposed to touch it 'cept her. If she catches us, we don't get our donut."

"It's okay. I've got special permission from the high sheriffs around here."

"Who?"

"The woman who works in the office upstairs."

"That's Mrs. Paisley and she's not a sheriff. My mom lets her answer the phone and stuff 'cause Mr. Paisley died and she gets sad. My mom's in charge of the office stuff."

"Fine, Mrs. Paisley told me I could play this piano."

"You can't climb on it, either."

"Tough, but fair. Now, young man, I have work to do, so if you could just leave me to it." Because with every minute that ticked by, Alexei became more and more anxious. He was not used to interruptions. Or crappy pianos. Or prying children.

He needed to focus. Clear his mind. Warm his fingers up.

But the child did not move. "My name's Holden."

Alexei let out a puff of exasperated air. "Right, Holden, listen, I really need to get to work."

"What's your name?"

"Alexei."

"That's a funny name."

"I'm from Russia."

"My dad told me that Russians are bad people."

"Oh?"

"They middle in American elections."

"Meddle."

"What does that mean?"

"To interfere. Like you're doing at this very moment. Why aren't you in school?"

"I'm sick. Mom says I can't stay home by myself so I haf'ta come to work with her."

"Please don't breathe on me, I cannot afford to get sick right now."

"I won't."

"I have to practice."

"Okay."

"You have to go."

"Why?"

"I need privacy. Besides, it's just scales. Very boring."

"Do you know any songs?"

Alexei threw back his head and groaned. "Yes, Holden, of course."

"Can you play me one?"

"No!"

" 'Kay."

"I need you to go and leave me alone. Is that clear?"

"Yes." Holden was six and he was a good kid. He was also an intuitive kid. Absorbing the change of tone, he made his way to the staircase without any further resistance.

Alexei was clear for takeoff. But there was something in Holden's unquestioning obedience that gave him pause. It bothered him. Some sadness tugged deep inside him. Alexei had no right to be impatient with a child who was merely curious about music.

"Holden."

The boy was halfway up the staircase when he turned around. "What?" he answered, threading his arms through the railing and leaning forward.

"I'm sorry," Alexei said.

"What you sorry for, Alexei?"

"I was rude."

"S'okay."

"No, it's not. Would you like to hear a song?"

An enthusiastic Holden nodded his head, then jumped down five steps and ran back to the piano.

"What would you like to hear?" Alexei asked.

"Mrs. Weatherby always plays 'Five Little Ducks.' "

"I'm not sure I know it but if you sing it I can figure it out."

"I don't want to hear that one," Holden said.

"Okay," Alexei said, "pick another."

"Mm, I can't remember the name of it."

"Is it a song from the radio?"

Holden shook his head along with his shoulders. "It's from a play we had at our school."

"What is the name of the play?"

"I don't know."

Alexei could feel his insides tightening like a drawstring. Still, he resisted the temptation to dismiss Holden a second time. "Can you tell me what the play was about?"

"It was about a girl who had to go to a place when you don't have parents. I don't remember what that's called."

"An orphanage? Was the name of the play *Annie*?"

"Yes! How did you know?"

"I know a lot of things."

"Like what?"

"Like how you need a tissue. Your nose is running."

Holden ran to the bathroom and came back with a clump of toilet paper.

"Right, here we go," Alexei said. "I'll play you a medley of the score."

"What's that mean?"

"It is a sampling of all the songs."

And then one of the world's best piano players played to an audience of one in a musty basement for a ticket price of zero dollars. Alexei played "It's a Hard Knock Life" and "Maybe" and the showstopper, "Tomorrow."

It sounded like shit on the terrible piano. Not to Holden, though. To him, it was nothing short of magical.

When Alexei finished, Holden stared at Alexei's hands as if he had the powers of a wizard. Then he said breathlessly, "I wish Mrs. Weatherby would let us touch the piano. I want to do that!"

"Tell your mother you want to take lessons."

"Does it cost money?"

"Yes."

Holden shrugged. "She won't let me."

"*Let* you?" For Alexei, it had never been a choice.

"Also, we don't have a piano."

"Don't let that stop you."

Holden wiped his nose and Alexei studied him for a minute. Oh, god, what was he about to do? He had to practice and he had no time for this. But something inside him was tugging and pulling and kicking at his heart.

"Holden, I'm going to give you permission to touch the piano, okay?"

"Will I still get my donut?"

"Absolutely. Would you like to learn a song?"

Holden nodded and gazed at the keyboard. There were so many keys, you couldn't tell one from another. But Holden was six years old. He was in the right place at the right time. Anything Alexei taught him, Holden's brain would soak up like watercolors on parchment paper. Such was the miracle of the young brain.

Alexei moved over and Holden climbed up on the bench. "Do you know your left hand from your right?" Alexei asked.

Holden held up his right hand and said, "This is the hand I write my name with."

Alexei took Holden's right hand and placed his thumb on middle C and the rest of the fingers on D, E, F, G.

"When I sing," Alexei instructed, "play the first note, then the next."

Alexei sang *do,* Holden played C, when Alexei sang *re,* Holden played D; and on up so that *do, re, mi, fa, sol* was C, D, E, F, G.

Alexei repeated the exercise. This time, Holden sang with Alexei *and* played the notes.

They did this together three times.

"Very good. Do you know 'Twinkle, Twinkle, Little Star'?"

"*Evvvv*erybody knows that song!"

"Well, let's learn how to play it," Alexei said. "I want you to sing 'Twinkle, Twinkle, Little Star' and press the keys. Let your ears direct your fingers. Don't worry if you press the wrong note at first. Your brain will correct itself. Mistakes are crucial to learning. But you have to sing, do you hear me? That is very important."

"Okay!"

Never was there a more suited or willing pupil. Holden's ears were as ready to hear as a perfectly ripe peach is ready to eat.

"I'm going to count to four," Alexei told the boy. "Listen to the rhythm of my counting and then try to play it like that."

"What's wriv . . ."

"Rhythm."

"Wrivum."

"Right. For now, just listen to how fast or slow I count. Then you play just like that."

It took just three tries. As if learning to ride a bike, something was tripped in Holden's brain. Having never played a note in his life, he learned "Twinkle, Twinkle, Little Star" in the time it would take to brush his teeth.

His life was forever changed.

CHAPTER FORTY-FOUR

Moon River

Prudence was waiting for Stuart to come home from work. She sat on the chaise and watched the sun's waning rays reflect the dust and pollution of the desert. It was an extraordinary display. The sky glowed like a jewel.

As the orange light faded to gray, a single star seemed desperately to call attention to itself, shining brighter than all the others. Venus? Mercury? She could never remember. But it was there, urgently winking as if to tell her something. Her mind went to Pierre Millet. She had to call him. She had to tell him that when she played the rolling arpeggios in the second movement of the Debussy piece she could hear each note separately and together at the same time. That abstraction, she discovered, was the draw of the piece. It was so wonderful to feel something new in the music.

Prudence dialed Pierre Millet's number. A woman answered. "Hello?" said the tired voice.

Prudence glanced at her phone to make sure she'd dialed correctly. "I'm Prudence Childs. I was looking for Mr. Millet."

The pause was so long that Prudence said, "Hello?"

Something was wrong.

"I'm sorry, Ms. Childs." It was the housekeeper.

"You're sorry?" asked Prudence. Sorry was not good.

"Mr. Millet passed away this afternoon."

"No!"

"I'm sorry."

Prudence's first reaction was disbelief. The housekeeper had gotten it wrong. "But he's supposed to play at the Ocean Club tonight. He told me this morning."

Another long pause. "I know, Ms. Childs. We were all caught off guard."

It was a stroke, the housekeeper said. He took his usual lunch of pickled beets and boiled eggs. He took his usual nap. That was it. He never woke up.

PRUDENCE HAD NOT yet dealt with the death of a parent, which is what Pierre Millet's death felt like. Unlike her absentee parents, he had believed in her and encouraged her. Because of him, she could finally begin to believe in herself.

"My *petite chienne, je ne sais pas,*" Prudence said to Mrs. Wintour. "How to go on?"

The little dog raised herself and placed her front paws on Prudence's knees. *A walk, my mistress.* Mrs. Wintour was very good at communicating these sorts of things.

"Yes, a walk," Prudence said. "Mr. Millet would be angry with me if I gave up now."

So they set out for a walk. They went down Pricklypoppy Lane and up Vista Verde Drive and around DeSoto Avenue. Prudence thought of all the things Pierre Millet had given her. How he was not only aware of her gift, but all her doubts, too. *Listen to the music as you play, all of what you need is inside. The music will draw it out of you. Listen closely enough and the music will never let you down.* He was the consummate mentor. The first time she could ever trust someone artistically. Pierre Millet had no agenda except to get Prudence to be the very best she could be, a startling contrast to Granny Paddington and her abusive ways. Prudence had imagined collaborating with him after the competition, someone to guide her for whatever came after. Like concerts and television performances and even endorsements.

And now he was gone.

Prudence and Mrs. Wintour returned to 10534 Pricklypoppy Lane. As they made their way up the driveway, her neighbor opened her door and stood in the threshold. Mrs. Castilla looked tired and sad. Her once perfectly coiffed page boy was overgrown and hung in loose tangles around her face. The silk blouses and chic pencil skirts had been replaced with faded shorts and a wrinkled shirt that wasn't properly buttoned. Prudence remembered that Tamara Quigley said the neighbors had been complaining. From the looks of things, Mrs. Debra Castilla was one of them.

As they stood outside their doors in the dusk, neither woman was sure of what to say. Which was strange because both of them very much wanted to say something. Mrs. Debra Castilla shifted nervously. Her mouth opened quickly and just as quickly shut again. Of course. If Prudence was sick of playing Debussy, Mrs. Castilla must be sick of hearing it. The effect on her neighbor was obvious. Prudence nodded nervously and hurried inside. She would have to find somewhere else to practice or this poor woman wouldn't last the week.

What Prudence didn't know was that earlier that evening, when Prudence had been practicing, Mrs. Debra Castilla had crept out onto her veranda and lay on the chaise lounge and closed her eyes and smiled. A single tear rolled down her cheek like a raindrop. Oh, sleep would come now.

Then the music stopped.

Mrs. Debra Castilla—well, the *former* Mrs. Debra Castilla—did not want the music to stop. When Mrs. Castilla saw Prudence returning from her walk, she wanted to tell Prudence how the music had saved her. She wanted to tell Prudence about her *annus horribilis*. How, last spring, her husband of twenty-five years had up and left her for another. The nasty divorce. The feelings of inadequacy. The blue days and the dark nights. The loneliness. The insomnia. The hopelessness.

Until one empty September night she heard the most beautiful music. It was three in the morning and insomnia had sent Mrs. Castilla outside to get the night air. The music was magical. It was comforting. Because someone else was up and she wasn't alone. That's all you need, sometimes. One other person. This realization got the former Mrs. Debra Castilla through September, and into October, as she sat on her veranda and listened to the sweet strains of Debussy and Beethoven and Rachmaninoff. Her own private concert. She was no longer lonely. No longer alone.

The music in the night gave her hope in the day.

It gave the former Mrs. Debra Castilla hope right up until Tamara Quigley stepped in.

Not one neighbor complained, as Prudence had been led to think.

The neighbor to the left of Prudence, Mr. John Porter, formerly of Chanhassen, Minnesota, had hearing aids that he removed at night. He wouldn't have been able to hear a bomb go off.

Further, all the houses on Pricklypoppy Lane were situated on one-acre lots and adequately spaced from one another. Unless Prudence pushed her piano out into the driveway, it wasn't possible for anyone to be disturbed by the playing save for the neighbor directly to the right and the neighbor directly to the left—Mr. John Porter and the former Mrs. Debra Castilla.

Once inside, the fear of losing her home set off a fresh wave of anxiety. Prudence pined for her children and the comfort and safety of her old life. She called Tess but it went to voicemail. Tess texted back: on a party bus, what's up?

Prudence began the reply: I miss you.

But then quickly deleted it and instead typed: Have fun.

Who wants to be on a party bus and get a mopey text from your mom?

Prudence then remembered the story of Puccini's death. He died without completing his final opera, *Turandot*. The evening of its premiere, the conductor Arturo Toscanini put down his baton at the end of the third act and said, "Here ends the opera, left incomplete by the maestro and his death." Neither the orchestra nor Toscanini had the will to go on.

At the next evening's performance, Toscanini gathered his strength and told the orchestra, "The maestro did not want the opera to die with him, he so believed in it." They performed the opera again, this time with a new ending, written by a loving and skilled admirer of the maestro. "Long live Puccini!" cried the audience in a swell of emotion.

Art must be stronger than death.

Prudence looked out on the glowing desert, the same place she brooded after dropping Becca off and feeling there was nothing left except death. She'd come so far since that afternoon. And it then occurred to her with stunning clarity. Mrs. Martinelli, a woman who so believed in Prudence, had offered up her own *Turandot* so Prudence could fully realize her talent.

She reminded herself of what her future could be. *A piece of music can be written with two different endings. The first time through you play the first ending, the second time through, skip the first ending as a final measure denotes a second ending.*

Hadn't Pierre Millet spent his final days leading her to this? The music would never let her down. Only the voices of doubt.

This is my second ending, Prudence thought. *The power to live the life of my dreams is, quite literally, in my hands.*

CHAPTER FORTY-FIVE

Charade

Prudence woke rested and ready, with electricity in her heart that extended like a current to her fingers. Two days to go. Their suitcases were packed, waiting by the front door. Stuart was upstairs shaving while Prudence sat before her piano one last time and played "Brahms' Lullaby." A surrealness had set in. She had not quite believed this day would come, like a much-anticipated wedding or graduation. Or an execution. All the practicing and planning, the late nights, the joy and the fear, the highs and lows, all of it filling the space between. But the day had indeed arrived. She would be leaving soon and couldn't quite wrap her mind around it.

Prudence's phone rang. It was Tess. She was somewhat emotional. Like her sister, she could not fly to California because of midterms.

"I wanted to wish you luck one more time," Tess said. "I wish I could be there with you."

"I know. I love you, sweetheart."

"I love you, too, Mom. I'll be watching."

Her daughters were about to see an entirely different dimension of their mother, one that had been kept from them until this moment. Now that they were coming into their own as adults, they could finally understand.

Prudence reached into the leather tote bag that held her sheet music and pulled out a child's bracelet, pink plastic beads strung together with a thin elastic band. A cheap drugstore trinket that had once belonged to Tess and that Prudence could not bear to part with. A nostalgic heirloom from a past life. Prudence slid the bracelet onto her wrist. There were no feelings of sadness and longing now. Only a rush of tenderness and love.

Stuart clipped downstairs, zipping his carry-on. "Are we ready to load up?"

"I am so ready!"

He embraced his wife. "Ah, my darling, I'm proud of you."

"I'm glad you'll be with me. I can't imagine doing this alone."

"Nothing can stop me from being by your side." His wife was going to blow the roof off the place on live television!

"Shall we?"

"Let's!"

They went out front where the car was parked. While Stuart loaded their bags into the trunk, Prudence walked Mrs. Wintour out to pee as the dog sitter would not arrive until noon. The little eight-pound dog bounced down the stone walk, sniffing around for a place to do some business.

Prudence had a lot on her mind. A great many things would be happening in the next two days and she was distracted. That's likely why she did not notice the rattler out sunning himself beside the lantana bush. Rattlers do not like to be bothered when they sun themselves beside lantana bushes. Alas, Mrs. Wintour did not know this. Coming across the creature, she gave a little sniff. The snake rattled his tail in hopes she would leave him be. The rattling sounded like one of her toys. She did not want to leave him be.

It all happened so fast.

Prudence heard the rattling and shot down the walk. "NOOOOOOO!" Stuart ran after her. But it was too late. Mrs. Wintour let out a high-pitched yelp as the rattler struck and then slithered back under the shrubbery.

"Oh, little love!" Prudence scooped up her dog.

THE SECOND ENDING 281

"Keep the bite lower than the heart," Stuart said.

"Lower than the heart," Prudence repeated, trying to remain calm. "Got it."

"The faster she gets to the vet, the better."

"Let's hurry, then!" Prudence said as she headed toward the Jaguar.

"Prudence, you can't come with us."

"But I can't leave her, Stuart."

"We don't have time to argue. I need to take Mrs. Wintour to the vet. And you have got to make your plane."

They both knew what was going to happen next. An antivenin would be administered, and for the next forty-eight hours, Mrs. Wintour would need to be watched carefully. Any sign of increased swelling, weakness, or seizures and she would have to be rushed to the vet once more. Otherwise, she would die. Someone had to stay with her. That someone would have to be Stuart.

The dog whimpered and her breathing became ragged. Prudence's heart broke. "I can't do this alone."

"You can," Stuart said. "If anyone can do this, it's you."

"But Mrs. Wintour!"

"I'll take care of her."

Tearfully, Prudence put her little dog in her husband's arms. Pierre Millet was dead. Mrs. Wintour's life hung by a thread. Her children were consumed with midterm exams. Her husband was needed somewhere else.

She took a last look at her beautiful house, the one that might not be hers once she returned.

It was the fight of her life.

And she was going into battle alone.

PRUDENCE SWITCHED ON her phone the moment the plane touched down at Burbank International Airport. A text from Stuart: Mrs. Wintour responding to antivenin. Swelling down, she is stable. And then, You got this.

Time would tell.

The driver took Prudence down the famed Sunset Boulevard. Here were the iconic nightclubs like the Whisky a Go Go and the Viper Room. Here were grand movie-star homes where buses full of tourists hoped to get a glimpse of celebrities taking out the trash.

Here was traffic. Lots and lots of traffic. Advertisers love the traffic on the Sunset Strip, where commuters have no choice but to gaze at the enormous billboards that line the entire two-mile stretch.

Today, on one of those billboards, was a fourteen-foot image of Prudence herself. Her fingers grazing piano keys the size of a city bus, her green eyes blown up to the scale of small moons. Next to her, and nearly ten stories high, was an image of Alexei Petrov draped over a tall building. Dressed in a crisp tuxedo, leaning against his Model A Salon Grand, his image towered. Emblazoned across both billboards were the words: THE PRODIGY VERSUS THE LEGEND: ALEXEI PETROV'S DUELING PIANO WARS! FRIDAY, OCTOBER 27, 8 P.M.

Looking closely, Prudence saw herself through the years—from prodigy to artist, from child to an almost fifty-year-old woman— each version encased in the other like a set of Russian dolls. Music had always been there, she realized, like the color of her eyes or the birthmark on her arm. Prudence had never not been a pianist. Walking away had never been an option. Not now. Not three months ago. Not forty-five years ago.

As PRUDENCE WAS making her way down Sunset Boulevard, Bobby Wheeler was waiting for Tamara Quigley at the Delta bag check in Terminal 3 at Phoenix Sky Harbor Airport. Bobby Wheeler had taken care to dress in something other than his cargo shorts and flip-flops. He wore a collared golf shirt, his best khaki chinos, and a pair of polished loafers. The plan was to check in together so she could give him his boarding pass before proceeding through security.

Bobby Wheeler waited.

And waited.

And waited.

He texted Tamara Quigley, but her phone seemed to be in sleep mode. *Probably in a dead zone,* he thought. It did not occur to him to check the departure screen right in front of him. Had he done this, he would have been unable to find the fictitious flight number that Tamara had given him, glaring evidence that he'd been conned.

For Tamara Quigley was not in Phoenix Sky Harbor Airport. At least not anymore. She had flown out that morning, with the manuscript tucked carefully into her carry-on.

Five hours after Tamara Quigley had departed, Bobby Wheeler considered that he might be at the wrong airline. That's why he spent the next thirty minutes wandering around the bag checks for every airline in Terminal 3. Including Hawaiian Airlines.

Maybe it wasn't a bag check at all. Was it a bar?

He spent the following half hour wandering through bars. Then stores that sold turquoise jewelry and key chains with scorpions encased in Lucite. Then he spent a half hour wandering the little markets that sold magazines and candy.

That final half hour, after dismissing the possibility that he got the day wrong, Bobby Wheeler bought a bag of chips and came to the slow but inevitable realization that he'd been tricked. Hoodwinked. Scammed.

Bobby Wheeler was not happy about this. Not at all. He got into the dusty Chevy Aveo, slammed the door, and put the gearshift in drive.

CHAPTER FORTY-SIX

Someone Like You

Alexei was in no mood to meet Prudence. He was wound up after an argument with his mother, who insisted on coming from Paris the next day. Alexei did not want his parents to come to L.A.—not the next day, nor the day after that. It wasn't just because he was still angry with them for betraying his trust. He feared their strong presence. How his mother took control of any situation, how his father backed her up, even when he knew she was wrong. Alexei had come so far and did not want to fall back into his submissive ways.

And now he was expected to meet Prudence.

Alexei did not like meeting his rivals before a competition. He remembered this from his youth, how meeting an opponent could turn into a real mind game. Like the time Alexei was in Beijing for a competition. A pianist from Ukraine sought Alexei out, coming into the practice room to announce, "If you haven't heard, I won the Chopin competition in Warsaw last month."

That's what they did, opponents, they resorted to intimidation. The stakes were even higher now, much more public, and Alexei wasn't sure how this one-on-one meeting was supposed to play out. He wanted to cancel.

Les Strom was having none of it. "How would that look, Alexei? Tell me, how would that look?"

Alexei Petrov knew how that would look. It would be insulting and rude, two things that he was not. So he arrived in the Beverly Wilshire bar at five minutes after five only to discover that the famed Prudence Childs was not there.

He shifted anxiously in the booth and thought about ordering a glass of white wine, but he wanted to practice for a few more hours afterward. He settled on a glass of pink lemonade.

It was nearly 5:30 when the waiter refilled his glass. If there was no sign of Prudence in the next ten minutes, he would leave. He would tell Les Strom the truth, that Prudence never showed. The more Alexei thought about this, the more he wanted it to come true. He wanted to go home to pet his little gray cat. Yes, that is what he wanted.

Alexei had just signaled for the check when he felt a change in the air, as if a door had been blown open by a sudden gust of wind. He turned and there she was, a breeze of glamour in a short cream dress. She was smaller than he had imagined, yet her presence filled the entire room.

"Prudence Childs," she said, holding out her hand.

"Alexei Petrov." His long, smooth fingers shook her battered ones, the torn places held together with clear nail polish.

A moment passed between them, both unsure of how to proceed. Prudence broke the silence. "Sorry I'm late," she said. "I had to check out the practice piano in the ballroom."

"Oh. How is it?" he asked her.

"Not bad."

"Steinway, concert grand?"

"Yamaha."

"Really?"

"I know. When's the last time you played a Yamaha? I mean, it's a beautiful piano. But it's not a Steinway."

Alexei smiled. "Playing a Steinway is the difference between driving a Mercedes and a Cadillac."

"Exactly."

The waiter appeared. "Good evening, ma'am. Something to drink?"

"Dirty vodka martini, straight up."

"Very good," the waiter said. Then, turning to Alexei, "Another lemonade, sir?"

"You're not drinking?" Prudence said. "How rude of me. I'll have a pink lemonade as well."

Alexei Petrov felt childish just then. Like a schoolboy. A fresh wave of resentment washed over him. He wanted to appear as worldly as his billboard on the Sunset Strip.

"I'll have what she's having," Alexei said. The waiter nodded.

"I love martinis," Prudence said.

"Me, too," Alexei lied.

Prudence was surprised at how shy he was compared to the brash confidence he showed on TV. She sensed his discomfort. "How are you doing?" she asked warmly.

It was the most genuine question Alexei had been asked all week. But he was not ready to let down his guard. "Marvelous."

"Oh, good." Although she suspected it wasn't true.

"How about you?"

"Nervous," she said. "It's been a very long time."

Silence followed as the two competitors sized each other up, each one unsure of what to give—or take—from the other.

Again, it was Prudence who spoke first. "Favorite living composer?"

"Easy. Philip Glass."

"Good choice."

"You?"

"Wynton Marsalis. The master in both jazz *and* classical music." Prudence dug an olive out of her drink. "If you could go back in time to meet one nonliving composer, who would it be? For me, it'd be Rachmaninoff. Dinner, drinks, a private concert."

"For me, it would be Bach," Alexei said.

"Well, drinks would definitely be out," Prudence said, popping the olive into her mouth. "I picture him being so serious, you know?"

Alexei liked this game. He was beginning to like Prudence. He knew she had actually met several famous composers when she was young. The big ones like Leonard Bernstein and Vladimir Horowitz. But she hadn't name-dropped. Not once.

"You said it's been a long time since you last performed in concert," Alexei said.

"I was nineteen," Prudence said. She winked at him. "And no, I won't tell you how long ago that was."

Alexei smiled. "And your first concert? Do you remember that?"

"Somewhat," she said. "I was five. I had a special booster seat on the bench so that I could reach the keys. I even had an extender—a box at my feet—so I could work the damper pedal. I remember I played a Bach minuet and a Mozart sonata, which started all that Mozart business, comparing me to him."

"That must have been difficult," Alexei said. "Even Mozart couldn't live up to Mozart. I think that's why he died so young."

"It nearly killed me, too. I turned eighteen and was completely lost, not knowing if I was really who everyone made me out to be, you know?"

Alexei did know. He thought not just about himself, but of all the musicians who had performed on his show. Even the most skilled pianist needed encouragement.

"You just have to envision your strongest moment, a moment you know you've played your absolute best—I'm sure you've had many of those—and hold on to it whenever you start to doubt yourself. And look, you did survive. You wouldn't be sitting here, Prudence, if you weren't a fighter."

Prudence liked hearing this. She liked being acknowledged for her strength.

"I suppose. My grandmother . . ." Prudence paused, looking into her glass.

"Go on." Alexei wanted to hear this. He wanted to know how such a young child became a worldwide sensation. It had to be more than talent.

"She was the original Tiger Mom. Unless you count Leopold."

"Who?"

"Mozart's dad."

"Oh. Right."

Drinks in hand, they sipped and talked. Prudence told Alexei about her childhood. About her parents taking off and her grandmother taking her in. About the whirlwind that followed and how Prudence ran away at eighteen. About her concert grand piano and how she dragged it around in her youth.

Alexei listened carefully.

"Did you ever see your grandmother again after you ran away?" he asked.

Prudence shook her head. "Cut her off. I had to."

"Because you were afraid of her?"

"Because I didn't trust myself around her. She was incredibly manipulative. She'd tell me I was a talentless brat one minute and then heap praise on me the next. Have you ever played a slot machine? You know, you feed it quarters and pull the lever and you get rewarded if three bananas or apples or sevens in a row pop up?"

"Of course. It's addictive."

"You know why it's so addictive?"

Alexei Petrov shrugged.

"You're always waiting for that payoff. Sometimes it happens, most times it doesn't. But it happens just enough to keep you trying. Some people sit all day at those machines and don't even realize it. That was me waiting for the praise." She took a sip of her drink and said, "I always had this urge to please her. Once I found the courage to break away, I knew I could never go back, you know?"

Did he ever. "Do you hate her now?"

"I don't think I could ever hate anyone."

Alexei picked an olive out of his drink because he could not look

Prudence in the eye. "How was it you were able to break away?" He had to know.

Prudence laughed. "I turned into a teenager! I rebelled!" She leaned into him as if telling a secret. "Rebellion is good."

Rebellion is good.

Alexei Petrov had felt that delicious rebellion four weeks ago when he woke up with his little gray cat. He, too, had considered cutting his mother off. "Do you have any regrets?"

"Nope." She drained her drink and signaled for another. "Not anymore."

By the time they got to this point in the conversation, Alexei had finished his martini. A warmth was flowing through him. There was something wise about Prudence, something safe. He wanted to trust her. He wanted to shed the confusing feelings he had about his mother.

Was it the martini that made him want to confess his vulnerabilities to this competitor?

Or was it this competitor?

Alexei watched a busboy clear glasses from an empty table. "Some days I wish I could just play the music without anyone knowing who I was."

To his surprise, Prudence said, "Me, too."

"You do?"

Prudence nodded. "People make too much of it, who's playing and what they're playing and how they're playing."

Alexei could see his own fears in her eyes. It validated everything for him. He had always been told he was lucky to be where he was, how few people had the opportunities he had been given. The expectation was to be grateful. Always. Never fearful. Never sad or angry. Alexei was never allowed to express his emotions. Never allowed to admit that the pressure was crushing him. In a different world, Alexei wanted Prudence as a friend, the friend who would tell him he was worth something beyond music. "I wish my mother understood that."

"Don't worry about your mother. Or your father. They'll love you even if you fail. Not that you'll fail, of course."

"You don't know my mother."

"I don't have to. I *am* a mother. There is absolutely nothing in this world you could do to lose her love." Alexei started to object, but Prudence wouldn't let him. "Just talk to her," she said. "She might surprise you."

CHAPTER FORTY-SEVEN

Surrender

Prudence sat before the Yamaha in the large ballroom sipping scotch and running through her program. Midnight. It was dark except for the sconce lights near the exits and, of course, the chandelier over the piano.

These would be her last moments alone.

But she wasn't alone. She was being watched. Prudence had run through her scales and her finger exercises and her program, unaware that she was performing to an audience of one. Only when she paused to tap out a response to Stuart's text—Mrs. Wintour is doing well, almost out of the woods. Missing you. XOXO, S—did she hear the soft breath of another person. The sound was unmistakable. An uneasiness washed over her.

"Hello?" Prudence called out into the darkness.

No answer, but she knew she wasn't alone. Maybe a janitor or a chambermaid had wandered in.

"Who's there?"

"I love this song, Peanut."

At the sound of his voice, every capillary in Prudence exploded. "You!" she gasped.

"Greetings," said Bobby Wheeler, from his perch on a Louis XVI chair.

"I'm calling security."

"Oh, please don't do that. I want to listen to our song."

"Don't ruin it for me. I've got to play it for fourteen million people on Friday and I don't want to be thinking of you. Leave."

Bobby Wheeler crossed one leg leisurely over the other. "I can't leave," he said. "I have some very important information concerning your performance."

Bobby Wheeler had time to think during that six-hour drive from Phoenix to Burbank, and he had come to the awareness that he'd been hoodwinked. Tamara Quigley, he now realized, was not a good person.

"What do you want, Bobby?" Prudence asked.

What did he want? He wanted to save Prudence, that's what.

Bobby Wheeler wanted to save her because his head and heart were stuck in 1986, the year he first tried to save her. He couldn't do it then. But he would do it now.

"You can't go on Friday night," Bobby Wheeler told her. "You're in danger."

"I'm in danger because of *you*," Prudence snapped.

This was not the reunion Bobby Wheeler had in mind.

"I'm trying to do the right thing here," he said. "I'm trying to save you." Bobby wanted to be a hero, never mind that if Prudence found out he had colluded with Tamara Quigley, he would not be the hero.

"I can save myself, Bobby."

Prudence started to gather her music.

"You won't be able to keep the money, anyway, not when everything gets out," he told her.

Prudence looked up at him sharply, knitting her brows together. "What do you mean, I won't be able to keep the money? Are you asking for more?"

He replied with a small "No."

Her suspicions aroused, Prudence pressed him. "What did you do with that manuscript, Bobby?"

"Peanut, all I can say is that someone is after you—someone who wants to see you punished. Please listen. You can't go on."

Prudence was worried. She had underestimated Bobby Wheeler's ability to fuck things up. It was quite possible the Pep Soda manuscript was in someone else's hands, beyond Bobby's control. Which heightened the reality of a high-profile lawsuit, the kind that are televised and followed relentlessly on social media. The show really would be her last chance to prove to the world who she was. She was now more determined than ever.

"No one can stop me from performing on Friday night. Get out of here before I call security."

"You wouldn't."

"Watch me," she said as she picked up her phone.

No way would Bobby Wheeler let that happen. He'd be thrown from the premises, his heroic mission aborted.

"There's not one goddamn thing you can do about it," she told him.

Yes, there was. There was one, and *only* one, goddamn thing he could do. And he did it. Rising from the King Louis XVI chair, Bobby Wheeler lunged toward Prudence and, grabbing her wrist with one large hand, began to squeeze her fingers with the other.

It does not take much to damage a pianist's fingers, the movements they make are so fine and delicate. You do not have to break any bones to disable them. The slightest twinge of a nerve could alter the most sensitive movement.

"Stop," Prudence breathed.

"Are you going to listen to me now?"

"*Stop,* you fool."

He looked down at her. "Look what you're making me do, Peanut. Now what did I tell you?"

A dull ache spread through Prudence's fingers. She tensed them in response, which made Bobby Wheeler squeeze harder.

"Let go!"

"Are you going to play?"

"Let *go!*"

If he did not stop, not only would she not play on Friday. She would never play again.

CHAPTER FORTY-EIGHT

La Donna è Mobile

Damn Bobby Wheeler and his mixed-up brain.

There was no way for Prudence to overpower him physically. He outweighed her by at least a hundred pounds. As she felt the nerves in her fingers scream for relief, the synapses in her brain fired back for a solution. There had to be a way to overpower him mentally.

What did Bobby Wheeler *really* want?

Pretty much what everyone else wanted: to be validated.

No matter how Bobby Wheeler got into this dumb mess—and the possibilities were endless when it came to him—Prudence knew that he would not want to be humiliated for his part in it. She would have to appear as if she believed he did have her best interests at heart.

Prudence pretended to humble herself. She uttered a simple "You're right."

She felt the pressure let up in her fingers.

"You think so?"

"Yes, I get it now. You're trying to help me." A little more of the grip was loosened.

"I can save you, Peanut."

"From this evil person."

"Yes!"

Bobby Wheeler stopped squeezing her fingers, but still he held them firmly. Prudence had to be very careful. He was holding her entire world in his hands. One wrong word and it would be over.

She got up from her knees and looked at his big, dumb face. "Look at us, together after all these years," he said, cracking a big dumb smile.

He had stopped squeezing, but her fingers were cramping because he was holding them too tightly in his sweaty hands.

"Are you in some kind of trouble?" Prudence asked.

Because Bobby Wheeler was always in some kind of trouble.

He applied some pressure to her fingers, causing Prudence to yelp in pain. "You're the one in trouble, remember? I'm here to help *you*," he said. "It's just like it was before, Peanut."

"Before?"

"That day your grandmother came to take you back. Remember? She was furious. Said I was only after your money."

"*She* was the one who was after my money."

Bobby Wheeler shook his head. "I thought that, too, at the time. I don't anymore. She wanted you home. She was desperate."

Prudence was surprised by Bobby's insight. "Maybe," she said. "It was probably embarrassing for her, me running away. Everyone ran away from her. I was neighborhood gossip, just like my mom."

"It was a small town," Bobby Wheeler said. "You were a big star. But this person, the one who's after you, I don't think she wants money either." Bobby Wheeler thought about Tamara Quigley and how, the day they met at the park, she was dressed in nice clothing and had driven away in an Escalade. He knew financial desperation. Tamara Quigley did not have it.

"Then what does she want?"

"Same thing as your granny. To take you down a peg."

Bobby Wheeler might've been dumb, irresponsible, and mixed up. But he was not always wrong.

"You need to let go of my fingers now, Bobby."

"We've got to get out of here. I will not let this person destroy you."

"You let me worry about that."

They were a few feet from an exit door. If she tried to free herself, he only had to apply a bit more pressure and her fingers would crack. He leaned into a metal bar and the door clicked open out onto a parking lot.

"Come on, Peanut."

"You cannot make this choice for me, Bobby. No one can." That said, she head-butted Bobby Wheeler so fiercely, he felt like he'd been hit with a brick. Where that came from is anyone's guess. It sure surprised the hell out of Bobby Wheeler, who moved his hand to his jaw and wailed in pain.

The relief was immediate. She could feel the blood pulse through her fingers.

But they were not the same.

CHAPTER FORTY-NINE

Scenes from Childhood

First Alexei had found a piano tuner for the Wurlitzer. Then he found his routine. He woke early, dressed, fed the little gray cat, grabbed his music, his metronome, and said good night to the baker who was coming in when Alexei was going out. Margaret had given him a key to the church so he could be at the Wurlitzer by six each morning. He was there until six at night, drilling his program, "Great Balls of Fire," the latter improving considerably under his new circumstances.

Holden's playing was also improving. When he wasn't in school, he was in the church basement. When Alexei needed a break, he let the child practice. He taught Holden two scales and three more songs. Holden was intuitive. He knew when he could talk and when to stay silent. He never disturbed Alexei when he was practicing. If he wanted to listen, he'd creep down the stairs, silent as a cat.

When Alexei finished, he'd turn to give Holden an exaggerated bow.

Alexei brought Holden donuts and Holden brought Alexei peanut butter and jelly sandwiches. He shared his Goldfish crackers. Which was good because Alexei was not eating properly. He did not have the time. Not even to shop or order out.

Alexei felt great. Energized. He hadn't felt this way in years. And his playing was better than ever. "Great Balls of Fire" wasn't perfect, but it was close. Very close. It was coming to him now. The anger, the passion, the fear . . . all were accessible.

He could do this.

He could do that other thing, too.

IT WAS 10:30 when Alexei's parents pulled up to the little house with the smelly carpets and the ugly brown couch.

Alexei was ready.

He peered through the bent window blinds, holding the little gray cat. His father parked the car, then opened the passenger door for his mother. They looked around at the shabby neighborhood and frowned. Alexei felt the twinge of their disappointment.

"Hello, Mother. Hello, Father," he said as he let them in the house.

They studied his rumpled clothing. They studied the little gray cat. They looked over his shoulder and into the bland living room, where fast-food containers and beer bottles littered the coffee table. A basket of unfolded laundry sat on the couch.

Alexei could not meet his mother's gaze. He could imagine what she thought of him then. That he wasn't taking care of himself. That he would fail. That he would lose everything she had built for him. He stared at the floor.

"Alyosha," she said. "Look at me."

He kept his gaze on the floor. "I'm still very angry with you."

"Alexei," his father said sternly.

He recalled Prudence's words. *Rebellion is good. They will always love you no matter what you do.*

"Father, let me speak." Alexei waited until he was sure his parents were listening. "I don't care what you gave up for me. I did not ask you to do that. You are the ones who made that decision, not me. Can you look at what you've asked of *me*? Of all I've had to give up for *you*?"

A leaden silence followed. He could hear his father fidgeting with the keys in his pocket. He could feel the pressure of their eyes on him.

He paused before he said his next words, hoping they would come out right. "I appreciate all you've done to get me here. But now it's time to let go."

"What does that mean?" his mother asked.

"You're fired. I'm signing with a talent agency to manage my career."

He was ready for the next question. "Are you punishing us?" she asked.

"What would that accomplish? Listen, if I win, I can get us out of our financial straits. If I'm able to sign on for another season, I can stay in America and you'll be eligible for family visas. I've done some research. There are resources here. They'll work with us. This is not Russia. I can handle these things."

Silence followed. A silence so deep Alexei feared he would lose his resolve. His instinct was to take back what he said. Say something to make his mother happy. Dilute the discomfort. But when he opened his mouth to speak, Prudence's words came back to him: *No matter what.*

He took in a deep breath. "I will always need you in my life. That will never change."

Alexei looked up, expecting the harsh glare of his mother's reproach. She smiled softly instead. She held him until a sob burst from his chest like a pinball in a chute.

After a long time, she let go, and said, "Okay."

The best thing she could've said.

He felt the comforting weight of his father's hand on his shoulder. And he felt a shift. That he had stood up to them. That they respected him. It would take time for them to get used to it, but he was willing to give it to them.

Prudence had been right.

CHAPTER FIFTY

The Matador

Here's the thing about courage. It grows from intention to action . . . to more action. After his parents had gone, Alexei Petrov sat on his brown couch and cuddled his little gray cat. He felt strong. Like a bullfighter.

His thoughts turned to Mia. He didn't know where she was in her life and with whom. All he knew was that he loved her, needed her. That wasn't being weak. That was being human.

He stared at his phone, wanting to say something to her. Anything. He tapped out several sentences but kept deleting them because they felt cowardly and wrong.

Corny. Dumb. Insincere.

Nobody ever lives their lives all the way up except bullfighters.

It came to him. He would text an apology. If she did not reply, he would not text her again. He would make an effort to meet new people, move on.

But he had to try. He had to know.

Please forgive me for the other night. I hope you are well.

Then he switched off his phone, because if he didn't, he'd be up all night waiting.

—

THE NEXT DAY, Alexei went to the corner store, where he bought a box of chocolate-covered donuts for Holden. He was excited to play "Great Balls of Fire" for his little audience of one. Holden always got excited by the music and when he heard something that got him excited, he wanted to play it. Just like Scott Joplin's "The Entertainer"; Alexei had taught the child a beginner's version of the song only four days ago. Already Holden could play it from memory. His timing was perfect. The child had an incredible feel for the rag's syncopated beat. Alexei even gave Holden an old MP3 player with a set of headphones so he could listen to all the music he was playing.

At 2:30, right on time, he heard footsteps on the stairs. But it wasn't Holden. It was a woman. Alexei guessed she was a few years older than he was, but it was hard to tell. She wore a cream blouse and cardigan, with black trousers and sensible black shoes. This was, Alexei knew, what Americans called "business casual."

She smiled at him, but there was sadness around the corners of her pretty eyes.

"Are you Alexei Petrov?"

"I am."

"Are you the one who's been teaching my son music?"

"You're Holden's mother!" He rose from the piano bench. "What a pleasure. Your son is very gifted."

Her smile bloomed and her face brightened. The look of a proud mother. But there was something else that Alexei could not pinpoint.

"You are the gift, Mr. Petrov. You offered my son what he needed, when he needed it."

"Ah, yes. Mrs.—"

"Mrs. Lawrence. Please, call me Ellen."

"Ellen," Alexei said, "your son is the perfect age to learn about music. The cables in his brain are not all connected yet. Not yet hardwired. Learning something like a foreign language or music is easiest at this stage. What is it the Americans say? He is . . . like a sponge."

Her expression turned serious. "Maybe, but what you are giving my son is much more precious."

Alexei couldn't imagine anything more precious than music.

"Holden needs a friend right now." She nodded at the Wurlitzer. "You've also given him something to look forward to every day."

"Oh?"

Ellen continued. "Holden's father died earlier this year in a car accident. It was so sudden." She looked very sad just then.

"Holden's father? I am so sorry. How awful."

"Yes, it was. It is."

Alexei struggled with what to say next. He was caught off guard. "How tragic for your church, two deaths coming so close to each other."

"Two deaths?"

"Margaret's husband," Alexei said.

"Jimmy Paisley!" She burst out laughing.

Alexei was confused. "I don't understand."

"Jimmy Paisley is alive and well. He's probably out in his garden right this second fussing over his tomatoes. What gave you the idea he had died?"

But Alexei didn't answer.

And Holden's mother didn't say a word.

Because they knew.

The pain of a small sensitive child had wound its way into a story. A story that made the unbearable a little easier to bear. The two adults shared a glance, and in it, an understanding. Children know what they need.

Alexei couldn't believe what this little boy had given him at a time when he, Holden, needed so much himself. Seeing how music had awakened something in Holden had awakened something in him. After all those years of being told what to do, this small child had liberated Alexei from the pressure of precision and had given him joy.

He turned to Ellen and offered the only thing he had.

"May I play for you?" he asked.

And he did.

CHAPTER FIFTY-ONE

I Got the Music in Me

Prudence Childs and Alexei Petrov stood tall at separate podiums. It would appear that these two great pianists, dressed identically in crisp black tuxes, were well matched. But there was a difference that went beyond the human eye, beyond the human ear and into the soul. Both were extraordinary musicians, but one was built and the other was born. You could feel it.

"Ladies and gentlemen," Les Strom announced, "please meet the world-famous Alexei Petrov of *Alexei Petrov's Dueling Piano Wars!* and his challenger, former child star Prudence Paddington Childs!"

Prudence winced. She didn't want to be introduced as a former anything.

Alexei Petrov took the first question.

"Mr. Petrov, the show is in your name. Are you feeling pressure to win?"

You can bet that Les Strom had coached Alexei for this question. Being a showrunner means having a vision, not just for the evening's extravaganza, but for a second season, and a third and fourth.

There would be spin-offs, franchises.

Licensed merchandise.

To make it work meant making it big. Which meant playing up the rivalry between the two pianists. "I'm sure Ms. Childs will give me a run for my money," Alexei answered. "But the show's in my name for a reason. I am the best there is and tonight I will prove it."

Alexei hated the words even as they were coming out of his mouth.

"What about you, Ms. Childs? Are you feeling pressured to live up to the hype of your storied childhood?"

Prudence gripped the sides of the podium. She had been expecting this question as well, but she had not been coached. She didn't need to be.

"Are you asking me now if there is pressure to be greater than I've ever been?"

"That's the question," quipped the reporter.

Just weeks ago, Prudence had been consumed with dying. Now, she was consumed with creating. She had left her past behind, and with it a desire to please. She was no longer the passive girl who would do as she was told. Prudence had learned and listened and worked. And worked and worked and worked. She was an artist deserving of the title.

"I am at the top of my game," she said.

"At the age of nearly fifty?"

"*Especially* at the age of fifty."

Tamara Quigley squirmed in her chair. Her suit itched.

A series of playful softball questions followed. Alexei was relieved that he did not have to keep up a sham of a rivalry.

"Who's your favorite composer?"

Prudence said, "That's like asking who your favorite child is."

"How many hours a day do you practice?"

Alexei said, "It borders on insanity. You're better off not knowing."

"Ms. Childs, at a press conference in 1981, when you were thirteen, you said you had a crush on Andy Gibb. Is that still true?"

"Absolutely."

"Beethoven or Mozart?"

"Mozart," Alexei said.

"Beethoven," said Prudence.

"Coke or Pepsi?"

"Neither!" both said at the same time, prompting laughter from the press.

Tamara Quigley made her move. "What about Pep Soda?"

The room tittered at the seemingly innocent question.

It took Prudence a second to place the face. Why in the world was the president of the HOA in this press conference?

Tamara Quigley said, "You must like Pep Soda to have written such a famous jingle about it."

The tone was accusatory, demanding. The ballroom fell silent except for the soft clicks of camera shutters.

"I wrote a lot of jingles back then."

"But Pep Soda was your best, wasn't it? Who could forget that melody! Unless . . . you didn't actually write it?"

A dull roar of confusion rose above the crowd.

"What's your question?" Prudence asked.

"Oh, I'm not asking, I'm *telling*. You did not write the jingle to Pep Soda."

Prudence suspected that this was the person Bobby Wheeler was trying to warn her about. Somehow, somewhere, and for whatever reason, a rendezvous between the two of them had taken place and the HOA woman most likely possessed the manuscript. But why? Prudence remembered what Bobby Wheeler had told her in the ballroom that night: *She wants to take you down a peg.*

But why?

The room buzzed.

"Ms. Childs. Ms. Childs!" a reporter called out. "Did you or did you not write the Pep Soda jingle?"

"If not you, then who?" asked another.

"Did you take credit for someone's work?" asked a third.

Tamara Quigley nearly sang the words. "I can prove she's a plagiarist. A fraud!" She locked eyes with Prudence. Tamara just needed Prudence to deny it in front of everyone so she could present her proof and take Prudence down.

Tamara Quigley had what she had wanted all along: attention.

Attention as she danced on a stage years ago, attention as the head of the HOA conference room table. Now she was getting attention from all the reporters, cameramen, and photographers. But it was the rapt attention of the show's star, the dapper Alexei Petrov, that prompted Tamara to show off. In fact, to upstage herself. "Ladies and gentlemen," she said, "I'm about to shatter one of the longest-standing myths in pop culture!" Pulling the Pep Soda manuscript from its plastic folder, she turned it over and read, "Dear Prudence . . ."

What followed was the sort of silence that makes hearts pound with uncertainty, that makes ears ring with anticipation. Tamara turned the letter over. "Ladies and gentlemen of the press, the original manuscript to Pep Soda, penned by a Mrs. Adeline Martinelli, the author of this letter."

The room erupted.

Tamara Quigley said, "The prodigy's nothing but a fraud."

Prudence locked eyes with Tamara. In that moment, a memory went off like a flashbulb. Prudence was fourteen. She was playing a Mozart sonata. Granny Paddington berated Prudence for her lack of pedal work. But Prudence knew she'd gotten the pedal work right. She knew Mozart rarely used the damper pedal except for emphasis in short bursts. Instead of cowering, Prudence rose to her full height. "You really don't know anything about Mozart, do you?" she had said.

This display of courage was unexpected. Granny Paddington then growled at Prudence, "I know more than you'll ever know, young lady."

The put-down was familiar. But there was an uncertainty in her grandmother's eyes that was new. Sometime after that, Prudence spied Granny Paddington attempting to play the piece, her face etched in self-loathing. She was forever trapped in her own well of inferiority. Prudence saw that same self-loathing in Tamara Quigley. The same uncertainty in the eyes. The same demeaning taunt: *You are nothing but a fraud.*

Bobby Wheeler was right. This woman needs to see me fail. But Prudence held her gaze and the corners of Tamara's eyes began to quiver. She gritted her teeth with a resentment so old and calcified it would never soften.

Prudence had been exposed now. A lawsuit was a real possibility. Yet she no longer cared. The Pep Soda jingle was no measure of who she was. Sure, she could lose her house, her property, everything in her bank account. But Prudence had one thing that couldn't be taken away in any court of law: her gift.

Over the last two months she'd spent twelve hours a day at the piano preparing for this moment. Four decades dreaming of it. Not only did she rediscover her talent, but she had learned how to harness it in a new way. Prudence believed everyone had a gift. And they must learn to never let it go to waste out of fear.

·The room turned its attention toward Prudence. She would not lie. But she wasn't going to confess, either. Not yet, anyway. "You're sure that letter is real, Ms. . . . ?"

"*Quig*ley, Tamara *Quig*ley! Yes, it is, Ms. Childs." Tamara held the document up once again for the room to see. But for all her careful planning, she had made a careless mistake. Someone from the *Hollywood Reporter* asked, "Can you verify this letter?"

"Of course!" Tamara said. "There's an envelope addressed to Ms. Childs, postmarked with the date." But when she looked in the plastic folder—nothing. Damn. Bobby Wheeler still had the postmarked envelope. She'd never gotten it from him that day at the park.

A murmur rippled through the room.

"I don't have it on me. But it exists!"

Prudence knew that the envelope did indeed exist. She also knew Tamara was no journalist. "What paper did you say you wrote for?" Prudence asked.

All eyes turned to Tamara Quigley. "Oh, uh, the *East Valley Journal*."

"The paper out of Scottsdale, Arizona?"

"Yes."

"Has anyone checked her press credentials? Because my subscription ended in 2012 when that paper went out of circulation."

At once, several reporters googled the *East Valley Journal,* its demise documented online. Now the room looked at Tamara as if she were the fraud, not Prudence. Tamara Quigley was escorted from the premises.

The show would go on.

CHAPTER FIFTY-TWO

You Ain't Seen Nothing Yet

An Olympic athlete and a concert pianist have a lot in common. Both require strength, drive, and a competitive spirit. Both must be fearless to play in front of an audience without error. But a pianist needs a heightened degree of emotional, intellectual, and physical control. She must play with as much sensitivity as strength.

This is why an athlete's prime is in his youth, while a pianist will continue to grow for the rest of her days. An athlete's goal is to win the race. A pianist's goal is to win the heart.

Age is on her side.

Unless, of course, the race is rigged.

THIS WAS EVENT TV, and the network had gone all out. They were going to make a star of Alexei, and they were going to make a star out of midlevel TV presenter Ricki Gest. A man who'd once had his own dreams of stardom—he last appeared in the 2010 remake of *The A Team* movie, as an extra—Ricki Gest was chosen to host this special episode of *Alexei Petrov's Dueling Piano Wars!* The diminutive Gest (five foot, four inches) didn't make it on the big screen, but network executives all agreed that he "had something," a *something* that landed him behind an entertainment news desk where he reported on million-dollar divorces and celebrity rehab.

Ricki Gest moved around backstage, no fewer than five people attending to him at once. Either trimming his already-trimmed hair or dabbing his already-made-up face with a sponge.

Les Strom was running around as if the building were on fire. Carrying an electronic clipboard and wearing large headphones, he snapped his fingers and barked at stagehands.

"Okay, and here we go!" he roared.

A cameraman counted to three, prompting a red light to pop on and a roar of club music to pump up the crowd. Columns of light shot from all corners of the studio, crisscrossing frantically to the beat. The audience clapped and whistled and cheered. They threw their hands in the air.

"Okay, let's do this!" Les Strom shouted backstage.

Ricki Gest was lowered from the ceiling by a flashing hydraulic lift. He jumped from the hydraulic platform onto the stage and danced to the intro music. The pint-size host stopped and pointed to someone in the audience, waving as if he knew them. Which he didn't. He danced and clapped some more to work up the audience. Then, on cue, he said in an oddly animated voice, "Prepare to witness a musical battle on this very stage! This, folks, is *Alexei Petrov's Dueling Piano Wars!*"

More clapping. More yelling. More hands in the air.

Ricki Gest stood between two shiny black Model M Steinways lit up by spotlights. The pianos faced each other and the keyboards were angled so the audience would be able to see the pianists' fingers.

"Are. You. READY?!" Ricki Gest called to deafening cheers. He pumped his fist in the air while simultaneously whirling it around like a helicopter blade.

"Let me introduce you to the star of the show, classical PIANIST and RECORDING ARTIST Alexei Petrov!"

Dressed in a $5,000 tuxedo, Alexei took center stage with Ricki

Gest and bowed. Girls screamed, overcome by his beauty and his sable-colored hair. Men clapped, envious of his beauty and his sable-colored hair. He sat down at the piano to the right.

"And now his COMPETITOR!" Ricki Gest bellowed. "Former CHILD PRODIGY and JINGLE WRITER, once hailed as the next MOZART, Prudence Childs!"

Everyone screamed, including those who were too young to recognize the name and those who didn't know what a prodigy was. Prudence came out onstage and took a bow. Ricki Gest kissed her hand, then launched into an explanation of the rules.

"All right, folks. These two are going to DUEL! Our first category is the contemporary era, songs by composers from the years 1900 to the present. Prudence will play a song and Alexei will follow. You, the audience, must text in your vote after each performance! Let's get ready to duel!"

Prudence's fingers trembled. She closed her eyes and thought about the power of fear and about the power of hope, and how those two forces will always fight each other and how fear will most certainly win if you let it.

She would not let it.

It would seem the way to calm the nerves would be to imagine the audience is not there. Shut them out. Focus on the music. But that would be a mistake. Prudence could not shut out the people she was trying to reach. She looked all the way to the back row. There sat a man with a stern face. His arms were crossed before him, his back rigid. *If I can reach him, I can reach all of them.*

Prudence concentrated on awakening some sort of memory in him.

A time when he'd loved someone from afar.

A voluntary detachment that caused both longing and pleasure.

Her fingers steadied as she began Debussy's "Clair de Lune." The studio hushed in anticipation and the first breezy notes flitted like butterflies skimming a field. Prudence then drove up the tempo, thinking of the man in the back and imploring him to remember this beautiful sadness. The man in the back was indeed thinking of another. His arms were no longer across his chest. His head fell to the side and the corners of his mouth drooped as if tugged by his heart.

Some in the audience were smiling. Some dreaming. Some weeping. Prudence controlled the room and drove the tempo to a fantastic peak as if the audience were about to take flight. The ending notes rose up and hung in the air until they fell as lightly as flakes of snow. There was silence, then the roar of applause.

Prudence was relieved that her fingers had not failed her. But the night wasn't over.

The spotlight switched to Alexei Petrov, cutting off the applause in a strategic programming move. The audience would not have time to reflect on Prudence's performance because Alexei launched immediately into Sergei Prokofiev's showpiece, Toccata in D Minor. A technically difficult piece, it was said that even Prokofiev had trouble playing it. Alexei's left hand leapt back and forth over the right. As the song went on, his hands crossed and weaved and bounced, which made for great TV. When he finished, there were oohs and ahs and cheers. Alexei rose from his bench and the lights flashed, giving him time to take three bows in a row.

Ricki Gest danced back out onto the stage. "We're taking a commercial break while you text in your vote! Prudence Childs or Alexei Petrov!"

Prudence fumed. She went backstage, where Les Strom was rushing around, meting out directions.

"What was that?" she snapped.

He looked up from his clipboard. "Prudence, dear, why so worked up?"

"You cut me off!"

"That's the show, baby! You duel."

Prudence's eyes narrowed. "You're making it very difficult for my pieces to resonate."

"It's television, dear. Your song ran over and, well . . ."

"It did not!"

"Look—" Les Strom started to speak, but he cut her off when a voice came through his headphones. "We're on in twenty seconds. Just go do your thing. You'll hit it out of the park, kid. I know it."

Alexei Petrov hated what had just happened. Stacking the deck against Prudence made him feel like an imposter.

Boom, boom, boom went the club music as Ricki Gest danced his way back onto center stage. The audience clapped and Ricki Gest bowed. "What a round! Totals are in and the winner of that round was . . . Alexei Petrov with 52 percent of the vote. Prudence with 48 percent. This is turning out to be a close one!"

More appreciation from the audience.

"Time for our next category. Each pianist must play a song from the romantic era, which must be a song composed between 1820 and 1900. Which of these great pianists will you fall in love with?"

Prudence was to play Tchaikovsky's "Pas de Deux." Alexei was to follow with Chopin's Nocturne in C Minor. It was a far more technically complex song, one that sounded impressive to the un-trained ear. If he got the dynamics just right, Alexei's performance could crush hers.

But Prudence was in no mood to be crushed. She sized up her opponent. She knew the amount of work he put into the Prokofiev piece. Alexei would surely stick to the program he had so rigorously prepared.

But she could play anything.

If Les Strom could turn the tables on her, she would do the same. When the lights went down, she did not play "Pas de Deux." She stayed within the Romantic category, but played a solo from Mendelssohn's frenetic Piano Concerto no. 1 in G Minor. It was a song that could be utterly explosive one moment and extremely gentle in the next. The audience gasped as her fingers bobbed up and down, working the keyboard like a sewing machine needle.

Alexei Petrov watched from his piano. As was his way, he did not like any sort of change in plans. Prudence's surprise performance threw him off, amped up his anxiety. His piece was slower, fussier. The audience might find it sedate in contrast. He looked at his parents and saw the fear in their eyes.

Prudence lost herself in the music without losing sight of where she was and what she had to do. She was ready this time. Knowing that she wouldn't be able to take a bow, she let the song do it for her. She made the most of the last measures, drawing out the notes as if she were plucking the petals off a flower and throwing them, one by one, into her adoring audience.

Alexei was terrified now. Prudence was the better musician. He could hear it in her playing. Certainly, the audience could hear it. He looked at his mom, hoping for a reassuring smile, but she gave him a look of helplessness, as if once the show ended, they'd be on a plane bound for Moscow.

Alexei played Chopin's Nocturne in C Minor and thought of Mia. He thought of her Instagram pictures. He remembered the way she laughed, how her hair smelled, how her hand felt in his. How so badly he wanted her back. He let all that heartache bleed from the piano. He played well. Again, he stood to a healthy applause and bowed and bowed and his parents beamed.

Les Strom was apoplectic. "What the *fuck* was that!" he said to Prudence when the show broke for a commercial. "You were supposed to play 'Pas de . . .'—the *Nutcracker* piece."

"It's 'Pas de Deux.' And change of plans."

Les Strom was minutes away from having a top-rated show. Minutes away from buying the latest Tesla. Minutes away from moving up the Hollywood ladder.

Too bad he had underestimated Prudence.

"You listen to me," he growled, "we have one final segment and you will stick to the program. If you don't . . ."

Prudence's eyebrows shot up. "If I don't?"

"If you don't . . . then, then I will dis*qual*ify you."

"But it's designed for me to lose."

"Of course it isn't!" Les sputtered. "What kind of a show would that be?"

"A rigged one."

"That's ridiculous." He scowled at her. "I want to hear the Beatles medley next and if I don't, we're going to have a real problem here, Prudence." Les Strom kept his eyes intensely fixed on hers for a beat before he turned on his heels and walked away.

"We'll see," Prudence said when he was out of earshot.

She had one last ace up her sleeve. It would be a gamble, not only because she wasn't sure if her fingers had been compromised, but because she had not prepared for it. She remembered Pierre Millet's words: *The music will never let you down.*

Meanwhile, Ricki Gest sipped his special water while someone combed his hair.

"Ten seconds, Mr. Gest," said the stage manager.

Ricki Gest marched up to Prudence, a parade of primpers in his wake. "I don't know what the hell is going on here," he snapped. "But I don't like looking like a dick. When I say you're going to play something, play it."

Oh, she would do a lot more than that.

Ricki Gest took his spot center stage as Alexei and Prudence went to their pianos. The music and the lights and the cheering ratcheted right back up to hysteria.

"Welcome back to *Alexei Petrov's Dueling Piano Wars!* Wow, that was quite a duel. It looks like Prudence gave our Alexei a run for his money. She took that round with 64 percent of the vote!"

A roar thundered up from the audience. Alexei gave Prudence an obligatory smile.

"The final segment for tonight is pop music. First up is Prudence Childs with a Beatles medley. Remember, folks, text in your vote with the number at the bottom of the screen. Take it, Prudence—"

Prudence thought about Tamara Quigley. Wherever that envelope was, it would validate the manuscript and undercut any victory Prudence might have. It would render her a fraud.

She could not give in to fear now. She looked out onto her waiting audience for inspiration, to give them everything she had. That's when she saw Stuart in the front row! She knew then Mrs. Wintour was okay—he wouldn't be here if she wasn't. Happiness, relief, and love—lots and lots of love—spread through her heart like a sunburst. He looked at her, his brown eyes as warm as she'd ever seen them. There was no trace of fear or uncertainty in his eyes. As if he already knew the outcome. She knew then she could do it.

She did not care about Tamara Quigley anymore. And because she did not care about Tamara Quigley, she did not care about Bobby Wheeler. And she certainly did not care about Les Strom and his silly rules.

It was finally time to leave her fingerprint on a star.

She had seven minutes.

Prudence flipped her tails and sat down and looked at the keyboard.

She launched into what was supposed to be the final song of the medley, "A Day in the Life." She played passionately, the chords as heavy as clock chimes, quarter notes light as raindrops on a tin roof. The damper pedal theatrically giving passages a haunting, echoing effect until the final violent chord. She had compressed the five-minute song into three minutes before suspending her hands above the keyboard.

A nervous, pin-dropping silence descended on the crowd.

"She's got four minutes left," Les Strom said nervously.

"Yeah, but Jesus, that was impressive," Ricki Gest muttered.

Prudence held up her two index fingers. "Ready for a classic?" she asked. The audience cheered in anticipation.

"What is she up to now?" Les Strom moaned.

Prudence smiled and began, simply, "Chopsticks."

Les Strom stomped up and down like a cartoon character, but the audience howled with laughter. After playing the simple notes with absolute precision, Prudence winked and riffed away, augmenting "Chopsticks" into a fantastic Bach-like fugue before turning it into an elaborate Broadway show tune. She brought it to a climax to let the audience catch its breath. She then turned to them, smiled slyly, and again held up two index fingers in the air. The audience cheered and she played the simple notes again before spinning the tune into a boogie-woogie jazz improv.

The crowd went crazy.

Never before had they seen such simplicity turned into wild entertainment. Prudence Childs would prove her immense talent with a song everyone could play. She performed as if holding the reins of a horse, galloping wildly and then pulling back before repeating the sequence.

She had three minutes left and her fingers were spasming and her forearms were locking up. But she knew what she had to play next. By far the hardest to manage with damaged fingers. A shot of adrenaline burst inside Prudence like a water balloon as she launched into "Bumble Boogie" at an incredible 180 beats a minute. The entire studio cheered, rising to their feet just a few measures in. It was sensational.

That was the moment Alexei Petrov understood the difference between them. He could never be Prudence Childs. He was the B-side of the record. Good, but second best.

And yet he needed to win. He needed the lucrative tux endorsement. He needed to stay in America.

He could not outplay Prudence, so he had to top her.

He had just the trick.

CHAPTER FIFTY-THREE

Are You Experienced?

The one thing Alexei Petrov had going for him was the excitement of the crowd.

Bring it, Alexei! Bring it!

He would have to bring it if he was going to win. But "Great Balls of Fire" was not as good as it needed to be. He had come to terms with this a few days ago, and that was before he had witnessed Prudence's electrifying rendition of "Chopsticks." Alexei was a classical pianist, not a rocker. But this was television. And television is all about spectacle.

Alexei had formed a plan a few days ago when it became clear that he could not deliver on "Great Balls of Fire." With the spotlight still on Prudence, he gave a signal to a slight young man dressed in black who sprinted onto the stage and gave Alexei what looked to be a water bottle.

When Prudence finished, Ricki Gest stepped back out onto the stage to cheers and hollers. "Alexei Petrov is gonna roar right back with the great Jerry Lee Lewis song 'Great Balls of Fire' like you've never heard it! Make sure you text in your vote."

The audience, already worked into a frenzy, roared as Alexei began the rattling chords to his final piece. He knew he was no Killer; still, he did his best, zipping his fingers up and down the keyboard, tossing his long hair around in exaggerated jerks. Just like a young Jerry Lee Lewis.

Everyone was too worked up to notice that Alexei Petrov was not quite on the beat. Not that they would have cared. The crowd had gotten to their feet and danced, filling the aisles, standing on seats. It was a free-for-all, the type that television adores. When the camera panned to Ricki Gest pulling a young female from the audience onto the stage, twirling her around, Alexei knew what he had to do.

He would have to time it just right, though. He would have to do it midway through the piece, when he could feel the song slipping from his grasp. He would do it just like he'd seen Jerry Lee Lewis do it. Just like he'd seen Jimi Hendrix do it at the Monterey Pop Festival.

At the right moment, Alexei Petrov stood up and kicked the piano bench back and the crowd exploded. He perched his left foot on the piano and, with one hand still banging away at the upper register, shrugged off his tux jacket and twirled it into the crowd. The cameras panned briefly to the audience, where a small crowd had set upon the garment as if their lives depended on it.

Alexei knew that his life depended on what came next.

When the moment was right, when he could feel the song slipping from his fingers, Alexei Petrov picked up the water bottle and held it up to the crowd, still pounding the bass line with his left hand. Only it wasn't water in the plastic bottle. It was lighter fluid. Without missing a note, Alexei doused the harp of the piano. He took a single match from the pocket of his trousers and flicked it across a matchbox.

When he held the flame up to the crowd, they cheered as if to encourage him.

Alexei threw the lit match into the piano and angry flames burst up from the harp. The audience had never seen such a thing and Alexei played the rest of the song, the cheers and screaming so loud that no one would be able to hear the wrong notes or the lagging tempo.

The harp of a piano may have been made of metal, but the piano was ruined. A small price to pay for a television spectacle that millions watched from their homes. And once the lighter fluid burned off, the flames went out just as Alexei finished the song. The timing was perfect. Text votes surged in Alexei's favor.

Les Strom was euphoric. Ricki Gest was as worked up as the audience. So much so, he missed his cue and had to be prompted by a stage manager.

Everyone was astounded by Alexei Petrov's performance.

Everyone except for Prudence.

She heard every wrong note. She felt the sluggish pace and the underwhelming dynamics over the cheers of the crowd. She pitied him a little just then because, in that moment, Alexei Petrov was the circus act, not her.

Ricki Gest danced back out to his spot and shouted, "Yeowwwww! Prudence Childs, what did you think of that incredible performance?"

But Prudence was not at her piano. She had vanished into thin air.

CHAPTER FIFTY-FOUR

The Morning After

Tamara Quigley refreshed her Google News page. Again and again and again.

Aside from the headlines reporting on the show's through-the-roof ratings, there was nothing about her, save for a brief mention in *Variety*: "At a pretaping press conference, an unnamed woman accused former child prodigy Prudence Childs of plagiarizing her iconic jingle to Pep Soda. No supporting evidence was offered for the claim, and Childs went on to perform on *Alexei Petrov's Dueling Piano Wars!*, in which she stole the show. The legend lives."

Unnamed woman?

The legend lives?

Tamara Quigley felt a skip in the record.

What just happened?

It wasn't as if she'd spent years harboring fantasies of revenge. Maybe in times of despair, sure, she would reach back to that dark place where she held on to such things and recall the Incident, ruminate on what might have been. But it would only be a moment, a brief interlude of self-pity before tucking it away and getting on with it.

That day in the conference room changed all that. One seemingly harmless mention of Prudence and Tamara Quigley was transported back some thirty years. She realized she had been holding on to this animus until it burst like a waiting storm, when the intense heat of a desert day builds and builds and builds until the pressure finally gives way to thunder and lightning, an explosive monsoon.

Once upon a time, Tamara Quigley felt that there had been something bigger in store for her—a creative life, with dance at its center.

What was it that had gotten in the way of her dream? A coach, a parent, a talent scout?

Prudence?

No, Tamara Quigley had gotten in the way of her own dream.

She gave up because she had a flawed expectation of the outcome—to be up on a grand London stage, her name at the top of the program. The end goal overtook the pleasure of dancing, of working through a number, learning the steps, mastering the routine. The goal was not in the glory. It was about finding that kind of satisfaction in each day.

Tamara Quigley loved her little family. Why couldn't she enjoy them for who they were and not what she needed them to be? Her husband was a good man, a hard worker. Her son was kind and sensitive. So what if he hadn't figured things out yet. How fortunate he was to have that exploration in front of him.

He will not be like me, she vowed. This is what mattered. Not stupid summer camp. Not some TV show. She looked around at her tidy home, traces of a good life all around—the sunflowers in the vase, the chess set, midgame, on the coffee table, the breakfast dishes drying in the sink. Everything was in its place, the day before her. It was enough.

Tamara snapped her laptop shut and went outside. She breathed in the fall air, then folded the letter into a paper airplane that she pitched into the afternoon breeze. Tamara Quigley watched as Mrs. Martinelli's tender words sailed over the cinderblock wall and into a neighbor's yard.

It was late October and the sharp summer sun had softened into the easy glow of autumn. The pleasant months had arrived and soon there would be cottony sunshine under cloudless skies. Having been sequestered by the heat for most of the summer, people would emerge from their houses. There would be dinners on the patio and walks around the neighborhood. The perfume of mesquite burning in outdoor fire pits.

Tamara Quigley stood on her back porch and felt the contentment all around her. *Let go,* it whispered, *let go.*

She closed her eyes and listened to a lone clarinet tease out the haunting melody. In comes the harp, giving the melody wings now. Then, in rapid succession, come the strings, then the horns. Oboes and cellos, and trumpets and tubas. Louder and louder. Higher and higher. *Let go, let go.*

The baritones thunder and the timpani roars, pushing the music into a powerful crescendo, where it bursts open and notes rain like confetti. Only then did Tamara Quigley realize she was dancing, once again, to *Swan Lake.*

Let go.

CHAPTER FIFTY-FIVE

I Can See Clearly Now

Now then, what of *Alexei Petrov's Dueling Piano Wars!*?

When Prudence disappeared before the winner was announced, the ratings went through the roof. Alexei would go on to host several more high-rated seasons. He was a classical pianist—a serious musician—but when he threw his jacket into the crowd that very first time, he had not realized the immortality of it. He would never reverse that image. Such overt showmanship was against Alexei's nature, but he learned to relax and enjoy it. Plus, throwing his suit jackets into the audience turned out to be very lucrative. He was rich now. And this time, he hired the proper people to manage his money.

His parents were bursting with pride. They admired this streak of independence. They could see now that he was capable of accomplishing great things on his own. Alexei Petrov assured his parents he loved them and would always need them. He made good on his promise to take care of them and arranged for a permanent home for Tatiana and Nikolai in the United States. But first he arranged for them to go on an around-the-world cruise that would take an entire year.

Inspired by Holden, Alexei Petrov endowed a tuition-free summer camp for children who might not otherwise have access to music lessons. Gabe Puente was a frequent guest instructor—as was Alexei's dear friend, Prudence Childs.

And what of the ache in Alexei Petrov's heart?

Well, one morning not long after the duel, a text popped up on his phone, sending involuntary plumes of pleasure through his veins.

Mia here. Can we talk?

They did.

The text turned into a phone call.

The phone call turned into a visit.

The visit turned into a union, which then turned into a child, a little boy with blond hair that curled like wood shavings, who loved baseball and adored his father.

Alexei Petrov never, ever played "Great Balls of Fire" again.

THE MORNING AFTER Prudence's performance, Bobby Wheeler was still in debt and still confused about how he kept blowing all his chances to turn things around for himself. He got into his rented blue Chevy Aveo and made his way back up to Redwood City along the coast of California, even though he knew the sheriff would be there, waiting for him. The ocean on his left churned blue and white and the hills on his right were yellowed and dry and the road ahead stretched endlessly, menacingly before him.

At last he was doing the right thing. And on his own terms, too.

MRS. WINTOUR WAS much hardier than her eight pounds would suggest. Fully recovered and back in her home, she jumped up on the large bed and slept on her mistress's pillow, waiting for her return. She never sought to play with a rattlesnake again.

THAT MORNING THE desert sky was clear and blue. Stuart steered the small Cessna down the runway, faster and faster, until he could feel he was no longer on the ground but in the air, an indescribable sensation. Below him he saw knotty canyons and mesquite trees that dotted the desert like flakes of parsley. He flew over the Superstition Mountains, so grand he thought he was in a dream. He was, his own dream come true. It was his first solo flight.

CHAPTER FIFTY-SIX

Dear Prudence

And what of Prudence?

Still in her stage clothes from the night before, she had approached the house. It was smaller than she'd remembered. In her child's mind, it had been a castle, three stories high and constructed entirely of red brick.

She stood on the sidewalk for a long while. The morning was chilly. The sun was just beginning to rise. Palm-size leaves the color of pomegranates lay on the ground like a wet carpet. Maybe Karen Martinelli would call her a thief and slam the door in her face. Regardless of her reaction, Prudence and her children would be repaying Karen and her children for the rest of their lives.

Prudence wanted this to be over. She wished a meteorite would fall to Earth on the very spot she was standing. But she had to give back what did not belong to her. She did not need it anymore. She had proven herself even in the wake of Alexei Petrov's win.

Prudence lifted the brass knocker and banged loudly before stepping back. The door creaked open and there stood Mrs. Martinelli's only child, older than Prudence by ten years. Her white hair surrounded her face like a halo. Karen Martinelli examined the tuxedo-clad Prudence with curiosity. "Can I help you?"

"Your mother was my first piano teacher."

"Aw," Karen Martinelli said, smiling. "Come in, dear. I love when her former students stop by."

She ushered Prudence into the old parlor. The two women stood where hundreds of children had learned how to play scales and create music with their fingertips. The old upright upon which Prudence picked out the tune to "Brahms' Lullaby" at the age of three was in the same corner, the rocking chair where Mrs. Martinelli held her by its side.

The simple gold crucifix above the piano.

"I hope you still play," Karen Martinelli said.

For whatever reason, maybe because Prudence thought perhaps she would not be believed, and, obviously, Karen Martinelli did not watch television, Prudence held up her battered fingers. "I do."

"My goodness, I guess you do. Wonderful. She hated when they gave it up."

"Well, I certainly tried to."

"Oh?"

The scent of the house, a mix of must and cedar and lemon oil, was exactly the same. Prudence was time traveling now, consumed with the grief of losing her beloved teacher and the realization of what she'd done for Prudence. The sheer luck at having connected with this woman. The right circumstances were everything and Prudence could feel the emotion rising up inside her like a vapor.

Karen Martinelli placed her hands on Prudence's shoulders. "Are you okay?"

"I'm Prudence."

Karen Martinelli gasped. "Prudence! I've been waiting for you for years. We always hoped . . ."

Prudence dreaded her next words, her heart beat like a moth stuck in a lampshade. But it was the only way to be free. "Ms. Martinelli, I have a confession."

"Of course, dear. What is it?"

"Your mother wrote the jingle to Pep Soda. Not me." Prudence waited for a bolt of lightning to strike.

But the most astonishing thing happened. Karen Martinelli smiled. "No, she didn't."

"You don't understand, it wasn't me."

"I do understand and, yes, it was you."

"No, you see, she sent it to me. In a letter. It made me rich."

"It saved your life."

Prudence shook her head in confusion. "Don't you want the money?"

"It doesn't belong to me."

"Well, it doesn't belong to me, either."

"Dear, *you* composed that melody."

"I did?"

"At the age of three. My mother saw you working it out on the piano. She thought it was immensely clever and wrote the notes down as you played them. That's when she knew for certain how gifted you were."

Prudence had no memory of this. For all she knew, Karen Martinelli could be lying.

But why would she?

Karen Martinelli continued. "Then your grandmother took you away and my mother's worst fear came true. Your talent had been exploited instead of nurtured. Like putting dynamite into the wrong hands. When you wrote to my mother of your situation after you dropped out of Juilliard, she remembered your little composition and thought it would make a great jingle. The rest is history."

And so it was.

Prudence had not ridden on the heels of another. She was not a fraud. Mrs. Martinelli believed in her. And when someone believes in us, it unlocks something inside. Something that pushes us to seek out the extraordinary. How many people, Prudence wondered, lose sight of a dream because of one careless comment from a stranger? When someone tells us we can't do something, why do we accept it? She thought of Tamara Quigley. She thought of Alexei Petrov. She thought of her grandmother.

Prudence sat down on the old piano bench and now felt immortal. Immortality, she realized, was in all of us, in some form or another. Because each of us lives on in the people we connect with, whether through music, or love, or a shared dream. And so she put her fingers on the worn keys, aged to the softness of cream, and began to play.

Acknowledgments

I'm indebted to my incredible agent, Stefanie Lieberman, and her fantastic team, Adam Hobbins and Molly Steinblatt, who believed in this story from the beginning. Thank you for plucking my manuscript from the slush pile and bringing it to life.

I'm grateful to Anne Speyer at Ballantine Books. Thank you for your flawless editorial guidance and your boundless enthusiasm for Prudence and the gang. A big thanks to Ballantine for publishing this book and to all those behind the scenes, including Kara Cesare, Jesse Shuman, Laurie McGee, Cindy Berman, Melissa Folds, Allison Schuster, Yewon Son, and Kathleen Carter.

To Todd Grossman, for sharing your vast musical expertise with me. To my terrific mechanic (twenty years, multiple vehicles, two teenage drivers), Dan Pensabene, whose extensive car knowledge helped finesse the McDowell Mountain Park scene. Thank you to my brother-in-law, Mark Weisbrod, whose banking expertise helped shape Stuart Childs's midlife crisis and looming bankruptcy problems. To Jennifer Johnson-Blalock, for directing me toward writing a high-concept novel and for being an early reader. To Miriam Landis, for graciously answering my ballet questions.

To my lovely parents. Thank you for introducing me to the arts at a young age and for tirelessly driving me across town to both piano and trumpet lessons for many years. You provided me with a never-ending stream of books, the building blocks of becoming a writer. *Please live forever.*

To my two little Mrs. Wintours, who were dedicated, card-carrying members of the Five A.M. Writing Club. There is never a more willing companion than a dog.

To my little family, who've tolerated years of scales and finger exercises coming from the very loud piano every morning. Drew, thank you for patiently (and frequently) talking me off the ledge by employing your savvy tech skills whenever I thought the computer ate my manuscript. Paige, thank you for making me laugh every day. You are one of the funniest people I know. To my husband, Steve, who makes life so much fun. Thank you for always believing in me and supporting me. I love you all so much.

I was fortunate to have some amazing piano teachers over the years. To my college instructor, Doris Lehnert, a child prodigy and Juilliard graduate. You chose the most exquisite arrangements, songs I continue to play to this day. You encouraged me to never give up the piano, if only to play for myself. In memoriam to Julian Leviton, my inspiration for Pierre Millet. You were an incredible pianist who made Rachmaninoff less intimidating. (So many notes, so few fingers!)

And to the late, great playwright Dale Wasserman, who once told me, "The power is in the dream, a drive that engenders the person dreaming it—he won't give up." Those words set this whole thing in motion.

PHOTO: © TONY TAAFE

MICHELLE HOFFMAN is a former arts and entertainment writer for the *Arizona Republic*. She began formal piano lessons at the age of five and now lives in Arizona with her husband, two spoiled shih tzus, and a very large piano.

Twitter: @MichelleHffmn

ABOUT THE TYPE

This book was set in Sabon, a typeface designed by the well-known German typographer Jan Tschichold (1902–74). Sabon's design is based upon the original letterforms of sixteenth-century French type designer Claude Garamond and was created specifically to be used for three sources: foundry type for hand composition, Linotype, and Monotype. Tschichold named his typeface for the famous Frankfurt typefounder Jacques Sabon (c. 1520–80).